say you're mine

The One I Want Book One

SIOBHAN DAVIS

ISBN-13: 978-1-916651-23-4

This book was originally published, in part, as The One I Want © July 2023.

This print edition © February 2024.

Critique and research by Jennifer Gibson of The Critical Touch
Edited by Kelly Hartigan of XterraWeb
Proofread by Imogen Wells of Final Polish Proofreading
Cover design by Shannon Passmore of Shanoff Designs
Cover image © Bigstockphoto.com
Interior cover imagery © Depositphotos.com

BOOK DESCRIPTION

I never intended to fall in love.

This girl had goals and guys were an unwelcome distraction.

Until I met Garrick, my sophomore year of college, and he blasted through the walls I kept around my heart, tearing them down.

He knew what he wanted, and he wanted *me*.

Falling hard and fast, I experienced the rollercoaster highs and lows of first love.

Until life threw us a curveball, and everything flipped overnight.

Now, I'm stuck in limbo. Falling apart as I try to be strong for my boyfriend.

But it seems fate has other plans.

Note From the Author

This is a an angsty, emotional, new adult romance, recommended to readers eighteen and older. Contains some distressing scenes and sensitive subject matter. For a list of triggers, refer to my website.

say you're mine

The One I Want Book One

Prologue
Stevie

"Hey," I whisper as I enter the room for what I know is going to be the last time.

"Hey, beautiful." His red-rimmed eyes shine with honest emotion, conveying so much without words. "Come sit with me."

I walk quietly to the window and sit beside him, memorizing the stunning view I have always loved.

He takes my hand, giving it a gentle squeeze. "I'm so sorry, Stevie."

"Me too."

"I never meant to hurt you."

"Nor I you."

"I was selfish and cruel and reckless with your feelings, and I won't ever forgive myself for it."

"Forgive yourself," I say without hesitation. "There's been enough hurt, guilt, and blame." I lean in and kiss his cheek with tears in my eyes. "I already forgive you."

"You shouldn't."

"I love you and care deeply about you. That won't ever change. A part of my heart will always belong to you." Removing the jewelry he bought me, I place it on the coffee table, and it makes it final.

This is the last time we will ever see one another.

As much as this needs to happen, it's sad it has come to this.

"But you love him more." Pain underscores his words, and I hate I'm the cause of it.

My inclination is to refuse to answer or deflect, but we're not tiptoeing around one another anymore. "I do."

Agony flares in his eyes, and it hurts, but I'm not sorry I was truthful.

"I will always love you," he says as we stare at one another through blurry eyes. "It's because I love you I am letting you go. We need to let what we had stay in the past and move forward along different paths. We're very different people now."

"We are," I acknowledge with a nod. "And it's neither of our faults we have ended up here."

"I thought we would grow old and gray together," he says with a sad smile.

I'm not sure I did, but it's hard to remember exactly what I was feeling at the time. "Things happen for a reason. Some lucky woman is out there waiting for you to find her. I hope she doesn't have to wait too long."

He brings our conjoined hands to his mouth and brushes his lips across my knuckles. "I want you to be happy, and he's your happy place. I see it now."

He is, and I hope it's not too late to reclaim what we had.

"I won't ever forget you," I say over a sob. "I will always cherish the time we shared. Be happy." I swipe at the tears streaming down my face. "It's all I want for you. Don't ever stop fighting for that happiness because you deserve it."

I don't protest or pull away when he leans forward and kisses me softly and briefly on the lips.

It's the only goodbye we can handle.

I hug him for the last time, and then I get up and walk out the door and out of his life.

Chapter One
Stevie

"Watch out! Coming through!" I holler over the almost deafening noise of the music as I attempt to maneuver my way through the heaving crowd. Lifting the tray over my head, I shimmy sideways, slipping nimbly between a rowdy group of frat boys. Some dickhole squeezes my ass, and I shriek, almost dropping the tray of empty glasses as I fight my way back to the bar.

The End Zone—the sports bar where I work Thursday and Friday nights—is popular with my fellow Oregon students. Live music on the weekends is a big draw, and the boss is particular about the acts he books. While the manager is careful who gets in the door, and we have a strict alcohol policy, this is a regular spot for juniors and seniors who like to party it up on the weekends in downtown Eugene. Some of them are known to get more than a little disruptive when booze is involved.

Most of the college freshman and sophomores stick to the other sports bar or the tavern closest to campus because both establishments are known to pass a blind eye to fake IDs and clearly underage patrons.

It's one of the reasons I enjoy working here. The management never allows it to get too wild, and the crew is tight. We look out for one another. If I'd seen who groped me, I could tell Manford, and he'd kick the perv out. But an ass squeeze is the least of my worries tonight. Navigating the packed bar, and surviving without any breakages or spillages, is priority number one.

Pushing through the thirsty students swarming the bar, I maneuver to the end of the counter, to the area reserved for staff, and set my tray down with a relieved sigh. Glasses rattle as Camila instantly grabs it, making brief eye contact with me before she takes it straight to the dishwasher. Everyone is working at max speed tonight, and the manager called in extra staff when he realized we were going to be packed to capacity.

"Hey, Stevie. Is everything cool out there?" Manford—the head bartender on duty tonight— asks as he lands in front of me on the other side of the bar. "It's pretty insane tonight."

"It's a goddamned jungle, but I've seen it worse." Not often, but enough to know I'll get through it intact. Brushing damp tendrils of red hair back off my brow, I fan my face with my hands in an attempt to cool down. I'm glad I wear my long, thick auburn hair up in a messy bun for work. Despite the AC working full throttle, it's hotter than hell in the room, and we're all feeling it.

"The new guy has them eating out of the palm of his hand," Manford says, jerking his head toward the stage in the back as he reads my next order from the tablet in front of him. We went digital a few months back, and there's no denying it's very helpful on busy nights.

Casting a quick glance over my shoulder, I stare at the dark-haired guy on stage. I can barely see him through the throng of students standing and dancing around the high tables on that side of the bar. He is sitting on a stool, strumming a guitar, and belting out the lyrics to some classic pop and rock songs with his eyes closed.

"He's good," I agree, pouring myself a glass of ice water from the jug Manford keeps topped up for the servers. I have been subconsciously listening to him play as I work the tables. "His husky voice is very distinctive, and he definitely knows how to work a crowd."

"Doesn't hurt he's easy on the eyes." Camila smirks as she wipes the sticky counter down with a damp cloth.

"I wouldn't know. I haven't had a second to look, and you can hardly see him from here. I'll just have to take your word for it." I guzzle water as I wait for Manford to finish my order for table five.

"Go see for yourself." Manford smirks, thrusting a bottle of water and a glass filled with ice at me. "Take them to Garrick. He's overdue a refill, and he'll be taking a break shortly. Got to keep the new talent happy. Boss already confirmed he wants to book him for the regular Friday night slot."

If this is the kind of attention he attracts, can't say I blame the boss.

Taking the bottle and glass, I navigate my way around the perimeter of the room, heading toward the stage. A line of girls, two rows deep, crams the front of the stage, swaying and singing along as Garrick works the crowd like a pro. I roll my eyes at their obviousness as they jostle one another, vying for the best position in the hope he'll notice them first.

Donny is part of the security team tonight, and he looks like a grumpy sentinel standing guard at the side of the stage. With a curt bob of his head, he steps aside to allow me to pass.

Garrick brings the song to a close just as I walk up the five short steps to the platform. The girls at the front scream and shout vulgar proposals as he opens his eyes and grins at the adoring crowd. "Thank you. I'm gonna take a short break," he says, tilting his head to the side as I approach. His eyes flit between me and the audience. "But don't go anywhere. I'm not finished with you yet!" He flashes a blinding grin at the crowd, and I swear I hear audible swooning.

Swiveling around on his stool, he fixes me with the same dazzling smile, showcasing a set of perfectly straight, perfectly white teeth behind a wide mouth and lush full lips. Dark hair curtains his handsome face, and the tousled strands look like he was repeatedly running his fingers through it. A few errant tendrils are stuck to his brow, and there's a light sheen of sweat coating his skin. The lights are strong up here, and my shirt is already clinging to my spine. Sweeping his chin-length hair back off his face, he lifts his eyes to mine, and my heartbeat speeds up.

Camila wasn't wrong.

This guy is totally freaking hot. Like model or rock star hot.

He's also younger than I was expecting. If I had to guess, I'd say he's in his early twenties. High cheekbones, smooth olive-toned skin, a strong nose, and a chiseled jawline with an artful layer of stylish stubble complete the features of his gorgeous face. He has the most mesmerizing hazel eyes, framed by long, thick black lashes. His grin expands, revealing matching dimples, as we stare at one another, and I smother a sigh.

Of course, he has dimples.

As if he wasn't already gorgeous enough.

I realize I'm being rude and obvious in the extreme, so I shake myself out of it and break eye contact. Clearing my throat and the brain fog from my head, I hand him the bottle of water and the glass. "Manford thought you might be thirsty." I have to shout over the noisy bar to be heard.

Placing his guitar aside, he reaches for the drink. His fingers brush against mine in the exchange, and our eyes lock together again. "That was thoughtful of you both. Thank you."

My breath hitches in my throat, and butterflies swoop into my chest as he pins me with another glorious smile. Dimples and stunning smiles should be outlawed as a lethal combination capable of annihilating the female race. I'm pretty successful at deflecting interest from the opposite sex, but give me a set of dimples and a gorgeous smile, and I'm as ovary punched as the next girl.

Garrick climbs off the stool, unfurling to his full height. He towers over my five-feet-nine-inch frame, proving he's well over six feet tall. His torso is lean, but his shoulders are broad and there is clear definition in his chest, abs, and arms underneath his fitted white T-shirt. Wrinkled jeans hug his long legs, and the dark denim hangs tantalizingly from his shapely hips. Worn tan boots encase large feet, and this guy truly is the full package.

It's just as well I've sworn off men and his effect will only be fleeting and temporary.

"Follow me," he says, snapping me out of my ogling. He's still grinning as he walks off, and I wonder if the guy ever stops smiling.

Confusion puckers my brow, but like a trained puppy, I trail him across the stage and through the small door at the back. It leads into a self-contained soundproofed area that was built specifically for the various entertainers who have graced the stage here. The main space, currently empty, holds a three-seater leather couch, a rectangular coffee table, a mini refrigerator, wall-mounted TV, and a table with snacks. Enclosed on the left is a small bathroom with a shower, and on the right is a private dressing area. It's compact but appropriate.

I close the door, instantly grateful for the silence as the noisy bar outside is muted. Standing by the wall, I watch

Garrick dump the bottle of water into the glass of ice and knock it back. The way his throat works as he drinks is sexy as hell, as is the way his eyes remain locked on mine the entire time. He has barely taken his eyes off me since I arrived on the stage, and I wonder if he's always this attentive with everyone he meets. When he's finished, he places the glass down on the snack bar with his gaze still attached to mine in a way that is starting to make me uncomfortable.

"Can I get you anything else?" I ask, my eyes darting to the door. It's crazy busy and I need to get back. I also wouldn't mind putting some distance between the two of us. His presence is magnetic, and it concerns me that I've noticed.

Little beads of sweat cling to his brow before he swipes them away with the back of his hand. His disarming smile is firmly in place as he stalks toward me. "Just your company." He moves in closer, and his breath tickles my face when he speaks. "What's your name, and do you go to school here too?" Curiosity lights up his handsome face as his inquisitive gaze probes mine.

"Why do you want to know?" I step sideways to create some distance between us.

"I'm just making conversation."

There's a weird tension in the air. A crackling charge ripping across the space separating our bodies, and I don't like feeling some freaky connection between us. "Well, I'm working, and they need me outside, so I should go."

"It's too quiet in here, and I don't like hanging around by myself." His earnest eyes are shielding nothing, and I know it isn't a lie or a ruse to trap me into spending time with him. "Not when I'm pumped full of adrenaline. Normally, my friends would be here, but they all had shit to do tonight." His eyes soften. "You'd be doing me a big favor if you kept me company." He flops down on the couch, still maintaining eye contact with me. He pats the space beside him. "I only have a short break, and I promise I won't bite." He flashes me another ovary-clenching smile. "I'm betting you haven't taken a break all night. Rest your feet and take a breather."

A break does sound nice, and he's right. I wasn't able to take my usual ten minutes earlier because it was too busy. Suddenly, my feet feel heavy, and my legs ache like they might go out from under me.

Garrick hops up and grabs two chilled bottles of water from the mini refrigerator as I lower my tired butt onto the couch. Fridays are always nightmarish because I have classes until lunch, then I work my shift at Butterfly Flowers, and run back to the apartment I share off-campus with my friend Ellen to grab something to eat and a quick shower before showing up for my shift at the bar. I usually sleep in late on Saturday morning, too exhausted to get up early.

"You look like you need this as much as me," he says, handing me a water.

"Thanks, and I do. It's hot out there tonight."

"It's a veritable sauna," he agrees. "If it's like this every Friday night, I might start showing up in nothing but shorts."

"That would be one way of keeping your fans loyal," I tease as I uncap the bottle.

"I'm here for the music, not the girls." He flashes me a flirty look, that seems to contradict his statement, before gulping back his drink.

"Said no rock star ever," I deadpan, fighting a grin.

"I'm not a rock star nor do I have any desire to be."

"How come? You must know you're good, and isn't it what most musicians dream of?"

He shrugs before draining his second bottle of water and tossing the empty in the trash can. "Not me. Music is a hobby.

It's a release. A way to indulge my creative side. It will never be anything more."

"It seems a shame to waste such natural talent, but I admire you for knowing what you want and sticking to your resolve."

"I still don't know your name." He twists around on the couch. His knee brushes against my jean-clad leg as he leans in closer, giving me his undivided attention.

It's unnerving, but I still can't force myself to get up and leave.

"And you didn't tell me if you go to UO too," he adds, looking at me like I'm the most fascinating person in the world.

"I'm Stevie, and yes, I go to school here. I'm studying floral management and just about to finish my sophomore year."

"Same here."

My eyes pop wide. I'm pretty sure there are no guys in any of my classes. Floral management is not really a guy thing.

He chuckles. "I meant I'm a sophomore. I'm majoring in family enterprise."

"Oh, cool. Does your family have a business?"

He nods as his tongue darts out wetting his lips. "My dad is CEO of Allen Lumber and Allen Wineries. I'll be joining the business when I graduate."

His tone is very matter-of-fact, and it doesn't seem like he's bragging. Wouldn't matter if he was. I'm hard to impress, and I can't think of any guy who has ever managed to do it. "I know Allen Wineries. The country club I used to work at back home buys their wine. So, you're from Seattle too?"

"Born and bred."

"What part?"

"Dad lives in North Bend, and Mom lives in Medina. I used to split my time between both homes." Air trickles out of his mouth as he drags one hand through his messy dark hair.

Something akin to desire pools low in my belly, but I ignore it.

"What about you? Where do you call home?" he asks.

"Ravenna. I live with my mom, and my nana is close by too."

"No dad?"

"I never knew him." I'm not about to get into it with a guy who is a virtual stranger even if he seems like an okay guy and the conversation is flowing easily.

"This feels a little like fate." His eyes sparkle with excitement.

"What does?"

"Us meeting like this."

I resist the urge to roll my eyes. "It's coincidence. Not fate. And it's not like there aren't a ton of people attending Oregon from Seattle."

"True, but I'm sticking to my convictions. You call it coincidence. I'm calling it fate." He attempts to dazzle me with that flirty smile again, and it almost works. Angling his body closer, he stares at my mouth like he wants to kiss me.

Which is crazy.

We only just met.

I can't deny I feel *something* between us, but I have zero intention of acting on whatever chemistry we share.

The spicy scent of his cologne calls out to me like a siren, and I scarcely resist the urge to lean into his neck and sniff him. He smells delicious because it's not enough that he's hot, has dimples and an amazing smile, is talented yet not stuck up his own ass, and seems like a genuinely nice guy. No, he has to smell incredibly tempting too.

It's just as well I'm a stickler for my self-imposed rules and a tough nut to crack.

Otherwise, this guy might smash through my shell and burrow his way underneath.

Garrick's eyes rise to meet mine, and it's so hard to concentrate on anything but him when he's fixing me with such a bewitching expression. His eyes are like magnets, drawing me closer, sucking me into his orbit, and making it almost impossible to break free of his spell. His warm breath fans across my face when he speaks, and I bite on the inside of my cheek to stop myself from groaning when his gorgeous scent swirls around me. "Do you have any plans tomorrow night, Stevie? Would you go out to dinner with me?"

A shudder works its way through me as his husky voice does funny things to my insides. I love how my name rolls seductively off his tongue, but I'm determined to remain immune to his charm. It takes considerable effort to sound unaffected when I reply. "I thought you were here for the music not the girls."

He chuckles. "I am, but I didn't expect to cross paths with you tonight." His eyes pierce mine, and I want to look away, but I can't.

Butterflies run amok in my stomach, and my chest heaves the longer he stares at me. Electricity crackles and snaps, and I am almost afraid to breathe. I bet Garrick has girls beating a path to his door without even trying.

"And just so we're clear, I'm not the kind of guy who goes around hooking up with different girls. That isn't who I am." The smile on his face and the look of appreciation in his eyes seem genuine, and if I was going to break my rules for anyone, it could be him.

But I can't.

"You seem like a nice guy, Garrick, and I appreciate the dinner invitation, but I have to decline." I move to get up, and he takes my hand, holding me in place.

"Please call me Gar. All my friends do. Tell me what I need to do to convince you to go out with me?" He cocks his head to one side, stabbing me with those stunning eyes that hold me hypnotized. His lips kick up at the corner. "I can be very convincing when I need to be."

"I don't doubt it," I murmur, shaking myself from my stupor and trying to retrieve my hand from his hold. His large palm dwarves my much smaller one as he holds my hand hostage. Calluses brush against my soft skin as warmth spreads from his hand into mine, radiating up my arm. His grip is firm, steady, and comforting, and it unnerves me. "Can I have my hand back now?"

"No."

"No?"

He lets loose an enormous smile while clutching my hand tighter. "Agree to go out with me, Stevie." His eyes drill into mine. "Please," he adds. "I promise I'll be the perfect gentleman, and if you don't want to continue dating, I'll back down."

"We would still see each other. You'll be playing here every Friday night."

"I promise things won't be awkward."

"You shouldn't make promises you can't guarantee you can keep."

"I have remained on good terms with my exes." He shrugs while his thumb rubs circles on the back of my hand. "This is all hypothetical anyway." His eyes twinkle with the weight of what he thinks he knows. "Just one date, Stevie. That's all I'm asking. It's not really that big of a deal."

Maybe not to him. Mention of ex-girlfriends suggests Garrick likes being in a relationship, and all it does is prove how incompatible we are. "You're wasting your time, Garrick. I don't date."

"It's Gar, and why not?"

"I don't have the time for distractions, and I really need to get back to the bar before Manford sends out a search party."

"What if I'm the best kind of distraction?" he asks, finally releasing my hand.

"You probably are, but I'm not changing my mind." Standing, I straighten a hand down the front of my tight-fitting black T-shirt. It's adorned with the bar logo on the front and my name on the back. All the staff have to wear them, but we can choose to pair it with whatever we like. I usually wear skinny jeans and black tennis shoes because I value comfort over sexiness any day of the week.

"Help a guy out here, Stevie." Rising to his feet, he stands in front of me, pinning me with puppy-dog eyes. "Just one dinner. That's all I'm asking. How distracting could that be?"

Tipping my head back, I peer up at him. I admire his persistence. But it won't alter my decision. "I have a feeling you could be the most distracting distraction of all."

"Just give me a chance."

I shake my head and take a few steps back. "There are tons of girls out there tonight who would love to go out to dinner with you. Ask one of them."

"I don't want to take any of them to dinner. I want to take you."

"We can't always get what we want." Stretching up on tiptoes, I press a soft kiss to his cheek, unable to resist a sly sniff of his intoxicating smell. "It was good to meet you, Garrick, and I'm flattered you asked me out, but it's not happening."

"We'll see," he shouts after me as I make my way toward the door. "I'm not the kind of guy who backs down at the first hurdle."

Chapter Two
Stevie

"Fuck off," I grumble, shoving my head under my pillow and ignoring the incessant vibration of my cell phone as it buzzes on top of my bedside table. It was just after four a.m. when I crawled into bed, and I have not had enough sleep. My cell continues to vibrate, and I spew a ton of expletives as I lift my head from under the pillow and reach for it. Whoever is calling is clearly determined, so I might as well face the music. I swipe to answer the call, squinting at the screen through blurry eyes. "This better be important," I mumble over a yawn as I haul my tired body up against the headboard and brush knotty hair out of my face.

"I'm sorry to wake you, sweetie," Mom says, and I instantly regret my snippy tone. "I just didn't know if I'd get a chance to call you again today. It's bedlam here."

Mom works Monday to Friday as the office manager for a Seattle architectural firm, and for the past few years, she has worked at Sand Point Country Club on alternate weekends as front desk manager of the restaurant. She only took on the second job to subsidize my college fund, and she refuses to quit until I have graduated.

I was lucky to receive one of a limited number of scholarships. It covers my tuition and books but not accommodations or food. I wanted to take out student loans, but Mom wouldn't hear of it. She doesn't want me saddled with huge debt coming out of college.

"Sokay, Mom. I just got in extra late last night, and you know what a grouch I am if I don't get enough sleep." I scrub at my heavy eyes, forcing them to open. My bedroom is pitch-black, thanks to the best blackout blinds money can buy.

Outside, car horns blare, thumping music pumps out through open windows, dogs bark, playful children laugh, and other sounds of normal Saturday morning activity ensure I won't be able to fall back asleep after this call.

Mom's tinkling laughter hits my ears. "You always loved your sleep. Even as a toddler, I often had to coax you out of your crib." More laughter trickles through the connection. "Can you believe I actually used to wake you if you slept too long? Until Mom discovered what I was doing and made me stop."

"You were doing your best," I remind her, my heart swelling with unconditional love for the woman who gave up all of her dreams for me.

"I tried, and look how amazing you are." Pride suffuses her tone, and warmth spreads across my chest. "Though I can't claim much credit. It's all on you. Being your mother is such a pleasure. You make it so easy."

I adore my mother, and we have a fantastic relationship. She was the only parent I had growing up. I'm super close to my nana too, but Mom was the one I lived with.

She was only twenty when she got pregnant. Basically, the same age I am now, and I don't know how she did it. The thought of being responsible for a tiny human terrifies me. I can only imagine how difficult it was for her. But she never complains or ever makes me feel like I ruined her life. She continues to put me first and make sacrifices for me, and I have never felt anything but loved and cherished. While I went through phases wishing I had a dad, I never felt his loss for more than fleeting moments in time because Mom was everything.

"It's entirely too early for mushy compliments, Mom, even if it's true." I'm smiling as the words leave my mouth, and my heart is full of love for my mother. "I won the mother lottery for sure."

"You make me proud, Stevie. Every single day. Never forget."

It would be impossible to. She is constantly boosting me up and very open with her emotions and her thoughts. "I don't think you called me to tell me I'm amazing. What's up?"

"I hate to ask this of you, honey, and I wouldn't if I had any other choice."

"What do you need?" Yanking the comforter off, I swing my legs out of bed.

"This is the first year of the new golf tournament, and it's been a massive success. Tomorrow is the final day, and it's going to be extremely busy. Unfortunately, a few of the servers have come down with a stomach bug, and I'm shorthanded."

"When do you need me to come in?" I stand and arch my stiff back as I stifle another yawn.

I worked at the restaurant in the country club for three years, on weekends, during high school to save money for college. Mom got me the job after she started working there. She could quit now. We saved up enough money, Nana insisted on making a contribution too, and I have a steady income from my two jobs here, so there is enough to cover the rest of my college costs. Especially if I keep accumulating credits and I can finish in one year instead of the standard two that are left. But Mom is stubbornly insistent, and she won't quit until I have my degree.

"Could you work a full day shift tomorrow?" she asks. "It will be at the premium rate, so it will be worth your while."

I still have two assignments to finish before classes end in a week. Exams start shortly after, but I'm well prepared so I can afford to forgo one weekend of study.

Even if I was behind, I would still agree.

Mom has sacrificed so much for me, and I would go out on a limb to do anything for her. "No problem. I'm gonna grab a shower and something to eat, and then I'll hit the road." It's a five-hour-plus car trip home, and I'd rather get into Ravenna tonight than get up early tomorrow and head straight to Sand Point. If Hadley is around, we could meet up for a drink. I haven't seen my childhood bestie in ages.

"You're an angel. Thanks, love."

"I'll see you tonight."

"Drive safe, and text me when you're leaving and when you get home."

"Aye, aye, Captain." I hang up with her laughter ringing in my ears.

I wander out into our main living space, in my panties and silk pajama top, still yawning and rubbing my eyes.

"Ahem." A pointed throat clearing claims my attention. My roomie is seated at the island unit enjoying coffee and breakfast with a good-looking guy with dark-blond hair and navy-blue eyes. Ellen's lips twitch as she rakes her gaze over my bare legs and the tangled bird's nest on top of my head. The strange guy sitting at the island unit beside her smiles behind his coffee cup.

"Shit, sorry. I didn't know you had company," I say, quickly backtracking. Mention of that word conjures up images of the hottie from the bar last night, but I punt the visual from my mind's eye, unwilling to go there.

"This is Will," Ellen says. "I did text you to say he was here."

"The bar was nuts last night, and I didn't get home until really late. I never thought to check my phone before I conked out." I wiggle my fingers in the air and smile. "Hi, Will."

"Hi, Stevie." He's fighting a smirk but purposely keeping his eyes fixed on my face, which I appreciate.

"I'm just gonna go put on more clothes," I say, making a hasty retreat out of the room. It's just my luck to meet Ellen's new boyfriend when I'm semi-naked.

Grabbing the robe off the back of my bathroom door, I wrap it firmly around my body and slip my feet into slides before I head back out to the kitchen.

We were incredibly lucky to get this place this year because student rentals are in high demand in Eugene. All freshmen have to room at one of the residence halls, which sucked butt last year. Except it's how I met Ellen. That was the only good thing to come out of it. We became instant friends, and it was a no-brainer to share a place off-campus this year. We both hated cramped dorm living and having to sneak guys into the building.

Our two-bedroom apartment is only a ten-minute walk from campus, and it's in one of the newer buildings, so it's modern and more spacious than a lot of student accommodations. We both have our own bedrooms with en suite bathrooms, and there is a large communal space, which is our kitchen, dining room, and living room.

"It's nice to meet you, Will," I say as I head toward the coffee pot. "I was beginning to think you were a figment of Ellen's overly active imagination," I quip.

"Nice to meet you too, Stevie. Ellen never shuts up talking about you."

"That's 'cause she's my boo."

Ellen smiles at me. "Ditto, babe."

I race over and give her a quick squeeze. A look of amusement washes over Will's face, and I'm not sure he knows what to make of us.

"What have you guys planned for today?" I ask while I fill a mug with rich coffee.

"A study date at the library," Ellen confirms before popping the last piece of waffle into her mouth.

"We're grabbing dinner at the taco place later. A couple of my friends are joining us," Will says. "You should come."

"Sounds fun, but I can't. I have to head home unexpectedly." I slide onto the stool across from the lovebirds.

Ellen frowns. "Is something wrong? Is Nana okay?"

"She's fine. Mom needs me to work at the country club tomorrow, so I thought I'd head home today and try to catch up with Hadley." I waggle my brows. "Meaning you have the place all to yourself tonight." My gaze flickers between Ellen and Will. "You're welcome."

***

"Girl, it's so good to see you!" Hadley squeals, throwing her arms around me and hugging me tight.

"I've missed you." I cling to her, squeezing her tightly, before breaking our embrace and looping my arm in hers. "You look amazing. Love the dress." My bestie has an eclectic sense of style I adore. She owns who she is and always looks stunning. Hads only ever wears dresses and boots. Never jeans, or sweats, or pants, or skirts. In the summer, when it's hot, she will exchange the boots for tennis shoes, sandals, or flip-flops, but that's her only concession. Tonight, she's wearing a patterned floaty dress, with a bird print, that skims the asphalt as we walk along the sidewalk, heading toward town.

"You look great too. A little pale from too much work, no doubt, but your makeup is on point, and I love your ripped jeans. They're very you."

We chat casually as we make the short walk into town, heading for our favorite diner. When we are settled in our usual booth at the back and the waitress has brought our drinks, we pick up our conversation. "How are things with Dave?" I ask, slurping my berry smoothie through a straw.

"Over." Hadley flicks her hair, and bouncy strands of long, messy corkscrew curls cascade over her shoulders and down her back.

Growing up, I hated my red hair and wished I had my friend's mess of brown curls. Now, I have embraced my glossy, thick auburn locks, and I'm proud to be a redhead. "Already?"

She shrugs, taking a sip from her soda. "You know me. I fall in and out of love and lust fast."

"Truth." I have lost count of the guys Hadley has gone out with. Most of them never last long.

"His dick was too small, and he suffered from premature ejaculation." She just voluntarily tosses it out there like she's commenting on something as mundane as the weather. "I felt sorry for the guy, but a girl has needs, and his inability to satisfy me in the bedroom killed the feelings I had for him."

"The poor guy."

"Enough about me. How about you? Anyone at UO catch your eye lately?"

I shake my head as images of Garrick resurface in my mind. I scowl for the umpteenth time today. It's like he has hijacked my brain all day, and I'm sick of thinking about him. Like, what is with that?

"Spill the beans, sister. I know that look." She props her elbows on the table, excitement skittering in her eyes as she stares at me. "Have you met someone?" Her tone notches up a few decibels, and she's grinning so wide she'll give herself lockjaw if she keeps it up.

"Keep your panties on. It's nothing to get excited about." I take another drink of my smoothie before I put her out of her misery. "The new singer at the bar asked me out last night."

"Oh. My. God." Hads is bouncing in her seat now like an excitable kangaroo. "This is awesome." Softly clapping her hands, she smiles with obvious glee.

"I turned him down."

She sighs as the smile fades from her lips. "Of course, you did." She shakes her head, looking at me like she'd love to throttle me—lovingly, of course. "How long are you going to keep this up?"

I shrug, holding back my reply when the waitress reappears. She slides our burgers and fries in front of us, offering a quick smile before she leaves. "You know the score. Guys are a distraction. I'm focused on my studies and my future career. I don't have time for boys."

"You are missing out on so much, Stevie. Before you know it, you'll be an old gray spinster with nothing but a houseful of smelly cats for company." She narrows her eyes before popping a fry in her mouth.

I dunk a few sweet potato fries in chili sauce. "I'm not missing out. It's not difficult to find a guy when I need a fuck, and that's the only kind of interaction I'm interested in right now with the opposite sex." Stuffing the fries in my mouth, I savor the taste and ignore the pitiful look on my bestie's face.

"You're not your mom, Stevie."

I chew my food, swallowing it before responding. "It's not about that."

"This is *me* you're talking to. Of course, it's about your mom." She reaches across the table, grabbing my hand. "Just cause your mom got pregnant and had to drop out of college does not mean the same thing will happen to you."

"I'm not an idiot, Hads, and do we really need to have this conversation again?" It's like Groundhog Day sometimes.

"Yes, we do." My stubborn bestie glares at me before biting into her burger.

I finish the food in my mouth, dabbing the sauce at the corner of my lips with a napkin before I speak. "It's not really about Mom getting pregnant so young and having to give up her dream career although I definitely don't want that to be me. It's more how she invests so much time and energy in every guy she meets only to be let down over and over again. I have mopped so many tears as she cried over some asshole who failed her. Why would I willingly put myself through that?"

Mom is an eternal optimist and a true romantic. No matter how many times she gets her heart broken, she keeps putting herself back out there, and she hasn't given up hope of finding "the one." I can't decide if she's incredibly brave or stupidly foolish.

"Not every guy is an asshole. There are good guys out there. And I invest energy into relationships, but you rarely have to dry my tears."

"You're abnormal. Sometimes I wonder if you're even human," I joke, wanting this conversation to be over.

"I worry you're missing out on the best years of your life, babe. College is a time to have fun. To date guys. Fuck guys. Have your heart broken. Break a few hearts yourself. You won't know when Prince Charming lands in your lap if you haven't dated a few frogs first."

"It's not part of my life goals right now. There will be time for guys and relationships later."

Hads eyes me skeptically. "Tell me about this guy."

"Why?" I dunk more fries in the sauce, shoving them in my mouth and hoping that will end this line of interrogation.

"Humor me. Did you even like him?"

I chew slowly as I contemplate whether I should lie. But I can't do that to Hads. That's not how we roll. "Yeah, I did. There was chemistry, and he's hot. He even has dimples and a killer smile."

"And you turned him down? I think I should have you committed." She takes another chunk out of her burger as I finish my fries.

"He's a stranger."

"That's what dates are for. Duh." She rolls her eyes. "What harm would it do to go out on one date with the guy?"

"If I didn't know better, I'd say Garrick paid you to hassle me. You sound like his clone."

"It sounds like he's talking sense." She pulls out her cell. "What's his last name?"

I consider not giving it to her for like five seconds. "Allen," I reluctantly supply before diving into my burger.

Her fingers fly over the phone as I eat. "Woah. Holy fuck. He is smoking hot, and you're legit insane for rejecting him."

"You go out with him then."

"He didn't ask *me* out."

"This conversation is over."

"For now." Hads jabs her finger in my direction as she points at me. "But I'm not letting this go. Not this time. Someone needs to talk sense into you, and that someone is going to be me."

Chapter Three
Garrick

"**S**up, dude?" I ask, lifting my head from the screen as Will walks into the living room of the house we share with Noah and Cohen. We all lived in the dorms on the same floor last year and became firm friends in no time. Noah is majoring in family enterprise too, and we share most of the same classes. "Did you stay at Ellen's place last night?"

"Yeah." Will drops down on the leather couch beside me. "I really like this girl."

"Good for you, dude." My fingers fly over the game controller as we talk.

"How did the gig go?" he asks, watching me kill a few rogue militants on the screen.

"It was good."

"It was more than good," Cohen says, jumping over the back of the second couch and landing spreadeagled across the cushions. "Manford said you killed it."

Noah wanders into the room, holding a large bowl and shoveling cereal into his mouth. Dude is addicted to the stuff, eating it at all times of the day and night. He has commandeered one entire cupboard for all his cereal boxes, and I think he single-handedly keeps Kellogg's in business.

I jerk my head in acknowledgment as Noah settles his butt on the arm of the couch Cohen is sprawled all over. My eyes meet Cohen's. "Your cousin is cool, man, and I appreciate him putting a word in for me with the boss." I return my eyes to the screen in time to witness my demise. "I appreciate you vouching for me too."

"Anytime, broski." Cohen gives me a two-finger salute before turning his attention to Will. "Are we still on for dinner?"

I finish the game and toss my controller down on the coffee table.

"Affirmative," Will replies. "But Stevie can't make it, so I'm not sure if you and Noah still want to come."

Sitting up straighter, I turn my head to look at my buddy. "Hold up there a sec. Who's Stevie?" Is it the same Stevie who has transfixed my mind and wrapped soft fingers around my heart? I haven't been able to stop thinking about the redheaded beauty since our paths crossed last night.

"Ellen's boo, bestie, and roomie."

"What's with the dinner invite?" I rest my ankle over my knee.

"We were planning a little matchmaking because Ellen says Stevie never dates and she needs a nudge in the right direction."

"Cohen doesn't date." I state the obvious as my friend smirks.

"I'm aware." Will shrugs before scrubbing a hand over his smooth jawline. "We were giving her different options."

"My invite must have gotten lost in the mail."

"Dude, you know I would've invited you if you weren't heading home tonight."

It's got to be the same Stevie, and there's no fucking way I'm letting Will set her up with Noah and especially not Cohen. Don't get me wrong. I love both guys like brothers, but if Stevie is being set up with anyone, it'll be me. I can't believe Will would even consider setting her up with Cohen anyway. Dude is a legend, and he's always got my back, but he's a dirty dawg, and he rotates through girls like they're a dying breed.

Cohen has no business putting his hands on a girl like Stevie.

I doubt she'd let him anywhere near her anyway.

She had no trouble standing her ground and declining my dinner invite last night, and I'm not a player.

"She wouldn't happen to be a tall, hot redhead with legs for miles and stunning green eyes?" I ask.

Will's brow puckers. "Yeah. That sounds like her. I met her this morning, and she's a sweetheart." He cocks his head to one side. "How do you know her?"

"She was working at the bar last night. I asked her out, but she turned me down."

Cohen bursts out laughing. "This is fucking priceless. Has the notorious Allen charm deserted you?"

I shove my middle finger up at him. "She confirmed she doesn't date, and I got a stubborn vibe from her."

"Let me guess." Will chuckles as he tucks his hands behind his head and leans back in the couch. "It only makes you more determined."

"Abso-fucking-lutely." I grin at my buddy. "You know I love a good challenge, but it's more than that. I might have only met her, but I really, really like her. She's sexy and sweet, and we just clicked. It was easy breezy."

"Until she rejected you." Cohen smirks.

I flip him the bird again. "That is only a minor obstacle, and she's the kind of girl worth making an effort for."

"If you say so." Cohen's stupid smirk is still firmly planted on his face, and a wave of irritation crests over me.

"I do, and I'm staking my claim now."

Will whistles under his breath, Noah almost chokes on a mouthful of cereal, and Cohen chuckles.

Calling dibs is the kind of douchey behavior Cohen is known for, not me, so I understand their reactions.

Noah hooks up occasionally, but he's not interested in dating. I think he's still hung up on his childhood sweetheart back home. She broke things off with him just before he left for Oregon, and I don't think he's gotten over her yet.

Will and I are into relationships, favoring dating over random one-night stands. I would not ordinarily make a claim on any girl 'cause it's a major dickhead move, but there is something about Stevie that makes me want to beat on my naked chest, throw her over my shoulder, and turn full Neanderthal. "We had insane chemistry, and I have never wanted to kiss a girl as badly as I wanted to kiss Stevie last night. I just want to see where this might go."

"Wow." Will grins. "Sounds intense."

"I think it could be."

———

"Your tie is crooked." Mom purses her lips as she strides across the large living room, making a beeline for me, when I materialize in the doorway.

"You look nice, Mom," I say as she approaches.

Ivy Allen-Golding-Smith doesn't look a day over thirty despite celebrating her forty-fourth birthday recently. Mom has her cosmetic surgeon on speed dial, and she spends an inordinate amount of time at the dermatologist's office and at the gym with her personal trainer, and it shows. Today, she is wearing an elegant, fitted navy lace dress with cream and gold high heels that accentuate her slim frame to perfection. Expensive pearls—gifted to her by Henry Golding during their short-lived marriage—adorn her neck, and she wears a matching bracelet on her wrist. Her dyed-blonde hair hangs in loose curls over her shoulder, and her makeup artist clearly paid a house visit.

She looks every inch the society belle she has molded herself to be.

Dad's current wife is the opposite of Mom. As if he purposely set out to find a woman who isn't anything like my mother. Dawn couldn't give a flying fuck what she looks like, and she's never seen the inside of a plastic surgeon's or a dermatologist's office. She favors jeans and yoga pants, and the only time I ever see her dressed up is when she attends an official business event with Dad. Dad married her three years after his divorce from Mom, when I was nine, and they have been happily married ever since.

I have a real laid-back relationship with my stepmom, and she's good people. She helps to balance the sometimes exhaustive high maintenance demands of my mother.

I love my mom, but she's hard work.

"Thanks, sweetheart." She fiddles with my tie as I arch my neck, look up at the ornate ceiling with the intricate molding detail, and try to resist rolling my eyes. Everything is about appearances with Mom. God forbid I show up to the country club with an askew tie. "Today is important. Your father is trusting you to represent the family, and you can't let him down."

Dad wouldn't give a shit about my crooked tie. As long as I show up, smile, shake a few hands, and say the right words, he'll be happy. Allen Wineries is sponsoring the inaugural golf tournament at Sand Point, and if it's a success, it will probably become a regular annual thing. Normally, Dad or my uncle would represent the company, but they are overseas meeting with clients, and they took their wives with them.

Dad asked me to fill in, instead of one of the management team, and I readily accepted. I need to start getting more involved in the business, and I'm proud to represent my family today. "Dad knows I won't," I supply as the doorbell chimes.

"Oh good. They're here early. We can have champagne on the terrace."

My eyes narrow to slits. "Who's here?"

She beams at me, the skin on her face remaining stationary with the motion. "Relax, darling." She squeezes my shoulder. "I just invited Cristelle and the governor." She brushes hair back from my face with an effort at a scowl. "I really wish you'd do something with your hair." If she had her way, it'd be much shorter and worn in a preppy style, and my wardrobe would consist solely of polo shirts, loafers, and dress suits and shoes.

"Is Pepper with them?" I ask although I suspect I already know the answer.

"Pepper will be accompanying us today too." Her smile widens, but I don't share her exuberance.

"Mom." My tone contains considerable warning. "Stop. Meddling."

"What?" She feigns surprise. Something that's hard to do when her brow barely lifts. "Pepper's a gorgeous girl. She's single. You're single, and you're both destined for amazing things. She's a great catch, Garrick. I don't know why you're resisting."

"I like Pepper," I admit. "She's a great *friend*." I enunciate the word in the hope it might finally get through to my meddlesome mother. "But friendly feelings are all we have for one another. You can't force something that isn't there, and you need to quit with all this matchmaking bullshit. I can find my own dates."

"Language, darling."

Air whistles out of my mouth in frustration. "Stop treating me like a little kid who can't make his own decisions. I'm a grown man, Mom, and you need to let me lead my life the way *I* choose."

"I'm only suggesting you keep an open mind. Feelings can develop over time, and the best relationships grow out of friendship." The sound of approaching footsteps echoes in the hallway behind me. Mom stops fussing over me and steps back. Her lips pull into a tight line. "Just look at your father. He's a ringing endorsement for friends to lovers."

"I don't know why you're still pissed at Dad. It was you who filed for divorce."

And you who had an affair, which broke up your marriage. I think it, but I don't articulate it. Everything that needed to be said on that topic was said years ago when the seedy truth came to light.

"You have repeatedly told me you weren't a good match," I continue. "You should be happy he's happy. I know that's all he wants for you." It's true. Dad doesn't have a bad bone in his body. He's content with Dawn, and he would love Mom to find someone she stays married to for more than a year or two. I think it's very generous of my father considering the hell he went through with Mom.

Sometimes, I wonder if she'll ever find true contentment and inner peace. She never seems happy even if that's the front she portrays. Deep down, I think she's riddled with insecurities and incapable of lasting happiness. It makes me sad. I remind myself of this at times when I'm close to losing my patience with her. She loves interfering in my life, believing she knows better than I do about what's best for me. Her meddling drives me insane even if I know she believes it's coming from the best place.

I'm not naïve. I know she would love me to get together with Pepper because her father is the governor, her mother is Mom's best friend, and there is talk of a future presidential run for Paul. Mom would love those kinds of bragging rights, but it's not happening. Pepper will never be anything more than a friend.

Chapter Four
Garrick

"Here. You look like you need this." Pepper hands me a bottle of beer as we make our way from the presentation room to the restaurant.

"Thanks. I have done as much schmoozing as I can handle today."

"It's exhausting at times though I mostly don't mind."

"You've grown up in political circles, so I imagine it's as natural as breathing for you," I remind her, holding the door open so she can walk through first. "Dad kept me sheltered from all the corporate bullshit that comes with the job until recently. He wanted me to have a normal upbringing."

"I envy you that, but I think you're being too hard on yourself. You're a natural. They were all putty in your hands," she says as we approach the woman at the front desk.

"Welcome, Mr. Allen and Miss Montgomery. We're so pleased you could join us today," the older woman says, smiling kindly. She's very striking with strawberry-blonde hair and warm green eyes.

"Thank you, Ms. Colson," I reply, discreetly skimming my

gaze over her name tag. "We are delighted to celebrate the inaugural tournament and hope to sponsor the event going forward." It was a resounding success, and I already know Dad will want to strike a deal. No harm in putting it out there now.

Pepper tilts her head and grins. "Natural," she mouths, and my lips kick up at the corners.

"If you would follow me, I will show you to your table," Ms. Colson says.

Pepper loops her arm in mine as I escort her across the large room, both of us tipping our heads at guests as we pass.

When we reach our table, I pull out a chair for Pepper, and Ms. Colson smiles warmly at me.

"There is water on the table, but can I get you anything else?" she asks, circumspectly eyeing the beer in my hand and the wineglass Pepper is lifting to her lips. I turned twenty a few weeks ago, and Pepper isn't quite twenty-one yet, but my father is sponsoring this event, and our winery is supplying all the wine, so no one is going to call us out for underage drinking.

"We're fine for now, but thank you," I say as I claim the chair alongside my friend.

"I'll send my best waitress to your table as soon as your party is fully seated. Enjoy your lunch."

"This place is nice," Pepper says after Ms. Colson has left. "The views are stunning."

I glance out the window at the sumptuous grounds bordering the large lake. The water is calm today, and soft rays of buttery sunlight glint off the surface. Imposing mountains loom majestically in the background. "They are. It reminds me of my dad's house in North Bend. It's on a large private plot facing the lake, surrounded by mountains."

"It sounds like heaven."

"It is. I loved growing up there. I spent my youth hiking, cycling, fishing, and kayaking. When I have time, I go home over the weekend to take my brothers out on the lake." Dad and Dawn had twin boys seven years ago. I don't get to see much of John and Jacob since moving to Oregon, but I try to make it home a few weekends during the year, and I am there for most of summer break.

Gradually, Mom, her date, Winston, Pepper's parents, and another couple take their seats at our table, and conversation is lively while everyone peruses the menu. I'm grateful for Pepper's company at events like this. It stops the boredom from setting in too early.

"Good afternoon," someone with a somewhat familiar voice says, and I whip my head up, startled to find a stunning redhead standing at the side of our table. She's addressing Mom and not looking in my direction yet. "I'm Stevie, and I'll be your server today."

A slow grin spreads over my mouth, quickly transforming into a full-blown smile. Things just got infinitely less boring. "Well, hello again, Stevie. I wasn't expecting to bump into you so soon, but it's a most pleasant surprise."

Her eyes pop wide when she notices me. Air filters through her slightly parted lips, and her jaw slackens, for a few seconds, before she composes herself. Stevie clears her throat. "Mr. Allen. It's good to see you again." I hate the fake smile she plasters on her face, but I can't fault her professionalism.

She is even more stunning under the full glare of the late-spring sunshine pouring through the large window. Minimal makeup paints her pretty face, and her beautiful auburn hair is tied back in a high ponytail, highlighting her stunning features. Gorgeous green eyes framed by long lashes coexist with a cute nose, defined cheekbones, full lips, and delicate porcelain skin with the tiniest hint of freckles across the bridge of her nose. Her skin is flawless, and my fingers itch with a craving to touch her. To discover if her smooth skin feels like silk under my hands. The plain white blouse and black pencil skirt hug her womanly curves in all the right places, and she manages to make the drab uniform look enticing.

Her eyes connect with mine, and a spark of electricity charges the space between us.

Just like on Friday night.

I can't remember ever feeling such an immediate attraction to any woman before.

I'm sure I'm staring like a dog in heat, but I cannot help myself.

She is breathtaking, and I am enchanted.

I have got to convince her to go out with me.

Letting her go without exploring the connection between us would be sinful.

"How exactly do you two know each other?" my mother asks in a prickly tone I'm all too accustomed with.

No doubt, she has picked up on the vibe between us, and she's not happy.

If she could scowl, she would be doing so.

"Stevie attends UO," I explain, not taking my eyes from the woman who has instantly captivated me. "She's a sophomore like me. We met at the bar where I was playing Friday night. She was waitressing there too."

"What a hardworking young woman," the governor says, and I couldn't agree more.

I wonder if this is why Stevie said she didn't need the distraction. Is it more the case she doesn't have the time to date? I don't see how she can have much free time if she holds down two jobs and full-time studies.

Yet, I won't let that stop me.

Stubborn determination is practically my middle name.

"We need more young people setting such good examples,"

the governor adds. "Well done, young lady." Paul is a good man, and I know he means well, but it's coming off a bit patronizing.

"Thank you, sir." Stevie's cheeks pink a little, and I can tell she's uncomfortable.

"We should let Stevie do her job," Pepper says, sending a friendly smile in Stevie's direction. "The restaurant is full, and I'm sure she's busy."

Stevie shoots a grateful smile in Pepper's direction. "What would you all like?"

You to go out on a date with me.

I think it, but I don't articulate it. No sense in riling my mother up further.

But if Stevie thinks I'm giving up, she has another think coming.

I have never been more determined to win a girl over than I am in this moment.

Chapter Five
Stevie

"I think you have an admirer." Mom lets loose a grin as she subtly jerks her head in the direction of the Allen table while I enter more orders into the system.

"Mom," I hiss, glancing up briefly. "Stop looking. He'll notice."

"Garrick Allen has not taken his eyes off you. I've watched him staring at you from across the room all afternoon. He looks smitten."

"I'm sure his mother loves that." I know who everyone is at that table because Mom and the club manager updated me so I would take extra care of the VIPs of VIPs.

The room is swarming with important people, but it's vital we keep the Allen family happy so they'll agree to sponsor the event annually. It's the only reason I didn't beg to be reassigned after I realized Garrick was here. Most of the experienced servers are out sick, and I didn't trust any of the others not to fuck it up. I loved working here. They were always good to me, and they treat Mom well, so I'm sucking it up and doing my duty.

"Ivy has dined here a few times in the past year," Mom says, lowering her voice so no one can hear. "She's a snooty bitch. She always finds something to complain about, and she's extremely rude. It's no wonder Hugh Allen divorced her. He's such a nice man. I don't know how he married her in the first place."

"Is Garrick their only child?" I ask despite my better judgment.

Mom nods. "Hugh has twin sons with his current wife. They're such a lovely family. I spoke with Garrick earlier, and I can tell he takes after his father. He has lovely manners and good taste if you have caught his eye!" She winks at me, and I roll my eyes. "He's very handsome too."

"Mom, just stop. I already got the same pitch off Hads last night."

Her eyes widen. "I knew there was more to this. Spill the beans, missy."

"Mom, I'm working."

"Fine, but you're not leaving until I get all the tea!"

The rest of my shift is busy, and I try to attend to my duties without thinking about Garrick Allen, but it's challenging when I feel his eyes trailing me around the room and he avails of every opportunity to engage me in conversation when I'm at his table. Much to his mother's clear annoyance. I was tempted to flirt back, purely to wind her up, but that would be counterproductive.

I need to discourage Garrick, not egg him on.

I feel sorry for his pretty date because it's obvious he's distracted and fixated on me.

True to form, his mother complains her steak is overcooked. I make a speedy retreat from the kitchen after returning her plate as the chef explodes with anger and a slew of obscenities.

I wouldn't be surprised if he spit on her freshly cooked steak before I handed it to her.

I breathe a sigh of relief when they finish their meal and make their way outside, but my relief is short-lived.

I'm clearing their table when I sense his presence behind me. My spine stiffens as I straighten up.

"I was hoping we could talk for a minute," Garrick says.

Planting a smile on my face, I spin around to face him. "I am working, and fraternizing with the clientele is frowned upon." I made that last part up, but it sounds plausible.

He chuckles. "You're determined to make me work for this."

"I don't know what you mean."

He flashes me one of his brilliant smiles, and those tempting dimples come out to play. Goddamn it. He doesn't play fair. I have been trying to ignore how freaking gorgeous he looks in his designer suit, and how delicious he smells, all afternoon. My limits are being severely tested with him all up in my personal space.

"It's okay, Stevie. I love a good challenge."

My mouth hangs open for a split second before I pull myself together. "I'm not a challenge or a game, Mr. Allen."

He takes a step closer, and I suck in a strangled gasp as his purely male scent hits the back of my nose. It's unfair for any man to look and smell this good. "I know you're not. You're so much more." His eyes seem more brown than green today, and they have stunning little amber flecks. "Go out with me, Stevie. Please." His eyes drill into mine.

"No, and you need to stop asking."

"I'll beg if I have to. I'll get down on one knee, right now, if that's what it'll take." He moves to lower himself, and I grab his arm.

"Don't you dare. All humiliating me will do is earn you a permanent spot on the top of my shit list."

"You're right." He straightens up, pinning me with the full extent of his hypnotic smile. "I should reserve the knee bend for more important occasions."

My eyes almost bug out of my head. He cannot mean what he's insinuating. "I think you might be crazy. Have you ever had your brain examined, because I think it's malfunctioning."

"There is nothing wrong with my brain or any other part of my anatomy." His eyes sparkle with mirth as his lips twitch.

"You're awfully cocky for someone I keep rejecting."

"Deep down, I know you want to say yes."

"There is that Allen arrogance again."

"You say arrogance. I say confidence." He leans in close to my ear. "I am going to uncover every single objection you have and smash them into smithereens."

"Good luck with that plan, buddy, 'cause you're gonna need it."

"Do you think I could leave now?" I ask Mom a couple of hours later as I collect my tips and remove the apron from around my waist. "I would like to get a head start before it gets dark." That's no lie, but I have ulterior motives. Like not wanting to elaborate on what Garrick said to me earlier or explain what went down on Friday night. Mom is already gushing over him, and I'm not in the mood.

Why won't he just leave me alone?

Mom glances around the room as staff members continue the cleanup. "We can manage it from here. I'd prefer you set out now rather than traveling so far in the dark." She pulls me into her arms and kisses the top of my head. "I know you're also avoiding, but it's okay. I'll grill you on the phone on Wednesday."

A groan slips from my mouth as I shuck out of her embrace, muttering about interfering mothers under my breath. Mom laughs. "He's a nice young man. You could do a lot worse."

"Bye, Mom!" I wave goodbye to the remaining staff as I make my way into the locker room to get changed.

Walking out the rear staff entrance with my bag slung over my shoulder, I wish I had brought my coat as a gust of wind rushes over me and a shiver whips through me. Despite the sun earlier today, it's been colder than usual for the end of April this past week. We should be welcoming warmer weather soon, and I'm looking forward to it.

Rounding the corner of the clubhouse, I slam to a halt at the sight awaiting me. "You have got to be shitting me," I grumble under my breath as I watch Garrick climb out of his car. Narrowing my eyes in his direction, I stride toward my silver Honda CR-V. It was a present from Mom and Nana for my sixteenth birthday. It's ten years old now, but I get it serviced regularly, and until I moved to Oregon, I didn't clock up many miles. She's in good condition and should last at least until I graduate.

"You really don't take no for an answer, do you?" I say as I unlock my car with the key fob and stop in front of the stubborn guy leaning against the side of a newish-looking Range Rover parked right beside my vehicle. "How did you know this was my car?"

Garrick's dimples make an appearance when he smiles. "I have my ways."

"And that's not stalkerish at all," I drawl, playing up the sarcasm.

He holds up his hands. "I'm just a lonely guy trying to get a pretty girl to say yes to a date."

I can't hold back my laughter. "You are ridiculous, and I'd hazard a guess rarely lonely." A guy who looks as good as Garrick is not short of female company. "I'm sure your lovely date from earlier would be upset to hear such statements."

"Pepper is a family friend, and it wasn't a date."

"I'm betting your mom wishes it was."

"You caught that, huh?" Reaching out, he tucks a stray strand of hair that has come loose from my ponytail behind my ear. His fingers brush against my cold cheek in the process, igniting a heady warmth under my skin. "Definitely not just a pretty face. I can add observant and intuitive to my list."

"You have a list?"

He nods, smiling as he maintains eye contact with me. "It's a long list and growing longer by the minute."

"You are so full of shit."

He chuckles. "Every interaction with you only heightens my interest, Stevie. You're funny, hardworking, intelligent, charismatic, and stunningly beautiful. If you want me to go away, stop being so captivating."

My pulse races, and my heart speeds up. It's a little OTT but still one of the sweetest things anyone has ever said to me. Not that I'm admitting to it or letting this go any further. "We should stop interacting then, Garrick," I say, turning around and opening my driver's door.

"Even the way you say my name enchants me."

I glance over my shoulder as he plants one hand against his chest and taps it.

"It gets me in here." His lips pull into a wild smile. "And other unmentionable places."

A laugh bursts from my mouth before I can stop it. "You have a certain charm. I'll give you that," I admit, and his face lights up. I am momentarily stunned, but I snap out of it quick, realizing what I've just said. "But it makes no difference. I told you already. I don't date." Climbing into my car, I get comfortable behind the wheel.

Garrick steps right up in between me and the open car door. He crouches down, and his face is so close I have an unhindered view of the stunning amber flecks in his eyes. "Make an exception for me."

"I can't. I'm sorry."

"I'm not giving up."

Air whooshes out of my mouth even as a shot of excitement races through my veins. "You should." Butterflies go crazy in my chest as I lock eyes with him. His gaze drifts to my lips for a couple seconds, and lust pools low in my belly. I gulp over the sudden dryness in my mouth.

What is this guy doing to me?

I do not have these reactions to men.

Garrick has me all flustered, and there's a teeny part of me questioning whether I shouldn't just go out with him.

Averting my eyes, I glance down at my lap as I struggle to regain my usual composure. When I feel in control, I lift my head and look at him. Garrick has straightened to his full height, and he's leaning his arm against the top of my open door, patiently waiting for me to reject him again.

"You seem like a nice guy, Garrick. If the timing was different, maybe I would agree. But it's not. I can't go out with you, and you need to accept my decision."

His smile fades as he slowly nods, taking a step back. "Okay."

"Okay?" I blurt, unconvinced he would give up that easy. Then again, why would he chase someone who keeps rejecting him? A guy like Garrick has no problem scoring dates. He's hardly going to pursue someone who keeps shooting him down. A pang of disappointment slaps me in the face, which is ridiculous.

I want him to give up.
This is a good thing.
I should be happy he's backing off.
So why aren't I?
"You know how I feel. Should you change your mind, let me know." He taps the top of my car. "Drive safe, Stevie."

Chapter Six
Stevie

The enticing smell of coffee lures me from my bedroom on Monday morning. Delicious scents of caramel and nuts reels me into the kitchen, and that can only mean one thing— Ellen grabbed takeout from Bumble Bees.

Have I mentioned how much I love my college bestie?

I float into the kitchen with a massive smile on my face, and it blossoms into a full-blown cheesy grin when I discover Ellen and her boyfriend in a charged embrace. My roomie is in love, for real this time, and I love seeing her so happy. Will has Ellen caged against the counter, and the look on his face is downright feral.

"Don't mind me," I say, moving seamlessly around them. "I'm just here for the coffee."

Reaching for the paper holder containing four takeout coffees, I remove the cup with a large S on top. "If this is a caramel macchiato, I will love you forever and ever, babe," I say, grinning at my bestie.

"Now that's what I'm talking about," someone with a rich, deep, decidedly male voice says from behind me.

All the fine hairs on the back of my neck lift as warmth hits my spine. I already know who I'm going to find before I turn around—the hot, charming guy occupying prime real estate in my head and holding a recurring role in my stubborn dreams these past few nights.

There is no ignoring the swarm of butterflies that swoops into my chest as I spin around and face him. Fuck, why does he have to be so irresistible? "What are you doing here?" I blurt, trying my best not to drool as my gaze skims quickly over Garrick.

His chin-length hair is hanging in tousled strands around his chiseled jawline, and a thin layer of dark hair adorns his chin and cheeks. Those mesmerizing hazel eyes simmer with pleasure and amusement as he fixes them on my face. Plush lips I am *not* daydreaming about tasting part as a trickle of air seeps from his mouth.

Ripped dark-rinse slim-fitting jeans mold to his long legs. A black designer hoodie with a splash pattern on the front emphasizes his broad shoulders, defined arms, and toned chest and abs. A worn pair of black and white Nike Dunks covers his large feet, and some kind of Garmin sports watch is strapped around his wrist.

It's clear the guy has money, but he doesn't appear to flaunt it. His look is casual and effortless, and he exudes confidence. Garrick owns who he is, and that's the most attractive thing about him.

I hate I'm finding more reasons to like him, but it's the truth.

No matter how much I want to evict him from my thoughts and my dreams, he has hijacked my mind and ensnared me.

"Garrick and Will grabbed coffees on their way over," Ellen

pipes up, looking slightly sheepish as she stares at me with pleading eyes. "Isn't that super nice of them?"

"It is," I acknowledge, lifting the cup under my nose. They obviously checked what we liked, and that kind of thoughtfulness speaks volumes.

If Garrick is trying to impress me, great coffee is a good start. I eyeball him with sincerity. "Thank you."

"You're welcome."

Closing my eyes, I softly moan as the delicious aromas of one of my favorite coffees tickles my nostrils, making my mouth water in anticipation. I lick my lips before raising the cup to my mouth and taking the first reverent sip.

When my eyes pop open, Garrick is staring at me with dilated pupils, and his lips are slightly parted as he drags a hand through his messy, dark hair. He loudly clears his throat and arches a brow. "Good?"

"Yep." I attempt to ignore the erratic beating of my heart and the fluttering feeling in my chest as I meet his heated gaze. "In general, the coffee is shit in Oregon compared to Seattle. But Bumble Bees has my heart—and a decent amount of my weekly paycheck," I add, laughing a little.

"Next to my family, great coffee is the thing I miss most when at college." Garrick smiles, and it lights up his entire face. "Though you're right. Bumble Bees is good. I won't drink coffee from any other local place."

"Don't get me started on the shit they try to pass off as coffee on campus." A shudder works its way through me. "I almost threw up the first day when I tasted it."

"It's nasty, for sure."

Before he can dazzle me with another panty-melting smile, I take a second sip of my coffee and tilt my head to the side. "You didn't answer me. How come you're here?" I'm guessing Garrick and Will are friends, but that doesn't explain Garrick's motives for showing up at my house with coffee.

"Will and I share a house with two other buddies a few blocks from here. He mentioned he was driving Ellen to campus today, so I thought I'd bum a ride and see if you wanted to come with us?"

Ellen and I usually take turns driving Monday through Wednesday, because our schedules align, but that doesn't mean I'm comfortable riding with Garrick and Will.

"Thanks, but I'm fine to drive myself."

The smile doesn't fade from his face as he says, "Parking is tight on campus, and it's cleaner for the environment to only have one car on the road."

"Garrick raises valid points," Ellen agrees, and I whip my head around, glaring at my treacherous best friend.

All sense of pretense is gone now as she grins at me. "I already checked, and the guys will be leaving the same time as us. We're on their route home, so it's a no-brainer."

"We should hit the road unless we want to drive around for ages trying to locate a parking spot," Will says, distributing the other coffees. "Let's make a move."

***

"I thought you were giving up?" I say in a low voice as I sit in the back seat of Will's SUV, alongside Garrick, heading in the direction of UO.

I drink my coffee as he turns to face me, his knee brushing against mine with the motion. Sincerity oozes from his face as he holds my eyes captive. "I told you I'd back down, and I meant it." His tongue darts out, licking his lower lip.

That shouldn't be hot, but it is.

"I never want to make you uncomfortable or disrespect

your wishes. You've made yourself clear on the dating front." His lips twitch. "That doesn't mean we can't be friends." A full smile blooms across his mouth. "Our best friends are dating. We're going to be seeing more of one another, so we might as well make the best of it."

I stare at him through narrowed eyes, and he chuckles. "Friends? You just want to be friends now?"

He shakes his head, sending strands of dark hair skating across his strong brow. "You know what I want, but I'll settle for friends if that is all that's on offer."

"It is!" I confirm, ignoring the devil whispering naughty thoughts in my ear.

"Okay." His smile is so wide it threatens to split his face in two.

"That *is* all that's on offer!" I rub at a tense spot between my brows, hating how flustered I feel in his presence. It is most unlike me, and I don't like it.

"I know."

"I hope you do, because if this is some kind of ruse to convince me to date you, it won't work. I don't break my rules. I haven't had a boyfriend since junior year of high school, and even then, the only reason I caved was due to peer pressure. I'm way more assertive now, and I don't let anyone pressure me into doing something I don't want to do."

"Understood." He flashes me a perfect smile, and I'm torn between wanting to scream at him and kiss him.

Purely to wipe the smug grin from his mouth.

That's all.

"I mean it," I warn, scooting over to the door to put as much space between us as possible.

"I'll be the perfect gentleman, and I promise I won't hit on you again." Leaning back against his door, he pins me with a searing-hot look that burns through my flimsy defenses, igniting every part of me. Resolve and confidence are written all over his face, and I feel like the only person in the room not getting the joke.

"What?"

He feigns innocence as his brows tip up, but that infuriating smile is still firmly planted on his tempting lips. "Nothing, *bestie*."

I'm waging an internal war with the excitement and adrenaline coursing through my veins. "It won't work. Whatever you're planning. You should give up now."

He lifts his coffee to his mouth. "I don't have a clue what you mean."

I legit growl under my breath.

He chuckles, still grinning at me, and I realize it's his superpower the same time I understand I'm far from immune to the effects.

Waggling his brows, he points at my half-empty paper cup. "Drink up before it gets cold."

"I'm divorcing you," I grumble at Ellen as we make our way through the packed cafeteria toward the table at the back. "I'm serious. You're supposed to be on my side, not helping Garrick with whatever his nefarious plan is."

"Of course, I'm on your side." She giggles before looping her arm in mine. "You can thank me by making me maid of honor at your wedding."

My mouth hangs open in shock for a few seconds. "You did not just go there."

"Girl, the sparks were flying in the kitchen and the car. You cannot deny you two have chemistry," she says, weaving a path around a group of obnoxious frat boys blocking our way.

A few guys whistle as we pass, their gazes roaming appreciatively over us, but we don't acknowledge them. "It doesn't matter. I don't have time to date Garrick."

"That's bullshit, and you know it. I'm as busy as you, and Will has a crazy schedule too, but we're managing. That's what you do when you like someone and *You. Like. Him.*" She levels me with a knowing look, pulling us to a stop a few feet away from the table where Garrick, Will, and a couple of other guys wait. "I saw the way you were looking at one another. Garrick is hot, he's crazy about you, and Will says he's the best guy he knows. What harm would it do to go out on one date with him?"

"It has the potential to get messy. What if I took a chance on him and it didn't work out? That would make things extremely awkward for you and Will."

She vigorously shakes her head. "Nope. You're not going to use that as an excuse. It has nothing to do with Will and me. Our relationship won't be affected whether you date Garrick or not." She sighs. "Look, I don't want to be an interfering old hag, so I'm not going to pressure you. I just think you could be missing out on something great, and I want you to be happy."

"I am happy, Ellen. I don't need a guy to be fulfilled."

"That's not what I'm saying, and you know it." She tugs me forward. "Just promise me you'll keep an open mind. That's all I'm asking."

"That's asking a lot."

She stops again, stabbing me with a serious expression. "No matter how much we want to map out every path on our life journey, there are always unknown turns and unforeseen dips in the road." She squeezes my arm. "You gotta roll with it, babe. You never know where this path might lead, and you won't find out unless you take that leap."

Chapter Seven
Garrick

"Incoming." Will sports a lovesick goofy grin as he nudges me in the ribs, tipping his head in the direction of the two pretty ladies coming our way. He quickly removes his backpack from the chair beside him so it's free for his girlfriend. It's the busiest time to grab lunch in the cafeteria, and the place is teeming with students and buzzing with the sounds of raucous conversation and boisterous laughter.

"They're both hot," Noah proclaims, in between monstrous bites of his burger, as we watch Stevie and Ellen make their way toward our table. They stop for a bit, locked in what appears to be an intense conversation, and I wonder what that's all about.

On the other side of our table, Cohen is deep in conversation with two of his football buddies. The jocks' table is behind us, and Cohen usually sits with them. Today, he has graced us with his presence because he's curious to meet the girls.

Cohen is facing away, with his back to us, so he hasn't noticed their approach. I already warned him to be on his best behavior, and I'll kick his ass if he steps out of line. The odds are already stacked against me, and I don't want him perving over Stevie or Ellen and giving them the wrong impression of me and Will.

"Hey." Ellen smiles, waggling her fingers at me and Noah before claiming the seat beside her boyfriend.

Will leans in, planting a kiss on her mouth, and she visibly melts.

Dude is totally smitten.

"Hey, Stevie." I attempt to reassure her with a smile as she stands awkwardly at the edge of the table, looking like she wishes she was any place but here. "I kept this seat for you," I add, patting the empty space beside me. "Sit. I promise I won't bite."

Unless you ask. Then all bets are off.

I keep those thoughts firmly trapped in my head because they're premature. I'm focused on developing a friendship with Stevie in the hope she'll lower the shield she protects so fiercely and let herself act on the obvious chemistry we share. I know I'm not alone in feeling this, but I promised I wouldn't keep pushing, and I'm a man of my word.

Irrespective of how badly I want her, I will let her set the pace.

The ball is firmly in her court.

"Unless you're into that kinda thing, and then I'm sure my buddy would be more than happy to oblige," Cohen says, swirling around in his seat to join our conversation.

I drill him with a heated glare. A not-too-subtle reminder that he needs to tone down his assholish ways. It's like he just can't help himself when he's around a pretty girl. I'm still watching when he looks over at Stevie, so I spot the instant spark of recognition the same time Stevie sucks in a small startled gasp. My eyes flick to hers as she finally sits beside me, setting a brown paper bag down on the table and dumping her book bag on the ground at her feet.

Nibbling on the corner of her mouth, she glances swiftly between me and Cohen, and it clicks with me instantly. A sour taste pools in my mouth, and knots form in my gut.

"You two know one another?" Will asks what I'm afraid to, now he's no longer sucking face with Ellen.

Cohen's lips twitch as his gaze roams leisurely over Stevie, and I don't like it one little bit. "If you mean know in the biblical sense, then—"

"Watch your mouth." I cut across him, working hard to keep my ass in the seat when I long to reach across the table and ram my fist in his face. "Show some respect."

Cohen loses the smirk, but his jaw tightens in clear aggravation as he levels Stevie with a neutral look. "Apologies, Stevie. I meant no disrespect."

"None taken," she says, recovering her composure fast. Her slender fingers open the paper bag, and she removes a wrap, a bottle of water, and an apple. She must have bought it from the deli on campus, and it's surprising we didn't bump into one another there.

"He can't help himself," Noah supplies, balling up the wrapper from his burger and depositing it on the tray along with the rest of the remnants of his lunch. "His default setting is stuck on asshole."

"Hey!" Cohen tries to defend himself. "I'm not that bad."

"I'm sure we don't want to get into all that here." Will slides his arm around Ellen's shoulders, attempting to defuse the situation.

"We're cool, Stevie, right?" Cohen leans back in his chair and smiles at her.

"I have no beef with you." Her smile is tight, but I detect no animosity. Just the same awkwardness the rest of us are feeling with the obvious elephant in the room.

"Awesome." Cohen offers her a tame smile before diving into his meatball sub.

A pregnant pause ensues, and it's cringing.

Clearing my throat, I slide one of the smoothies in front of me across the small gap to Stevie. "I got you this. Ellen said you like them."

"That was extremely thoughtful. Thank you, but you don't need to keep buying me things. Unless you're like this with all your friends?"

Cohen almost chokes on his sandwich. Is it bad, for a fleeting second, I wished he did? I don't want to start shit with my buddy, especially for something that happened before I met Stevie, but knowing he's probably hooked up with her sticks in my gut.

"Gar is a generous guy," Noah says before adding, "I'm Noah, by the way."

"Nice to meet you," Stevie says. "How do you guys all know one another?"

"Cohen and Noah are the roomies I mentioned," I confirm. On the other side of me, Ellen and Will are whispering, which is rude, but whatever. I'm kind of over this lunch already.

"And Gar and I are both family enterprise majors," Noah confirms. "You're a sophomore too, right?"

Stevie nods as she picks at her wrap.

"What's your major?"

I am uncharacteristically quiet as I finish my sandwich, lost in my thoughts, but I'm listening to the conversation around me.

"Floral management." She confirms what I already know in between drinking sips of the smoothie.

"That's an interesting choice," Cohen says. "What made you pick that?"

I fight the urge to snarl at him, which is unfair because he's not hitting on her and he's trying to be sociable, which is a big concession for a guy like Cohen. I'm pissed at whatever has transpired between them in the past, but I'm not asshole enough to blast either of them for it. I know Cohen isn't any competition. If he'd been interested in pursuing her, he'd have done it already, so I wish I could snap out of this funk.

"My nana runs a garden center back home in Ravenna. Her parents set the business up in the nineteen twenties, and she took it over when they retired. I've been helping her out since I was a little girl, and I always find it peaceful surrounded by nature and plants and flowers." She shrugs, sending waves of glossy red hair cascading over her shoulders, and my fingers twitch with a craving to touch the silky strands. "I guess it's in my DNA."

The awkwardness dissipates as the conversation picks up at the table, but I'm quieter than usual as I listen to everyone talking, too lost in my head to properly engage. Breathing a sigh of relief when lunch ends twenty minutes later, I gather all the trash from the table onto my tray and walk off to throw it away. I need some space to shake myself out of my bad mood.

So what if Cohen hooked up with the girl I'm crushing on?

It was in the past.

Everyone's got a past. I know that. So why does this hurt? Why does it matter so much?

The normal me would be able to let it go, but Stevie has me twisted into knots, and I'm not acting like myself.

When I return, everyone is ready to go. "We'll meet you out by the car at six," Will says to Ellen before planting another kiss on her swollen lips. My buddy is infatuated in a way he hasn't been before. From what I have seen, it appears mutual, which is good, because Will is a decent guy, and he doesn't deserve to be jerked around if Ellen doesn't share his feelings.

"Thank you for the smoothie and for saving me a chair, Garrick," Stevie says as she slings her bag over one shoulder.

"No problem, and it's Gar. All my friends call me Gar," I remind her, desperately wanting her friendship, because if it's the only way I can get close to her, I'll take it.

She tilts her chin up, and a soft smile ghosts over her mouth. "I like your full name. If you don't mind, I'd much rather call you Garrick."

Now I know it's not because she's keeping me at arm's length, I love that she calls me that. "I don't mind."

"Cool." Threading her arm through Ellen's, she waves at all of us before walking off.

"Gar." Cohen steps beside me as we head off in the other direction, toward the rear exit.

"I don't want any details," I say, shoving my free hand in the pocket of my jeans. "But were you with her?"

There's a brief pause before he confirms it. "Yeah, it was a couple of months into freshman year and—"

"I'm not trying to be an asshole, but that's as much as I need to know."

"Stevie is great, but I'm not going to hit on your girl. I know I'm a jerk at times, but I'd never go there."

"I get it, and it's fine." I push out through the door, joining other students leaving the cafeteria. "And for the record, she's not my girl."

"Yet." Noah slaps me on the back. "It's only a matter of time before Cohen and I'll be flying solo while you two are all wifed up."

Chapter Eight
Stevie

"Are you in a rush, or could we go inside to talk in private?" I ask Garrick the second Will kills the engine curbside at our apartment building.

Garrick slowly turns his head, his brownish-green eyes scrutinizing my expression for a few beats. I see no hint of gold in his irises today, and I miss it. He truly has the most arresting eyes. It's no wonder I'm having trouble concentrating when he fixes his peepers on me.

"Sure." He nods, and I release the breath I was holding as I climb out of the back seat of the SUV. Garrick was quiet at lunch, and quiet on the ride home, and I suspect I'm the reason for it.

I about died when Cohen turned around at the table and I realized who he was. I know I don't owe Garrick any explanation, but I don't want things to be strained between us. Especially when he's been so sweet and thoughtful today. I wonder if he feels differently about me now he knows I engage in random hookups.

That thought shouldn't send panic racing through my veins like it does.

But if he's going to turn all judgmental, then it will help my cause. I won't apologize for who I am or how I live my life. And I'm certainly not apologizing for something that happened before we knew one another. Especially when we're not dating. I know he likes me, and I get it probably pisses him off I've hooked up with his friend. Honestly, if the tables were turned, I would feel the same. Which is why we need to have a conversation.

Will and Ellen have their arms wrapped around one another in the elevator as we make our way up to the fifth floor. Ellen shoots concerned glances our way as we stand silently side by side, the tension accelerating with every passing second, and I'm glad when we reach our floor and the doors ping open.

Will and Ellen make a beeline for the couch after we close the door to our apartment, stopping to grab snacks and drinks on the way. I busy myself making coffee while Garrick hovers in the background, doing a good impression of a brooding rock star. "Cream or sugar?" I ask after I've poured coffee into two mugs. "We have a sugar substitute too, if you prefer?"

He shakes his head. "I'll take it black."

"It's not Bumble Bees, but it's decent," I say, handing him a mug.

"Thanks." His appreciative smile is sincere, and I don't think Garrick is the type of guy to stay grumpy for long. At least I hope he's not.

After stirring some sweetener in my coffee, I dump the spoon in the sink and jerk my head for him to follow me. His footsteps are quiet as he trails me down the hallway and into my bedroom. I close the door behind us, purely for privacy. Ellen is a nosy bitch, and she loves getting all up in my business. I wouldn't put it past her to try to eavesdrop even though she knows I'll tell her everything later.

Gesturing for Garrick to take the seat at my desk, I plonk my butt down on the end of my bed and just go for it. No point in pussyfooting around the subject. "We need to discuss Cohen. I didn't want to say anything at lunch, because it wasn't the time or place, but I'd hate for things to be awkward between us."

"It's cool," he says, wrapping his large hands around his mug. "You don't need to say anything."

"I know, but I'd prefer to clear the air all the same."

He takes a healthy mouthful of his coffee as his eyes invite me to continue.

"I met Cohen at the first frat party I attended, about a month into freshman year. I was with a few of my classmates. Ellen wasn't there." I don't want him thinking my roomie knew and was keeping it from him. It's important to Ellen that she gets along with Will's friends. "I overindulged, and I was fairly tipsy. Not to be disrespectful to your friend, but he's not my usual type."

Truthfully, I usually run a mile from jocks.

I know they aren't all promiscuous idiots, but enough of them are for me to avoid taking one to my bed.

"Not to be rude, Stevie, but I don't want to hear all the details."

"I would never kiss and tell," I calmly reply.

"Cohen wouldn't either. I know he's no saint, but he doesn't dish the dirt. He hasn't told me the specifics, and I would never ask."

It says a lot about the kind of man Garrick is that he'll defend his friend even when he's clearly angry with him. "It was a onetime drunken hookup. I barely remember it, to be honest, and I'm sure it's the same for him. It didn't mean anything." I square my shoulders and look him in the eye. "But he's not the first guy I've hooked up with, and he most likely won't be the last. I might not have time for a relationship, but I've still got needs. When I need sex, I go and get it. It's no different than when a guy does it, but if you think differently of me now or—"

"I'm not judging you, Stevie, and I don't think differently of you."

"Yet, you're upset."

Putting his mug down, he claws a hand through his hair and leans forward with his elbows on his knees. "I am upset, and honestly, it surprises me. This isn't my usual MO. I'd be a dick to hold something in your past against you. I know that, but I can't shake this feeling. I've been mulling over that more than anything. But I'm not upset with you or Cohen for hooking up before either of you knew me. I'm not an asshole. It is what it is. It's just..." He trails off, his eyes lowering to the hardwood floor.

"It's just what?" I ask in a gentle tone, coaxing him to let it out.

Lifting his head, he drills me with a confident look I'm more used to seeing on his face. "I'm jealous."

I thought it might be jealousy except this seems nuts when we've only known each other a few days. "Does it strike you as odd how potent our reactions are to one another?"

His lips curl at the corners, and I'm glad to see it even if I slipped up by admitting the truth. "It's not usual for me, if that's what you're asking. It's—"

"Do not say fate!"

His smile expands. "Wouldn't dream of it."

"Ugh." Tilting my head back, I stare at the ceiling wondering what the hell I'm doing.

Like, legit, what the fuck am I doing?

"It's good to know you're not totally in denial," he says, reclaiming my attention. A full grin slips over his mouth, and his dimples come out to play.

Yep, just kill me now!

"You know it—"

"Changes nothing."

I flip him the bird, and he chuckles, picking up his mug again.

A comfortable silence descends for a few seconds while we both drink our coffee and contemplate whatever the hell is going on between us.

He breaks it first.

"Can I ask you something?"

Although wary, I nod.

"Why are you so against relationships?"

Air expels from my mouth. This is a pretty heavy convo for such a new friendship, but I'm not going to hide from him or lie. I move up to the top of the bed and rest my back against the headboard with my mug in my hands. "Come join me." The words have barely left my mouth, and he's striding across my bedroom, eating up the space quickly with his long legs.

Garrick gets comfortable beside me, and I angle my head so we're face-to-face. "I'm the first to admit I'm a bit of a control freak," I say.

He fights a smirk, and I level him with a dark look. "I've only known you five minutes, and I can already tell you like things orderly." His gaze skates around my tidy bedroom. "Case in point. I don't think I've ever seen a student's room so neat, tidy, and regimentally organized." He brushes hair out of his face, smiling in amusement while he peers at me. "If you ever end up in my room, I'll have to blindfold you so you don't see the mess."

"Oh no. That's it." I shake my head. "We can't be friends."

He chuckles. "Maybe you'll be a good influence on me."

"But will you be a good influence on me? That's the million-dollar question."

"What if I want to be a *bad* influence?" Heat flares behind his retinas as he pins me with a suggestive look that has me discreetly squeezing my thighs together. I playfully push his chest. He's solid and warm beneath my touch, and it's almost impossible to resist the urge to crawl into his lap and siphon some of that body heat.

"Stop with the innuendo." It takes massive self-control to withdraw my hand from his chest. "We're just friends, remember?"

"Of course." The grin is firmly planted on his face, but it's good to see it. I only realized I missed it when he was quiet and sullen this afternoon. "And you were going to tell me why you're allergic to dating."

A laugh spills from my lips. "I guess that's one way of putting it."

He finishes his coffee and puts the empty mug down. Moving closer, he reaches out, softly threading his fingers through my hair. "Sorry, I know we're trying to have a serious conversation, but I can't hold back any longer. You have the most beautiful hair, and I've been dying to touch it."

I'm in a daze as I stare at his lush mouth while he rakes his fingers in my hair.

"I wondered if it would feel soft as silk, and now I know."

Our eyes meet, and attraction smolders in the small gap between us. It would be easy to bridge the distance and press my mouth to his. I know he wouldn't turn me away, but I can't get distracted by his full lips, those naughty dimples, or the warmth and vitality brimming in his eyes.

I do not do this.

And I need to get a grip.

Scooting over to the edge of the bed, I drink the dregs of my now lukewarm coffee and give myself a silent pep talk. Anything to avoid surrendering to the feelings simmering under the surface of my skin.

"Is it fear?"

My eyes meet his.

Concern glimmers in his eyes. "Did someone hurt you?"

I place my empty mug on my bedside table and lie down on my side facing him. "No one hurt me, but I suppose fear plays a small part."

Garrick mirrors my position except he tucks a hand under his head as he waits for me to elaborate.

"My mom got pregnant at twenty, just before the start of her sophomore year at UO. She wanted to be a doctor until she met a handsome sailor one night in Seattle, and they had a wild night together." A shudder works its way through me. I peer directly into Garrick's eyes, loving how he clings attentively to everything I say. "Those were her words, not mine, and yes, it's gross, and I'd rather she hadn't overshared, but it's good to know I was the product of fun if I wasn't borne out of love."

"I'm sure your mother loves you. I imagine it'd be impossible not to."

And there he goes again. If I didn't know better, I'd swear I conjured Garrick out of my vivid imagination—a mashup of every book boyfriend I've ever swooned over.

"My mom is great." I pluck at the comforter as I smile. "You met her actually. She works the front desk at the Sand Point restaurant."

"Ms. Colson." He bobs his head. "I don't know why I didn't spot the resemblance. You look alike."

"I have her eyes, and we share the same stubborn streak though it manifests in different ways." I run my fingers back and forth across the comforter as we speak. "Mom is an eternal optimist and the biggest romantic. She had to sacrifice her dreams when she became pregnant with me. I know she doesn't regret it, but it's hard not to feel guilty sometimes. Especially when I have to endure watching her falling for the wrong guy, over and over, and I can't help wondering if things would be different if she wasn't a single mom."

"That's not your burden to bear." Reaching out, he touches his pinky against mine.

"I know and I don't carry it. Sometimes, I shoulder it, but mostly, it feels like a lesson to be learned."

He hooks his finger around mine, and my heart pounds against my rib cage. "In what way?"

"Mom was always chasing boys and yearning for love, and ultimately, she sacrificed her career because she wasn't focused on the right things. It feels wrong to call it a mistake, as if I'm acknowledging I am a mistake, which I know I'm not, but I don't want to follow the same path. I want to make something of myself. I have career goals and a plan for the next ten years of my life."

"And if you let any boy distract you, your life might veer off track?" he surmises, threading his fingers fully in mine.

"Exactly. I'm not saying I don't believe in love or that I don't want to get married and have kids one day, because I do, but that's not even remotely in the cards now."

"How old are you, Stevie?"

"I'll be twenty in June."

"You are so mature and way more determined and self-aware than most girls your age, and I don't mean that to be insulting to you or other girls."

A laugh bursts from my lips. "I know. I sound ancient. Ellen and my friend Hadley are always telling me that."

"There is nothing wrong with being goal-orientated or knowing what you want from life and going after it. I have goals too, but I live by the motto you should work hard and play hard. When do you get to play, Stevie? When do you have fun?"

The insinuation I don't have fun rubs me the wrong way, and I yank my hand back, sliding it between my knees. "I find *that* insulting." Fire burns in my eyes. "I know how to have fun, and I have plenty of it. I'm not some boring bitch who is all work and no play."

I sometimes hang out with the crew at The End Zone on Friday nights after our shifts end. It usually involves copious Patron shots and drunk dancing until the early hours after the bar is officially closed. I always go out Saturday nights, either to a party or a movie or I head home to hang out with Hadley. I've had wild one-night stands. I have cliff jumped and skinny-dipped, and I'm game to try anything once. I could say all that, and a lot more, but I don't have to explain myself to a guy who is virtually a stranger.

"I'm sorry. I didn't mean to offend you or imply anything. I'm just trying to get to know you. To understand your motivations and what you're passionate about. You know I think you're fascinating. I already told you and I'd never lie."

I pull myself back up until I'm sitting against the headboard. It feels too intimate lying side by side, and I need to mark clear boundaries between us if we are to become friends. Tucking my hair behind my ears, I attempt to leash the sudden rush of anger his baseless assessment has induced. "I know I'm not your typical college student, but that doesn't mean I'm some nerdy bore."

"I didn't think you were. I see how hard you work, and you're clearly very driven. I just wanted to know if you make time to relax." He sits up and raises his palms. "I swear that's all I meant."

"I've shared stuff with you today I don't readily talk to

others about," I truthfully admit. "It shocks me that I opened up so easily to you, and now I'm wondering if I should have."

"Please don't say that. I'm honored you felt you could talk to me about it."

"You seem to own who you are, and I admire and respect you for that. All I'm asking is for you to give me the same courtesy."

"I admire and respect you a hell of a lot, Stevie."

"Even if I have casual sex instead of committed relationships? 'Cause it seems to me we both have very opposing views in this regard."

He exhales heavily. "God, I'm making a mess of everything." Dragging his hands through his hair, he shakes his head. "Now you think I'm a judgy asshole, and I'm not. I swear I'm not. I'm just an idiot who seems to have forgotten how to speak to a woman he likes."

The edge slices off my anger. I might not know him well, but I think I'm a pretty decent judge of character, and Garrick *is* a good guy. I haven't exactly been making it easy for him either.

"It's fine. I probably overreacted. I get defensive when people get on my case, and my friends and my mom are always nagging me. I think I was the only seventeen-year-old in the whole of Seattle who had their mom begging them to go out and party instead of staying home to study."

He chuckles, and it helps to break up the tense atmosphere. "Your mom really did that?"

I nod. "All the damn time. She was always worrying I was wasting my youth." I roll my eyes. "One time, she locked me out of the house and threw a bag out the window at me. This was after having called my best friend Hadley to come take me to a party one of our classmates was throwing. She refused to let me back in until I'd gone for a minimum of an hour and kissed at least one boy. And I needed to provide photographic proof."

Laughter rumbles through his chest, emitting as a loud booming sound as he cracks up. "I knew there was a reason I liked your mom. She's awesome."

"She really is."

"So, did you do it?" His smile is back in place, and I'm hypnotized all over again.

"Do what?" I blurt, the picture of confusion as brain fog sweeps through my head.

He rubs his chest, attempting to smother his laughter this time. "Kiss a boy and provide photographic proof?"

"Hell yeah." Now it's my turn to smirk. I can't keep the grin off my face when I say, "I kissed three and had the pics to prove it."

Booming laughter erupts from his mouth, and I love how his whole persona lights up when he laughs.

Garrick truly is a beautiful man, and I must be insane to deny him. But my self-imposed rules are there to keep me on track, and I can't lose sight of that. "There is one really important thing you should know about me," I say.

Dimples wink at me as he holds his smile. "Let me guess. You never back down from a challenge?"

"Never back down and always raise the stakes. If you test me, I'll test you right back." I flick his nose. "And that's the only warning you're getting."

Chapter Nine
Garrick

"We should put a date in the calendar for our camping trip," Hudson says as we talk Wednesday night on the phone. It's the first day of May, and there are officially only four weeks until school is out, so we are making plans for summer break like we did last year.

"I'll need to talk to Dad and Dawn, check my work schedule, and find out if Mom has planned anything on the weekends, so I'll get back to you."

Swiveling on my chair, I drum my fingers on top of the desk in my bedroom. Books are scattered around me, and my laptop is open on my final assignment of the year. It's due next Monday, and I'm trying to finish it before my gigs over the weekend. The guys are coming on Saturday, and it'll probably turn into a session. Our last blowout before we knuckle down to study and take exams.

Glancing around the messy room, I smile as I imagine the horror on Stevie's face if she was here. She'd probably have a coronary. I've never paid much attention to the organized chaos that surrounds me until a gorgeous redhead showed up in my life, turning it upside down. Shit, I really need to clean up my act before I completely blow my chances with her.

"Is Ivy still trying to set you up with Pepper?" Hudson asks, yanking me from my inner monologue. To say my best friend is not a fan of my mother is an understatement. He can't stand her and hates how she tries to manipulate me.

I shrug even though he can't see me. "It's like talking to a brick wall, but Pepper is cool. She gets it, and it could be worse."

A few beats of silence pass before he clears his throat, refocusing the conversation on our trip. "I'm available any time except for the last two weeks in July," my childhood buddy from North Bend confirms. "That's when I'm going on a post-divorce trip with Dad."

"Is he still depressed?"

"His wife was having an affair with her personal trainer, who happens to be fifteen years younger, and she walked out on her marriage for him. I'm pretty sure it's going to take Dad more than a few months to get over it."

"I was too young when my parents divorced to notice whether either of them was depressed, but I'm sure everyone who experiences it goes through it. Your dad will pull through." I know Hudson has been worried about him, and he's still not talking to his mom, so he's focusing all his energies on his dad.

"I'm just glad I got him to agree to a vacation. He's been pulling crazy hours at the hospital, and I know he's throwing himself into work to avoid dealing."

"Can't blame the man."

"I still can't believe my mother has done this."

"Yeah, it sucks. I can relate." When I was fourteen, I discovered my mother's second husband was the man she'd been having an affair with while still married to my dad. I didn't speak to her for over a year that time, only relenting when Dad encouraged me to let go of the past like he had.

"I remember how angry you were, and I feel the same way. I'm so pissed at my mom and worried about Dad."

"This could end up being a good thing for your dad though. Look how happy mine is now. Sometimes, things happen for a reason."

We end the call, promising to catch up before the weekend and agree on a date for our trip. I have only just turned the page on my leadership development book when Dad calls. "Hey, Dad. What's up?"

"Just calling to check in. How's school, and are you all set for your exams?"

I lean back in my chair, stifling a yawn. "It's good. More than good."

"Tell me more." I can hear the smile in his tone.

"I met a girl."

He chuckles, and I know what he's thinking.

"Stevie is special. Things feel different with her. Good different."

"I can't wait to meet her."

"I just have to convince her to go out with me first."

Laughter filters down the line. "She's making you work for it. Good for Stevie. I already like her."

"You're going to love her, and I have faith in my ability to win her over."

"I have no doubt you will. You love big, and you don't give up when you want something. I admire those traits in you."

"Thanks, Dad. How are Dawn and my troublesome brothers?"

"Dawn is good. The twins are still troublesome, but some-one's got to keep me on my toes!"

"Tell them I miss them and we'll hang out over the summer."

"They miss you too, and that's why I called. I didn't put you on the roster for the first week. Figure you need some R & R after your exams."

"Thanks, Dad." I have learned about balance from the man who raised me. Dad works hard, but he always makes plenty of time to destress. His family and his health come before the business, and I don't think there are many CEOs who could make the same claim.

"If you like, you can join us in Cyprus. We'll be there for the month of June."

Dawn's great-grandparents were from Cyprus, and when Dad took her to Paphos, in the early years of their marriage, they loved it so much they bought a vacation home there. It helps that it's in a five-star golf resort with an award-winning course and a bunch of amenities on site. You can even see the clubhouse, driving range, and the first tee from the upper level of our house. Dad is like a little kid on Christmas morning whenever we vacation there.

"Thanks for the offer. It's tempting. But I'll pass. I want to hang out at home and do a bit of hiking."

"The place is open all of July, so feel free to avail of it. I can take you off the schedule for a week or ten days."

My heart swells with love for my old man. "I'll keep it in mind." Perhaps Stevie might be up for a Cypriot vacay.

"One last thing, I've split your schedule between the winery and the lumberyard this year. Alternate weeks. You need to gain a firmer understanding of both businesses."

I have worked with Dad at the lumber company every summer since I was fourteen. It's like a home away from home. The winery was a fledgling business back then, only in operation a few years, but its growth has been nothing short of miraculous, and it now accounts for twenty percent of the Allen Company overall annual gross income. So, it makes sense I need to get more involved.

"I look forward to it."

"Good man." Pride suffuses his tone. "You can stay at the cabin there on those weeks if you don't want to drive in and out every day."

I chuckle. "Dad, it's only a forty-minute drive to Woodinville. It's not like I'd be driving to Oregon every day."

"I stay over sometimes, and it's nice not to have a commute occasionally. I'm just saying it's an option."

"I hear you, and I've got to go. This assignment won't write itself."

<hr>

I'm up early the next morning for a run, but I ditch my usual route through Hendricks Park in favor of a shorter route around the area where we live because I've got an early morning tutorial.

When I round the next bend, a smile spreads across my lips as I spot the distinctive redhead walking a few yards in front of me. Stevie is pounding the sidewalks, moving at an energetic pace, her long legs striding easily as her arms swing at her sides. Wearing a sleeveless running top and tiny little running shorts, she is a vision for my tired eyes. Damn, her ass looks good in those shorts, and my dick wholeheartedly approves.

I jog faster to catch up to her, noticing the ink on her neck for the first time as her ponytail swishes side to side. Slowing my pace, I walk the last few steps toward her so she hears me and isn't surprised. But I didn't realize she's got AirPods in.

Stevie jumps and emits a startled scream when I appear

alongside her. Stumbling, she almost trips over her feet, and I hold her elbow to steady her.

Tugging the pods from her ears, she rubs a hand across her chest. It takes considerable effort not to lower my eyes. I've noticed she's got a killer rack, and her chest is heaving from exertion, so not peeking is monumentally difficult. But I don't ever want to objectify her or make her think what we have is purely physical. My attraction to her is way deeper than how she looks or the electrifying chemistry we share.

Everything about Stevie Colson enchants me.

"Fucking hell, Garrick. You almost gave me a coronary." She thumps my upper arm. "You can't go creeping up on people like that."

"I wasn't creeping. I stopped running so you'd hear me walking up. I didn't realize you were listening to music."

"I'm listening to a podcast actually." Her eyes skim over my training top and shorts as we walk at a brisk pace. Her tongue pokes out between her lips, and her eyes widen when she notices my hair is tied back in a man bun. I fucking hate that term. The only time I rock this look is when I'm exercising and I need to keep my hair out of my eyes so I don't trip and crack my skull or drop a weight on my foot.

"Which one?" I inquire.

"It's a true crime podcast. I listen to a bunch of different ones. If I'm not listening to music when I run, I am usually listening to this."

"Sounds interesting."

Her eyes narrow in suspicion. "How are you here? This feels semi-stalkerish."

I laugh. "If I'm going to do something, I go all in. If I was stalking you, you wouldn't know it. I'd be all about the stealth."

She rolls her eyes. "I'm not sure I believe you."

"It's the truth. I usually run at the park, but I need to be on campus early today, so I decided to run locally."

"So, it's just a coincidence we bumped into one another then?" Her expression conveys her continued wariness.

"You call it coincidence. I call it—"

She blocks her ears with her hands and starts singing, "La, la, la."

Warmth spreads across my chest as I chuckle. She's too fucking cute. I wait until she stops singing and lowers her hands. "Fate, but we're not labeling shit, so pretend I said nothing." After our heart-to-heart on Monday night, we agreed to not put any labels on anything and to just hang out.

"You're incorrigible."

"You get what you see." I gesture toward myself, pleased when her eyes drink me in like a cold refreshing drink on a hot Texas day.

"I didn't know you had ink," I say, purposely changing the subject. "What is it?"

She slams to a halt and turns around. "See for yourself." Lifting her ponytail, she bends her head so I can see the small design.

The artwork is sublime, and whoever tattooed it is clearly talented and master level. Encased in a black circle is a triple spiral symbol in a rotational pattern. Gold and silver are entwined with the black to create a stunning visual. "It's beautiful." I sweep my fingers over it. "Is it a Celtic symbol?"

"Yes." Her one-word reply comes out in a throaty whisper.

"What does it mean?" I ask, removing my hand and freeing her ponytail from between her fingers.

She turns to face me. "It's called a triskelion or triskele, and it's a complex ancient Celtic symbol that can mean many things like life, death, rebirth. Father, mother, child. Past, present, future. Power, intellect, love. My dad was of Irish ancestry. That was something he divulged to Mom that night."

I want to ask her about him. To understand why he's not in her life. But it's a bit too heavy for six thirty a.m., so I dampen my natural curiosity.

"I wanted to get a tattoo of something that would represent my father," she continues, "so I had a piece of him with me but also something that had deeper meaning for me. It's an emblem of resilience and determination in the Celtic culture, and I knew this was what I wanted when I found it."

"It's perfect for you, and it's a stunning tattoo. Why hide it where no one can see?" I hadn't seen it at The End Zone or the country club, and she was wearing her hair in a ponytail on both occasions. But her hair is thick, and the ink is small, so it's well hidden from prying eyes. I am guessing that's probably the point.

"This is just for me."

God, this girl. The more I learn about her, the more I like her.

Stevie moves to start walking again, but I place my hand on her lower arm to stop her. Delicious tremors dance across my skin from where we're touching and it's like I've been tasered.

No one has *ever* affected me like this.

"I need to show you something." I whip off my shirt and point at the tattoo over my left pec. Her eyes are out on stalks as she checks out my bare chest. I run, work out at the campus gym, and I'm an outdoors person, hiking and biking when I get the time. I know I'm in good shape, and I like that she seems to approve.

Her hand hovers over my chest, and her eyes lift to mine. "Can I touch it?"

"Of course." My lips tip upward. "I probably should've asked before I touched yours."

"It's fine," she says, and I try not to flinch as her soft fingertips coast over my tattoo. Warmth seeps underneath my skin at her touch, and I try to think of gross things when I feel my dick twitching in my pants. I'm only wearing light running shorts, and they do nothing to disguise a boner.

"This is Celtic too," she surmises, inspecting the design up close. Her face is right by my chest, and heat rolls off her body, washing over me in heady waves.

My dick stirs, and panic sets in. I need to keep things friendly between us. Sporting a semi from the slightest touch is not cool, and I silently plead with my body to get with the program. Thankfully, Stevie is too engrossed in my ink to notice how badly I'm struggling to maintain control.

"What does it mean?" Tilting her chin up, she stares at me with her gorgeous, big emerald-colored eyes, and I could easily drown in the way she's looking at me.

Fuck. I really have it bad.

"It's a Trinity knot," I explain, my voice gruffer than usual. "It's one of the earliest symbols of Christianity. Not that I'm religious. I chose it because it symbolizes father and son."

Her eyes attentively hold mine, and it's hard to breathe, but at least it's distracting the snake in my pants.

"Technically, it symbolizes Father, Son, and the Holy Ghost," I continue. "I'm close to my dad, and I wanted to get something that represented him and our relationship. There's Irish ancestry in my family on my dad's side." Something else we have in common. "So, this seemed appropriate, and it called out to me. If I'm going to permanently mark my skin, I want it to mean something, and I need to be comfortable looking at it for the rest of my life."

"I totally get it. It was the same for me though I have to look in the mirror to see mine."

Does it make me a pussy that I feel like crying when she removes her hand and takes a step back?

"I constantly find myself touching it," she admits. "At times when I need comfort, or often, I'll just absently touch it. It gives me a sense of..."

"Inner peace."

She bobs her head. "Yeah. That's it."

Silently, I pull my top back on, and we set off walking at a more leisurely pace.

"The Trinity knot is in the Book of Kells in Dublin. Someday, I want to go to Ireland and visit it."

Her eyes spark to life and she's almost giddy as she looks up at me. "Oh my god, yes! Me too. The Triskelion is found at the entrance to Newgrange, which is this ancient stone passage tomb, in Ireland. It's on my mug list to go there."

My lips twitch. "Mug list?"

She giggles. "It's my version of a bucket list."

"I like it," I say as we round the next corner, and her apartment building materializes in the near distance. "And you know what this means?" I let a wide grin loose on my face.

She groans, thumping me in the arm. "Do not say fate or kismet or anything else cheesy, or I'm liable to thump you somewhere a lot less pleasant."

Chapter Ten
Stevie

"I don't know how I let you talk me into this," I shout in Ellen's ear as she bounces around on her stool at our table close to the stage. A large speaker is right in front of us. Add that to the noise of an enthusiastic crowd, and it's almost impossible to speak. At least without shouting directly in someone's ear.

"It's one last blowout before our heads are stuffed in books and we're drowning in study and exams. The gang is all here. You couldn't have sat this one out." Nudging me in the side, she grins like a loon as she directs her attention to where Garrick is performing on stage.

It's Saturday night, and he must be exhausted because he also played a set at The End Zone last night. I was on shift. My last one until next semester because I'm finishing up early to concentrate on my upcoming exams, and then I'm heading back to Seattle for summer break.

Last night was even busier than his opening night, if that's possible, and it was pretty hellish. I was dead on my feet by the time I flopped into my bed at three a.m. I barely got a second to myself all night, and the only break I managed to grab was a ten-minute breather with Garrick during his interval.

We've settled into an easy friendship despite the frisson of electricity that threatens to zap us every time we're together. I'm sure it will die down in time. Right now, I like hanging out with him, and I'm not inspecting that further.

Garrick asked me to come out tonight, and I initially said no. This sports bar is on the other side of town and notorious for underage drinking and bar fights. I tend to avoid it. Besides, I had planned on studying until Ellen badgered me into coming out. It was that or listen to her relentless list of reasons why I should go on a repetitive loop all afternoon.

Seemed counterproductive, so here I am.

Squeezed into a tight-fitting black lace crop top that makes the girls appear bigger and ripped black skinny jeans with high heeled boots, I know I look good. My hair hangs down my back in soft waves, and my makeup is on point. I'm in a great mood, on a buzz and enjoying myself, though that could be the three beers I've had or the stream of heated looks leveled my way from the gorgeous man on the stage.

When his eyes aren't closed, lost in a song, Garrick has been keeping me in his sights. He has barely taken his eyes off me, and the girls shoving and pushing one another at the front of the stage, competing for his attention, are starting to notice. The next time he looks over here, I make a slicing motion across my neck in a "cut it out" maneuver.

Sitting up there, with the lights shining down on him, a guitar on his lap, and a mic at his lips, he looks like he was born to be a rocker. The sleeves of the tight black shirt he's wearing are rolled up, showcasing delicious arm porn, and a hint of smooth skin peeks out from the unbuttoned opening at his neck. A few leather bands wrap around one wrist, and a thick silver chain rests low on his collarbone. I'm fascinated by the veins in his arms and the way his muscles flex and roll as he plucks the guitar strings. Watching his long slim fingers expertly work the guitar sends a tremor of heat shooting through my nether regions.

Not that I'm imagining those fingers working their magic on me.

I'm not imagining that at all.

Friends don't have those kinds of thoughts about friends.

And that's all we are.

F.R.I.E.N.D.S.

I hate that I keep needing to remind myself.

Garrick's messy hair hangs around his gorgeous face like tangled dark sheets. Navy denims and scuffed black boots complete the look. It's understated, and I doubt it took him long to get ready, but he's one tempting package, that's for sure.

He belongs up there.

It's a shame to waste such talent, but I would never tell any person how to live their life. Garrick is close to his family, and he's proud of their business. Sparks glow in his eyes when he talks about them, in the same way it does when he talks about music. It's clear he's not being forced into the family business. He has chosen it, and I sense it's a source of pride for him. There is nothing wrong with that. Even if I look up at the god on the stage and wonder how he can turn his back on something that could be a major deal for him.

Garrick announces a break, and Will and Cohen head to the bar to grab more beers before we join him in his dressing room backstage.

Noah barges into the room without knocking. "Oh, shit," he exclaims as the rest of us pile into the small space. "I didn't know you had company." Rubbing the back of his neck, Noah glances at me with a slightly apologetic expression.

I swallow over a lump in my throat at the scene in front of

me. A stunning girl, with long sheets of straight golden-blonde hair, is pressed against Garrick, smiling up at him like he put the stars in the sky. She's teeny and petite, and if it wasn't for the skyscraper heels on her feet, she would barely reach his chest. Dainty hands rest on his bare lower arms where they hang at his sides. Her delicate curves are draped in a black bandage-style minidress, and she looks every inch a rock star's princess.

The chicken I ate at dinner threatens to make a reappearance, so I turn around, mumbling about needing the bathroom, and hightail it out of there.

I berate myself the entire way across the crowded bar for acting so recklessly. I should have gritted my teeth, forced a fake smile, and stood my ground. Now, I look like I care more than a friend should.

I am an idiot, I grumble to myself, ducking away from a clearly drunken guy who stumbles toward me and racing into the safety of the bathroom. It's busy, but there is one stall free at the end. Girls are huddled against the sinks on my left, fighting for mirror space, as I pass by them. A girl with a crop top and minuscule matching skirt eyeballs me through the mirror, scowling as she gives me a once-over. "Bitch," she says before I dive into the stall and shut the door.

That is all I need. Garrick's groupies targeting me in a place known for fights.

I knew I should not have come out tonight.

Whatever buzz I was feeling is long gone.

But I won't go home sind look like even more of a loser. To save face, I've got to get back out there.

This isn't an issue. It's a good thing if he's planning to hook up with that girl. It helps solidify the friendship line between us.

"Stevie!" Ellen shouts to be heard over the noise in the bathroom. "Where are you, babe?"

"In here," I say as I open the door.

Ellen pushes me inside, and I sit on the closed toilet seat as she locks the door behind her. "Talk to me." Leaning against the wall, she crosses her arms over her chest. "What's going on?"

"I'm an idiot."

"You're not an idiot."

"I am. Ugh." I bury my face in my hands for a few seconds before looking up at her. "I have told Garrick I don't want to date him, that I just want to be friends, so that scene shouldn't have upset me."

"But it did."

I nod. "Like I said." I poke myself in the chest. "Idiot."

"You like him, and that scares you."

"I don't *want* to like him."

She crouches down in front of me. "You can't help how you're feeling. Even if you try to control it, try to push it away, it's not going to change how he makes you feel."

"I have made a fool of myself."

"You haven't, and I don't think it's what it looked like either. It seemed pretty one-sided to me, and Garrick was upset when you took off."

"I don't know why. We're only friends. He's free to date or hook up with who he likes."

"True, but he seems to only have eyes for you." She stands. "Do you want to leave?"

I consider it for a few seconds.

"I'll go with you. We can call an Uber."

I climb to my feet and hug my bestie. "I love you, and I'm not tearing you away from your man. Nor am I leaving." I release her and straighten my spine. "I had a moment, but it's over now. I'm good, and I need to save face. Running away is something a coward would do. We're staying."

"That's my girl."

———

Garrick is back on stage when we return, and I spend the second part of his set avoiding eye contact with him, unsure what I'll see and unable to face it. My bravery only stretches so far.

"Hey." Cohen moves his stool in closer to mine. "You okay?"

"Fine." My smile is as fake as my lashes.

"You sure? You looked upset back there."

"I wasn't upset," I lie. "I just needed to use the restroom."

"Okay." He sips his beer as he turns to face me. Our knees brush in the exchange, and there is no shiver coasting over my body like when Garrick touches me. "This is why I don't do relationships. Too much shit. Casual hookups are much less hassle." His slightly glassy blue eyes bore into mine before dropping to my chest.

"My face is up here, buddy," I say through gritted teeth.

"And what a pretty face it is." A suggestive smirk materializes on his mouth as his eyes rake over my features.

"Whatever you're doing, don't."

Out of the corner of my eye, I spot Will frowning and Ellen watching with concern.

"I'm just trying to have a conversation." He waves his hands around, almost dropping his bottle of beer. "You know, clear the air and all that jazz."

"There is no air to clear. We're cool."

"I like you," he proclaims, his words slurring a little.

I don't dignify that with a response, staring straight ahead and sipping from my beer in the hope he'll get the hint.

He doesn't.

Leaning in closer, he pins me with a flirtatious look. "I've been known to return for repeats when it's prime pussy. So how about it?"

His leering grin is like acid crawling up my throat. How could I have slept with this jerk? And how are Will, Noah, and Garrick friends with him? They are all decent guys, and Cohen isn't.

"You're disgusting. Get away from me. I wouldn't touch you again if you were the last man standing." I'm tempted to say more, but I don't want to start an argument either.

"Sure, you wouldn't." His sleazy smirk expands. "You were all over me like a rash, bouncing up and down on my dick like you were riding a bucking bronco." One hand drops under the table. "Fuck, I'm hard just thinking about it."

"You make me sick." How can he claim to be Garrick's friend and then proposition me?

"Quit lying. You loved every second of it. I hate sluts who enjoy a good dicking and then pretend like they're above it. News flash, doll. You were so into it you came all over my dick after creaming all over my fingers and my mouth. It's too late to pretend you're a stuck-up prissy bitch." He presses his revolting lips super close to my ear. "I remember every second of our night together, and you fucking loved it."

"You're a pig, and I'm glad I have no recollection of that night." I don't care if he's one of Garrick's best friends. I won't put up with this misogynistic bullshit. "I was clearly too drunk to make a sound decision, because, trust me, if I'd been sober, I never would have lowered my standards and ended up in bed with you."

The smirk slips off his mouth, replaced by a cold nasty expression. "Bitch, you're lucky I lowered *my* standards and gave you a turn on my cock. If I'd been sober, I wouldn't have given you a second glance." He rakes derisory eyes over my body, and I feel ill that I let this asshole anywhere near me. It's a lesson in never getting so drunk my judgment is impaired. I hate he has carnal knowledge of me, but at least my brain wiped all memory of that night in what was clearly a protective mechanism.

I am disgusted with myself. I wish I had a time machine so I could return to that night and turn the jackass down.

"Hey, Stevie. I'm doing a bar run, and I need an extra pair of hands." Noah plants himself in between me and the douche, so Cohen has no choice but to back off.

"I'll have another beer." Cohen levels a glare at his friend as a muscle pops in his jaw.

"You're cut off." Noah returns the glare and then some.

"Fuck off, Dad." Cohen slides off the stool, swaying a little. "I'll get my own beer." He takes off, and three seconds later, a girl with jet-black hair and bright red lips is tucked under his arm like she'd love to live there.

Poor bitch.

"I'll help." I stand, keeping close to Noah's side as we navigate our way to the bar.

"I know you probably think the worst of Cohen, and I don't blame you, but he's not a bad guy when he's sober. He's a perfect example of someone who shouldn't drink. He turns into a raging asshole with alcohol in his veins."

"That isn't an excuse, siand I honestly don't know how you can defend him or how any of you can be friends with him."

Noah claws a hand through his hair, looking contemplative. "Maybe we make too many allowances for him. Maybe we should hold him more accountable." Hooking his arm around my waist, he steers me away from a group of unruly frat boys. "I hate this place. I'm glad this is Gar's last night playing here." He automatically releases his protective hold on me when we are clear of the idiots.

"I'm not fond of it either," I agree as we stand in line behind two girls waiting to be served at the bar.

"Every time I've been here, there's been a fight," he adds. "Make sure you stick with one of us at all times."

"I can handle myself, but I appreciate the gesture."

After we get our drinks, we return to our table a few minutes after Garrick has finished his set. I'm tempted to slink off home to avoid an awkward conversation, but that would be a shitty thing to do. So, I hang around, biting the edge of one nail as I sink another beer and chat with Noah. Ellen and Will are making out like high schoolers on a first date and Cohen has, thankfully, made himself scarce. If I never had to see that asshole again, I'd die happy.

When Garrick emerges from the side door, he's immediately deluged as a gaggle of girls swarms around him, shoving and pushing one another as they try to get close to him. Noah guffaws and shakes his head. "Can you imagine what it'd be like if he was a bona fide rock star? He'd have to carry a stick to beat them away."

Although music is pumping out of speakers now, it's not as loud as earlier, and it's a bit easier to speak without shouting. My dry throat thanks whomever lowered the volume. "For sure. He's magnetic when he's on a stage. Far too good for small-town bars. It's a shame he won't pursue it."

"Music is a hobby for him. I don't think Gar will ever stop playing, but he truly doesn't want the big stage. We've talked a lot about it, and he's very sure about what he wants from life." Noah clinks his bottle against mine. "Like someone else I hear."

Garrick chooses that moment to appear at our table, saving

me from having to respond. "Hey." His greeting is for the table, but his eyes lock instantly on mine.

I hold his stare for a few beats, flashing him a soft smile as I attempt to forget my earlier embarrassment. "You were amazing up there, and the crowd loved you."

"Thanks. That means a lot." A tinge of concern lingers at the back of his eyes as he returns my smile.

He accepts congratulations from the others as he swipes a bottle of water and a beer from the table. Noah switches stools, leaving the one beside me free for his friend. Garrick sits and pulls deeply from the water.

Watching his throat bob as he drinks shouldn't be sexy, but it is.

Nerves fire at me from all angles, so I drink my beer faster than is wise.

Garrick drains his water, picks up the beer, and spins on his stool so our legs are touching. It's like dipping my limbs into flames as scorching heat sears me through my clothes. Lowering his head, he leans in closer, peering deep into my eyes. "Can we talk?"

"I'm sorry for making it awkward earlier," I blurt. "I was just being silly. Ignore me."

He eyeballs me for a few seconds. "You were jealous."

I open my mouth to dispute his allegation, but I can't. "I was," I whisper, rubbing at my temples. "I didn't like it."

He peers deep into my eyes, like he's trying to drill a hole in my skull and extract my innermost thoughts. "Will you be mad if I tell you I do?"

"Depends on why."

"It means you care, and I like that."

Or I'm certifiable. I think it, but I don't say it.

He opens his mouth to add more but clearly thinks better of it, drinking a mouthful of beer instead.

"I have no claim on you, Garrick. I have no reason to be jealous. You are free to date or hook up with whoever you like."

Setting his bottle down, he licks his lips, and it takes serious self-control not to follow the motion with my eyes, but I succeed, and I'll consider that a win.

"I'm not interested in Carrie. She's an ex," he explains. "I dated her for three months at the start of freshman year. We parted ways amicably, and she's been dating a basketball player for the past year. He's here with her tonight, but she stopped by to say hi. We were just catching up. It wasn't anything more, and I'm sorry if it upset you."

Relief washes over me. "You don't need to explain yourself to me, but I'm thankful you did. Sorry for being an idiot."

"No need to apologize. I just want to ensure we're okay."

"All is good." This time, my smile is sincere, and I silently berate myself for being such a dumbass.

His thumb brushes against the corner of my mouth, shooting tingles across my skin. "You had a drop of beer there." Lifting his thumb to his mouth, he sucks on it while piercing me with a heated look. His eyes are a smoldering warm brown tonight, and they are glued to mine like he physically can't pull away. I can't either, and I wonder who I'm kidding with our friendship pact.

He continues sucking his thumb, and it's seriously turning me on.

Holy fuck. I squeeze my thighs so tight I might have given myself muscle strain.

"What was Cohen saying to you?" he asks a minute later, breaking whatever spell we were under. His hand wraps around his beer again, and I loosen my thighs and breathe a little easier.

"Are you sure you want to know?" I don't want to start an

argument within his friend group, but he should be aware exactly how much of a dick Cohen is.

"I wouldn't ask if I didn't want to know. I could tell he was making you uncomfortable. If he was rude to you, I'm gonna kick his ass all over the bar."

"I'll tell you, but I think we should park this conversation until tomorrow when we're all sober." I'm not going to lie to Garrick. He deserves to know his friend was propositioning me and how nasty he turned when I didn't entertain it. However, I don't think it's wise to have this conversation when we've all been drinking. I don't want it to turn into World War Three in a place that is notorious for mass-scale fights. The last thing I want is Garrick getting hurt. I'd have less concerns about Cohen. Perhaps a few punches to the head are just what that asshole needs.

Garrick scrutinizes my face. "I know he's a friend, but I won't tolerate him disrespecting you for a single second. If it's something I need to know, I want to know it now."

Before I can reply, I'm almost pushed off my stool as a girl with long, wavy blonde hair shoves past me, flinging her arms around Garrick and smacking a hard kiss against his lips.

Chapter Eleven
Stevie

Garrick grabs the girl by the arms, yanking her lips off his, and forcibly creates distance between their bodies. "What the hell, Simone?"

"Baby, I have missed you so much." She attempts to get close to him again, but Garrick keeps her at arm's length as his eyes meet mine.

I'm two seconds from leaving. I need additional drama like a hole in the head, and I've had a gutful tonight. My temples throb in a combination of stress, frustration, and the aftermath of drinking too many beers.

"Don't leave." Garrick stares at me as he astutely reads my intention. "Let me handle this, and then I'll explain."

"What the fuck, Gar?" Simone spews, glancing over her shoulder at me with a poisonous expression. "Why the hell are you even with her?" An ugly sneer crawls over her face as her gaze skims me from head to toe. She snorts out a laugh, and all it does is highlight her unattractiveness. "She's a fucking *ginger*. You cannot seriously have ghosted me for this ugly bitch?"

Keeping my tone level and my expression neutral, I

respond before Garrick gets a chance. "If you think I give two shits about a single word that comes out of your nasty mouth, think again. Envy really isn't a good look on you."

"Shut your stupid ugly face!"

"That's enough!" Garrick snaps. He stands, looking like he wants to throttle Simone. It won't take any convincing for me to help him. He jerks his head at someone or something over my shoulder before leveling her with a cool glare. "Stevie is a friend, and I'm not letting you insult her out of petty jealousy. As for ghosting you, that's a fucking lie. I told you I didn't want to see you again. I couldn't have made myself any clearer. But let's set the record straight for good."

One of the bouncers appears, and Garrick hands the girl off to him. "One sec, Rex."

The beefy dude nods, struggling to hold on to a wriggling Simone while she screeches her outrage at the top of her lungs.

Garrick folds his arms as he eyeballs her, a frown creasing his brow when he notices the people around us pointing, whispering, and taking out their phones. "You are drawing attention, and unless you want to be broadcast all over social media, I suggest you stop fighting Rex, stay quiet, and listen carefully."

"Gar, come on." Simone sniffles as silent tears stream down her cheeks, and she deflates in the bouncer's grasp. The girl is a hot mess. "I love you!" she wails. "Why are you doing this to me? You can't seriously be picking her over me?"

"I'm not interested in you, Simone," Garrick calmly explains, purposely keeping his voice low. "We went out one time, and I tried to let you down gently. But now I'm spelling it out. I don't want to date you. I don't even want to speak to you. We aren't compatible, and we have no future. You need to quit messaging me, quit stalking me on campus, and quit hanging around me at gigs. This is your final warning. Next time, I'll ask the management to permanently ban you. For now, you can cool your heels outside." Garrick nods at the bouncer, and he starts ushering the blonde away.

"Fuck you, Gar! No one rejects me for a ginger!" She's still screaming abuse when the bouncer throws her over his shoulder and pushes his way through the crowd.

"Never a dull moment," Will deadpans.

I had almost forgotten we had an audience.

"Your crazy radar must have been on the blink when you took that raving lunatic out," Noah adds.

"You're telling me." Garrick sighs, looking contrite as he slides back on his stool. "I'm sorry about that, Stevie. She was way out of line."

"Does drama follow you everywhere?" I work hard to lighten my mood when the truth is I'm done.

"Not usually. I swear."

I shrug, finishing the last of my beer. "None of my business anyway."

Garrick ensnares my gaze as he explains. "I went out with her once, a few weeks ago, before I met you. I knew instantly it was a major mistake. She's in one of my study groups, and she seemed normal. But she freaked me out, talking about weddings and babies and how she's had the biggest crush on me since last year and she knew if she was patient I would finally notice her."

"She's a legit creeper," Will supplies as Ellen snuggles into his side while shooting concerned looks in my direction.

"I was polite but firm when I told her I didn't want to date her," Garrick continues. "I don't lead girls on. But she's not backing down. She seems to think it's some kind of challenge."

"You should report her for harassment to the university," Noah says. "That should get her off your back for good."

"I didn't want to get her into trouble with UO, but it looks like she's leaving me with no choice."

"I would definitely report that crazy bitch before she turns nasty on you or whomever you date next," I say.

"The only woman I'm interested in dating is you," Garrick replies, breaking our self-imposed rules already.

"I'm not an option!" I don't mean to snap, but my patience reservoir is running on empty now. "And redheads are clearly not your type."

"That's not—"

I cut across Garrick before he can finish his sentence. "You should date Carrie again," I suggest, finishing my drink and standing. "She might have a boyfriend, but she's obviously still hooked on you." Grabbing my bag, I clutch it to my chest as I cast a glance at Ellen. "I'm so over this night," I say. "Are you coming home or staying at Will's?"

"We'll come with you," Will says, helping Ellen to her feet.

"Stevie, please. Don't go. Let's talk and I'll make sure you get home safely." Garrick reaches for me, but I step back, avoiding his hand.

"I'm capable of making my own way home, and you should stay. Find some other blonde to date, and leave me out of your woman drama."

I wait to emerge from my bedroom the following morning until after I hear Will leaving. I slept fitfully, and I'm grumpy. A dull ache slices across my brow, and my tongue is partially glued to the roof of my furry mouth. Ugh. I am *never* drinking again.

"Hey." Ellen thrusts a paper cup at me when I emerge in the kitchen. "I was about to knock on your door and see if you were alive. Garrick just picked up Will. They're planning to work through their hangovers at the gym. He stopped off at Bumble Bees on the way and grabbed us all coffee.

There are pastries too," she adds, pointing at the box on the counter.

"He makes it so hard to stick to my resolve," I murmur while popping the lid on my coffee and inhaling the delicious aroma.

"He's a good guy." Ellen rests her elbows on the counter as I hop up onto a stool. "But after all that drama last night, maybe you're right to relegate him to the friend zone."

"Yeah, I have zero desire to become a target for his crazed fans and lovesick exes." I lick the froth off the top of my cinnamon caramel cappuccino as I remove a poppyseed pastry from the box, realizing Ellen must've given Garrick a list of my Bumble Bees favorites.

"However." Ellen draws out the word as she watches me rip a piece of pastry and pop it in my mouth. "What happened last night wasn't really his fault."

"Except for questionable judgment in relation to some of the girls he has dated," I supply in between mouthfuls of the luscious pastry.

"True, but he dumped the crazy after one date, and it's not on him if his ex has lingering feelings. You probably didn't notice before you hightailed it, but he wasn't encouraging her. Carrie was the one all over him."

"You sound like you're back on Team Garrick."

She jabs her finger in my direction before swiping a vanilla Danish from the box. "Girl, I'm always Team Stevie. Just trying to put things into perspective."

I'm still mulling over her words later as I set out on foot to meet Garrick at the coffee shop closest to the campus gym. He'd texted me while I was nursing my hangover and attempting to study, asking if we could talk. I figure some fresh air would do me no harm, and I don't like how I left things last night with him. I was probably a little harsh, and he's been nothing but nice to me all week. I at least owe him an opportunity to defend himself.

Garrick is sitting in the corner by the wall when I arrive, his eyes peeled on the door. His legendary smile is toned down today but still welcoming. I hurry across the semi-busy room toward him. He stands and pulls out a chair for me. "Hey, thanks for coming."

"I'm glad you reached out to me," I say, sitting down as he reclaims the seat across the table.

A waitress arrives at our table. She refills Garrick's coffee as she asks me what I'd like. "I hear you're partial to caramel macchiatos, and we do a great one," the older woman says as she shares a conspiratorial look with Garrick.

"Don't tempt me," I groan. "This guy already hand-delivered my favorite cappuccino and pastry earlier. My blood sugars will be through the roof if I ingest any more sweet stuff."

She pats Garrick on the shoulder. "This one's a keeper."

Yeah, I'm not touching that.

I smile up at her. "I'll have an unsweetened chai latte if you have it."

"Coming right up, sweet cheeks."

"Another fan?" I ask when she's out of earshot, quirking a brow.

Scrubbing his hands down his face, he sighs heavily. "I'm not making a great impression, am I?"

"Women seem to gravitate to you like moths to a flame, and that's really not my scene."

He leans forward, straining toward me across the table. "I swear I'm not into the whole rock star groupie thing. I'm only up there to play my guitar and sing my favorite songs. I'm not interested in any of the other bullshit."

"I believe you, but I loathe drama and tend to run a mile from it. You seem to attract it wherever you go."

"I don't purposely invite it."

"I know it comes with the territory," I admit, sweeping my hair over my shoulders. "You don't have a choice, but I do."

"I'm really sorry, Stevie. You got caught in the crossfire last night, and it wasn't fair."

"It wasn't, and if that's the way it always is, I won't ever be hanging out with you at gigs. I won't be a target."

"I won't let it happen again, and though it'll be difficult, I'll stop watching you when I'm on stage."

"Yeah, that doesn't help. I was on the receiving end of some hostile looks in the bathroom from girls who noticed your attention was on me."

"Can I be honest with you?" he asks as the bubbly waitress returns with my latte.

I wait for her retreat before answering. "I always want honesty—no matter how much it might hurt."

"I'm trying to respect your wishes and be your friend even though we both know I want more. But you're sending out mixed signals. Last night, you were pissed, and it's not really what I'd expect from someone who says she's only my friend."

"I'm a little conflicted, but you're right. It's not fair to give you mental whiplash. It won't happen again, I promise."

He looks a little crestfallen as he nods, and I feel like a bit of a bitch. "Can I ask *you* something?" I inquire as I taste my drink.

"I always want honesty too, and you can ask me anything at any time."

"Why are you so into relationships? Most guys I meet are more interested in working their way through the entire female student body than dating and getting attached to any girl. You and Will aren't like that, and I'm curious." I know not all college students are interested in partying and playing the field, but based on my limited experience of college life, Will and Garrick are more the anomaly than the norm.

Leaning back in his chair, he shrugs. "I've never given it much thought. I'm just not into the whole hookup scene. Girls throwing themselves at me, purely for bragging rights, breaks me out in a cold sweat. I was too young to remember much about my parents' relationship, but I've grown up watching my dad with my stepmom, and I think deep down I've always tried to replicate what they have. They're happy. Unlike my mom who recycles boytoys and husbands on a regular basis. That's not what I want for my life. I want intimacy and someone I can connect to on multiple levels. I want something real, not tempo-rary gratification."

"Wow. That's hardcore for someone so young."

He shrugs again, and his mouth kicks up at the corners. "I told you I know what I want, and I always go after it." His gold-ish-brown eyes convey everything he's not saying as he stares at me with steely determination before dropping his gaze briefly to my mouth.

"We've both been influenced by our parents' experiences." I swirl a spoon in my latte as I contemplate it. "I'm determined to not be like my mom when it comes to relationships, and you want a relationship like the one your dad has with your step-mom. Those goals are not in sync."

"I don't see it like that at all." He rests his hands on top of the table as he holds my gaze. His long, slender fingers gently tap out a silent beat. His grin returns full force along with those damned dimples. I swear he knows what they do to me, and he does it on purpose to fuck with my head. "If you really think about it, it all boils down to the same thing. We both want something meaningful and long-lasting."

"That doesn't mean it wouldn't be distracting."

"The right guy won't be a distraction. He'll be a support. This might sound a little cheesy," he adds, shooting me a goofy grin. "But he'll want you to soar to dizzy heights and do what he can to help you reach them."

Pushing my empty mug to one side, I concede he's good at this. Perhaps he should be a lawyer. He almost has me believing it. I wet my lips and just put it out there. "And you think that's you?"

He doesn't hesitate to reply, exuding the confidence I now associate with him. "I think that guy could be me, yeah." Stretching across the table, he removes a stray strand of red hair from my face, tucking it tenderly behind my ear. Sincerity oozes from his pores when he says, "We're a lot more compatible than incompatible. You just need to open yourself up to the possibility we could be so damn good together."

Chapter Twelve
Garrick

A bell chimes as I step through the door of the floral shop in Eugene. Butterfly Flowers is one of several florists in the area, but the only one the woman I seek works at. Stevie is behind the counter, chatting with an older coworker as they wrap up an order. Her head lifts at the sound of approaching footfalls, an automatic smile already painted on her lips. It could be my imagination, but I swear her eyes light up and her grin expands when she sees it's me.

"Garrick, hey. What are you doing here?"

Her coworker's eyes are out on stalks as she blatantly checks me out. The blue-haired woman wears quirky glasses with purple frames, and a flirtatious smile toys on her thin lips. Both women are wearing branded T-shirts and jeans behind their aprons.

"I'm in the market for flowers, and I've heard there's a discount for friends of the staff," I joke, not giving a flying fuck about any discount. I just needed to see Stevie. Now classes are out, and we have some time off before exams start, I've had no excuse to see her this week. Though it's only Wednesday and we had coffee on Sunday, I'm suffering huge withdrawal symptoms.

I have it bad.

"You have been misinformed." Stevie's smile looks forced as she straightens her spine.

"Oh, I don't know about that." Her colleague licks her lips as she continues giving me a thorough once-over. "I'm thinking a hottie discount is in order."

"A *hottie* discount?!" Stevie splutters, her eyes popping wide as she stares at the pint-sized woman like she's sprouted an extra head. "Please tell me my ears are deceiving me and you did *not* just say that." Pink colors her cheeks.

"Said it. Meant it." The blue-haired pixie nudges Stevie with her hip, pushing her to the right a little, and then she grabs my hand and pulls it toward her. "Such manly hands. Firm and strong and powerful."

A chuckle filters from my mouth.

Her fingers explore the back of my hand before moving to my palm. The fine lines at the sides of her eyes crinkle as she grins at me. "These hands are solid and steady, and they create magic. I bet you know how to put them to good use too. Am I right, or am I right?"

"Oh my god, Sharon." Stevie slaps a hand to her brow. "You are legit insane. I feel like I should call Tim this minute and tell him he needs to take you in for a psych eval."

Ignoring Stevie, she clings to my hand and pins me with a naughty look. "If this idiot won't go out with you, I will."

Stevie rolls her eyes. "You're married."

"Tim will understand," she fires back, showing no signs of letting my hand go.

"You're acting like a creepy stalker. Let his hand go."

Amusement bubbles in my chest as I watch them face off. This is priceless, and I love it. I also love that she told Sharon about me. It's got to be a good sign she is talking about me, right?

"I'll release his hand when you agree to a date with him." Tearing her gaze from mine, Sharon flashes Stevie a mischievous smile. "There is only one legit insane person around here, and it's not me! If anyone's getting committed, it's you!"

"I like you, Sharon. You talk a lot of sense."

"That's what they all say. Among other things." She winks at me, and I roar laughing.

"I deserve a bonus for all this additional stress. Employers are not supposed to harass their staff," Stevie says, fighting a smile as she finishes taping the bouquet they were working on when I walked in and interrupted them mid-flow.

"Pfft." Sharon lets my hand go, albeit reluctantly. "It's not harassment. It's life advice, missy." She prods Stevie in the chest. "Advice you'd do well to listen to before this fine specimen of a man is snapped up by some other lucky woman."

"You're incorrigible, and quit it. You'll give Garrick a big head."

I kid you not, but Sharon, matriarch and employer, leans across the counter and ogles my crotch. "No sign of any big head yet, but the evening is young."

"Oh my fucking god." Stevie buries her head in her hands but not before I see the laugh dying to break free. "I just can't with you." Her face is flushed when she lowers her hands and pins her boss with a stern look. "Go out back and work on the accounts before I permanently quit."

"You wouldn't dare." Sharon squeezes her arm. "Give the poor guy a break, and go on a date with him. If I was younger and Tim-free, I'd be scaling that mountain and conquering the peak in record time." Tossing one last flirty wink over her shoulder as she walks off, she sashays her curvy hips and wiggles her ass before disappearing into the room at the back.

I bend over, clutching my stomach, as I convulse in fits of laughter. Stevie joins me, and we're both cracking up and wiping the dampness from our eyes. "Damn, she's a hoot. I only came in to buy flowers!"

"Sharon is insane in the best possible way," Stevie says when she's composed herself. "There is never a dull moment around here."

"I get that. She's a cool boss."

"She is, and she's been very flexible with my hours, which I appreciate. Today's my last shift till school is back, and I'm going to miss her." Stevie leans in closer, pressing her delectable mouth to my ear. "Don't ever admit I said that though. I like to keep her on her toes."

"Your secret is safe with me."

We trade a mutual grin, and there's a definite shift in the air the longer we stare at one another. "You look very pretty with your hair like that," I say, shoving my hands in the pockets of my jeans before I do something reckless like grab her to me and plant one on her. Her hair is wrangled in a messy bun on top of her head, and wispy strands frame her stunning face, only serving to showcase her exquisite features. She has barely a lick of makeup on, and she's flawless.

"I'm sure I look a hot mess, and you're clearly biased, but thank you." Propping one hip against the counter, she clears her throat. "Did you actually come to buy flowers, or was there another reason you dropped by?"

"I came to buy flowers."

She straightens up, losing the easy demeanor, and I can guess why.

"For my mother and my stepmom," I add.

"Oh." Her shoulders relax, and I do too.

"Is there a special occasion?"

"Nope." I shrug. "I just felt like sending them flowers. I

tend to do it a couple times a year, just to remind them how much they mean to me." I might have ulterior motives this time, but it's no lie. My father buys Dawn lilies and chocolates every Friday on his way home from work. They aren't expensive or extravagant, by any means, but the way Dawn's face lights up you'd think they were. Even after all these years, and copious bouquets and chocolates, she still cherishes the gesture.

Stevie stares at me as if she's seen a ghost. Shaking herself out of it, she drags her lower lip between her teeth before releasing it. "You are so bad for my heart, Garrick," she whispers, like the words might hurt her. "Stop being so sweet."

"I only ever want to be good for you," I admit, hoping she hears the sincerity in my tone. "Now, what would you recommend?" I inquire, changing the trajectory of the conversation on purpose.

I leave the store twenty minutes later with a gorgeous, big, colorful bouquet. I placed a delivery order for Dawn's flowers but refused delivery for the second bunch, making up an excuse Stevie seemed to buy. Placing the bouquet down carefully on the back seat of my SUV, I drive around town, listening to music and fastidiously watching the clock until I know Stevie's shift ends. Then I circle back to the shop, park at the curb, and wait for the enchantress to show her beautiful face.

When she walks outside, zipping up her raincoat, her feet falter as she spots me exiting my car. "Need a ride?" I ask, already knowing she does. Light rain falls as I stride toward her. Judging by the stormy gray clouds in the sky, it won't be long before it turns heavy. "I know your car is in for service, and I thought I could drop you home."

Tipping her head back, she stares at the darkening sky and the tinkling rain tumbling from above. I expect her to fight me, and I'm pleasantly surprised when she doesn't. "Thanks, Garrick. A ride home would be great."

I open the passenger door for her, closing it softly after she climbs inside. Running around the hood, I jump behind the wheel just before the rain turns heavy and a deluge falls from the heavens.

"Perfect timing." Stevie rubs her hands together as I crank up the heating.

"I've been known to have my moments." A trademark grin crosses over my face as I power up the engine.

"I love your car. Nana has an older Range Rover, and I drive it sometimes. They're solid."

"They are," I say as I maneuver out onto the road. "Dad got me this last year when I moved to UO. I protested, because these babies aren't cheap, but he insisted. He knew I'd be driving back and forth a lot, and he wanted me to be safe."

"Your dad sounds awesome."

"My dad is as awesome as your mom." Delicate floral notes stretch across the console, tickling my senses, and I can't deny how much I love Stevie sitting in my car beside me. She looks comfortable and like she belongs there. I intend to ensure she knows it one day too.

Taking the next turn, I risk posing the question lingering on my tongue. "Are you hungry? Want to grab something to eat?"

She shakes her head just as her tummy emits a loud rumble.

The grin that skates across my mouth is so wide it threatens to rip my face apart. "I think your body has spoken," I say, taking the next right and heading in the direction of the taco place that is popular with UO students. "How about some tacos? I don't know about you, but I could murder a few."

She runs her hands through her hair, glancing out the window, before she concedes. "Tacos sound good. I had a small salad at lunch, and I'm starving."

Ten minutes later, we are huddled at a table in the back near the window. It's not too busy today because classes are finished and most students are studying at home or the library, trying to cram last-minute knowledge into overtired brains.

"Was this your plan all along?" Stevie asks, eyeing me over the rim of her glass after we've placed our order.

"I'm sure I don't know what you mean." My lips purse as I smother a grin.

"Are you trying to tell me this wasn't intentional?" Cocking her head to one side, she peers deep into my eyes.

I could stare at her beautiful face all day and all night and never grow tired of it.

"Not really." I take a sip of my soda before continuing. "I'll admit I came to the store because I wanted to see you, and I knew you didn't have your car today, so I was hoping to drive you home, but I didn't plan this. Would have if I thought you'd go for it."

"Guess you got your date after all."

Leaning across the table toward her, I ensure her eyes are locked on mine when I speak. "If this was a date, you'd know it and we sure as fuck would not be here."

"Where would we be?" she blurts, looking like she regrets the words the instant they leave her mouth.

"At that nice steakhouse or the new sushi place. If we were in Seattle, I'd take you to the winery."

"What's wrong with here?" Her gaze trips around the long narrow room.

"Nothing. I love this place, and the tacos are to die for, but it's only a diner. If I'm lucky enough to score a date with you, I'll be taking you to a nicer place. You deserve to be treated like a queen."

"Fuck me," she moans before resting her brow on the table.

With pleasure. The snake in my pants reacts immediately to her words, and I silently talk the beast down. I would give my left nut to fuck Stevie but only when it means something to both of us. I have zero desire to be friends with benefits or a one-night stand. With someone as special as Stevie, I want both of us to be all in.

The waitress arrives with our food, and Stevie sits back up, eyeing me curiously. I wait her out as the server sets plates in front of us, taking long pulls of my soda as I silently plead with the universe to help me out.

I have just picked up my silverware when she speaks. Warmth floods her tone and fills her eyes as she holds my gaze. "You make me want to break all my own rules, Garrick."

"You say that like it's a bad thing."

"It's a dangerous thing."

Reaching across the table, I tentatively place my hand on top of hers. "It doesn't have to be. It could be the greatest thing of all."

Chapter Thirteen

Garrick

Pulling up outside the apartment building Stevie lives at, I pray she invites me in because I'm not ready to say goodbye to her yet.

I'm aware I'm acting like a lovesick teen, but I don't care—guilty as charged.

I am certifiably crazy about this girl, and I don't care who knows it.

The conversation flowed easily at the taco place, and it's like I've always known her. It just seems so natural with us, and it's rare to find that kind of connection. I get the sense Stevie is feeling this too, and though she's still fighting the attraction, there are holes in her protective shield. I plan to poke them until they grow bigger and eventually become nonexistent.

"Thank you for the ride and dinner."

"You can't thank me for dinner." I wanted to get the check, but she insisted on paying half. I didn't argue even if the old-world manners instilled deep inside me protested. Stevie likes her independence, and I like that about her. I'm not about to be *that guy.* The one who claims hurt male pride because his date insists on paying her share of the meal.

Stevie lifts her head with confidence. "Of course, I can. It's not about who paid. Thank you for taking me there."

"You're welcome."

"And Sharon said to say thanks for the business. She was thrilled."

A smirk dances on my lips. "I appreciated the hottie discount." I was given a fifteen-percent markdown, which was kind of Sharon.

Stevie rolls her eyes. "You're never going to let that one go."

"Damn straight."

"I'm considering proposing it as an official discount." A grin runs across her face. "Some permanent eye candy at the store would be nice."

I fake a scowl as I unbuckle my seat belt. "Sharon will never go for it. It was a onetime thing because she likes me."

"Doesn't mean I can't try."

"If you need permanent eye candy, I can make myself available." I lean back in my seat and shoot her a flirty smile.

"Nice try, Casanova, but no. I'd never get any work done if you were always around."

I'm taking that as a win. Before I can celebrate, her hand curls around the door handle as she prepares to make her escape, and instant panic sets in. "Do you want to hang out some more?" I blurt, hoping I don't sound as desperate as I feel.

This girl has me acting like an inexperienced first-timer with zero game.

"Sorry, no can do. I need to glue my eyeballs to my retail floristry operations management book, or I won't be prepared for that exam. What about a rain check Saturday night? I think Will and Ellen are planning takeout and a movie at our place. We could gate-crash."

"I'm down with that plan."

"Great." Her enthusiastic smile does weird things to my insides. "Thanks again, Garrick. I'll catch you later." She slides out of the car before I can get her door.

Hopping out my side, I open the back door and grab the bouquet. Stevie is halfway to the building when I call out after her, running to catch up. Turning around, she frowns, looking confused as I thrust the flowers at her. "These are for you."

"What?" she splutters, looking between me and the bouquet with a crease between her brows. "I thought these were for your mom?"

"I might have told a little white lie. I hope you can forgive me." I don't bother telling her my mother would scoff if I showed up with anything that wasn't the most expensive roses, gardenias, or orchids. There is nothing wrong with this bouquet. It's exquisite, and Stevie is talented, but Mom is as snobbish with flowers as she is with most other things in her life.

Dawn will love her delivery like I know she'll love Stevie when she meets her.

"These are for *me*?" Stevie stares at them in a bit of a daze, like she can't believe they're for her.

"Hasn't anyone ever bought you flowers?"

"I'm surrounded by flowers, thanks to my nana," she admits, her fingers tracing reverently over the bouquet that is still in my hand. "But no one has ever bought me flowers before."

"I'm glad to be the first," I truthfully say, gently pushing them at her. I hope it's the start of many firsts we have together. Stevie doesn't know what it's like to be in a committed relationship, and I look forward to educating her. To spoiling her as she deserves.

Cradling the flowers against her chest, she buries her nose

in the scented petals and inhales deeply. "You're chipping away at my resolve," she softly admits, looking up at me with a tender sheen in her eyes.

"There is no ulterior motive." My fingers wind through the wispy strands of hair cupping her face. "I wanted to buy you flowers, so I did. I expect nothing in return."

"Thank you so much, Garrick. I love them, and it was really thoughtful."

"You're welcome." Though I hate to walk away, I want to prove to her I won't be a distraction from her life goals. "Good luck with your studying." I press a light kiss to her cheek, relishing the feel of her soft, satiny skin against my lips. "I'll see you on Saturday."

The air in the kitchen plummets a couple of degrees the instant Cohen steps foot inside it on Saturday morning. Will and I have been giving him the cold shoulder since Stevie informed me of the vile things he said to her last Saturday night. Noah is tiptoeing around all of us, hating the tension and trying not to pick sides. He was angry when he heard the truth, but he's trying to play mediator in the hope we can reconcile.

I'm not sure that's possible.

Since all this has gone down, I am reconsidering everything I thought I knew about my friend. Blaming alcohol is no excuse, and I realize we have been making excuses for Cohen from the moment we met him. His behavior is not acceptable, and it's time we stopped sweeping it under the rug. Stopped enabling him.

"How long do you plan to keep this up?" he asks, sounding bored as he pours coffee into a mug while eyeballing me.

"This isn't a game, Cohen."

"I'm well aware." He points at the colorful bruising surrounding his left eye.

"You deserved that," I calmly reply, drinking my coffee and schooling my features into a neutral line.

"You deserved more than a black eye," Will says, entering the kitchen with a yawn.

"You're both overreacting, and you know it. We always said we'd never let any chick come between us, yet here we are." Folding his arms, he slouches against the counter and drills me with a sharp look.

I finish my coffee and stand. "We are here because you are way out of line. With Stevie and with other women. You have no respect, and we've been letting you get away with it for far too long. I can't speak for the others, but I won't stand by and tolerate it anymore."

"I'm with Garrick." Will edges around the island unit and heads for the refrigerator.

"Of course, you are. As long as you're sticking it to Stevie's friend, at least."

"Watch your fucking mouth." Will glares at him. "This is the exact kind of shit we're talking about."

"You're such hypocrites!" His voice elevates a few notches. "All of a sudden, I'm no longer good enough for the mighty Garrick Allen and his sidekick?" He scoffs at us, letting out a laugh, as he pushes off the counter. "At least have the balls to admit this is nothing to do with how I treat women and everything to do with the fact *I* nailed the girl who keeps rejecting *you.*"

His nasty smirk and crude words rub me the wrong way and I clench my hands into fists at my side. "Ever had a light bulb moment, Cohen? 'Cause I had a big fucking bright one when you hit on the girl I like after you promised me you wouldn't. The way you spoke to Stevie was disgusting, and while this *is* about her for me, it's about way more. You treat women like shit, and we were wrong to laugh it off. I'm ashamed I called you my friend when you were behaving like the biggest fucking asshole."

"Tell me what you really think," Cohen snarls, and the mean contempt on his face makes me question how I ever liked the guy. I fucking hate he had sex with Stevie because no guy has ever been more undeserving of a woman.

"Guys, please." Noah stalks into the kitchen with a towel wrapped around his waist and water dripping down his chest. "Do we have to do this again?"

"No, we don't." Snatching my keys and wallet from the table, I bend down and grab my bag from the floor. "I'll be making myself scarce for the day and for the rest of the time we have left," I add making a beeline for the front door.

I'm still all riled up hours later as I stand outside the door to Ellen and Stevie's apartment, waiting to be let in.

When the door swings open, Stevie stands before me like a fiery goddess in a simple black dress with short sleeves and a knee-length hemline. It molds to her tempting rack, clings to her trim waist, and curves around her slim hips. Her beautiful hair hangs in glossy soft waves over her shoulders and down her back, and she has her usual light makeup on. She steals the breath from my lungs as she smiles at me, her stunning green eyes vibrant and full of life as she drinks me in. I'm just wearing jeans and Nikes with a plain white tee under my open black shirt, but her appreciation is obvious, and it helps to dispel the lingering threads of my bad mood.

"Hey, you," she says, in a soft throaty voice that sends a shot of lust straight to my dick.

I have a feeling tonight is gonna be an extreme test of willpower, and I already gave my libido a stern talking to on the walk over here.

"Hey, yourself," I say, finally finding my voice. I dart in and kiss her cheek. "You look beautiful."

A flattering blush blooms across her skin, and it's clear Stevie isn't accustomed to praise from the opposite sex. Another thing I intend to remedy. "Thank you. You look pretty good yourself."

I hand her the bag I'm carrying. "I brought some drinks and snacks."

"Great, thanks." Taking the bag, she steps aside. "Where are my manners? Come in."

"I bumped into Will and Ellen at the library earlier," I say as we walk into the kitchen. "Are they here yet?"

Stevie sets the bag down on the counter and shakes her head. "There's been a change of plan. They went out to eat, and I have a baked ziti in the oven for us. I hope you like it?" She removes the bottle of white wine from the bag along with the goodies for the movie.

"Love it," I reply, sliding onto a stool. "Dawn makes it every week, and it's my brothers' favorite pasta dish."

"That's funny," she says, going to the refrigerator. She places the wine I brought on the interior wine shelf and removes a couple of beers. "I used to make it weekly for my mom and my nana." She hands me a cold beer, and our fingers brush in the exchange, sending a tingling sensation shooting over my hand and up my arm.

"Thanks." I lift the bottle to my lips as she opens the oven door to check on dinner. Tempting aromas hit the back of my nose, and my stomach rumbles appreciatively. "It smells incredible."

"It should be ready shortly," she says, closing the oven door and walking to the counter where a chopping board and ingredients are laid out. "I'm just making a salad and some garlic bread to go with it. Will that be all right?"

"Anything you cook will be amazing. This is a first for me," I admit with a wink.

Her brows climb to her hairline. "Are you saying none of your girlfriends cooked you a meal?"

"Nope, not a single one. The only woman who has ever cooked for me is Dawn."

"Wow."

"Most girls I have dated were clueless in the kitchen."

"My mom is a disaster." Stevie pops the top of her beer, taking sips as she finishes the salad. "She only has to glance at the kitchen, and the fire alarm goes off." Her light laughter is music to my ears, and I'm obsessed with watching her hands as she prepares the rest of our meal.

"Is that how you learned to cook?"

"My nana taught me. She tried to teach Mom when she was a little girl, but that was an utter failure. It was either I learned or we starved." She laughs again and my cock jumps behind my zipper.

"You sound super close to your nana." She has mentioned her before, and it's clear to see the admiration on her face and hear it in her tone.

"I am." Sliding the salad in the fridge, she removes a bowl with butter. "My nana was as much my mom as my mom growing up. It's why I never felt like I missed out with my dad." She continues talking as she moves around the kitchen. "Mom and Nana ensured they were there for me for everything. Nana had breast cancer a few years ago, and it was so scary. The thought of ever losing her terrifies me."

"Is she okay now?" I ask.

She bobs her head as she slices bread. "Thankfully, yes. She's in remission, and her health is good."

We continue chatting about everything and anything as she places the garlic bread in the oven and sets the small table in the corner. We quickly finish our beers, and she grabs the now chilled wine from the fridge, inspecting the label.

"It's one of our best bottles," I explain. "Ellen said you preferred white to red and that pinot gris or sauvignon blanc were your favorites."

"They are, but I tend to drink New Zealand wines if I want a sauvignon." She walks toward a cupboard and removes two wineglasses. "I thought most Seattle wineries produced chardonnay or riesling?"

"They account for eighty percent of white wine production in Washington, but other variations are becoming popular. We produce a wide variety, but Dad is focusing heavily on new-world wines because he believes they will become just as popular. Our sauvignon is more like a full-bodied French wine than a crisp Marlborough, but I think you'll like it."

"It smells delicious," she says while pouring wine into both our glasses. "And you clearly know your stuff."

"Thanks," I say, accepting the glass. "I wish I did, but the truth is, I know very little about the winery side of the business. Something I hope to rectify this summer."

"You're going to be in Seattle over summer break?"

I nod, savoring the citrusy apple-scented flavor of the cold white wine as it fills my mouth and glides down my throat. "I have worked at the lumberyard every summer for years. This year, I'll be alternating my weeks between the yard and the winery. What about you? What are your plans?"

"I'm heading back to Ravenna. I help Nana out with the business every summer."

"We have that in common too." I can't help mentioning it as

I like to reinforce our similarities in the hope it'll shatter her belief our interests aren't aligned.

"I guess we do," she says with a shrug, and I wonder if I might possibly be getting through to her.

Dinner is sumptuous, and I have second helpings and clear my plate. After, we top off our wine and head into the living room to watch a movie. There is still no sign of Ellen and Will.

Not that I'm complaining.

I'm enjoying having Stevie all to myself.

We have the lights turned off so the only illumination in the room is from the TV screen. I couldn't tell you what movie we agreed on or what we're watching because I'm highly attuned to the woman sitting close to my side, and I can't focus on anything but her.

Tension slithers into the air, but it's the good kind. Sparks crackle around us, and I'm conscious of every little puff of air that slips out of her mouth and how her tongue darts out, tracing a line back and forth across her full lips. I track the way her chest heaves up and down, how her fingers dig into the side of her thigh, and every movement of her long shapely legs as she crosses and uncrosses them.

I'm wound tight, afraid to move a muscle in case I lose hold of my tenuous control, grab the back of her neck, and pull her mouth to mine like I'm dying to do. When I can't take it any longer, I turn my head and blatantly stare at her as I inch a little closer on the couch. Our thighs brush, and she sucks in a subtle gasp, letting me know I'm not in this alone.

Warmth seeps through my clothes and skin, embedding deep. My cock stirs, eager for action, and there is no talking myself down this time. Deliberately, I hook my pinky in hers, willing her to turn and meet my obsessive gaze.

I know she knows I'm looking at her.

Her pulse jumps in her neck, and I can almost hear her

heart thumping wildly against her rib cage. Blood rushes all over my body, and my heart pounds in my chest as butterflies swoop into my stomach, turning somersaults and cartwheels as I unwind her tense fingers and link them with mine.

Slowly, she turns toward me, and time seems to stand still. I stop breathing. My pulse thrums in my ears, and my heart beats out of control as our gazes lock and hold tight. Liquid heat radiates from her eyes as they drift to my mouth. I wet my lips and stare at her mouth, dying to taste her and understanding there will be no going back if I do. My cock is rock hard, straining against my jeans and leaking precum behind my boxers.

I am painfully attracted to Stevie, and not kissing her, not touching her, is the worst form of torture.

But I gave her my word, and I'm already testing it.

I can't be the one to push us over the edge.

She has to give me a sign or meet me halfway.

We continue staring at one another as the movie plays in the background and electricity hums in the air. She gulps, twisting her body ever so slightly as our eyes connect again. My heart is beating so fast I fear it'll beat right out of my chest. Her lips part, her chest rises, and I spot the moment she makes her decision.

Stevie grabs my shirt, ready to pull me toward her, when the front door swings open, slamming noisily against the wall as Will and Ellen crash into the apartment and ruin the moment.

Chapter Fourteen
Stevie

I stare at my best friend and her boyfriend in a kind of slow-motion daze. I'm still clutching a handful of Garrick's shirt as we turn and watch our friends stumble their way around the kitchen, frantically tearing at their clothes as they kiss passionately against the counter, the island unit, and up against the wall. It's hot and a fleeting pang of jealousy stabs me in the chest. Will grabs her leg as he plasters the full length of his body against hers, hooking her leg up and around his waist while grinding his hips against hers. Ellen lets out a gravelly moan, yanking clumps of his hair as he buries his face in her chest and his hand slips under her skirt.

That snaps me out of my shock, and I let go of Garrick, briefly sharing a look with him before I loudly clear my throat. "Ahem, guys. You have an audience. As much as I love porn, I'm not down for a live performance in the kitchen."

"Oh, shit," Ellen mumbles, slurring her words. Her head pivots in the direction of my voice. She squints through blurry eyes. "Um, sorry. We might be a teeny bit drunk." She giggles, looking deliriously happy and more than a little tipsy. Will chuckles as he lifts his head from her chest. "And horny," she adds, sending him a scorching hot look we all feel. "So fucking horny."

Will molds his lips to hers, thrusting his pelvis against her as he dry fucks her into the wall, and I squirm on the couch, uncomfortably turned on and about ten shades of awkward. Garrick is staring at them with a mix of amusement, horror, and something akin to...envy? "Get a room," he drawls a few beats later in a decadently deep voice that sends shivers all over my body. "For the love of god, please get a room."

Will removes his lips from Ellen's mouth and his hand from under her skirt, lifting her effortlessly, and her legs automatically circle his waist. "Oops. Our bad," he says with a grin, looking in no way apologetic. Ellen's arms go around his neck, and she digs her fingers in his hair while whispering something in his ear. From the way his pupils dilate and his hands squeeze her ass I'd say, it was something dirty.

Good for Ellen.

At least one of us is getting some.

You could be too, the devil on my shoulder taunts, and I know it's the truth. I was literally seconds away from throwing caution to the wind and mauling Garrick.

I should probably thank my bestie for the timely interruption.

Will sprints down the hallway toward the bedrooms, and I breathe a sigh of relief when the door to Ellen's room slams shut.

However, it's only temporary relief.

The banging starts almost immediately.

A rhythmic *thump, thump, thump* as the headboard slaps repeatedly against the wall.

It does nothing to quell the awkwardness or the simmering tension in this room. It's like throwing gasoline on a small flame. Heat blooms in my cheeks, and the throbbing between my legs is now a crescendo of potent need.

I sense Garrick looking at me, and I know if I look at him this inferno will explode. I'm confused, horny, and scared, and it feels like I'm coming out of my skin. I hop up, avoiding eye contact with him, as I force a laugh out of my lips. At any other time, we'd probably both be cracking up at the scene we just witnessed, but we're too highly strung. Too amped up on the fiery desire crackling and burning in the space between us. "I don't know about you, but I need a drink. Or some noise-canceling headphones," I mutter under my breath as I stalk toward the refrigerator.

More alcohol is not the solution, but I desperately need something to occupy my hands and my mouth before I pounce on the gorgeous guy sitting on my couch, no doubt staring at me like I'm crazy.

The thumping of the headboard continues, accompanied by a chorus of moans and groans, and I could happily murder my bestie right now. How come I never realized the walls were paper-thin before?

"Hey." Garrick wraps his fingers around my wrist just as I reach the refrigerator, and I jump about ten feet in the air, not noticing he'd walked up behind me. His low chuckle washes over me like an aphrodisiac, and I'm seconds away from throwing my self-imposed rules out the window. "I have a better idea."

"What could be better than alcohol?" The giggle that bursts from my mouth is borderline hysterical, and inside, I'm cringing.

Garrick's hands land lightly on my hips, and he turns me around, tipping my chin up with one long finger until our eyes meet. "Let's dance."

I stare at him in utter confusion, sure I must have heard him wrong.

His fingers thread through mine as he smiles. "You need a distraction, and drink isn't it. I know you have plans to study tomorrow, so more alcohol probably isn't a good idea." Heat flares behind his eyes, and I know what else he isn't saying. I know if I drink more my inhibitions will fly out the window and we'll be making out before I've drawn a breath.

My heart swells with the realization he's saving me from myself.

Garrick is putting aside his own needs to prioritize mine, and that only makes me like him more. It's time I accept this thing between us is inevitable. I am on this train, whether I wanted to be there or not, and there's no getting off.

I don't want to.

Deep down, I know I want this.

Garrick is right.

I'm afraid.

Afraid of losing my heart and getting it broken.

Terrified he'll become my entire world and nothing else will matter.

"Stevie, breathe." He squeezes my hand. "It's okay."

"I'm terrified, Garrick."

With his free hand, he traces his fingers down my cheek in an infinitely tender gesture that warms my heart and cranks my arousal a level higher. "I know you are, but there is no pressure, and nothing is going to happen tonight. We're going to put music on. Loud. Really loud," he adds when Ellen screams Will's name from the top of her lungs.

Laughter bursts from my lips. "I am going to fucking kill her for this."

Garrick chuckles. "We both know it's funny, and it's great to see our friends so in love. I'm happy for them."

I step a little closer and our chests brush. "Me too. You're such a good guy, Garrick Allen."

"I try my best." He waggles his brows and grins, clasping my hand tighter as he pulls me into the living room. I cling to his hand as he hooks his iPhone up to our sound system, and loud rock music blares from the speakers, drowning out the sounds of our best friends banging their brains out.

The music instantly unlocks some of the tension in my stiff limbs, and we rock it out, throwing wild moves and crazy shapes, laughing and shouting the lyrics as we dance around the living room like we're connected to the electrical supply. Elation is the only emotion I'm feeling as we work up a sweat, and I haven't had this much fun in ages. I can be myself around Garrick, and he appears to be the same. He's goofing around, causing me to emit deep belly laughs, and nothing has ever felt more natural or more real.

Unexpectedly, the music changes, and my eyes pop wide as Karen Carpenter's distinctive voice belts out around the room. "You listen to The Carpenters?"

"You know who they are?" he asks, sounding incredulous as he walks toward the sound system.

"Don't turn it off!" I blurt. "They're my nana's favorite band. I grew up listening to them and Abba on repeat."

Garrick lowers the music a little, and we stare at one another from a few feet apart. "My stepmom would love your nana. She loves all the music from that era. It was Dawn who introduced me to them. She's the reason I have a playlist on my phone." He looks a little sheepish, and now I'm intrigued.

"I sense a story."

He rubs the back of his neck and grins. "I was taking my first crush to winter formal, the year I was a freshman, and I couldn't dance."

I find that so hard to believe because Garrick is a fantastic dancer, and it seems innate, like his musical ability.

"I asked my mom to teach me, but her suggestion was to arrange formal dance lessons with a private instructor. It was a shit show, and I canceled after the first lesson. Then Dawn stepped in. She taught me to dance to the backdrop of The Carpenters." A tinge of pink stains his cheeks, and it's adorably cute. "At Christmas, I usually end up dancing with her around the kitchen. It's kind of tradition now."

I think that's the moment I give myself full permission to fall.

I can't deny it any longer, and I don't want to.

Closing the gap, I walk toward him and hold out my hand. The opening notes to "Close to You" start up, and it's like a sign from the heavens. "You never cease to amaze me, Garrick. That is one of the sweetest things I've ever heard. If it's okay to start a new tradition with me, I would love to dance with you to my favorite Carpenters song."

"It would be my honor." He takes my hand and gently reels me into his body.

My arms encircle his neck as his hands gravitate to my lower back. He applies soft pressure, pulling me in flush against his body as we sway in time to the music. Heat seeps from his body into mine, and I'm acutely aware of his solidity and masculinity as we move in perfect tandem. My heart is so full when he softly twirls me in his arms before drawing me back in close. His attention is solely focused on me, and his smoldering golden-colored eyes bore sinto mine, pinning me in place as I melt in his embrace, feeling cherished and adored in a way I have never felt before with any man.

Butterflies run amok in my chest when he starts singing, peering deep into my eyes as he serenades me, and I fall even deeper.

More Carpenters songs flood the room as the playlist goes on, and we continue dancing. Garrick swirls me around as he sings. He never misses a lyric, and he never moves his attention from me.

I'm enraptured, and it's one of the most romantic moments of my life.

I never want it to end.

And I never want to stop feeling the things he makes me feel.

Chapter Fifteen
Stevie

"Oh my god, that is so romantic," Mom swoons over the phone the following night when I recount the details of my magical night with Garrick. He was a perfect gentleman, and despite the explosive chemistry we share, the night ended without any making out. We danced, sang, and exchanged longing looks and lingering innocent touches—over clothes—and yet it was still the most intimate night of my life.

"Your nana is gonna love him!" Mom's blatant excitement breaks me out of my head.

Everyone is gonna love him.

It's impossible not to.

"You should bring him to her birthday party next weekend!"

Her gleeful shriek has me momentarily covering my ears. "Mom, calm down, seriously. You are getting too carried away."

"My little girl is finally in love." Her delight filters down the line. "You don't know how much I have prayed for this moment. I'm so happy for you!"

"Woah. Hold your horses, crazy woman. I did *not* say that."

"You don't need to. I hear it in your voice."

"Mom, I say this with the greatest respect, but you're insane. And delusional. I told you I like him and I think I'm ready to give this thing between us a shot. No one said anything about the l-word, and you need to dispel that notion right now. Unless you want to freak me out and have me end it before it's even begun."

"It's okay to be scared, honey. Feeling vulnerable is part of being in love. You can't open yourself fully to another person without it."

"Mom, we haven't even kissed, and you are totally overreacting. Right now, I really like him, and even admitting that is a big deal for me. Nothing will happen until after my exams anyway. I already told him I couldn't get distracted before then, so he knows the score."

"You can't place limitations on love, sweetheart. The heart wants what it wants, and practicalities just don't come into it."

Maybe that's true if you're Monica Colson.

But I am not my mom, and whatever happens with Garrick will happen on my terms and my timeline.

I won't be rushed into anything by anyone.

The next week, in the run up to exams, is hectic, but Garrick and I manage to find time to hang out every day. We either cohabit the library companionably or study at my place. I avoid his place like the plague. I have no desire to bump into that asshole Cohen. I saw him in the cafeteria on Tuesday, sporting a fading black eye, and Will confirmed Garrick gave it to him because he was talking shit about me. Perhaps I shouldn't silently applaud such behavior. Nana always says violence is not the answer, but I won't criticize any guy who uses his fists to defend me when provoked.

On days where we need to be on campus, Garrick picks me up in his Range Rover with a coffee from Bumble Bees. We ride there to the backdrop of The Carpenters, Abba, the Bee Gees, The Beach Boys, The Monkees, The Rolling Stones, The Doors, and a host of other popular bands from the sixties and seventies.

The ride home is usually accompanied by contemporary sounds as Garrick educates me on indie rock and pop. We talk about everything and anything, and I wake up every day excited to see him.

We eat together most evenings, grabbing dinner on campus or at one of the local diners or I cook something at home. Ellen and Will join us occasionally. Garrick seems to enjoy my cooking, and I like making food for him.

It's all very domesticated, and I'm shocked at how much I don't dislike it. Nothing is official, but we already feel like a couple except there's been no touching or kissing. We share plenty of sultry looks, and I know he's as eager as I am to move things to the next level, but abstaining only heightens the anticipation.

I almost cracked last night when he showed up with flowers and a bottle of wine. The fact it was Friday didn't go unnoticed by me. Is Garrick emulating his father? I can't even be mad he stole the idea because I'm overjoyed at his thoughtfulness and giddy at the prospect of weekly flower and wine deliveries.

I nearly caved and planted one on him.

I think he was the same a few hours ago when I handed him a Tupperware container of homemade cupcakes and cookies. Garrick does so much for me, and I wanted to do something nice for him too, so I got up at the crack of dawn to bake. I hated having to kick him out at lunchtime, but I had laundry to do, and I needed to pack a bag before making the trip home for Nana's birthday.

Something that is now appearing less and less likely. I turn the engine on my CR-V again, and it splutters and chokes before dying. "No!" I groan, resting my head on the steering wheel and cursing the shit timing. I had my car serviced recently, so this should not be happening. Glancing at my watch again, I already know I'm cutting it close. I could take public transportation, but it's over six hours on the train and almost seven on the bus, and that's before I make it to the station and wait for the next available train or bus. Then I'd have to grab an Uber from Seattle to Ravenna, and I'd be lucky to make the tail end of Nana's party.

Briefly, I consider calling Ellen, but she's out in Sutherlin, meeting Will's family for the first time. She could be here in an hour if I could reach her—but I'm not sure if she has cell phone coverage while hiking the North Umpqua Trail. I know she'd come if I asked, but I don't want to ruin my bestie's day.

That only leaves one other option. One other person. As I take out my cell to call Garrick, I console myself knowing he'll be delighted to spend all this time with me, steadfastly refusing to acknowledge how much I'll enjoy spending the time with him too.

GARRICK

"It's no problem, Stevie. I don't have any major plans for the rest of the day." That's no lie. I was just going to hang out in my room. Now, she's saving me from an evening of avoiding Cohen.

"Are you sure? I wouldn't ask if it wasn't important. I have never missed Nana's birthday."

"Honestly, it's fine. Let me grab a shower, and I'll be over as quick as I can."

"Thank you, Garrick. I really, really appreciate this."

"See you in a few," I say before hanging up.

"That didn't take long," Cohen says, creeping up behind me.

I didn't realize he was here. Will is hiking with Ellen and his folks, and I left Noah at the gym as he has a boxing lesson. Ignoring Cohen, because I'm not in the mood to argue with him, I grab a glass out of the overhead cupboard and reach for the tap.

"You're so fucking pussy-whipped already it's pathetic," he continues, trying to get a rise out of me as I fill my glass with water. He pops the top on the bottle of beer in his hand.

Grinding my teeth to the molars, I work hard to compose myself before I turn around to face my ex-friend and soon-to-be ex-roommate—if I have my way. "I don't give a shit what you think." I drill him with a dispassionate expression while I drink greedily from my glass.

"She giving up the goods yet, or are your balls still bluer then blue?" He smirks before taking a mouthful of his beer.

"Fuck off," I snap, losing my cool. "My relationship is none of your business." I drain my water and stow the empty glass in the dishwasher.

"Unless I make it my business." He folds his arms across his bare chest and smirks.

I jab my finger in his chest, and it takes considerable self-control not to punch him in his smug face. "Stay the hell away from Stevie, and stay the hell away from me."

I'm still fuming as I stand under the steaming-hot shower a few minutes later, wondering how I was ever friends with that douche. Cohen has shown his true colors these past few weeks, and alcohol can no longer be used as an excuse. Even Noah is fed up with his childish moods and nasty digs. I don't think it'll take much more for Will and I to convince Noah that Cohen needs to transfer to the frat house with his jock buddies for junior year. Neither of us wants to live with him any longer.

Will and I have discussed possibly getting a place with the girls. I told him it's premature on my side, but I'm open to it. Stevie and I are both returning to Seattle for summer break, and I'm hoping it'll be the turning point in our relationship. She told me last week she's onboard, but she wants to wait until our exams are finished before making anything official, and I'm fine with that. I was prepared to wait as long as it took to convince her to go out with me, so I'm thrilled we both seem to be on the same page now.

Not touching her is slowly driving me insane. The more time I spend with her, the more I long to hold her in my arms, lay claim to her lips, and worship her body like the temple it is. But I can be patient for a little bit longer.

Stevie is worth it.

All it takes is visualizing her gorgeous face in my mind's eye, and I'm hard as a rock. Wrapping my fingers around my aching dick, I close my eyes and imagine Stevie is in the shower with me. I jerk off fast as the fantasy plays out in my head, and it's not long before I'm coming hard, spraying jets of cum all over the tile wall.

At least that should tide me over for the long journey ahead. While I relish the idea of spending hours in close confines with the woman occupying a starring role in my dreams, it's also the sweetest torture. Being near to her and not getting to touch her is killing me softly.

"This is really sweet of you, Garrick, and I owe you big time," Stevie says, buckling her seat belt as I kick-start the engine.

"I'll add it to my Stevie list, and we can work out a reward later," I tease, pulling out onto the road and peeling away from her apartment building.

"You and your list." She rolls her eyes, but she's smiling as she looks across the console at me. "Will I ever get to see this infamous list?"

"It's a mental checklist, but I can type it out if you like." Taking my eyes off the road for a split second, I flash her a flirty grin.

"I'm not sure which would be best—seeing the list or just imagining what's on it."

"Depends on how vivid your imagination is." I level her with a dirty look in case she missed the innuendo.

"I have a pretty vivid imagination." She coolly stares me down with a hint of mischief glinting in her eyes. "I'll see your dirty and raise you depraved."

I bark out laughing, wishing I could pull over and impale her on my throbbing cock. "Damn, Stevie." I adjust myself behind the zipper of my jeans. "You can't say shit like that to me when I'm driving. I'm liable to drive us into a ditch."

"Sorry." Her lips curve up, and she looks completely unapologetic as she shucks off her coat and tosses it in the back seat.

My eyes are out on stalks as I rake my gaze over her pretty sage dress. It's draped across one shoulder, ruched at her slim waist, and fitted over her hips, ending just below her knee. One side has a slit, revealing an expanse of creamy skin, and my eyes trail the length of her shapely legs, admiring the sparkly silver sandals on her pretty feet. Her toenails are painted a glittery blue color matching the polish on her fingernails. "You look beautiful," I say over the lump wedged in my throat. "Your dress is gorgeous."

Her cheeks flush with my compliment, like I've noticed they always do. "Thank you."

"So, ugh." I clear my throat. "Tell me about the party. Is this a special occasion birthday?"

She shakes her head, sending waves of auburn hair cascading over her shoulders. I think I have an unnatural obsession with her hair. The few times she's let me run my fingers through it has only enhanced my addiction. My favorite shower fantasy is imagining my hand fisting her hair as I yank her head back and ram into her gorgeous body from behind.

And now I'm leaking precum like a horny teen.

This drive just got infinitely longer.

"What are you thinking about?" she asks, craning forward a little in her seat. "Your face is all flushed."

"Trust me, you don't want to know."

Her mouth forms an O shape, and now I'm thinking about driving my cock between those tempting lips, and it's a miracle I haven't blown my load already.

So much for the one I rubbed out in the shower providing relief.

My balls are fit to burst.

"Tell me about the party," I say, desperate to talk about non-sexy shit to regain my control. "Is it a special birthday?"

"Every birthday Nana celebrates is a special occasion to me. She is sixty-seven today. Our birthdays are exactly two weeks apart," she explains.

Ellen already mentioned it was Stevie's twentieth birthday in a couple weeks. Apparently, her friend Hadley is organizing a night out in Seattle, and she personally asked Ellen to invite me. I'll be there, but only if Stevie invites me. So far, she hasn't mentioned it, and I'm not pushing.

"That's cool."

"It is." Stevie kicks off her sandals, throwing her bare feet up on the dash. "For a period when I was little, I used to insist we have a joint birthday party, and Mom and Nana always humored me."

"That's cute."

"Not sure my friends appreciated hanging out with a bunch of oldies, but I always got a kick out of it."

"Will there be many at the party?" I inquire, taking the exit for the I-5. It's straight on the highway all the way to Seattle. It's a boring drive, but I don't mind. If I'm alone, I welcome the time to listen to music and think about stuff. With Stevie, it means I can put the car in cruise control, and we can talk the entire ride.

"Nah. Just a few of my nana's friends and neighbors, my mom, and Hads." She worries her lower lip between her teeth before turning her head to mine. "You're welcome to come in."

I was hoping to be invited, but I didn't want to presume anything. I also don't want her to feel obligated to invite me. "I don't want to intrude."

"You wouldn't be, and the least I can do is feed you before you set out on the return journey."

"I'm going to stay at my mom's tonight." Like Stevie, my exams don't start until Tuesday, so I can afford to lose a few study hours. I'm as prepared as I can be anyway. There isn't much more I can cram in my brain with the time I have left.

"That makes sense," she agrees, bobbing her head. "Medina is what? A twenty-minute drive from Ravenna?"

"Yep, so don't worry about me."

Lowering her feet to the floor, she sits up a little straighter before turning on her side. "Look, I'm just going to put this out there. There is no chance my mom or my nana are going to let you leave when they know you drove me home. You have zero possibility of escaping this party."

I smile as I settle back in my seat, removing my foot from the accelerator when I switch on cruise control mode. "Why exactly is that?"

She bites down on her lip before sighing. "Mom is all excited because I told her about you. She's adding two plus two and getting fifty."

My smile expands into full-blown grin territory. "I already told you I liked your mom, and now I like her even more."

"Heads-up, Monica is going to flap and fuss over you like you wouldn't believe. My nana won't be so obvious. She'll quietly observe to see what you're made of. They can both be pretty intense in completely different ways."

"I can handle it, but don't feel forced to invite me." I'm probably underdressed in my white T-shirt, jeans, and boots, but I doubt Stevie's friends or family will mind too much. It's not like I'm rocking up to one of my mother's friend's houses dressed casually. Mom would have a coronary if she saw what I'm wearing and knew I was attending a party dressed like this.

"I don't," Stevie says, yanking me out of my head.

"I will be there if you want me there, but otherwise, I'll head on to Medina."

A pregnant pause ensues for a few tense moments. "I'd like you there," she admits in a soft tone. "But you don't have to come if it's not your scene."

"I wouldn't want to be anywhere else," I truthfully reply, reaching out to touch her hand. "In case you haven't noticed, I'm finding it hard to be anywhere but by your side."

The most glorious smile lights up her face, and I want to spend a lifetime looking at it.

Some might call me crazy. Hell, most would, but I feel it in my bones.

Stevie is *the one*.

I refuse to let anyone sway me from the truth—I have found my forever.

Chapter Sixteen
Stevie

"You should be writing love songs for a living, Garrick. You have a beautiful way with words." It's the truth. With any other guy, what he just said might sound cheesy, but Garrick is too genuine for it to come across as anything but sincere. "And a beautiful voice to match."

"I'd rather reserve all the words for you."

See what I mean? This guy has already wormed his way into my life and into my heart, and I'm in real danger of giving the whole damn thing away.

"Are you like this with all your girlfriends?" I ask before I can stop to question the wisdom of it. "Not that I mean I'm your girlfriend or anything. I'm just curious."

He drills a hole in my head as he drives with one arm, coasting at a consistent speed in the slow lane of the I-5, like he wishes he could extract the thoughts from my mind.

"I don't want to talk about my exes, and they all fade into nonexistence when compared to you. I have never felt this strongly about any girl before, and that's the truth."

"Have you ever been in love?" I blurt, and I don't know why I'm asking questions that have the power to hurt, but it's like I've lost all control of my mouth.

He wets his lips before clearing his throat and eyeballing me again. "I thought I was one time, but it wasn't the real deal. It was infatuation and nothing more."

I'm tempted to probe further, but I'm also keen to avoid getting too heavy for fear I'll scare myself into regressing.

"Have you?" he asks even though he already knows the answer.

"Nope."

"Not even with your one and only high-school boyfriend?"

I vehemently shake my head. "I told you that relationship was me caving to peer pressure. All my friends had boyfriends, and I went and got myself one to fit in. He was a nice guy but way more into me than I was into him. When he told me he loved me, I broke things off, and it was such a relief."

"Wow, okay, I'll add that reminder to my list."

I can't tell if he's teasing or sincere. "I was a kid then. It's different now."

Garrick pushes his dark hair behind his ears, looking deep in thought as he stares out the windshield. A couple beats later, he turns to face me, keeping one eye on the road and one on me. "I know you said you didn't want to put any labels on us or move things to a new level, not until after our exams, but do you think you'll want to be my girlfriend?"

Ugh. So much for not wanting things to turn heavy. "Do we really have to do this now?" Hurt splays across his face, and I feel like an evil bitch. Taking his free hand in mine, I lace my fingers through his. "I like you a lot, Garrick." My chest heaves as I stare into his eyes. They look more green than brown today. He is so gorgeous, and sometimes it's so hard to not touch him. "I think the answer to that question is yes, but I haven't processed it all yet. I have an all-consuming personality, and if I start thinking about it now, it'll distract me. I know that probably sounds stupid to you, but I swear I'm not stringing you along. I'm being honest. Just let me get through my exams this week, and then we can talk."

"I'm sorry for pressuring you. I shouldn't have said anything." He squeezes my hand, and warmth spreads across my skin. I love holding his hand, and I love being in his arms. He makes me feel safe and loved. For a new-to-me emotion, I'm embracing it wholeheartedly and not letting guilt do a number on me.

I know when I give in to Garrick I will give him my all.

I just need to ensure I'm fully ready for it.

The last thing I want to do is hurt him and hurt myself in the process.

"You aren't pressuring me, and don't apologize. You've been letting me set the pace and taking the scraps I throw you. If anyone should be apologizing, it's me. I know I'm not like other girls. I know it's most likely really frustrating for you, but when I decide to do something, I give it my all. I never jump lightly into anything, especially where it pertains to my heart." I pull my legs up under me and clutch his hand tighter.

Garrick's gaze alternates between me and the road. "Those are all reasons why I like you, Stevie. I like that you're cautious. I'm just impatient to get to the next part because I haven't ever felt like this about anyone before."

"I haven't felt like this before either. It's totally new. I'm not used to being so vulnerable. It scares me as much as it excites me."

"You can trust me. I won't ever do anything to deliberately hurt you. That's not who I am."

"I know, Garrick. You have shown me that already. That doesn't mean I won't get hurt though. Or that you won't."

"No one knows that or can make any guarantees when they enter into any kind of relationship with another person. You risk getting hurt every time you open yourself up to others." Raising our conjoined hands to his mouth, he brushes his lips against my knuckles. "But that is life, and that is love. You risk far more by not putting yourself out there. You risk never knowing the pure elation of loving another person so completely you'd take a bullet for them. You risk never knowing true happiness and contentment."

"How are you so wise?" I ask as he lowers our hands.

"I'm not wise, nor am I experienced. Not when it comes to love. But I know what I've learned from my parents. My mother never truly opens herself up, and that's why all her marriages fail."

I suspect her rotten personality is the reason for marital failure, but I keep those thoughts to myself. After all, I've only met the woman once. I don't think my first impression is wrong, but she did give birth to Garrick, one of the most amazing people I know, so she can't be all bad.

"My father is vulnerable with Dawn, and watching how they support one another through the bad shit is even more inspirational than seeing them happy and glowing in the good times."

"I watch my mother risking herself for love all the time and getting burned," I quietly admit, rubbing circles on the back of his hand with my thumb. "I see her being vulnerable, and it backfires every time." I lift my eyes to him. "I am cynical and skeptical. I know that, but for the right person, I am willing to try." Gulping back nerves, I force the remaining words out of my throat. "I think you're the right person, but I want to be sure before we make that step. I owe it to both of us to have fully thought it through. I'm eighty percent there."

Garrick presses a kiss to my brow. "That's good enough for now."

"Are you sure you're okay to do this?" I ask one final time before we get out of Garrick's car. He parked his Range Rover beside Nana's older version in front of the house, alongside a row of other cars. I spot Hadley's in the mix, so even if she hadn't already texted me to say she'd arrived, I'd know she was here.

He chuckles as he tweaks my nose. "Relax, Stevie. It's fine."

"Okay, but don't say I didn't warn you," I singsong, curling my hand around the door handle.

"Wait!" he exclaims, and I pause mid door opening. "Let me get that."

Before I can protest, Garrick jumps out, races around to my side and opens the door.

I peer at him in amusement.

"I'm making it an official rule," he says, taking my hand and helping me down. "You don't get in or out of this car unless I'm opening the door for you."

On instinct, I reach up and kiss his cheek, lingering a few seconds longer than necessary. His spicy scent is delicious, and I have a sudden urge to lick him like a popsicle. "And they say chivalry is dead." I beam up at him, and gosh, he really is fucking hot.

I deserve a medal for not pouncing on him yet. "For the record, I have no issue agreeing to your rule. It's sweet." I pat his chest. And yes, I am using the opportunity to salivate over the hard muscles flexing under my palm.

"Good." Without warning, he hauls me into his arms, and I don't protest, falling easily against him and resting my head on his chest. He dots kisses into my hair, and I silently swoon as I grip his waist and savor the moment.

A girl could get used to this.

"Let me write this card super quick." Easing out of our embrace, he places the birthday card he insisted on buying at the store on Main Street down on the hood. Pulling a pen out of his jeans pocket, he writes a message in neat penmanship before sealing the card in the envelope.

I grab the cake box and bag with Nana's gift from the back seat as Garrick opens the trunk. He reappears with two bottles of sparkling wine carrying the Allen Wineries label. "Do you just happen to have wine in your trunk, or did you bring them on purpose?" I ask.

"I brought them for your nana. Even if I wasn't invited in, I planned to gift them to her for her birthday. You're only sixty-seven one time," he adds with a grin.

I could kiss him for his generosity and his thoughtfulness. He makes it so hard to stay away from him.

Light pokes out between the curtains in the open living room window, and the sounds of lively conversation and background music filter out into the nighttime air. Just as I'm opening my mouth to reply, the front door swings open, and I figure the welcoming committee has run out of patience.

Honestly, I'm surprised Mom didn't rush out the door the second Garrick's car pulled up.

"Darling." Mom runs toward me, flinging her arms around my neck as I stand awkwardly with a cake box in one hand and a gift bag in the other. "I'm so glad you're here. Nana would've been devastated if you hadn't made it."

"I'm just lucky Garrick was available to drive me," I say, kissing Mom on the cheek.

"Thank you so much for bringing our girl home," Mom says, giving Garrick a quick hug.

"It was no problem, Ms. Colson. Getting to spend time with Stevie is never a chore."

Mom positively beams at him as she loops her arm through his and swoons. "Please call me Monica, and I know what you mean. My daughter is a delight."

Oh my freaking god. I just know she's going to embarrass the hell out of me tonight. I must be insane to even consider bringing him inside, but it's too late now. This shit show is already in motion.

I'm all but forgotten as she drags Garrick through the door. "Did Stevie ever tell you about the time..."

I'm glad I don't hear the rest because I'd rather not know which humiliating childhood story she's telling him first. I shuffle in through the door, closing it behind me before heading toward the kitchen where I deposit the cake I baked this morning.

Then I walk into the main living room, at the front of the house, where everyone is congregated. Nana's neighbors and friends descend on me en masse, enveloping me in a cloud of floral perfume, sticky kisses, and motherly hugs. Over their heads, I spot Garrick being interrogated by my mom, her best friend Julie, Hadley, and Nana. He looks relaxed and not in need of rescue.

Yet.

Mom is busy pouring the sparkling wine into flutes while she keeps one ear on the conversation. She gives me a none too subtle thumbs-up, and I don't hold back on the eye roll. Playing it cool does not exist in Mom's vocab.

Nana's friends bombard me with questions about UO, my jobs at the bar and floral shop, my summer plans, and mostly about the handsome stranger I brought with me. Me bringing a guy around is a novelty, and no one is letting me leave without telling them everything about Garrick.

When Mom hands me a glass of wine, I knock half of it back in one go, wondering how I can extricate myself without seeming rude.

Nana comes charging to the rescue, squeezing her way in between her friends to claim me in a bear hug. "Little Poppy. Come show your nana some loving."

Bending down, I wrap my arms around her, burying myself in the familiarity of her hug.

"I've missed you, sweetheart."

"I've missed you too. Happy birthday!" Although I call Nana once a week, it's been six weeks since I last saw her. We break our embrace, but she grasps my hands in her smaller ones as she looks me over, ensuring I'm in one piece. "It's almost summer break. You can glut yourself on me soon," I say, laughing.

"I'm looking forward to it," she says as I hand her the gift bag. "Silly girl. What have I told you about buying me things?"

"It's your birthday. If I can't spoil you on your birthday, when can I?"

"You spoil me with your presence, and that is all I need." She's starting to sound a lot like Garrick.

"You look stunning, Nana. I love the dress. Is it new?" Her wine-colored velvet dress has little gold birds dotted all over it, cute cap sleeves, ruched detail at the bust, and it flows softly from the waist over her small, slender frame. Sparkly gold shoes with a low heel adorn her tiny feet. Her long gray hair is pulled into an elegant chignon, sind I spot my mother's handiwork. I always say Mom could have been a hairdresser. She has never formally trained, but she cuts a lot of the neighbors' kids' hair, like she used to do mine as a child, and she's a magician with up styles.

My nana is the epitome of a glamorous granny. Mostly, she

wears work pants, shirts, sweaters, and heavy-duty boots, but she loves an opportunity to dress up for an occasion.

"It was your mother's birthday gift. We went shopping on Monday," she explains.

"I wish I could have been there."

"Next time, dear. We're long overdue a good shopping trip." Threading her arm in mine, she steers me over toward one of the purple velvet couches. Garrick is now wedged on the other couch, nestled snugly in between Mom on one side and Hadley on the other. They look like they're firing questions at him, and he's starting to look a little uncomfortable.

Ha! I'm almost proud of my mother and my bestie for rattling my man.

My man.

Look at me tossing that out without hesitation. I've got to admit it has a nice ring to it.

"You look smitten," Nana says, pulling me down beside her on the couch. She looks over at Garrick with a contemplative expression on her face.

"I fear I am," I truthfully reply, watching as she settles the bag on her lap.

"'Nothing in life is to be feared. It is only to be understood,'" she replies, carefully unpacking the cross-stitch materials in the bag.

"Who said that?"

"Marie Curie. A very smart woman. First woman to win the Nobel Prize. First person to win a Nobel Prize twice, and first person to win a Nobel Prize in two scientific fields."

Nana is the most amazing woman. She always has an appropriate inspirational quote for every situation and conversation. How she remembers all of them astounds me. I struggle to remember the contents of the chapter I studied this morning on planting design and maintenance, and there's Nana with a whole encyclopedia of knowledge stowed away in her head. She is truly remarkable, and she will always remain the most inspirational woman to me.

"I'll try to heed her advice."

"This is too much." Nana shakes her head as she surveys the supplies covering her lap.

"No, it's not. I love you. It's your birthday, and I can never repay you for everything you've done for me."

She kisses my forehead. "You give me so much joy, Stevie. That's all the repayment I ever need."

"I'm looking forward to coming back to work. I learned a few new things from Sharon I thought we could try."

A slight grimace slides across her face, but it's gone fast. Still, I know Nana. "What was that look for?"

"It's nothing we need to talk about now."

"Nana." I fix her with my fiercest expression. "Tell me now."

"I don't want you to worry, but we had a bit of an incident this week. The roof caved in on the barn, destroying most of the shop and supplies."

Nana's floral business is not your typical floral business. She used to buy flowers from the market and sell them from the barn her grandparents set up as a floral shop years ago. This property is on fifty acres of land, and most of it was going to waste until Nana established a flower farm fifteen years ago to grow her own flowers. It was a way to ensure a variety of flowers and to keep the prices down. She hired a guy to help her develop the farm, and he recommended these specialist greenhouses that mean we can grow cut flowers all year round. It was quite cutting edge at the time, but most flower farmers use this method now.

The barn was remodeled at the same time. A large area contains shelving where buckets of various flowers are stocked daily. Customers can pick the exact flowers they want for their bouquet or purchase one of the ready-mades. A variety of accessories are for sale, and at the back of the room is a small seating area where customers can avail of snacks, baked goods, and coffee, all supplied by local businesses. One of Nana's friends manages it. It's proven to be a great draw for locals who sometimes only come here for coffee but end up walking out with flowers.

"Oh no. Will the insurance cover the costs?"

"Unfortunately not. The last safety inspection we had noted a weakness in the left side of the roof. Because I failed to act on it in a timely manner, the insurance company is refusing to pay out."

"Why didn't you get it fixed?" I cry, horrified at what this might mean for the business. That kind of damage will cost thousands to fix. Another horrifying thought flits through my mind. "You couldn't afford it, could you?"

She pats my hand, her gaze flicking to Garrick intermittently as we talk. "I don't want you to worry. I'll figure out a way to resolve it. We'll have to manually repair most of the damage to the shop ourselves, so prepare to get your hands very dirty."

"You shouldn't have given me that money for college," I protest, mentally calculating how much I have in my savings account. "I have money I can give you. It's not going to make a dent, but it's a start."

"Absolutely not." She clasps my face in her hands. "Listen to me, Stevie, and listen to me good. This is my problem to fix, and fix it I will. I gave you that money because I wanted to contribute to your future, and that still stands. I will not take a penny of your money, and don't insult me by attempting to offer me anything but your labor." Air expels from her lips as her features soften. "This is why I didn't want to have this conversation tonight. And we're not discussing it anymore. I don't want you to worry, honey." She kisses both my cheeks as she pulls me to my feet. "This is a party, and I'll have no glum faces." Tucking her arm in mine, she leads me toward Garrick. "Now, let's go rescue this young man of yours."

Chapter Seventeen
Garrick

"What about anal?" Hadley asks, popping a square of cheese in her mouth and fixing me with a cool expression like she hasn't just put that out there. "Into it or not?"

I stare at her like she just sprouted horns from her head.

She could be the devil.

It sure seems like she's only here to torment me.

"Kidding." She smirks before slurping her vodka cranberry through a straw. "Kind of." She giggles. "You should see your face right now."

"I'm not used to being drilled on my kinks while sitting beside my future girlfriend's mother."

Man, I wish I didn't have to drive.

I could use a beer or ten.

Stevie wasn't joking when she warned me. These women are nuts. The shit they've been asking me must be heard to be believed.

"Don't worry, Garrick," Monica says, turning around and patting my hand. "I only have half an ear on your conversation, and I'm not easily shocked." Monica and her friend spent fifteen minutes peppering me with questions while Stevie was surrounded by a fawning group of elderly women who clearly adores her.

"I'll keep that in mind," I say, reaching for the bottle of wine. I hold it up in front of Stevie's mom. "Would you like a top off?"

"That would be wonderful." Monica grabs Julie's glass, holding both wineglasses out to me. "And you were right about this vintage. It's delicious. I will be recommending this year to the restaurant manager at Sand Point when I'm on shift."

"I'll be starting work at the winery the week after my exams finish. Let me organize to send you a sample of this and some of our new-world wines, and you can sweet-talk the management into bumping up their order." I fill both glasses up to the halfway mark.

"Sounds like a plan." She winks. "Throw in a couple of bottles for yours truly, and we have a deal."

"Put in a good word with your daughter, and I'll keep you permanently supplied," I fire back with a grin.

Her smile is wide as she hands a wineglass to her friend. "I'm only finding more reasons to like you, Garrick, and I was already sold. Any guy who puts that big of a smile on my daughter's face is worthy of my seal of approval."

We all look over at Stevie as if it was planned. She's sitting on the other couch, deep in conversation with her nana.

"She is positively glowing," Hadley agrees, smiling before narrowing her eyes at me. "You better not have knocked her up."

Fucking hell.

I'm unsure what to make of Stevie's childhood best friend. I don't know if she's being outrageous to put on a show, if she has no filter and is just always like this, or she's testing me to see if

I'm good enough for her best friend. Maybe it's a combination of those things. I'd like to point out sex would have to be involved to knock Stevie up and, given how we haven't so much as kissed yet, it's impossible, but I won't be rude, and what has or hasn't happened between Stevie and me is private.

Monica almost chokes on her wine. "Sheesh, Hadley. Anyone would think you don't know your best friend. Stevie will probably make poor Garrick triple bag it before he gets anywhere near her lady parts."

I'm not easily embarrassed, but I'd quite happily sink into the ground and disappear if it was an option.

"Oh dear," someone with a soft lilting voice says. "Have they been terrorizing you?"

I look up at Stevie and her nana, thrilled at the timely intervention.

I scramble to my feet in record time as if my ass is on fire. The women behind me snicker, clearly enjoying my obvious discomfort. I'm most definitely of the view this was a test, and I only hope I passed. I clear my throat. "It's been interesting, ma'am." Stepping aside, I gesture toward the couch. "Take my seat."

"Nonsense, and I told you to call me Betsy," she says, waggling her finger in her daughter's face.

Stevie's nana said hello earlier but otherwise was a silent observer while her daughter and Stevie's best friend proceeded with their Spanish Inquisition.

"Scoot, missy," she tells Monica. "You've tormented this young man enough for one night." Her gaze flits to Hadley. "You too, little Miss Mischief."

"Moi?" Hadley stands, looking the picture of innocence. "I'm sure I don't know what you're talking about."

"Please tell me you didn't grill him on his sexual preferences or start a debate over biodiversity or the overexploitation of natural resources," Stevie says, pursing her lips and eyeballing her friend.

"We were just getting to the end of the kink portion of the interrogation though it's worth noting Garrick avoided answering the anal question."

My cheeks heat in an uncharacteristic blush. I can't believe she said that in front of Stevie's nana. I don't think it's for show either. I get the sense these kinds of conversations occur naturally when Hadley is around.

"Anal is overrated," Betsy says, scoffing and waving her hands around. "Unlike DP. Now that's an entirely different conversation."

I have a feeling my face is as red as a tomato and the sweat beads forming on my brow are visible.

Stevie is trying hard not to laugh. "I did try to warn you," she says, resting her hand on my forearm.

"Your warning was lacking in detail," I murmur in her ear as Monica, Julie, and Hadley walk away to mingle with the other guests. Thank fuck for small mercies.

"You survived," she says, letting a giggle free. "I promise they're not always quite that intense, but Hadley is unnaturally invested in my sex life, and I can't promise she won't get inappropriate again."

Betsy pats the space beside her on the couch. "Come sit by me, Garrick, and don't mind little Hadley. That one missed out on the sixties, and she's determined to make up for it by living her best free-love high-spirited hippy life."

"Hadley is very passionate about sexual freedom and equality, the environment, books, and ridding the world of injustice," Stevie explains, sitting on the arm of the couch, right by my side. "I'll get her to tone it down next time you meet."

"Now I know what to expect, it's cool. These are not the kinds of conversations I'm used to having at parties." I chuckle. "I would love my mother to meet Hadley. The look on her face would be more than worth the lecture I'd receive after."

"That can be arranged." Stevie smirks. "Though it's probably not advisable if I want to get in her good graces. Something tells me I'll have my work cut out for me with your mom."

I thread my fingers through hers. "She'll come around when she sees how much I care about you."

"My Little Poppy hasn't told me much about you, so I want to know everything," Nana says. "Start from the beginning. How did you two meet?"

"So, are you scarred for life after that ordeal?" Stevie asks an hour later when we step outside.

"It wasn't so much bad as unexpected, and I think I'll be fine." I squeeze her hand and grin down at her. "After hours of intense therapy."

She throws back her head and laughs, and I'm glad to see it because she has seemed a little tense. "I'm sorry. I probably should've warned you more thoroughly, but I was dying to see how you'd hold up."

We linger by my car. "Did I pass the test, or should I be worried?" I ask, raising our interlinked hands to my lips and brushing my mouth against her soft skin.

A gentle shudder ripples over her body, and I silently fist pump the air.

"You passed with flying colors. I knew everyone would love you, and I was right."

"Your mom's a hoot. Your nana is adorable, and well, the jury is still out on Hadley, but if she's your oldest friend, I know she's a good one." I pull her in close to my chest, resting my hands lightly on her hips. "You wouldn't be friends with anyone who wasn't good to their core."

"Hads *is* good people. She's just...an acquired taste. Like absinthe, brussels sprouts, and liver." A grimace crawls over her face, and I laugh.

"Will I ruin everything if I mention I love brussels sprouts?"

"Yes. Absolutely," she says, making no effort to extract herself from my embrace. She beams up at me. "Though I'll probably cope as long as you don't try to kiss me after eating those hideous things."

My eyes lower to her lips on autopilot, and my dick suddenly realizes how strategically we're aligned, springing to life. It's becoming problematic around Stevie. I am so turned on by her. Sometimes she just has to look at me, and I sprout a boner.

My tongue darts out, licking my lips as I note how her pupils dilate, and she strains toward me. Her gaze is fixated on my mouth, and tension bleeds into the small space between our bodies. Abstaining is the ultimate test, and I'm not sure I'm going to pass. "I want to kiss you so badly right now," I admit, desire seeping into my gruff tone.

"Me too," she whispers, tentatively lifting one hand to my face. "You're so gorgeous, Garrick, and I really like you." Her soft fingers brush against the light stubble on my cheeks. "But I'm afraid if we kiss now, we'll never stop, and making out in your car in front of my nana's house is not how I picture our first time."

Pulling her to me, I press a kiss to the top of her head and briefly close my eyes. "Nor me. I think I should go."

"Yes," she agrees, albeit reluctantly.

Clasping her face in my hands, I tilt it up to look at me.

"Before I go, I just want to ask if everything is okay. You seemed a little preoccupied back there."

"You caught that, huh?"

I nod, and she sighs. "Nana told me some bad news. The roof of her barn collapsed, destroying her shop and ruining thousands of dollars' worth of supplies. The insurance won't pay out, and she doesn't have the money for repairs and replacements. I'm worried about her business."

"That's not good."

"No, it isn't." She sighs again, and I hear the pain behind the exhale.

"Is it far from here? Can you show me?"

"It's only a ten-minute walk, and yes, if you like. I wouldn't mind seeing the damage for myself."

Stevie retrieves her overnight bag from my car and darts back into the house to change her shoes. She reappears a few minutes later wearing boots and a cardigan. After grabbing my hoodie from the car, we set out on foot, hand in hand, and Stevie points out things as we walk past row upon row of greenhouses.

I draw to a stop when we reach a large field of poppies, blowing gently in the dark nighttime breeze. "Does this have anything to do with Betsy calling you Little Poppy?" I ask, pulling Stevie in front of me as I turn us to face the field. My hands skim around her waist as I hold her flush against my chest and rest my chin on her shoulder with my face pressed against the side of hers.

She places her hands on top of mine, and I hold her a little tighter, feeling like I never want to let her go. She fits perfectly against me, like she was made especially for me.

"Yes. This poppy field has been here for eons. As a little girl, I used to love running into it and rolling around. When friends came over, we'd play hide and seek in there, and I was always picking the poppies and decorating my bedroom with them. Nana gave me the name, and it stuck." Her back rumbles against my chest as she laughs. "Hads spent a year calling me Opium Poppy after a local farmer was caught growing a poppy field and manufacturing opium from it for sale. She tried to convince Nana to permanently change my nickname, but she was having none of it." Amusement and nostalgia underscore her tone. "Those were fun times."

"It seems like you had a great childhood."

"I did. Mom and I lived here for the first few years of my life before she bought the house we currently live in. Even after we moved, I still spent time here most every day. This is as much my home as our house is."

"What about your grandpa? You never mention him."

"He ran off with Nana's best friend when Mom was five, and he didn't come back. They never divorced, and she was notified twelve years ago when he died. We don't talk about him, and I never think of him. Hard to think of someone you never knew."

"I know I have only just met her, but your nana is an amazing woman. How anyone could desert her, and their own flesh and blood, makes no sense to me."

"Same here." She shivers, and I quickly shuck out of my hoodie, ignoring her complaining as I put it on her.

"Come on. It's getting colder." We pick up our pace, and it doesn't take long to spot the barn. Even in the dark, and from this distance, I can see the devastation wrought on the large structure.

"Fuck. It's way worse than I imagined." Unhappiness laces her tone as we approach the damaged barn. A giant-sized gaping hole in the roof is admitting the elements, and when we open the door, it's clear everything inside will have to be gutted and replaced.

Bits of the roof and weather-strewn debris cover the interior floor. Chairs, buckets, garden accessories, and other supplies are scattered around the place. Puddles of water, from recent rainfall, are dotted all over the ground ensuring there is no recovering anything inside. A large plastic sheet hangs down from one side of the hole in the roof, and it's obvious whoever tried to tack it up didn't do a good enough job.

It's a mess, and Stevie is right to be concerned.

"This is so bad," she says in a low voice, clinging to my hand.

"Yeah, it's not good."

"I don't know how we fix this, but I'm going to find a way." Steely determination resonates in her previously dejected tone as an idea forms in my mind. "Nana is not losing her family business." She looks up at me with a face steeped in determination. "Not if I have anything to say about it."

Chapter Eighteen
Stevie

I push through the crowded cafeteria with my heart pounding in my chest, my eyes darting everywhere, searching for the man I came to find. Ignoring the curious stares of the students I pass, I pick up speed when I spot Garrick in the corner of the large room, leaning against the wall as he talks with a short stocky guy with a mass of jet-black hair. Behind him, seated at a table, are Will, Noah, Ellen, and two other guys I don't know.

Butterflies careen around my chest, and my heart is so full it feels like it might burst. Tears prick my eyes as I race toward him, wondering how I could have ever considered rejecting this man.

Garrick Allen is a god among men, and I am so fucking lucky I caught and held his attention.

A smile ghosts over his mouth when he spots me approaching, and I lose all self-consciousness and self-control as I full-on run toward him, uncaring what anyone thinks. His brows climb to his hairline when I throw myself at him, snaking my arms around his neck and yanking his head down to mine as I smash my lips to his.

Garrick doesn't disappoint, winding his strong arms around my back and holding me close as I kiss him. Our surroundings disappear, and it's only the two of us in our own little bubble. Angling my head, I trace my tongue along the seam of his lips, demanding entry. His lips willingly part to welcome me, and we both groan as my tongue slides into his mouth and tangles with his. Garrick takes control. Tightening his hold on me and deepening our kiss, he meets every stroke of my tongue with a caress of his own, and his full velvety-soft lips worship my mouth in a way that exceeds my every fantasy.

Butterflies are running riot in my chest and blood is pumping through my veins as liquid lust combusts in my lower belly, and an almost painful ache throbs between my legs. Garrick keeps me close, kissing me passionately like he never thought he'd get to do it. His hard length presses into my stomach, and knowing he wants me as much as I want him thrills me. My fingers thread through his gorgeous hair as we kiss, and I pour everything I'm feeling into every sweep of my tongue and every brush of my lips.

Kissing Garrick is everything I dreamed of and more.

I never want to stop, but reality comes crashing back when a chorus of whoops, hollers, and calls of "get a room" break the bubble we're in, and I'm instantly aware that I'm devouring his mouth in full view of a packed cafeteria.

I don't really care. The moment called for this, but I'm not about to give them more of a show.

Garrick must reach the same conclusion at the same time I do because we both pull back in sync, keeping a hold of one another as we break our kiss. He rests his brow against mine. "Fuck, Stevie." His warm breath fans over my face like magical mist, and I kiss him again, because now I know what he tastes like, I don't think I can stop. "If we were anywhere but this cafeteria," he growls over my lips, leaving the rest of the statement unsaid because we both understand what he means.

"I know." My voice comes out all raspy and seductive. Clasping his face in my hands, I force him to look at me. Our eyes meet, and mine fill with fresh tears. "Thank you." A single tear trickles out of the corner of my eye and runs down my face. "First my car, and now this." Garrick called in a favor with a friend, and by the time we returned to Eugene on Sunday, my CR-V was back in full working order.

This guy has stomped all over the shields I usually keep around my heart and laid siege to it—in the best possible way.

"It's not a big deal," he says, softly wiping the dampness from my cheek.

"Don't downplay it. It's a huge deal, and you know it. Nana told me about the visit from your dad. How you're going to repair the barn free of charge. That you would do this for us." I slap a hand over my chest, and I'm close to breaking down. No one has ever done anything so amazing, and I'm all up in my feels. "I can't ever repay you for your kindness."

"I'm sure I can think of a few ways." He flashes me a flirty smile, and I laugh. It helps to break up the heavy emotion of the moment.

"I'm sure you can, and you can bet I'll raise the stakes."

"I look forward to it, beautiful." He kisses the tip of my nose, and I swoon in his arms.

I'm in so much trouble with this guy.

"All joking aside, Garrick, what you have done is nothing short of miraculous. I just." I pause, all choked up, unable to articulate my thoughts or say what I want to say. "I can't thank you and your dad enough, but I'm going to try."

"We're glad to help." He moves us farther into the corner away from prying ears. He plays with my hair as we lean against the wall, so close there is barely any space between our bodies. "And it wasn't completely selfless. At least this way, we get to spend more time together."

I arch a brow.

"I'll be part of the crew working on the barn next week," he confirms.

"I thought you were taking a week off to chill out and catch up with Hudson?"

"Plans change." He shrugs, and his selflessness blows my mind. In this moment, I don't feel worthy of Garrick Allen. "Hudson has agreed to help too. Between everyone, we'll get the barn fixed up and have Nana back in business in no time."

You are so getting laid.

I think it, but I don't say it. Not yet. It's only Wednesday, and exams aren't over until Friday. We're hitting The End Zone to celebrate, but Saturday night, he is all mine, and I'm going to commit to him. It's no longer a choice. I am all in now and dying to dive in with both hands. Wild horses couldn't separate me from this amazing man.

I want to be Garrick's, and I want him to be mine, and I'm done denying both of us what we so desperately need.

By the time Saturday night rolls around, I'm a bundle of nervous excitable energy as I dash around the kitchen putting the finishing touches to the special dinner I cooked for Garrick in between packing. Ellen left for home this morning with Will in toe. I'm heading home tomorrow, and I need to take most of my shit with me because the apartment has been sublet over the summer. Thankfully, we secured a lease for our junior year, and it's good to know we'll be coming back here, but it's a pain we can't leave everything behind.

Still, I count our blessings. Places like this are in high demand, and we're lucky we get to keep it for another year.

I am so glad exams are behind me, and now I have the whole summer to look forward to. A summer with Garrick. I'm itching for him to get here so I can confirm what I suspect he already knows—I'm ready to officially be his girlfriend.

I have just covered the dinner to keep it warm when the doorbell chimes. The biggest, goofiest grin spreads across my face as I sprint to the door and fling it open. We move as one, our arms and lips meeting as I pull him to me, and he claims my mouth in a fervent kiss I feel all the way to my toes. Since our first very public kiss in the cafeteria on Wednesday, we've been kissing any chance we get and struggling to keep it PG-13. But with exams and studying, there was no time to indulge in anything else.

Now the obstacles are gone, I look forward to taking our relationship to the next level tonight.

"Something smells good," Garrick purrs against my neck after we end our kiss. "And I'm not just talking about dinner."

"You smell delicious yourself," I admit, burying my nose in the gap between his neck and his shoulder and inhaling the purely masculine smell emanating from his pores. His scent is a mix of citrusy shower gel and spicy cologne, and I can't get enough.

"Invite me in, little minx, before we give the neighbors a show." He drags his nose up and down my neck as a door opens and closes behind him.

"Stop being so fucking hot, and I won't lose my head," I say, grabbing him by the shirt and yanking him into my apartment.

He backs me up with his body until my spine hits the counter. Placing the box of chocolates in his hand down beside us, he leans in and kisses me sweetly. One, two, three times, and I virtually melt into a puddle of goo at his feet. "I missed you."

"We didn't part until the early hours of the morning," I remind him.

Garrick showed up last night to collect me for our night out with our crew, with flowers and a bottle of wine, and it's a miracle we managed to make it to The End Zone because I basically attacked him with my lips and my hands, and it took mammoth self-control not to trap him in my bedroom and have my wicked way with him.

"So?" His brows crawl up his face. "That was hours ago. In case you've forgotten the memo, I miss you every second I'm not with you."

I place my hands on his trim waist. "I'm so into you, Garrick Allen."

"I'm glad to hear it," he says before stealing another kiss. "Because I'm so hooked on you, Stevie Colson."

We grin at each other like lovesick fools, and the pure elation charging through my veins is like nothing I've experienced before. I have fallen headfirst into this whirlwind with Garrick, and there isn't a single molecule of my body that regrets it.

"We need to eat before dinner is ruined." I trace my fingers through the stubble on his chin and cheeks. "But I promised you an official answer today, and I don't want to wait a second longer." I cup his handsome face. "I'm all in, Garrick. I want to be your girlfriend. Nothing would make me happier."

His answering kiss is deep, decadent, and hypnotic, and I'm barely capable of standing when we finally break apart, both of us panting and flushed with matching cheesy grins.

"Told you I'd convince you to go out with me," he says, shooting me a smug look.

"You did, and you were right." My arms glide around his neck, and I stretch up on tiptoes to kiss him. "Thank you for not giving up on me," I add when I end the kiss.

"That wasn't ever going to happen, beautiful. I had no intention of giving up."

The adoring look on his face as he messes with my hair does wonderful things to my insides. I think about how easy it's going to be to love this man, and while the thought still holds a modicum of fear, I'm ready to fall deep. Nothing has ever felt so right.

"You were always going to be mine, Stevie, and now you are." His lips glide over my mouth in a soft featherlight kiss, sending delicious tremors rippling across my skin. "Thank you for giving me a chance, and I promise you're not going to regret it. I'm going to be the best boyfriend because failing you is not an option. I'm in this for the long haul, and I'm going to worship the ground you walk on because you deserve everything and more."

When he hauls me into a hug, cradling my head against his strong chest, I close my eyes and absorb his words, letting them sink skin-deep as I relish the feel and smell of him. He's so solid and warm and all man. Nothing feels insurmountable if I have Garrick by my side. I don't have to lose my independence or any of my goals just because I'm in a relationship. I know Garrick won't ever let that happen. I can be a better version of myself with him in my life, and I'm excited for this summer and all the possibilities it offers.

Garrick is mine. I know I won't stop pinching myself to believe it's real for a while, but I'm determined to fully embrace our relationship because making him happy is now one of my goals.

And once I set my heart and mind to something, there is no going back.

Chapter Nineteen
Garrick

"That was delicious," I say, rubbing a hand across my full stomach as I push my empty plate away. Stevie went all out with filet steak, shrimp, a homemade garlic sauce, and gratin potatoes, and she even made me brussels sprouts—cooked to perfection, soft and mushy, just how I like them. For dessert, she made a berry meringue roulade, and if I eat another bite, I'm likely to keel over and die.

"I'm glad you enjoyed it." She reaches across the table to take my hand. "I wanted to cook something special to thank you for everything."

"Getting to be with you is all the thanks I need."

"How did I get so lucky to meet you?" She squeezes my hand and smiles.

"It was fate." I laugh when she predictably rolls her eyes. "You won't convince me otherwise."

"Believe what you like, but you'll never convince me. Fate is how lazy people explain inaction or an abstract notion clung to by stubborn people who refuse to believe in coincidence." She grins and then releases my hand. Her chair scrapes across the tile floor as she abruptly stands and begins gathering up the dinnerware.

"And the cynic is in the house, ladies and gentlemen," I tease, climbing to my feet and snatching the plates from her hands. "You cooked. I'm on cleanup duty. That's always how it worked in my house." Well, my dad's house. Dawn maintains no son of hers will grow up spoiled, and we all had daily and weekly chores. My brothers constantly complain, as I did when I was younger, but Dawn is right, and I'm glad she was insistent. At least I can cook and clean and fend for myself. If I'd grown up solely with Mom, I'd be a spoiled little prick, waited on by staff for my every whim.

"You have good manners." She darts in to kiss my cheek. "And I'm never one to look a gift horse in the mouth."

After stacking the dirty dishes in the sink, I return to the table to top off her wineglass. I lean in to snatch a quick kiss, but she's quick to shove me away. "Not a chance in hell until you've rinsed that brussels sprout taste from your mouth."

I chuckle as I swat her ass. "It's not like I carry my toothbrush with me wherever I go."

"You can borrow mine," she says, "or just rinse your mouth with mouthwash."

"If that's what it'll take to steal more kisses, so be it." I whistle under my breath as I head off in the direction of the bathroom.

"Oh, and Garrick?!"

I spin around on my heels to face her.

"I'm not cynical. I'm pragmatic, and I'd much rather believe in unplanned coincidental events than supernatural predetermined nonsense that can't ever be proven."

When I return a few minutes later with minty-fresh breath, I find my girl spreadeagled on the couch, trawling through movies on Netflix. Leaning down, I claim her lips in a brief tender kiss. "Better?" I murmur before brushing my lips against hers again.

"Much." She reaches up to kiss me, but I pull back and straighten up with a smirk.

"I'm on cleanup duty, remember."

"Leave it," she coaxes, pinning me with a seductive smile. "Making out is a far better use of your time."

"I don't doubt it, but I never shirk my responsibility."

She pouts, and I laugh as I make my way into the kitchen and clean the place in noteworthy time.

When I return, Stevie is sitting upright on the couch and sipping her wine.

"Thank you," she says, when I flop down beside her, setting her wineglass on the coffee table and crawling toward me. "You really didn't have to do that, but I appreciate it. The more Garrick layers I uncover, the more impressed I am." She climbs onto my lap, straddling my hips.

"It's only fair." I glide my palms up her thighs. "We're both tired after finals, and you've been slaving away over a hot stove all day. I wanted you to relax."

"I am relaxed," she purrs, looping her arms around my neck as she grinds down on me. "I think it's time you relaxed too." An impish grin crests along her mouth as she bends down and puts her face all up in mine. "I have a few ideas in mind."

"I like where this is going," I grit out as my fingers breach the hem of her dress and creep up underneath it.

"I'm so horny for you," she whispers, kissing one corner of my mouth. "All week, I've been getting myself off daydreaming about your hands on me."

"Only my hands?" I quip as she plants another teasing kiss to the other side of my mouth.

There is zero hesitation in her response. "Your tongue and your cock too." Her thumb traces a path along my bottom lip, and I'm like steel in my pants as she slowly rotates her hips and pivots against me.

My fingers move up toward the Holy Land, the tips grazing the edge of her lace panties, and she sucks in a needy gasp. "I've been fantasizing about you too," I admit, holding her gaze as I trail my fingers back and forth against her lace-covered crotch. A shiver works its way through her as she holds her hips up a little, granting me better access. "Kiss me," I demand, and she groans into my mouth as I push her panties aside and run my finger up and down her slit.

Her lips plunder mine as I continue teasing her with one finger, slowly dragging it back and forth against her wet folds, until I can't hold back any longer. Driving my finger inside her, I almost come in my boxers when I feel her warm walls gripping my digit and holding it tight.

Our kissing intensifies, and she's whimpering against my lips as I add another finger and pump them in and out of her pussy. She feels like heaven on my fingers, but it's not enough. I need more. I need to feel her arousal on my tongue. Breaking our kiss, I nip at her jawline and her earlobe before whispering, "I need to taste you. Can I?"

"God, yes. Please," she rasps, grinding on top of me before smashing her lips to mine and devouring me with the same potent desire I feel churning in my veins.

My dick is begging for release, dying to plunge inside her and make her fully mine, but I want to get on my knees for her first. This is about Stevie's needs, not mine, so I reposition her on the couch and slide to the floor, parting her thighs and licking my lips. Keeping my eyes on her, I reach under her dress, hook my thumbs in the side of her panties, and carefully drag them down her legs. I remove her heels, one at a time, and discard her panties.

Her chest heaves, and her breath huffs out in exaggerated

spurts as I glide my palms slowly up her legs. Starting with her perfectly formed feet, moving over her shapely legs, along the curve of her knee, and up along her satiny-smooth thighs.

"You're killing me here," she pants over a moan as I lean in and press a kiss to the side of one thigh.

"Good things come to those who wait," I tease, fighting a chuckle when she flips me the bird. "That's what I constantly told myself these past few weeks as I waited for us to be on the same page."

Something close to adoration paints her face as she stares at me. "You're about to get your reward."

"I would have waited forever for you, Stevie. I hope you know that," I truthfully admit as I push her dress up to her waist and expose her most intimate parts to me.

"I know." Her voice is a throaty whisper that cranks my desire to a new level.

Her thighs tremble as I push them farther apart so I can see all of her. "Show me your pussy," I instruct. "Give me my reward. I want to see every bit of you."

She gulps audibly as she lowers her hands to her cunt and pulls her folds back with shaking fingers, showcasing her glistening clit and the tempting wetness of her soft pink flesh.

"You're perfect, Stevie," I say, leaning in for a closer inspection. Her arousal tickles my nostrils, and my dick is throbbing in anticipation. "Such a pretty pink pussy. So beautiful and all mine." I lave my tongue up and down her slit, lapping up her juices and licking her fingers where they open her up to me. She tastes divine, like the sweetest nectar, and I sense a new addiction forming. "Touch your tits," I say before diving in with my tongue and my fingers, working her soaking cunt as she gropes her tits through her dress. I shove my tongue inside her warm tight channel while I rub her swollen bundle of nerves with two fingers. Then I alternate, pushing three fingers inside her as I suck on her clit, moaning against her quivering flesh as she rocks her hips, writhing above me, with her eyes closed and one hand on her boob.

"Look at me, baby," I command a few minutes later when I feel she's close. "I want you to watch me eating you out as you come all over my face."

"Fuck, Garrick," she mumbles, arching her back and grinding her cunt on my face as she loses herself to lust.

"Eyes on me, Stevie," I demand, curling my fingers inside her and hitting the perfect spot.

"Oh, god, Garrick. That feels so good. Don't stop. I'm so close."

"I know, beautiful. Keep your eyes on me, and fall apart on my fingers and my tongue." I wait until her eyes are fixed on mine to press down inside her at the same time I gently bite her clit, and she crests the peak. Screaming my name repeatedly, Stevie rocks against my face, writhing and moaning, her thighs spasming and her pussy quaking as she comes and comes on my tongue.

I milk every drop of her desire, even after she's gone quiet and stopped moving, unable to tear myself away from her magical cunt. Sounds cheesy as shit, but it's the fucking truth. I am utterly addicted to this woman. She has cast a spell on me, and it's one I never want to emerge from.

"Garrick." Her fingers roam through my hair, exploring and tugging, and it sends fresh tremors of need crawling all over my body. "That was the best thing anyone has ever done to me. Holy fuck."

Reluctantly, I pull my face away, feeling her arousal coating my lips and dripping onto my chin. I crawl up her body, holding onto the back of the couch as I lower myself down over her and claim her lips, letting her taste herself on me. Driving my tongue into her mouth, I explore and devour as my cock aches painfully behind the zipper of my jeans.

"Your turn," she says, palming my dick through the denim and piercing me with a searing-hot look.

"I won't say no." I'm physically incapable of turning her down, such is my need. My dick is so hard it could hammer nails. Pushing off the couch, I strip out of my jeans, boxers, and socks in record time, and then I yank my T-shirt off over my head, standing before her completely naked.

Her eyes are bugging out of her head, she's licking her lips, and her pupils are blown with the depth of her arousal. Not gonna lie. It does wonders for my ego.

"You're so beautiful, Garrick," she says, sliding to the edge of the couch. Her dress falls down around her upper thighs, and the sight of her fully clothed while I'm butt naked makes what we're about to do even dirtier.

"Spread your legs and lean back," I say, stroking my erection as I stare at her gorgeous mouth. I'm already salivating at the prospect of those plump lips wrapped around my cock. Stevie gets into position, and I stand between her thighs as I lean forward and rest my hands on the back of the couch, my dick straining and leaking precum as it bobs in the vicinity of her face. She scoots down a little until the angle is right, and then she circles her soft fingers around my dick and guides it to her mouth.

She licks the tip, groaning as she sucks down the beads of precum at my crown. Closing my eyes, I curse under my breath as she takes her time caressing my hard length. Nibbling, sucking, and lightly grazing her teeth along my shaft, she moans in appreciation while worshiping my dick like it's the best thing she's ever put in her mouth.

My hips jerk of their own accord, desperate to slam into her and craving release. Stevie reads my cues, hollowing her cheeks and sucking me down as far as she can go. When my cock hits the back of her throat, a guttural moan rips from my lips, and I fist her hair in one hand and take control.

Our eyes meet, remaining locked on one another as we work in tandem to drive me to blissful oblivion. I thrust my hips and pump in and out of her mouth as she widens her lips, stretching her jaw as far as it will go, sucking and licking like a fucking queen. Tears spill from her eyes and saliva leaks from her lips as I quicken my pace and tighten my hold on her hair.

Stevie stays with me the whole time, and I'm watching her carefully for signs she's uncomfortable, but I see none. The heat in her eyes and clear joy on her face tell me to keep going, so I do. Until my balls pull up, a familiar tingle snakes up my spine, and I know I'm close. "I'm going to come." I loosen my grip on her hair a little, peering deep into her emerald eyes. "You want me to pull out?"

She shakes her head over a mouthful of my dick, and the visual sends me steamrolling toward my climax. I detonate in her mouth, shooting jets of hot cum down her throat as I shout out my release, calling her name in worship as I empty everything inside her. Stevie doesn't let up until I've stopped thrusting and my cries have died out. My dick slides from her mouth with a loud pop, and I collapse in a sated heap, holding her as I maneuver onto my back, lying lengthways on the couch, with Stevie on top of me.

Her bare pussy rubs against my softening shaft, instantly hardening it again.

"Was that—"

"Fucking incredible," I confirm before she's even finished her sentence. I kiss her deeply, rolling my tongue inside her mouth as I hold her head firmly between my palms. "You're amazing." I dust kisses all over her face. "So fucking amazing."

"Want to take this into the bedroom?" she suggests,

waggling her brows while gyrating her hips and rubbing her pussy against my fresh erection.

Keeping her in an embrace, I sit us up and lay her legs sideways across my thighs as my feet plant on the hardwood floor. Nuzzling my nose into her neck, I inhale her sweet scent while my arms tighten around her waist. "More than anything," I finally reply, looking her straight in the eyes. "But that's exactly why I think we shouldn't."

Her eyes pop wide as she stares at me. I tuck her gorgeous hair behind one ear. "I don't want to be a casual fuck."

"You aren't, Garrick." Gently, she places her small hand on my bare chest. "You never could be."

I can't believe I'm going to say this, but it feels like the right thing to do. "I need you to be sure, Stevie. It wasn't that long ago you were adamant relationships weren't for you. I couldn't handle being a fling. Not when I'm so invested in you."

"I'm invested in you too, and I'm sure, Garrick. I swear. I told you when I go for something I give it my all. I didn't say that lightly. I'm fully on board."

I kiss her soft cheek. "I'm glad to hear it, but I still think we should wait."

Hurt flickers behind her eyes, and it guts me. I don't want her thinking it's a rejection when it's not. I'm just trying to do the right thing for both of us. "Listen up, beautiful." I hold her closer. "You mean everything to me. I want to fuck you so bad my balls are throwing a pity party right now. But I want our first time to be special. It's a moment that will stay with us for the rest of our lives. I want it to be memorable so it always brings a smile to our faces and tears to our eyes. I have no doubt if I took you back to your bedroom now it would be amazing, but I want more than that for us. I want to make it magical. I want it to be romantic and somewhere that means something to us and preferably surrounded by candles, not packing boxes." I try to bring some humor to the moment to lighten it.

"Is that the truth?" Her eyes probe mine.

"Absolutely. I would never lie to you."

"I don't like it, or agree, but only a bitch would say no to wanting it more romantic. You've patiently waited for me, so I guess I can summon patience from somewhere to wait for you."

I chuckle at the grumpy look on her face. "It won't be forever. Trust me when I say I can't wait long, but just think about how amazing it's going to be when we've waited and planned it for the perfect moment." I rub my thumb along her swollen lips, basking in the beauty of the woman sitting on my lap. Stevie has never looked more gorgeous than she does now with tangled hair, flushed skin, and a resigned pout on her delectable mouth. "A wise woman once told me anticipation makes it all the sweeter, and I'm sticking by that."

Chapter Twenty

Stevie

"Why the grumpy face?" Nana asks as we unpack the boxes of supplies that have just been delivered.

"I thought having Garrick here this week would mean lots of time together, but I've barely seen him."

On Monday, we joined Garrick and his crew, along with friends and neighbors, to clear out the barn, tossing everything into industrial dumpsters because nothing was salvageable. It was painstaking back-breaking work, and I collapsed in a heap that night, covered in sweat and grime and aching all over.

Garrick has been traveling to Ravenna with a team of workers from the lumberyard every day, and they leave promptly at six. We barely manage to grab lunch and a quick kiss in the middle of the day.

Nana chuckles. "You sure have changed your tune."

"You know me." I shrug as I cut through packing tape on one of the boxes and extract some cute vases and exterior wall hangings. "Once I set my mind to something, I give it my everything."

Last week, I set up a donation page online to raise funds to restock the shop, and everyone rallied around. We ended up tripling the donation target, and I'm glad because it's taken the pressure off Nana. There is enough to replace all the damaged items and to pay the staff this week even though most of them haven't been needed after Monday.

Garrick and the Allen Lumber crew have been working alone Tuesday, Wednesday, and Thursday to repair the roof and reinforce the structure so the barn is more robust and less likely to suffer damage in the future. Garrick promised to show up with double the crew tomorrow to finish the interiors before lunchtime on Saturday so we can get ready for the celebrations planned for later that night.

It was my idea to throw a barn party to thank everyone for riding to the rescue. Hadley canceled the bar booking she made for my birthday night out in Seattle, inviting my friends to come here instead, so it'll be a double celebration.

As soon as Garrick found out, he roped a few friends he knows, who are in a country music band, to play at the party. Hadley called a friend from college, who is a national line-dancing champion, and she's going to put us through our paces on the night. Nana's friends and a few local restaurants are providing the food. Mom got Sand Point to provide some complimentary booze, and I know Garrick will show up with boxes of wine.

The dress code is country and western, and I went shopping with Hads last night for a new outfit. I bought a navy, brown, and orange paisley print dress with elbow-length sleeves and a full swishy skirt that ends just above my knees. It came with a gorgeous crochet-style belt and a navy straw cowboy-style hat, and I bought my first pair of cowboy boots to wear with it. I love it, and I can't wait for Garrick to see me in it.

"Earth to Little Poppy." Nana snaps her fingers in my face, a look of amusement glittering in her eyes. "You're miles away."

"Sorry, I was just thinking about the party, and I guess I zoned out."

"Happiness looks good on you, sweetheart," she says, removing some garden decorations from a box and arranging them on the long table in front of us. We tidied up the barn she uses as a stockroom, to make way for the new supplies, over the past couple of days, and we've been unpacking daily deliveries in between making up bouquets for prepaid orders. Hadley and I have been driving around town delivering them most evenings.

"I have never felt like this about any boy before. Is it normal to obsessively think about him all the time?"

Nana chuckles. "I'd be worried if you weren't obsessively thinking about him." She fans her face with one hand. "Have you seen those muscles in his arms and the way they flex and roll in his back as he's working? Sheesh." She fans her face with both hands now. "If I was forty years younger, I'd be challenging you for him!"

I burst out laughing. "Nana, stop. At least I now know why you're always taking water and iced lemonade to the workers."

"I've got to get my kicks where I can." She swipes sweat off her brow as she winks at me. "All that young naked flesh on display is giving this old woman the thrill of a lifetime."

"We aim to please." Garrick's deep voice floods the space as he strides into the barn, grinning like all his Sundays have come at once. He's bare chested, like most of the workers, because it's been unseasonably hot these past few days, and they're not working under ideal conditions. A wrinkled T-shirt is stuffed in the back pocket of his dirty jeans as he ambles toward me.

"If that was the case, you'd be working buck-ass naked,"

Nana replies, staring my boyfriend straight in the eye without as much as a blush.

"Nana!" I shriek as Garrick busts out laughing. "Good god. Between you and Hads, you'll send me into an early grave."

Garrick slides his arm around my waist, pulling me into his sweat-slickened chest. "Don't worry, beautiful. The only eyes feasting on my naked body are yours."

I trail my fingers over the Trinity knot ink on his chest. "I wish. We've barely had time to talk this week, let alone anything else." I'm still so fucking hot for my boyfriend and dying to bounce on his cock.

He kisses me sweetly, uncaring Nana is watching, though he does keep it PG because we have an audience. "I'm planning to rectify that right this second. I drove today and was hoping you'd want to grab dinner?"

"Sounds great," Hadley pipes up, sauntering into the barn after finishing her flower deliveries. "Hudson and I will join you. It can be a double date."

Hads has decided Garrick's best friend from North Bend is her next victim. I have tried talking her out of it, but my free-spirited bestie is as stubborn as a mule, and she's set her sights on him, so there's no persuading her otherwise.

An hour later, the four of us are seated at a cozy table in the back of a local Italian restaurant, nibbling on bread sticks and sipping ice-cold Limonata. Nana let the guys shower and change at her place while Hads and I went back to my house to freshen up. Mom wasn't home yet from work, but I left her a note telling her I was out on a date. I whipped her up a chicken salad and left it in the refrigerator. I'll grab a tiramisu to take home to her before we leave.

Hads chattered excitedly about Hudson as we got dressed. I didn't bother warning her to behave, because she wouldn't listen, and anyway, I never want to clip her wings. What you see is what you get with my bestie, and if Hudson doesn't like her direct approach, I'm sure he'll let her down gently. Garrick says he's a good guy, and I trust him. I'm glad we got this opportunity tonight. There hasn't been much time to get to know Garrick's childhood friend thus far, and I'm hoping to change that now.

Garrick slides his arm along the back of my chair as he scoots in closer to my side. I look up at him, grinning like a loon as he bends down and pecks my lips. "You look beautiful," he says, toying with the spaghetti straps on my white summer dress. "Like a ray of sunshine." His fingers wind in my hair as he stares at me like I put the sun in the sky. I've noticed he always seems to be touching my hair, and I love it. Every time he puts his fingers on any part of me, I tingle all over.

"You two are so stinking cute I could puke," Hadley says, beaming at me. I know she's thrilled I've found a guy worth risking a relationship for.

"I agree." Hudson's deep voice reverberates in the busy restaurant. "You make a good couple." Hudson has dark hair, worn longish and loose around his face, like Garrick. But that's where the resemblance ends. His pale silvery-blue eyes are the opposite of Garrick's warm hazel ones, and he's a few inches shorter in height. Though they are both muscular, he's stockier than Garrick's lean build. I can see why Hadley has her panties in a bunch. He's a good-looking guy with a smoldering presence that's hard to ignore.

"I know." Garrick's smug tone is laced with pride as he wraps his arm around my shoulders and pulls me in close to his body. "Life doesn't get much better than this."

My heart thumps wildly against my chest wall as he peers

deep into my eyes, conveying so much with that one look. Falling this deeply and this quickly is scary, but when his protective arms are around me, I feel like I could scale mountains and nothing seems insurmountable.

Including my own entrenched fears.

"When they get married, I'll be maid of honor to your best man," Hadley tells Hudson, instantly claiming my attention.

My jaw slackens, and I silently pray for her to drop this line of questioning. Garrick and I have only started dating, for fuck's sake, and mentioning the m-word is like waving a red flag in front of a bull. My palms are sweaty as I grip the edge of my chair, wondering what is going to come out of her mouth next.

Life is never dull when Hadley is around, that's for sure.

"We'll probably end up banging then, so we should do a trial run." She pops an olive in her mouth, drilling him with a pointed look. "See if we're sexually compatible."

I breathe a sigh of relief, relaxing against my amused boyfriend as I wait to see how Hudson responds. To give him credit, he barely looks ruffled. I'm guessing Garrick forewarned him. "I'm down to fuck." He shrugs and rubs his neatly trimmed beard. "Just tell me the time and place, and I'm there."

"Awesome. No time like the present." Hads slaps a fifty down on the table and eyeballs me. "Get our food to go, and drop it by my place on your way home." Tugging on Hudson's arm, she stands. "Come on, mountain man. This pussy waits for no penis."

Garrick's chest rumbles with laughter as we watch them exit the restaurant in a hurry.

"Did that really just happen?" I turn to look at him as the waitress brings our pasta dishes. I quickly explain the situation, and she removes Hudson's and Hadley's plates to box them up.

"How did you and Hadley end up best friends when you're

polar opposites in so many ways?" Garrick asks, removing his arm from around my shoulders.

"I think that's why it works." I twirl creamy spaghetti around my fork. "She encourages me to break free of my rules, and I rein her in when she gets too crazy. We balance each other out." I stifle a moan as I chew my food, the flavors bursting on my tongue, and it's a close second to sex.

Which reminds me.

Glancing at Garrick, I admire his side profile, wondering if the guy ever looks bad. I run my fingers through the scruff on his cheeks, loving how I can touch him at will now. "Right now, I'm envious of my bestie because she's getting cock while I'm over here with my weeping pussy and a constant throbbing ache between my legs."

Garrick almost chokes on his meat cannelloni, and I smirk as I hand him a napkin quickly followed by a glass of water.

"I take it back," he says, tweaking my nose when he's composed himself. "You two are more alike than I realized." He tucks a piece of hair behind my ear. "It's as hard for me, you know. Literally." Discreetly, he pulls my hand under the table and slides it across to his crotch. He places my palm atop the obvious bulge in his jeans. "All week, I've been walking around in pain. The second I see you, my dick springs up. If you walk past the barn and your scent tickles my nostrils, I'm hard. When your laughter wafts through the air, I'm leaking precum and angling my body so the crew doesn't see I've got a boner." He leans in, pressing his mouth to my ear, as he returns my hand to my lap. "I'm dying to fuck you, my sunshine, and I have a plan."

"You could have led with that," I tease, snuggling into his side, more interested in touching my boyfriend than eating. We're picking up some curious glances from other patrons, but I couldn't care less.

"Do you think you could get away early next Saturday and come stay with me at the winery?" he asks. "The cabin is cozy and romantic and very private. It's surrounded by woodland, and the river transects our property, so we can go swimming or kayaking or hiking on Sunday. I think you'll love it there, and it's perfect for what I have in mind for Saturday night." He pins me with a suggestive look that has me visibly squirming on my seat and squeezing my thighs together.

"That's a whole week away," I grumble, resting my chin on his shoulder.

He chuckles, leaning in to kiss me as our food goes cold. "I promise I'll make it worth the wait."

I cup his handsome face. "I already know that." I peer deep into his eyes. "I know I'm bitching and whining, but it actually means a lot to me that you've put thought into this." All week, I've been thinking about what he said back in Oregon. He wants to make this different from every other time I've had sex because what we share is like nothing I've experienced before. He wants to ensure we give our relationship the respect it deserves and that we are starting out on the best footing.

As sexually frustrated as I am, I can't fault him.

It only intensifies my feelings for him.

We're new as a couple, but already, he cares so much. He has proven how willing he is to put my needs first. In this, I bow to the fact he knows more about what I need than I do. And I already trust him with my heart, so it makes sense I should trust him with my body too.

"I don't want to scare you, Stevie, but I already know you're my forever." His fingers sweep over my cheeks while I internally battle euphoria and panic. "The memories we're making now will stay with us for a lifetime." His lips brush against mine. "I only ever want to give you the most magical memories, and it starts from the very beginning."

Chapter Twenty-One
Stevie

The barn is bustling with activity, and my heart is swollen behind my rib cage. All the food and drink are laid out on two long rectangular tables, buffet style, so everyone can help themselves. Everywhere I look, people are enjoying themselves and having a great time. Laughing, talking, dancing, singing, eating, and drinking is happening in abundance, and I'm drunk on all the feel-good endorphins flooding my system. I was a little stressed out earlier. Worrying we wouldn't be able to pull this off in time, but it came together better than I expected.

Garrick and I are taking a well-earned breather, sipping beers from our position at the side of the dancing area as we watch everyone having a good time. I'm pressed against his side, and his arm is around my shoulders, and I've never felt more content. Seeing everyone I love in one place is amazing. But the cherry on top is noticing how relaxed Nana is now. It's like the weight of the world has been lifted from her shoulders. My eyes seek her out, finding her and Mom nestled in the center of the jiving crowd on the new hardwood floor. They are laughing as they loop arms and dance, and it brings tears to my eyes to see them so happy.

It's been a stressful few weeks for our family, and I'm glad we were able to put it behind us. It's a shame Garrick's dad and stepmom are on vacation. It would've been lovely to have them here. I'd like to meet them, and I know Nana wants to thank the man in person.

Shared tears of joy were shed this afternoon when Garrick's crew finished the barn remodeling and we saw the wonders they had worked inside. Overhead, sturdy beams prop up the solid new roof. Rows of new lighting have been installed, illuminating the large space. New shelving units and matching tables jut against either side of the front of the structure, ready to house flowers, displays, and accessories.

The coffee area at the back has been completely transformed. An L-shaped counter runs the length of the back with a host of brand-spanking-new kitchen appliances fitted against the rear wall, ensuring it's a complete kitchen so Nana can offer more than just snacks, if she chooses. Comfy chairs, tables, and couches occupy the long space on the left while two new customer bathrooms are tucked into the space on the far right.

Glistening wide hardwood planks cover the entire floor space. They are currently being put to the test by boisterous partygoers as they dance to popular country songs played by the talented band recruited by Garrick.

"Come on," my boyfriend says, setting both our beer bottles down on the table behind us. "I want to dance to this song." I let him steer me into the middle of the dance floor, looking around in amazement at the incredible transformation. The barn looks virtually unrecognizable now, and I still can't wrap my head around it.

The Allen crew went above and beyond, and what they managed to achieve in a week is nothing short of miraculous.

They had help from local tradesmen, who gave their time for free and provided parts at cost. Nana is well regarded in the town, and the way the community came out to support her only proves it.

My heart is so full tonight, and the fact it's my twentieth birthday accounts for none of it. It's all thanks to the man, twirling me around the dance floor, smiling at me like I'm a precious jewel. Garrick looks superhot in a plaid blue, red, and white shirt, open over a tight-fitting white tee. Dark jeans hang temptingly from his toned hips. Scuffed boots and a cowboy hat complete his ensemble, and I'm ready to climb him like a jungle gym.

Yanking his body into mine, I stretch on tiptoes and shout in his ear. "I feel like you should get lucky tonight. How else can I repay you for everything you've done?"

"Nice try, sunshine," he says, wrapping his strong arms around my back and dipping me down low.

For some inexplicable reason, he's started calling me his sunshine in recent days. In the past, I have always gagged at couples who have pet names for one another, but I can't deny how much I love Garrick's term of endearment. Cheesy as it is, I'm lapping it up like it's manna from heaven.

"We're not caving to wild monkey lust." He straightens us up as his words and the resolve behind them burst the erotic fantasy bubble playing out in my head. "Anticipation. Remember?"

He cups my face in his large palms, and his mouth descends on mine before I can protest or attempt to convince him to throw away his plan.

I lose all semblance of thought, like I do every time he kisses me. My hands find purchase on his hard, warm chest, and I swoon as he devours my mouth in a very public display of affection. Garrick's kisses consume me to the point where nothing else exists. I get lost in him and the powerful sensations he entices from my body until the only things I'm conscious of are his lips gliding against my lips, his tongue tangling with mine, the heat rolling off his body as he presses flush against me, and the possessive way he firmly holds my face as he makes love to my mouth.

Keeping his lips locked on mine, he lowers his hands to my hips and sways us in tune to the music. My arms encircle his neck, and a sigh of contentment eases through our joined lips. The band is playing a slower song now, and I grind my body against his, reveling in the feel of his hard-on against my stomach as we kiss and dance and basically dry-hump in the middle of a crowd of neighbors, friends, family, and coworkers.

Hadley must be proud.

When the song ends, whoops, hollers, and catcalls ring out, finally breaking us out of our little sexed-up bubble. Garrick's chest rumbles with laughter as he breaks our kiss, holding me tight to his chest. "I think we might have been making a scene," he mumbles against my ear, half laughing.

"I'm thinking I don't really care," I truthfully reply, but my words are muffled against his chest.

The song ends, and the band calls him to the makeshift stage. He drags me with him, but I don't complain. I'd challenge anyone to physically separate us right now.

Mom, Nana, Hadley, Hudson, Ellen, Will, and Noah are crowded beside the side of the stage, grinning and screaming encouragement.

My eyes flick to Garrick as he grips my hand in one hand and accepts a guitar in the other. "What are you up to?" I ponder when he turns to face me.

"You'll see." His eyes radiate mischief as he rests the guitar against the stool propped in front of the mic and lifts me onto an adjoining stool. "Just hold still, and let me do my thing." He kisses me, and it's no chaste meeting of lips, and the crowd goes nuts again. Mom and Hads are jumping up and down while Ellen has her phone out and pointed at my face.

Garrick sits on his stool with his guitar on his lap. After adjusting the mic, he introduces himself. "Now, I know we're all here tonight to help Betsy celebrate the relaunch of her business, but it's a double celebration. Tonight is also my girlfriend Stevie's birthday, and I want to sing a song for her."

A chorus of oohs and aahs rings out around the room before a reverent hush descends.

"This song reminds me of you, babe," he says, moving his fingers into position on the strings. "Of us. Happy birthday, my sunshine." Tears well in my eyes with the way he's looking at me, and how considerate the gesture is. Everything else fades away in this moment and Garrick is all I see. "This is 'You Make it Easy'."

He starts singing, ignoring the audience as he stares into my face, pouring his heart and soul into the lyrics. It's exquisite, and I'm enchanted. I haven't heard this song before, but the words are beautiful, especially when sung in such a heartfelt way. Garrick's distinctive husky voice wraps around me, and I'm reminded how talented he is.

When he gets to the guitar riff portion of the song, my chest is heaving, and I'm struggling to hold my feelings inside. A tear slips out when he sings about sunshine and being his better half, like God made me for him, and I can't control my emotions anymore.

This guy is unreal.

I didn't think men like him existed outside of books.

He's almost too perfect.

Certainly, when compared with my imperfections and fears about relationships.

I wonder if someone like me could ever permanently hold on to someone like him.

As soon as that thought lands in my brain, I mentally swat it away, unwilling to let any of my insecurities ruin this beautiful moment. Swiping at the tears spilling from my eyes, I smile and gaze adoringly at him as he finishes the song.

Garrick gets rid of the guitar, scoops me up into his arms, and kisses me passionately as the crowd roars their approval around us.

"Garrick," I choke out when he finally puts me down and releases my swollen lips. "That was so romantic and one of the most beautiful things anyone has ever done for me."

He brushes the dampness on my cheeks as his arms tighten around my back. "I plan to serenade you every day for the rest of my life, sunshine."

Now I understand the meaning behind the word, I practically melt into a puddle of goo. Garrick undoes me in the best possible way. "I love the song, but I don't think I've made it all that easy for you." My fingers trail up his solid arms as I lean back and stare up at him.

If ever there was a pinch-me moment, it's now.

I cannot believe I landed a guy like Garrick. I must have done something right in this life to deserve him because he's like the manifestation of my every dream and then some.

"That's not how I see it." He rests his brow against mine. "You make me into the man I want to be. A man worthy of you, and it's as easy as breathing being with you. You feel like the other half of my soul, Stevie." He slaps a hand over his chest. "I've never felt so whole, so complete, so content."

"Stop it," I say, half laughing, half crying. "You're too perfect, and I'm the one who isn't worthy."

"How about this," he says, moving his mouth to my ear so I

can hear him over the noise of the crowd. "We are worthy of each other, and we won't ever stop to question it."

"I like that," I say, clutching his waist as I sense movement behind me.

Garrick turns us as one, pulling my back against his chest as he circles his arms around me from behind. Mom and Nana lift a small table with a large birthday cake onto the stage.

Garrick has spoken plenty about moments and memories, and I know this one is one I will cherish forever. Enveloped in the arms of the guy I'm falling in love with while my mother and my nana join my friends and our neighbors in singing happy birthday to me.

As I blow out the candles, I make a wish.

Wishing to always remember how loved I am in this moment and to never be without this feeling.

Chapter Twenty-Two
Stevie

"You were right. It's beautiful here, and I love it," I truthfully admit after Garrick has given me a tour of the vineyards and winery in Woodinville. It's their flagship operation and the most successful one under the Allen Wineries brand. The setting is idyllic, nestled on acres of mature lush land. The sleek wood and glass modern building at the front of the property houses the tasting room, a restaurant, and a massive shop. A small function room is tucked into the back with floor-to-ceiling windows offering breathtaking views over the exquisite grounds. Garrick explained it is rented out by wine clubs and book clubs and for small parties and weddings.

The building faces the high ornate wrought iron entrance gates and the road at the front, but it's walled in on both sides, ensuring security and privacy. The entire rear of the structure surveys the sweeping landscaped gardens abundant with neatly trimmed shrubs and colorful flower beds. In the distance, bracketed by dense woodland that appears to run the perimeter of the estate, are several large barn-like structures where the wine production takes place, and beyond that, barely visible from here, are rows upon rows of vineyards. Sweet floral notes waft on the warm evening breeze, comingled with earthier tones, tickling my nostrils, and tempting my palate.

"I'll give you a tour of the vineyards tomorrow," Garrick says, threading his fingers in mine after we drop my weekend bag off at the cabin. The three-bedroom wooden cabin manages to be luxurious and homey at the same time. Visions of drinking wine in front of the open fireplace, naked after making love on the rug, was the first thought to accost my mind when I stepped foot inside. From the way Garrick looked at me, I suspect he knew exactly where my mind had gone. Nerves fired at me as he showed me around the place I'm staying the next couple of nights, which is another first for me.

"And I thought we might go hiking and take a picnic," he adds, yanking me out of my inner monologue. "The weather forecast is good."

"That sounds great. I'm happy to do whatever." This is Garrick's territory, and I trust him to show me the best time. Hopefully, there will be many more weekends in Woodinville before summer ends.

This place automatically feels like home, and I could easily get used to hanging around here more often. It's serene with no outside world interferences, and I felt instantly relaxed the second I arrived. It's like a little corner of heaven in Seattle and our own private getaway.

Garrick points out places on the grounds as we stroll from the cabin back to the commercial side of the property. He's as animated as when he is on stage, and I can tell his enthusiasm is coming from a genuine place. He truly loves it here, and he's passionate about his family business. It's one of his most endearing qualities, and I'm happy to sit back and let him do all the talking.

It's still light out, though nightfall is encroaching, and a gentle scented breeze swirls around my bare shoulders as we take our time meandering the grounds of the winery. My white cardigan and Garrick's sweater are draped over his free arm as we walk. Garrick's palm is solid and comforting against mine, and I'm blooming with happiness as I listen to his husky voice and his obvious pride.

Our feet crunch on the stones underfoot as Garrick leads me around the main building heading toward a cute outside area. I'm glad I wore white tennis shoes with my dress. I had a sense wearing heels on the grounds of a winery might be challenging. I'm also glad I opted for pretty over sexy with my choice of dress.

Tonight's a special night. The night we're going to have sex for the first time, and I agonized over what to wear. In the end, I ignored Hadley and chose this pale green and peach patterned ankle-length summer dress over the tight black minidress she was suggesting. If we'd been having dinner at a trendy spot in the city, it would have been perfect, but it wasn't right for this setting. I'm glad I listened to my gut, and I feel on top of the world in this dress. It has delicate straps and gentle ruching at the bust, and then it skims over my hips and waist in floaty chiffon that sways along my legs as I walk.

I left my hair down, because Garrick loves it like that, but Hadley used the curling iron on my tresses, and it hangs in soft glossy curls down my back. The heart-shaped locket Garrick gave me for my birthday rests delicately in the curve between my collarbone and my chest.

"We're lucky this area wasn't booked tonight," Garrick says, ushering me toward the most beautiful outside area.

A wide, tall wooden gazebo covers the space, protecting it from the elements. Enclosed by tall hedges and shrubs, it offers complete privacy in a very romantic setting. Stunning purple and pink flowering plants creep like ivy along all the posts and wooden frames. Tinkling spotlights are interwoven between the flowers, casting dancing reflections across the myriad of glass-topped tables. Little candles and vases with colorful flowers adorn each of the twelve tables, centered around a small stone water feature.

"It's stunning." I stare in awe as Garrick leads me to the only table set for dinner. He pulls out a wicker chair with comfortable cushions, waiting for me to sit before pushing my chair in. He's such a gentleman. Tipping my head back, I pucker my lips, and he doesn't disappoint, kissing me tenderly and sweetly from above.

"Not as stunning as you," he replies when we break our kiss. Garrick moves around the table to the silver wine cooler and removes a bottle of sparkling wine. "You're so gorgeous I won't be able to take my eyes off you tonight," he adds, filling two wineglasses with the bubbly liquid.

"You don't look so bad yourself." He's wearing black pants with a white shirt rolled to the elbows and open at the top so the edge of his tattoo peeks out. An expensive silver watch is strapped to his wrist, and his hair has been tamed with hair gel and tucked behind his ears. "You scrub up well, Allen," I tease as a server appears carrying a tray.

Garrick reaches across the table, linking our hands as the woman sets a bread basket down with olives and oils and a bottle of sparkling water.

We chat amicably as our meal is served, and any anxiety I was feeling on the drive here has long since gone. At least for now.

After a sumptuous meal of sage and butter ravioli, hake and ratatouille, and the most devilish chocolate fondant, we grab a bottle of wine from the store and set out hand in hand for the walk to the cabin. Nightfall has descended, but the stone path is lit by spotlights embedded on either side guiding our way.

Nerves prick at me when we arrive at the cabin, and a swarm of butterflies is stumbling around my chest like they're drunk or high.

"Don't be nervous, sunshine." Garrick places his hands on my shoulders and smiles. "I'm going to take care of you, and you don't have to do anything if you've changed your mind."

"I haven't." I rest my hands on his trim waist as a lump rises in my throat. "I want this with you, but it's different than what I'm used to." Anticipation has been building all week, which I love, but it also means I've been thinking more than I usually do, and it's left time for insecurities to rise to the surface.

Garrick palms one side of my face. "It's why I wanted to do it like this." He drops feather-soft kisses on my lips until I melt against him and relax. He reels me into his chest, and his smile is laced with adoration, before tucking me under his chin. "You make me feel so much, Stevie," he whispers against my hair. "I'm scared too because I don't want to mess this up with you. I want it to be perfect. Memorable."

I dance my fingers along his spine before tilting my face up to his. "I already know it will be. I adore you, Garrick." My heart is beating so hard, and I know that's not the totality of what I'm feeling for this man. "I trust you, and I trust in us. Nothing that feels this good can be wrong. I can't ever remember feeling this happy. My heart permanently feels like it's going to burst."

"You're already my everything, Stevie," he whispers against my face.

All the words we haven't said linger in the tiny gap between us, but we silently acknowledge tonight is for a certain first and the other first can wait.

As I stare into his eyes, I know I'm committed to giving this man all my unclaimed firsts. With that acknowledgment comes confidence, and my nerves flitter away. Placing my hand on his chest, right in the spot where his heart is beating as frantically as mine, I say, "Make love to me, Garrick. Make me fully yours."

I sip wine on the couch while Garrick readies the bedroom, my eyes skimming over the myriad of family photos lining the mantelpiece and the walls. Tucking my bare feet underneath me, I savor the warmth of the homey room as I drink it all in. Every item seems carefully chosen, and I spot tons of ornaments and decorations from foreign travel. The Allens are clearly well traveled, and I wonder if that is something Garrick and I will get to do one day.

"It's ready," my man says, and I whip my head around. Garrick pads soundlessly across the floor in bare feet, smiling as he approaches. He stretches out his arm. "Come, my sunshine."

Setting my wineglass down on the end table, I take his hand and let him pull me to my feet. Garrick instantly wrangles me into a bear hug. "Any cold feet?" he inquires, peering deep into my eyes as we embrace.

"My feet are toasty warm." I press a kiss to his chest through his shirt as I look up at him. "I want this, Garrick. There are no hesitations or doubts."

He heaves a sigh of relief. "Good." Taking my hand, he places it on the bulge straining against the zipper of his pants. "I might have died from blue balls if you'd changed your mind."

I stretch up and nip at his jawline as I give his cock a gentle squeeze. "We can't be having that."

"I'm crazy about you," he says before diving in and claiming my lips in a passionate kiss I feel all the way to my toes.

"I'm crazy about you too," I readily admit when he breaks our lip-lock and threads his fingers in mine.

Chapter Twenty-Three
Stevie

We don't talk as he leads me upstairs to his bedroom, making me close my eyes when we reach the landing. Butterflies swoop into my chest, and excited adrenaline courses through my veins as he positions me how he wants me and says, "Open your eyes."

"Oh my god, Garrick." Tears prick my eyes as I look from the bedroom to him and back again.

Scented candles line the floor on all sides and occupy empty space on the shelves and bedside tables. Soft light flickers against the wooden walls and vaulted ceiling, and notes of jasmine, orange, lavender, vanilla, and sweet floral smells waft around the room, drawing me inside. Red rose petals form a path from the door to the giant king bed dressed in luxurious white bedding. More rose petals cover the bed, and it almost seems a shame to disturb it. A freestanding silver bucket holds a bottle of expensive champagne, and Garrick produces two flutes from somewhere behind him. Sensual music plays in the background, adding to the overall romantic ambience.

It's stunning and set against the backdrop of the hauntingly beautiful forest visible through the wide unrestricted windows; there is no place that could be more perfect for what we're about to do.

"This is..." My voice cracks with emotion as I turn around and fling my arms around him. "Utterly amazing. So romantic and perfect, and I'm going to cherish this night forever."

"No pressure then," he says over a chuckle, leaning down to kiss me slowly and seductively.

"Thank you, Garrick. This is incredible, and I've never felt more special in my life."

"Nothing but the best for my girl." He laces our fingers and pulls me farther into the room.

We drink champagne, sharing the bubbly, amber-colored liquid between our mouths as we dance around the room, careful not to knock over any of the candles. It seems Garrick has crafted the perfect soundtrack for our first time, and every song that plays heightens my emotions and cranks my arousal to new levels. Some songs I recognize; others Garrick has to educate me about. It's an eclectic mix of new and old, romantic and sexual, and by the time we've finished our drinks, I'm high on champagne and Garrick and more than ready to take our relationship to the next level.

"Turn around," he whispers as "Good for You" by Selena Gomez begins to play.

Garrick sweeps my hair over one shoulder before starting to unzip my dress at the back. He dusts kisses along my spine as he lowers the zipper, sending a river of delicious tremors cascading across my skin. Lowering one strap at a time, he pushes the dress down my arms until it pools at my feet, leaving me in only a flimsy pink lace thong. "You are so beautiful," he whispers, his fingers slowly investigating every inch of my skin and leaving simmering flesh in every spot he touches.

Leaning my head back against his shoulder, I moan as his

hands mold to the bare cheeks of my ass. Thrusting his pants-covered erection against me, he confirms he's as turned on as me, and I'm quickly losing my sanity to mind-blowing desire. My breath oozes out in exaggerated spurts when his fingers traipse over the curve of my hips, skate across the band of my thong, and move upward with purpose. I arch my head back more, leaning fully against him, as he rocks his hips, pressing his hard-on firmly against my back. "Your skin is like satin under my fingers," he murmurs against my ear, and I feel his hot gaze skimming over my bare breasts.

"You're perfect," he rasps when he reaches my breasts. His fingers flick over the hard peaks of my nipples before he fully clasps my boobs in his hands, squeezing and caressing with tender care. "These are perfect." Closing my eyes, I rotate my hips, feeling warmth flood my thong as his hands go on the prowl again. When his fingers dip under the lace, he cups me down there, and my legs almost go out from under me. His amused chuckle raises all the fine hairs on the back of my neck as his breath fans across my sensitive skin. "You want me, baby?" he whispers, sliding two digits into my slippery cunt.

"So bad," I whimper, already enthusiastically riding his hand.

"Get on the bed, get rid of the thong, and spread your legs for me," he instructs, and I don't hesitate to oblige. Garrick relocates some of the candles, ensuring they are safely out of the way, while I get into position.

"Fuck, look at you." He stands at the end of the bed, raking his gaze over every overheated inch of me.

"Please, babe," I purr, writhing on the bed as I pin him with my sexiest look. "Fuck me now. I can't wait a second longer."

He chuckles as he slowly removes his clothes, drinking me in with his heated stare. "You are exquisite, Stevie. So fucking perfect," he says, crawling onto the bed naked.

"I can say the same for you." I lick my lips as I ogle his straining cock, imagining how incredible it will feel inside me. Garrick is thick and long, and I can already tell he's going to fill me to the max. "Come up here." I wiggle my fingers. "I need to touch you, taste you."

Garrick slides his body purposefully against mine as he moves up and over me, straddling my face with his powerful thighs. A satisfied moan leaks from his lips when I wrap my hand around him, enjoying the feel of his velvety-soft skin as I stroke him languidly. His hips thrust forward, and his thighs clench as I explore his shaft, enjoying seeing him come apart at my touch. A soft hiss flees his mouth when I cup and fondle his balls, replaced with a shout of agreement when I take his hard length into my mouth.

Giving Garrick head is top of my list of favorite things to do. I freaking love seeing my man so lost to the ecstasy I'm giving him. Veins throb in his neck as he tilts his head back, groaning, cussing, and thrusting his pelvis, while I suck and love on his erection with enthusiasm. His natural earthy scent mixes with the minty, citrusy essence of his shower gel, making for a potent combination as I draw him deeper into my mouth. He tastes divine, and I can't get enough of him as I hollow my cheeks and suck him greedily while fondling his balls and running a finger along his taint.

He pulls out unexpectedly with a loud pop a few minutes later, leaning down to slam his lips against mine. "I fucking love how you suck my dick, but I want to come inside you."

"I need you," I whimper, grabbing fistfuls of his gorgeous hair as I nibble on his lips.

"And you shall have me." His eyes shimmer with lust and mischief. "After I've made you come all over my face and heard you scream my name."

Garrick shoves my legs up against my chest, spreading me

wide, before he dives in with his tongue, lips, and fingers. I come in record time, leaking cum all over his face as I scream his name from the top of my lungs, just like he wanted.

He wastes no time after that, and it's almost like a race to get a condom on.

Holding himself still on top of me, with his tip notched at my entrance, he's ready to turn my world upside down. "You're so beautiful to me, always, but never more so than now." Bending down, he kisses me softly a few times, and my pussy clenches and unclenches as I feel his crown press a little inside. A strangled moan rips from my mouth when he eases his head back. His lips tilt at the corners as he stares directly into my eyes, balanced on top of me by his elbows. "Do you still want this?" he asks, and I love how he's making sure I'm fully comfortable even if he can tell by how my body is responding to him.

"I do." I stretch up and peck his lips. "Make love to me, Garrick. No more holding back."

Maintaining eye contact, he eases inside me, inch by slow inch. Feeling the man I'm falling in love with fill me so carefully and completely is the most alluring and sensual moment of my life. We stare at one another as we connect in the most intimate of ways, both of us barely breathing by the time he buries himself to the hilt. My pussy hugs him greedily, and the feel of him throbbing inside me is indescribable.

"Jesus, Stevie," he whispers. "You feel incredible."

Words hover in the gap between us, but I'm too scared to let them loose. I'm overwhelmed and coming undone underneath this beautiful man. Emotion floods my eyes, and I spot the same reflection in his heated gaze.

"It's okay." He sweeps his fingers along my cheek. "I've got you, sunshine. Always."

Garrick moves then, and no words are spoken for some

time. I wrap my legs around his waist as he pivots his hips, driving in and out of me in breath-stealing slow strokes that unravel me. We kiss as we rock against one another, our hands exploring every bit of flesh as we discover one another. My hands roam over his back, reveling in the defined muscles and solidity of his form. My fingers dig into his ass cheeks as I try to drive him deeper inside me, desperate for more even when he's giving me everything. He sucks on my neck, his tongue tracing the path of my collarbone, and his expert fingers pluck and tweak my nipples and grope my breasts.

Garrick pushes my legs back more and picks up his pace, pumping his hard cock inside me as he slams in and out. A line of sweat drips down his back, matching the one tiptoeing down my spine. Our kissing grows more frantic as we both chase our highs. My back lifts off the bed when his lips latch on to my nipple and his teeth graze the sensitive tip.

Flipping me over, he fucks me from behind while urgent fingers rub my clit. The moans escaping my mouth don't even sound like me as I lose all inhibition, surrendering to the blissful sensations he's coaxing from my body.

"Tell me when you're close, baby," he pants, doing a hip-gyrating maneuver that has him hitting my G-spot, causing me to cry out as stars burst behind my eyes and my orgasm creeps up on me.

"I'm close," I cry, ramming back against him, needing him deeper, deeper, deeper.

Garrick flips me around onto my back again, thrusting inside me in one powerful lunge I feel deep in my core. "Need to see you come on my cock," he rasps, grabbing my legs and placing them over his shoulders.

At this angle, he buries himself even deeper, and I'm whimpering and moaning every time he pulls out and slams back in hard, hitting the perfect spot over and over. I'm cresting the mountain, getting closer and closer, and the anticipation is almost killing me, such is my need to come. His eyes bore into mine as he drives hard and fast inside me. My breasts jiggle, and my body is jostled along the bed as he fucks me into oblivion.

"Garrick," I scream as intense pressure builds to a crescendo in my core. "I'm going to come."

His fingers move to my clit, and he ruts into me with renewed feverish thrusts. Sweat beads cling to his brow and his chest, and the veins on his neck strain as he roars out his release the second he pinches my sensitive bundle of nerves, and I detonate all over his big cock. I'm crying and screaming as the most intense orgasm rockets through me, barely conscious of the grunts coming from Garrick as he shouts my name, falling apart on top of me as his release powers through him.

We collapse on the bed in a heap of sweaty tangled limbs, and he instantly reaches for me, curling into my body as he holds me tight against him. After a couple minutes, he gets up to dispose of the condom before climbing back under the sheets with me. No words are spoken as we cling to one another, waiting for our bodies and our hearts to fully recalibrate.

Garrick dots kisses into my hair as we embrace, and my heart is a mushy pile of goo behind my rib cage. I have never felt so close to another person as I feel in this moment with him. I press kisses to his sweaty chest as I hold him close, never wanting to let him go.

"Are you okay?" he asks a few beats later, tilting my chin up with one finger.

"I'm perfect." I smile at him as I inspect his gorgeous face with my fingers. "That was amazing, Garrick, and I already want to do it all over again."

His answering smile renders my entire body to Jell-O. I'm putty in this man's hands. He could ask me for anything right now, and I'd give it to him. "You're amazing, and that was the most incredible experience of my life." His lips claim mine in the tenderest kiss that also manages to be possessive. "You're mine now, sunshine." His arms envelop me in a bear hug. "Mine to protect, love, and shower adoration on." His dick twitches against my crotch, and fresh need coils low in my belly. "I'm nowhere near finished with you." He squeezes my ass, sliding one leg between my thighs and pulling my pussy in flush with his erection. "I hope you have stamina because you're going to need it."

Chapter Twenty-Four

Garrick

The weeks fly by, and I wish I could slow them down. I spend my working days alternating between the lumberyard in North Bend and the Woodinville winery, and my nights all belong to Stevie. We are inseparable, spending every spare minute together, and I am so crazy in love with this girl. Date nights are usually dinner or a movie, and they always end with me buried balls deep inside the woman of my dreams because we're ravenous for one another, and I can't go a day without touching her.

It's challenging at her place even if Monica is laid-back and she's given me permission to stay there. We are loud in the bedroom, and I hate having to hold back. Stevie does too. So, the weeks where I'm at the winery, Stevie usually stays at the cabin with me. It's only a thirty-minute drive from Ravenna, so it's doable. North Bend is a little farther, and I don't like how the burden is always on Stevie to make the trip, so the weeks where I'm working at the lumberyard, we usually just spend weekend nights together.

Stevie has come to dinner at Dad and Dawn's numerous times, and as I predicted, they love her. My twin brothers have kiddie crushes on her, and they drive her insane when she drops by, begging her to play video games or watch them play basketball. She's a good sport and readily gives them her time.

Betsy invited my family to dinner at her place after Dad and Dawn returned from Cyprus, and she wouldn't take no for an answer. Stevie's nana put on a lavish spread, and she was profuse in her gratitude. Weekly flower deliveries are now the norm, and Nana personally drops in every Monday with them. Stevie usually accompanies her, sometimes with her mother in tow, and they stay for coffee and cake or occasionally dinner. Dawn and Monica became instant friends, and I couldn't be happier our families have gelled.

Well, at least part of my family has.

My mother is another matter entirely.

"You should go." Stevie circles her arms around me from behind, snapping me out of the depressive thoughts starting to swirl through my head. "I can't hog you forever, and we've just had the most amazing vacation where I had you all to myself."

I gave Stevie plane tickets to Cyprus as the second part of her birthday present the morning after we had sex for the first time. She refused them at first, like I knew she would. But I talked her around.

Although she has a passport, Stevie had never been out of the US, and I loved getting to share that first experience with her. Briefly, I toyed with the idea of inviting Ellen and Will, and Hudson and Hadley, to join us for a few days, but I'm utterly selfish when it comes to my girlfriend, and I didn't want anyone encroaching on our alone time.

"I wish we could've stayed there forever," I admit, turning around in her arms. I kiss her lips, wishing I didn't have to leave. Getting to live every second of the last ten days with her was sheer bliss. If I had my way, we'd be moving in together when we return to UO in three weeks, but that's an argument to be rehashed a different day.

"I know. It's so idyllic there. Every day, I woke feeling like I was living a fairy tale." Her arms wind around my neck. "Thank you so much for taking me. It was incredible."

"Please stop thanking me. All I did was book a flight." I wanted to pay for everything, but Stevie wouldn't hear of it, insisting on paying for our meals and excursions because I'd provided the airfares and the accommodations. I love that she's independent, but I know money is tight, and I hate she was using money saved for her next semester of college to fund our vacation.

We had the worst argument about money before we even stepped on the plane. At one point, I thought she'd back out of the trip altogether, so I had to concede. Biting my tongue when we were in Paphos was hard too, but I knew not to go there again.

I loathe that money is a contentious issue between us. I have more than enough, so why can't I just pay? We'll be returning to campus soon where Stevie will resume her two jobs, and we'll barely have time to see one another. If she had let me pay for things all summer, she would have saved enough to only have to work one job around her studies, and we'd have more time together. I don't see how it was selfish of me to suggest it, but she went crazy, leveling that accusation when I put it to her like that, and I eventually had to drop it.

"Well, I'm grateful," she says, easing out of my embrace to return to her unpacking. "And I was brought up to never take anything for granted, so you'll have to get used to me thanking you until the end of time."

Monica pops her head through the bedroom door. "Are you staying for dinner, Garrick? We can order in. I won't subject you to my cooking. I'd probably poison you, and my only daughter would hate me for eternity."

"That's not an exaggeration." Stevie grins at her mother over her shoulder.

"Thanks for the offer, but I'm heading to Medina to see my mother." I rub at the tightness in my chest. "Under duress," I mumble under my breath, and Stevie's head whips around to mine.

"Another time then." Monica smiles before leaving us alone.

"I don't want you falling out with your mother over me," Stevie repeats, linking her pinky in mine. "She hasn't seen you for weeks, and it's not too much for her to ask."

"She needs to stop being such a bitch to you." I clutch her hand, bringing it to my lips to kiss her knuckles. "I have made so many excuses for her over the years, but this is the final straw," I admit, releasing her hand.

"Babe." Stevie steps in front of me, moving her hands up my body to rest on my chest. She peers at me through pleading eyes. "Don't go to war with your mother because of me. I'm begging you. She will hate me forever if she thinks I'm the reason you're pulling away from her. The best way to alter her opinion is through perseverance and patience."

"She won't even meet you," I grumble, hating how horrible my mother has been to my girlfriend. "If she did, she'd see everything I do." I grip her hips, hauling her in flush against me. "Maybe you should come tonight. Just show up on my arm and force her to interact. She won't make a show in front of the snooty rich crowd or the press."

"That's a terrible idea," Stevie says, "and besides, I have

nothing to wear to a charity ball and no way of getting gala ready in time."

"I swear that's why she sprung this on me at the last minute." She knew Stevie wouldn't be able to attend without notice, so she waited until I was getting on a plane to demand my presence tonight. "It's not like she gives a shit about Autism Awareness. It's all about schmoozing with the right people, trapping Winston into marriage, and shoving me at Pepper any chance she gets."

I'm lucky my girlfriend isn't the jealous type. Mom has tricked me into attending two other events over the summer, knowing full and well that Pepper would be there with her father, and she was as subtle as a brick with her matchmaking, ensuring Pepper and I were seated together and deflecting anyone else from approaching us so we spent the night talking alone.

I told Stevie all about it, and I'm grateful she's cool with the situation.

I'm not sure I'd be so understanding if it was the other way around.

I'm an insufferable jealous prick when it comes to my girl, and I won't apologize for it.

When you find the one, you hold on tight with everything you've got.

Stevie tilts her head to one side, sympathy splaying across her pretty face. "I know it'll be a nightmare, but she's your mother, and it's only one night." She pats my chest. "You'll survive."

"You look miserable," Pepper says, walking up to me with a crystal tumbler in each hand.

Around us, the gala is in full-on party mode now the boring dinner and speeches part of the night is over. I'm hoping I can make an escape shortly. I showed up, smiled, and made nice with people. Mother cannot throw shade at me for ditching early when I played my part. Especially when I'm still on Cypriot time, and it's basically the middle of the night according to my body clock. It's a miracle I'm not curled in a ball sleeping in a corner someplace. Not that Mom would give me a free pass. I'm seriously getting tired of her excessive demands and questioning why I always bow to her whims.

"Please tell me one of those is for me," I plead, tugging on the collar of my pressed white shirt. I hate wearing a tuxedo, and I'm on a countdown until I can get this damned suit off.

"Of course." Pepper hands me a tumbler of whisky with ice. "It's Laphroaig 18. They don't have any Macallan."

"Bloody heathens."

"Don't be ungrateful. This is a rare bottle. They discontinued making the eighteen in 2015. I had to promise the bartender a date to get us these."

I swirl the nectar in my glass and raise it to my nose, inhaling the woodsy scent with a hint of fruity citrus and sharp pepper hidden underneath. I've learned a lot about wine this summer, and my nose is better trained now to sniff out the essence of any alcohol. The Laphroaig reminds me of the cabin. Currently my most favorite place on this earth. "You should always prostitute yourself for good scotch," I tease, clinking my glass against hers.

"Asshole." She nudges me in the side with a smile on her face. "I bet you wouldn't say that to Stevie."

"Hell no. Although the punishment might be worth it if she tried." I let loose a grin as Pepper drops her head and fixates on her drink. I take my first sip, letting the full, rich, sweet flavor roll around my tongue. A sharper smoky taste hits the back of my mouth as it glides easily down my throat.

We might be known for our wood and our wines, but Dad is somewhat of a whisky connoisseur, and I've tasted more than my fair share in recent years.

"I thought she might be with you tonight," Pepper adds, lifting her head and nodding at an older couple who walks past us.

"Mom sprang it on me at the last minute, but even if she didn't, you know Stevie wouldn't get an invite."

"She's still being difficult?"

I bob my head, swallowing hard over the lump in my throat. "My happiness clearly doesn't mean much to her. She knows she's hurting me by continually refusing to acknowledge Stevie's place in my life, and denying her invitations, yet she keeps doing it."

"I'm sorry, Garrick. That sucks." Sympathy is etched upon her pretty face. "Ivy is such a snob at times."

"Ivy *is* a snob, period." I take another mouthful of the whisky hoping it will disguise the sudden sour taste in my mouth.

"What are—"

"There you are!"

Speak of the devil.

Mom rushes up to us, cutting across whatever Pepper was about to say. "I've been looking for both of you. The photographer is waiting because we want to get some group shots."

"Of course." Pepper drains her drink, urging me to do the same with her eyes.

I knock my scotch back, dreading this next part. I don't know how socialites, influencers, and celebrities do it. I hate getting photographed at events as much as I hate wearing this monkey suit.

"You look stunning, dear." Mom sweeps her eyes up and

down Pepper's fitted red dress. With her jet-black hair and her gorgeous face, she really does stand out in the crowd. "Gucci? Am I right?"

"Yes. Daddy's assistant organized it as I was far too busy this week to go shopping." Pepper smiles at me. "Unlike some who were lazing around under a hot Cypriot sun."

I'm tempted to tell her it wasn't even close to lazy. Stevie and I fucked like rabbits nonstop the entire vacation. Our sex life is off-the-charts hot, and I'm a very lucky man. The only rooms we didn't christen were Dad and Dawn's room and the twins' bedrooms. We even fucked in the pool, out on the loungers, and on the balcony in the dead of night when we were sure no one was around.

As much as I'd love to see Mom's face if I said all that, I won't disrespect Stevie by discussing our private business. It wouldn't help our cause either. Mom would only feel justified labeling her a gold-digging whore. "It's a tough life for sure," I say, smirking.

"Doesn't Pepper look gorgeous?" Mom says, pinning me with a sharp look as she puts me on the spot.

"Pepper always looks lovely," I say, not wanting to embarrass my friend by saying nothing. The truth is, I barely notice what Pepper wears although I know she is always impeccably dressed. You can't grow up the way she did, or mix in the circles she does, and not look the part. "Red is definitely your color, and the dress really suits you."

Her face lights up at my compliment. "Thanks, Garrick."

"You two look striking together. Think of how pretty your babies would be!"

Pepper grimaces, looking awkward in the extreme, and I grind my teeth to the molars, wondering if I'd get away with gluing my mother's mouth shut.

When neither of us dignifies her remark with a comment,

Mom loops her arm through Pepper's and smiles at her with deliberate fondness. I've seen that look on her face before, and I can't decide if Mom genuinely likes Pepper or it's all an act. It's getting harder and harder to tell these days. Mom ushers Pepper forward and glances over her shoulder. "Garrick. Get a move on. We can't keep the governor waiting."

Pepper's parents are already in the room cordoned off for official press photographs, standing in front of the large Autism Awareness logo affixed to one wall. Freestanding heavy-duty lighting is arranged around the area, and a group of about ten photographers is lined up in front, like vultures, waiting for the money shot.

Mom steps into the frame alongside Cristelle Montgomery while Pepper gravitates to her father's free side. I move over beside Mom, and she attempts a scowl. "What are you doing?" she hisses, grabbing my arm. "Go stand beside Pepper!"

"What difference does it make where I stand?"

"Don't start with me, Garrick. I ask so little of you, and I've hardly seen you all summer thanks to that—"

I glare at her. "Say one nasty thing about my girlfriend, and I'll walk. I swear."

"Just go stand beside Pepper," she says, shaking her head as she looks behind me at someone.

"I'm not being photographed beside a woman who isn't my girlfriend," I reply, working hard to keep my tone calm.

"The jealous type, is she?" Mom sneers, and I clench my fists at my sides.

"Stevie isn't jealous at all. She trusts me. She knows I only have eyes for her."

Mom waves her hands in the air. "So, what's the problem then? It's only a picture, Garrick. It's not like I'm asking you to take her to bed."

"Sorry I'm late, dear." Winston shuffles in between me and

Mom, planting a beefy arm around her shoulders. Noxious cigar fumes waft from his fleshy mouth, and his beer gut is straining over the waistband of his too tight dress pants.

Winston heads up a global TV network, and I know he's mega rich and successful, but the guy is loud, obnoxious, hugely self-centered, and clearly only with Mom because she looks good on his arm. He's at least ten years older than her usual prey, and with his thinning gray hair and weather-beaten face, he could pass for her dad.

Mom is angling for an engagement, and I'm praying daily that it never happens. She might be top of my shit list right now, but I'd hate to see her tied to such an egotistical jerk. I have liked all of Mom's ex-husbands. They were decent guys and kind to me, for the short period they were in our lives, but this idiot breaks the mold. I have nothing in common with him, and he clearly has no time for me either, so I'd rather she didn't saddle me with him for a stepfather.

"Garrick!" Mom snaps, giving me a push in Pepper's direction. "Stop acting like a toddler, and go and stand beside Pepper."

There is no point fighting any longer, so I walk over beside my friend with steam practically billowing out of my ears. Pepper's brow is puckered as I line up beside her. She leans in, and I lower my head to hear her. "Is everything okay?" she whispers, looking into my eyes with evident concern.

"My mother is getting on my very last nerve," I whisper back.

Pepper reaches across my body to squeeze my hand. "She'll come around."

I've been telling myself that for weeks, but the truth is, I don't think she will.

Say You're Mine

I know, when it comes down to it, I'm going to have to decide between my girlfriend and my mother. Right now, as I watch my mother suction herself to Winston and primp and preen for the cameras, I despise her for forcing me to make a choice. Especially when it won't end up in her favor.

Chapter Twenty-Five
Stevie

"So." Hadley draws out the word as she drives Nana's Range Rover away from the greenhouse, loaded up with deliveries.

"So, what?" I ask, stifling a yawn. I'm still on Cypriot time, and my body clock is all messed up. I stayed awake all day yesterday, not that it helped much when I was overtired and couldn't sleep last night. At least I got all my unpacking and laundry done.

Nana told me to take today off, but I've been gone for almost two weeks, and I don't like slacking. The decision was made for me when Nana's main delivery guy called in sick today, and I was needed to fill in for him. It's not like driving to and from the shop, and making house calls, is any real chore. Although, I was thrilled when my bestie showed up ten minutes ago and offered to help. I'm struggling to keep my eyes open, and it's safer if Hads drives.

"It's as I figured. You don't know." Her mouth pulls into a grimace.

"Know what?" My brow puckers in confusion as she slows

down, pulling over at the curb and killing the engine. "Why are we stopping?"

"I need to show you something." She plucks her cell from the cubbyhole in the console. "Have you spoken with Garrick today?"

I shake my head as worry pricks at my nerves. "I missed a call from him at lunch, but I haven't had time to call him back yet." I sit up straighter, drilling my bestie with a sharp look. "Is this something to do with him?"

She nods, and sympathy splays across her face as she hands me her cell. An image of Garrick and Pepper fills the screen, and acid crawls up my throat. From the caption, it's evident the photo was taken at the charity event last night. It's a close-up of their faces as they lean into one another in an intimate pose that looks like they're having an intense private moment or getting ready to kiss. Bile coats my mouth as I gulp over the messy ball of emotion clogging my throat. "He wouldn't cheat on me," I croak, finally forcing words out my mouth as I stare at the picture in a kind of dazed horror. Stabbing pain pierces me through the heart, and I'm struggling to breathe.

Hadley smooths a hand up and down my back in a soothing gesture. "I don't think he would," she agrees. "But this looks pretty damning."

"It does." I rub at the tightness spreading across my chest as tears prick my eyes. I thrust her cell back at her, unable to look at it anymore. "Has he been playing me for a fool? Have I turned into my mom?"

"I don't think you can jump to conclusions, but if he has, he deserves a fucking Oscar for his performance. The guy is nuts about you, Stevie. Hudson told me he's never seen Garrick like this with any girl before. I spoke to him earlier, and he swears this is innocent. That Garrick doesn't have feelings for Pepper."

"He would say that if he wanted to cover for his best friend."

"True." Hads sighs as she leans back in her seat. "But unless Hudson is delivering an Oscar-worthy performance too, I believe him."

Hadley and Hudson have been hanging out a lot this summer. Fucking a lot. Unusual for her, they are not exclusively dating, and she seems to be working hard to keep it casual. It takes one to know one, so I see what she's doing. I suspect she's afraid of developing real feelings, so she's keeping distance between them. Hadley is in complete denial. I think she likes him a lot.

But I get it.

Hudson is returning to Brown in a couple of weeks while she attends UW. There is an end date in sight as they have agreed to end their fling then. I get not wanting to do the long-distance thing, especially when they have two more years of college left.

"How does Garrick know her?"

"Her mom is best friends with Garrick's mom. They have known one another for years. I have tried to be cool about Pepper because Garrick genuinely seems to only consider her a friend, but it's been challenging when I know his stuck-up bitch of a mom wants him with her. She tries to force them together any chance she gets."

"What's she like?" Hadley's corkscrew curls tumble around her shoulders as she turns sideways to look at me.

"I only met her one time, briefly, at Sand Point. She seemed decent, friendly, and she didn't eye me like I was a threat, but I don't know her. It could have been an act."

"Or it's not, and this is all completely innocent." Hadley drums her fingers on the steering wheel. "You won't know until you speak to Garrick, and there is no point second-guessing."

Her pretty eyes bore into mine. "You need to look him straight in the eye and ask him if something is going on with Pepper."

"I know." I exhale heavily as the tightness in my chest almost becomes unbearable. Tears prick my eyes again at the thought of losing Garrick. I don't know how I'll survive it. Not when he's become so embedded in my life. "This is what I was afraid of," I admit, resting my head against the window. "Becoming too invested in a guy and him letting me down."

"Don't do that, babe." Hads grabs my hand, squeezing it in a comforting gesture. "Don't assume the worst, and don't put those guards back up. Not unless it's justified. Then I'll help you stack them into place."

We make our deliveries in relative silence after that, and I'm grateful when Hads drops the topic and puts music on. She knows I need to retreat into my head and think this through.

Pulling out my phone, I discover a ton of missed calls from Garrick in the last hour, so he has clearly seen the evidence and knows how bad it looks. I don't return his calls, deciding to go home, get showered and changed, and head out to North Bend to see him.

Except I don't need to. Because he's already beat me to it. When Hads pulls Nana's car alongside the house an hour later, Garrick is pacing back and forth in front of the door, repeatedly dragging his hands through his hair, looking panicked and agitated and concerned.

Good. I'm glad I'm not the only one upset.

"Do you want me to stay?" Hadley asks as she parks and powers off the engine.

I shake my head. "Thanks, but I've got to do this alone. I'll call you later."

"Just hear him out." She hauls me into a hug. "I stand by my assertion he's a good guy and he's head over heels for you."

"I hope you're right." I force a weak smile as we break

apart.

"If I'm not, I'll help you dispose of the body." She waggles her brows and grins wickedly.

That raises a genuine smile on my face. "Love you, babe."

"Right back at ya, beautiful." She hugs me one final time as Garrick watches our interaction through the window. He's not approaching the car, and I don't know if that's because of a guilty conscience or his fear of Hadley. He constantly denies it, but I think my bestie scares him. Hadley is intense and fiercely protective of me, and he knows it.

"Call me," she reiterates as she opens her door and climbs out.

My heart is tripping over itself as I slide out my side, and an anxious fluttering feeling has taken up residence in my chest. Hadley narrows her eyes at Garrick as he moves in my direction, stalling for a moment to drill him with a pointed look. His Adam's apple bobs in his throat as he keeps his gaze firmly locked on mine, but I know he feels the tense charge in the air and the weight of Hadley's stare.

"It is not what it looked like," he says, striding to my side. His usual deep voice contains an undercurrent of panic as he reaches for my hand.

I yank it back, shoving both hands into the pockets of my jeans. Lifting my chin, I channel my inner Nana as I stare at him. Pain radiates from his eyes, and a crestfallen look washes over his face. "I swear there is nothing going on with Pepper. She's only a friend. Nothing more. Please believe me, Stevie." His voice cracks a little. "I would never cheat on you. I deplore cheaters. It's personal for me after what my mom did to my dad."

He confided in me on vacation how his mom had been having an affair before she filed for divorce from his dad. I didn't need additional reasons to loathe that woman, but I got them. She's such a selfish bitch. I remember the hurt when he talked about it, and his words go some way toward reassuring me. "Take a walk with me?" I suggest.

"Of course. I just want an opportunity to explain."

"I will give you that," I confirm, striding forward in the direction of the poppy field. "But before you say anything, I need you to understand how much this has hurt me." I look up at him, shielding nothing. Pain eviscerates me on the inside, and it's hard not to collapse into tears. Except I'm made of sterner stuff, and I refuse to break down over any man. "Do you have any idea how humiliating it is to see my boyfriend in a compromising position with another woman and for it to be splashed all over newspapers and on social media? I've had calls and texts in the last hour from tons of people commiserating with me because they believe you have cheated on me with the governor's daughter. I look like a fool." I don't mention the cruel text I received from Cohen as that will only sidetrack us, but I don't plan on hiding it from him either.

"Nothing happened, Stevie. Please say you believe me." Agony is supplanted across his handsome features, and he looks genuine, but am I just a sucker who has taken everything he's given me at face value when I'm being played all along?

"Who is Pepper to you, Garrick? I need you to be completely honest with me. Is something going on with her, or has it in the past?"

"She's just a friend, Stevie. I don't have feelings for her." His eyes penetrate mine, flickering with a host of emotions. "We have never touched, or kissed, or had sex, or had anything but a friendship. That is the whole truth."

"I want to believe you, but this has me questioning everything that has happened between us."

"Don't say that!" he exclaims, reaching for my arm as I turn left into the field. Bittersweet, smoky, nutty scents accost my nostrils as I plow through the poppies, confused and hurt and disappointed and feeling a host of other things.

"I won't lie to you, Garrick," I say, turning around and spinning to a stop. My fingers trail the tops of the flowers, skimming over the soft red petals as they swish and sway against my thighs. "I always promised you honesty, and this has shaken me. I'm wondering if I've been played all along."

"I promised not to lie to you either, Stevie." He firmly clasps my face in his hands, forcing me to look directly into his eyes. "Nothing happened with Pepper. Not last night or ever. She's a friend. That's it."

"Does she know that?" I hiss, letting hurt imbue my words. "Because she's looking at you in that picture like you hung the stars in the sky just for her."

"The photographer twisted it to make it look like that! She doesn't have those feelings for me either. She could tell I was upset, and she was just inquiring if I was okay. We were lined up with my mom and Winston and her parents in the shot. Ivy was giving me shit because I wouldn't stand beside Pepper."

His earnest eyes plead with me for understanding that is in limited supply right now. My thoughts are consumed with the way their faces were super close and the intensity in their eyes as they stared at one another. I think it will be imprinted on my brain for eternity. Although I am humiliated, I care less about what others think. I'm more concerned with the way they were looking at one another.

It fucking hurts to see my boyfriend looking at another woman like that.

"I didn't want to get in a photo beside any woman who wasn't you, but you know how my mother gets, and I just relented to get it over and done with. I had no idea they would twist it or that they would cut out the others and plaster us all over the internet." He cradles my face in his hands, and tears well in his eyes as he stares at me. "Please, sunshine. Please believe me. Don't let this come between us." Steely determination glints in his eyes, and that's the only warning I get before he presses his mouth to mine in a hard possessive kiss.

I don't return the kiss. I'm still too hurt and too confused.

He pulls back, looking wretched. "Stevie, I'm so sorry. The last thing I ever want to do is hurt you. I should have refused my mother and gone home." He loosens his hold on my face, brushing his fingers across my cheek. "You're the most important person in my life, and I'm done letting her come between us. I'm giving my mother an ultimatum. Either she accepts you and stops trying to push me at Pepper or I'm done with her."

"I don't want you to do that," I softly reply. "She'll only hate me even more."

"I don't care. I've let her dictate my life too much, and it stops now. I can't lose you. I won't lose you." He reels me into his arms, and this time, I don't protest. His arms wind around my back as he holds me close against his body. Arching my head back, I peer into a gorgeous face I love so much. Garrick's eyes are more green than brown today, but they are clear and determined as he stares at me. Electricity surges in the air around us, a reminder of the potent connection we share.

"I have wanted to tell you this for a long time, Stevie, but I held back out of fear over how you would react. But I'm done repressing my emotions."

Gentle fingers dig into my lower back as he leans in, gliding his lips gently against mine. Emotion shines in his eyes when he eases back a little, never losing eye contact. Dimples wink at me as he smiles through his tears. "I love you, Stevie. I love you so freaking much, and I'm not letting anyone, not Pepper, not my mother, or anyone else, tear us apart. You are it for me. You're my one and only, and I'll get down on one knee right now if that's what you need for me to prove it to you."

Chapter Twenty-Six

Garrick

Stevie stares at me in shock, her mouth opening and closing like a fish out of water. It's a fitting analogy because it looks like she's drowning in my words. I'm not sorry I spoke my truths. I only wish I'd spoken them earlier. Maybe then she wouldn't be analyzing everything and rethinking our entire relationship.

I'm in full-on panic mode.

I cannot lose her.

She means the world to me.

I was sick to my stomach when I saw that picture and further sickened when it started popping up all over the net. I don't get the exaggerated interest. So what if the governor's daughter is apparently dating the heir to the Allen Empire? Who the fuck cares? It's not like my family is that big of a deal.

"Are you serious?" she blurts, eventually finding her voice.

"About loving you or wanting to marry you?" I splay my hand flat against her lower back, and it's killing me to show restraint. I want nothing more than to lay her down in this field, strip us of our clothes, and bury myself so deep inside her I eradicate every single doubt written across her beautiful face.

"Both, I guess."

"I am speaking nothing but the truth, sunshine." I trace my finger along her plump lower lip. "I have loved you for a long time. I was afraid to tell you in case it scared you away, but I regret it now because I see the doubts in your eyes, and maybe they would not be there if you knew the intensity of my feelings for you."

Tears glisten in her eyes as she slides her hands up my chest. "You swear you're telling me the truth? You swear you don't have feelings for her because a picture speaks a thousand words, Garrick, and I don't like how you are looking at one another in it."

"I know how bad it looks, but I am not lying to you, Stevie. If I wanted to be with Pepper, I'd be with her. If I wanted to have an easy life and not clash with my mother, I'd be with Pepper. But I'm not with her because I don't want to be with her." I tug her flush against my body, needing to be as close as possible so she sees, hears, and feels my truths. "I want to be with *you*. I don't love her. I love you." I punctuate the words, praying they embed deep. "I love you so fucking much, Stevie."

"I love you too," she whispers as a tear runs free down her face.

Relief courses through me at her admission. I envelop her in a mammoth hug, dotting kisses into her hair as I repeat how much I love her over and over again. A fine layer of stress lifts from my shoulders, but I'm not out of the woods yet. I know how deep-seated Stevie's fears are about men and relationships, and this has, undoubtedly, set us back. But I won't ever stop fighting for us because she's my woman and I'm her man, and that is the only truth that matters.

"You're my forever, Stevie. I've never been surer of anything. If I had my way, we'd get married right now."

Her head jerks to mine, fresh shock seeping from her pores. "You cannot be seriously saying you know you want to marry me when you're only twenty, Garrick. That is the definition of insanity."

"I know what is in my heart, and it won't ever change. I know, categorically, that I want to marry you. My age or the passing of time has nothing to do with it. I knew I wanted to marry you yesterday. Like I know I want to today, and I'll know tomorrow and every day after that."

She wrestles out of my arms, stepping back and clawing her hands through her hair in jerky motions. "Woah, you need to slow down. This is way too intense."

"Is it?" I bridge the gap between us, gently unfurling stiff fingers from her hair. "You need to know if I'm being truthful, and that's as truthful as it gets. I won't apologize for finally admitting the totality of what's in my heart. It's fine that you're not on the same page yet. I will wait for you to get there."

She chews on the edge of her lip. "This is a lot to take in in one day. My emotions have veered from one extreme to the other."

"I get that." I clasp her hands in mine, squeezing gently. "But it doesn't change how I feel. I want it all with you now, Stevie, but I'll settle for moving in together."

Her brows pinch together as she scowls at me. "You really want to do this again?"

I shrug. "Might as well get it all out on the table. You know how I feel, so I'm hoping it means you'll consider our living arrangements more seriously when we return to Eugene." I tuck her hair behind her ears. "I want to wake up beside you every day and go to sleep at night with you curled around my body."

My eyes probe hers for any sign she's relaxing her stance on the subject, but she's giving nothing away. We had this conversation before, and it turned into a steaming argument. "We're not going to see a huge amount of each other between college and work commitments. At least this way, it'll make it easier to spend time together." My fingers caress her soft cheeks. "If you need proof of my love and my intentions toward you, it doesn't get any clearer than this. Share my life with me, Stevie. Move in with me, baby." I press a kiss to her brow. "Please."

Strained silence ensues as we stare at one another, and I can almost see the wheels turning in her head. Pain stabs me all over when she breaks free of my embrace and shakes her head. "This is too much, Garrick. You're moving too fast, and I can't think straight."

Pain drives my next angry words. "What do you want from me then, Stevie?" My voice elevates a few notches. "One minute, you're accusing me of lying to you and hiding secret feelings for Pepper, yet when I lay it all on the line...when I lay *my heart* on the line and tell you I want a future with you, you shut me down! I don't know how to make it any clearer. I want a future with you that involves marriage and kids and growing old together. I have never been surer about anything in my life. It's a future I want to grasp now with both hands, starting with moving in together." I throw my hands in the air. "I really don't get what the issue is? If this isn't what you want from me, then what is?"

"I don't know," she whispers with tears streaming down her face. She swipes angrily at them before jutting her chin up. "I need space. Time to digest all this and work out how I feel."

The last thing I want to do is give her space to talk herself out of a relationship with me. My anger instantly subsides, replaced with abject fear. "You're killing me, sunshine." I hear the dejection in my voice, but I won't shield it from her. "I don't know what else I can do. I just want to be with you. That's it."

"And I want to be with you." She steps up to me, carefully circling her arms around my neck. "I do love you, Garrick." She presses a feather-soft kiss to my lips. A sheen of tears clings to her lashes as she stares at me. "I don't mean to confuse you, but I'm confused too. Just give me a few days to mull everything over. I promise I will give your proposal about moving in together serious consideration."

"I need to tell Noah tomorrow if we're in or out." The lease on our old place is available, and Noah has asked Will and me if we want to live with him again. Cohen is, thankfully, moving into the frat house for junior year. Noah is the only one who has been in contact with him over the summer. Will and I have cut him out of our lives, and I haven't lost any sleep over it. "He has to give the landlord an answer, and he doesn't want to agree unless he knows Will and I are in."

"Okay. I will let you know tomorrow."

Stevie turned me down. Citing distractions and independence and how I need to back off because I'm scaring her with my intensity. Not going to lie. It hurt. A lot. I know she loves me. She shows me in many ways, but I feel like she's erected some of those shields again, and she's more cautious with her heart. She's trying to apply the brakes when I want to go full throttle.

When I'm with her, everything is amazing, but when we're apart, doubts creep in because I know she's purposely creating distance between us. And that can't be good.

Ellen chose to live with Stevie instead of Will. I knew she wouldn't abandon her bestie even if Will's girlfriend was open to moving in with him. So, Noah, Will, and I are back living together again, and the girls are in their apartment a few blocks away.

It's as I predicted. We are struggling to find time to see one another between work and college, and I'm terrified she's slipping away from me. It's only October, a couple months into classes, but the course load is savage this year, and I'm already drowning under numerous assignments.

I'm getting ready for my gig at The End Zone Friday night when my cell vibrates with an incoming call. Pain lodges at the base of my throat when I see who the caller is. My mother hasn't attempted to reach out to me since we had our fateful argument at the end of July. I gave her my ultimatum, like I promised Stevie I would do, and my mother reacted as expected.

I stare at my cell for a few seconds, wondering if I should pick up or not. If she's offering an olive branch, maybe I need to hear what she has to say. So, I press accept before the ringing stops.

"Garrick."

"Mother."

She sniffles. "I hate this."

"You brought it on yourself."

"I know."

Surprise shuttles through me, but I don't react.

She clears her throat. "I know now I was in the wrong. You are old enough to make your own decisions, and I need to respect that."

If I was sitting, I'd probably fall off my chair. Ivy Allen-Golding-Smith rarely apologizes, and I feel like I need to record this moment for posterity.

She coughs again. "In my defense, I have only ever had your best interests at heart, but I went about it the wrong way. For that, I am sorry, and I hope you can forgive me."

"That depends," I say, propping one hip against the wall as I tap out a quick text to Stevie letting her know I'll be five minutes late picking her up.

"On what?"

"On whether you're willing to accept my choice and accept my girlfriend."

A pregnant pause ensues for a few beats. "I didn't give Stevie a chance, and I understand your anger and frustration. I'm willing to make amends now. If you'll let me."

Relief flows through my veins and the corded knots in my shoulders relax a little. "I would like that. Stevie would too."

Stevie hates how fractured my relationship is with my mom, but she acknowledges I had no choice, and I know she's pleased I defended her. Yet, she can't help feeling guilty. What she doesn't understand is, I don't have the same kind of relationship with my mother that she has with hers. I never have. It would be sad not to have my mother in my life, but I'd get over it. I have Dad and Dawn, and Dawn supports me fully on this. Dad doesn't like rocking the boat, and he's been encouraging me to try a mediation approach, but I knew this was my best shot at getting through to my mother, and it appears to have worked.

"Wonderful. Thank you, darling. I have missed you so much. Perhaps we could have lunch on Sunday? Just the two of us?"

"I'd like that."

"And I'd like to invite you and Stevie to dinner here with Winston and I on Thanksgiving."

I alternate special occasions between my parents, and it's Mom's turn to share Thanksgiving with me this year while I'll be with Dad for Christmas. "I will ask her."

"Make sure to do it soon so I can instruct the caterers."

"I'll ask her tonight, and speaking of, I need to go." I grab

Stevie's flowers and wine and my jacket off the back of the chair in my bedroom. "I have a gig, and Stevie won't want to be late for work."

"I won't keep you, darling. Be here at one on Sunday, and you can update me then."

"This is a good thing," Stevie says, reaching across the console to squeeze my hand as I drive us to the bar where we're both working tonight. "I'm so glad she has come around, for your sake. I hate coming between you and your mother."

"It was never your fault." I lift our conjoined hands and kiss her fingers.

"I know, but I was still the reason."

"What do you think about Thanksgiving?"

"I'll talk to Nana and Mom, but I think they'll be fine if I'm not there this year. Nana usually invites a few friends and neighbors, so they won't miss me too much."

"That's highly debatable, but I won't say no if it means you get to spend Thanksgiving with me."

"Your mom has extended an olive branch, and I'm not going to turn it down."

"Thank you for being so gracious about this. I know she hasn't made it easy." I park the car outside the bar and lean over to kiss her.

She clings to my chest, angling her head and kissing me deeply. "I'm happy for you, Garrick," she says, smiling at me when we break apart.

"I love you." I peck her lips as Manford appears in the corner of my eye.

"I love you too," she replies, rolling her eyes as Manford makes kissy faces at us through the window.

"You're an idiot," I say to the bartender when I hop out and race around the hood to open Stevie's door. As much as he likes to wind me up, I like the dude. Thankfully, he's nothing like his cousin Cohen.

I wanted to knock the fuck out of my ex-friend when Stevie showed me the nasty text he sent her the day that photo of Pepper and me aired, but my girlfriend talked me off the ledge, convincing me ignoring him is the best way of handling him. And so far, she's been right.

"I want an invite to the wedding." Manford waves his finger between us. "I was the one who played matchmaker after all." He puffs out his chest and grins, not sensing the glimmer of tension crackling between me and my girlfriend at the mention of a wedding. I haven't gone there again as it's a very touchy subject.

Stevie is skittish.

I understand why, and I know I'm abnormal.

It's unusual to know you want to get married this young.

But when you have found the girl of your dreams, why wait is my motto. I'm only holding back because I don't want to scare Stevie off.

I convinced her to go out with me, so I know I'll eventually convince her to marry me.

I just need to channel patience for a while.

Chapter Twenty-Seven
Stevie

"Whore!" The word is hissed in my ear the second I exit the cafeteria after eating lunch with Garrick. He went out the rear door with Will and Ellen, so I'm alone for this encounter with Simone.

A heavy sigh escapes my lips. I'm not in the mood for this shit today. I'm quickly running out of patience with this girl, but I'm also conscious she seems to have a mental health issue, so I try to tread carefully whenever she accosts me. Something that is occurring more regularly in recent weeks, and I'll have to take serious action soon if she doesn't stop.

Garrick made a report to the dean at the end of last semester after the shit that went down at the bar and the vile things she said to me. I reported her at the start of this semester when it became clear she had switched her harassment from him to me. I blocked her number and her email after she sent me several abusive messages. Manford spoke to the boss at the bar, and Simone is permanently banned from The End Zone, and Sharon banned her from Butterfly Flowers, but I still see her around campus. I can't quite call it stalking, but it's enough to piss me off despite trying not to let her rile me up.

"Simone. I'm not doing this with you again," I say as she steps in front of me, blocking my path. "You need to get over this, and I highly suggest you sign up for therapy." I attempt to move around her, but she mirrors my position, thwarting my attempt to break free. "Move out of my way, Simone." I'm already cutting it close for my shift at the flower shop, but Sharon will be cool if I'm a little late.

"You're drugging him," she snaps, spittle flying from her mouth. "It's the only reason that makes sense. He should have kicked you to the curb by now. You have nothing on me," she adds, raking her gaze over me in a derisory fashion I'm well used to by now. "Nothing."

I'm tempted to tell her to take a look in the mirror because the girl looks like shit. The only reason I don't snark back is because her outward appearance hints at the state of her troubled inner mind, and I don't want to set her off or have her harm herself because of my actions. I never let her words affect me. They coast over my head every time. I feel sorry for her more than anything else. But she's a fucking nuisance, and Garrick and I are both short on patience now. I know the college spoke to her, but I don't know what else may or may not have happened.

Whatever the intervention was, it's clearly not working, and something else will have to be done.

I am not putting up with this harassment for much longer.

I make one last attempt to get through to her. "You need help, Simone. Garrick isn't interested in you. Whether I am his girlfriend or not doesn't change that fact." I deliberately use a soft voice and talk to her like I'd talk to a child. "You are wasting your college experience on a guy who will never return your interest. You need to forget about him and concentrate on yourself."

"I don't take advice from gingers," she screams, and the wild look in her eyes has me stepping sideways. But I'm not fast enough. "How dare you patronize me!" she yells, throwing herself at me and taking us both down.

My body slams into the asphalt as I land heavily on the ground with the crazy bitch on top of me. My bones rattle, and pain splices through my head as my skull meets the hard ground. Stars whizz before my eyes. I cry out when stinging pain radiates across my scalp as the bitch yanks on my hair, roaring in my face and yelling obscenities.

"Fuck, Stevie. Are you okay?" a man with a somewhat familiar voice asks as Simone's weight is suddenly gone from on top of me.

My eyes are blurry, and a metallic taste lands on my tongue as it darts out, dabbing over a small cut on my lip.

A strong arm goes around my back when I'm gently lifted into a sitting position. "Are you hurt?"

I attempt to take stock of my injuries as the guy converses with a few other voices. I'm vaguely aware of Simone screeching in the background.

"I'm going to call Garrick," he says as I raise trembling hands to my face and brush hair away from my eyes.

Gradually, my sight and my hearing return to normal as the adrenaline coursing through my veins calms down. My back aches, and pain throbs in my skull, but I don't think I'm seriously injured.

"Garrick is on his way," my savior says, and I blink profusely as I stare into Cohen's concerned face.

"You," I croak, immediately clearing my throat. "Get away from me," I add, suddenly aware his arm is still around my back and he's keeping me propped up. A small crowd has formed around us, and I spy two campus policemen approaching. Two of Cohen's jock buddies are restraining a thrashing Simone as she cries, shouts, and writhes like someone on the verge of a nervous breakdown.

I should hate her for what she just did, but pity is my predominant emotion as I look at her. I'm super pissed as well, but hopefully, this is the end of the harassment and I can breathe easier around campus. The girl needs psychiatric help, and perhaps now she'll get it.

An earnest expression materializes on Cohen's face. "I'm not leaving you alone until Garrick gets here." Remorse floods his features. "I owe you an apology, Stevie. Several, actually."

"You do, but that's the least of my worries right now." I attempt to get up, but my sore limbs protest.

"Let me help. Please." Cohen seems sincere, but I don't want him touching me. However, my overriding need to get up off the ground before some asshole records the scene supersedes my distaste, so I nod and let him help me to stand. Cohen guides me over to a bench just as campus police arrive. Cohen sits beside me as I give a quick verbal statement. He corroborates my story because he and his buddies witnessed the unprovoked attack.

Pounding footsteps approach, and then Garrick is there, crouching down in front of me, inspecting my face with worried eyes. "Jesus, Stevie. How badly are you hurt?" His eyes flicker to my cut lip and the way I'm hunched over with my arms crossed around my middle. "I am going to ensure the book is thrown at that crazy bitch, and don't even consider not pressing charges," he says through gritted teeth.

Cohen obviously fully updated Garrick on his call. "I'm okay." I take his hand, needing him to ground me right now. "I'm more shocked than anything."

"I about died when I got Cohen's call." He presses a tender kiss to my brow. "I was so scared, sunshine."

"I'm fine, babe." I cup one side of his face. "Stop worrying. I'm a little sore, but it's nothing some pain pills, time, and a few hot baths won't cure."

"She needs to be medically assessed by a paramedic," one of the policemen says to Garrick.

"And we'll need you to make a formal statement," the other one adds, glancing over his shoulder at where Simone is being strapped to a gurney and carried to one of two ambulances now parked on the grass. I hadn't even heard them arriving.

"Can it wait?" Garrick asks, perching his butt on the arm of the bench and gently sliding his arm around my shoulders. "She really needs to rest."

"That's fine." The taller of the two policemen hands Garrick his card. "Call me in a couple days, and we'll arrange a time."

They leave as a female paramedic arrives to inspect me. I ask Garrick to call Sharon and explain the situation before I go with the paramedic to the second ambulance. I sit up on the floor at the open back of the vehicle with a blanket wrapped around my shoulders while the nice lady asks me a bunch of questions and conducts a few quick checks.

Garrick and Cohen stand off to one side, talking in hushed tones. Though it looks like they are having an intense conversation, Garrick's eyes never wander from mine.

When I'm done, he's by my side in a nanosecond, gently cradling me against his body as we listen to the instructions from the paramedic. "You have a mild concussion, Stevie, and you need to take it easy for a few days and rest at home. If you experience any nausea or vomiting, you feel repeatedly dizzy or light-headed, or you have any issues concentrating or remembering things in the next few days, go straight to the emergency room. For now, take these painkillers and go home to bed."

Over the course of the next week, Garrick fusses over me like you wouldn't believe. He moves in—temporarily—to take care of me, but I don't protest. I have a permanent headache, and my body is sore all over, so it's nice having him here. He won't let me lift a finger, and he insists I skip all my shifts this week, making me promise I won't return to either job or classes until I'm feeling well enough. I've built up a lot of credits, so I can afford to miss a few classes. I know I have the time to catch up.

Mom and Nana drive down on Sunday to check on me, and a girl could get used to being mollycoddled.

After we patch things up with Cohen, he apologizes profusely to me and the guys, finally admitting something we all know—he's got an alcohol problem. He is attending an outpatient program, around classes and training, and he's moved out of the frat house and into a single dorm. He's quit partying and is focusing instead on his studies, football, and his recovery. He seems sincere, and we are giving him the benefit of the doubt. I don't think Garrick will ever have the same relationship with him, but at least it's amicable now, and we don't have to dodge him around campus.

Simone is gone for good. It turns out she was doing this to three other guys and their girlfriends. The college was already taking steps to kick her out when her parents showed up and took her home. The last we heard, she is receiving psychiatric care, and I hope it helps.

I didn't suffer anything more than aches, pains, and bruises, and I can't find it in me to hold a grudge against her. Garrick isn't as charitable, and he wasn't pleased I dropped the assault charge. He is entitled to his feelings, and I understand it. I'd feel the same way if he was the one who'd been hurt, but I prefer to put it behind us and move forward.

Things are finally back on track with us after a few rocky weeks, and life has settled down.

Before I know it, Thanksgiving has arrived. Which means today I'm finally getting to meet his mother officially.

I'd be lying if I said I wasn't a complete basket case.

A lot hinges on today, and I want it to be perfect.

I already know the odds are stacked against me.

Despite the assurances she has given her son, I expect Ivy is only doing this to humor Garrick. I very much doubt she has changed her opinion of me or given up on her plans to marry her son to the governor's daughter. But I owe it to Garrick to give her the benefit of the doubt, so I'm attending Thanksgiving dinner with an open mind.

"Are you sure this dress is good enough?" I ask for the umpteenth time as we exit my house.

"You look gorgeous." Garrick's slow perusal as he drags his eyes the length of my body brings a blush to my cheeks.

He has been staying over at my apartment a lot lately—I refuse to sleep at his place because his bedroom is a mess, and it gives me anxiety anytime I set foot inside it—and the sex is insanely good. He's learned how to turn me on with one sultry look, and I walk around in a state of near-constant need.

Regular sex on tap is definitely a perk of being in a committed relationship. I never realized sex could be like this. Sleeping with someone I love is intense and intimate, and I feel it on a transcendental level. I never feel closer to Garrick than when he's buried deep inside me, looking straight into my eyes, as he summons pleasure from my body like a skilled magician. Postcoital snuggling is heavenly too, and I love going to sleep wrapped up in his warm embrace.

He hasn't mentioned marriage or moving in lately, and I appreciate he is respecting my wishes and toning things down.

It's not that I don't love him.

I really truly do.

He makes me incredibly happy.

I love having someone to support me. Someone who will listen when I've had a shit day or someone to share exciting news with.

Garrick was there to hold my hand when I sent off my DNA test to that ancestry place, and he was there to console me when the results showed no paternal connections.

Having talked to my boyfriend about it, I've decided to make a concerted effort to find my father. Garrick knows the background story now. How Mom had no contact details for my dad and how uncooperative the Navy was when she reached out to them. All she knew was his first name and the date his ship was docked in Seattle. The Navy agreed to forward some letters she wrote, but we have no proof if he ever received them. Or maybe he did, and he chose not to contact her. To this day, we don't know.

It's not that I need him in my life, but I need to understand if he even knows about me. I don't want this unresolved question to hang over me my entire life, so I'm taking proactive steps to find answers I need.

I haven't told Mom yet. I know she wouldn't stop me from trying to locate him, but I'm not sure how it will make her feel. Dragging this history up again might upset her, so I decided not to say anything unless the results showed a connection.

Garrick gave me the strength to pursue this, and I probably wouldn't have done it without his support and encouragement.

I could not ask for a better boyfriend.

He is so devoted—showing up regularly with my favorite coffee and pastries from Bumble Bees, always making time to grab lunch or a coffee on campus during the day, and escorting me to and from work when his schedule permits it. Every Friday, he shows up to drive me to work at the bar, and he always has wine and flowers for me.

He constantly showers me with love and affection, and I try to do the same. Getting up early on weekends to bake him his favorite cookies and cupcakes. Battling the annoying groupies every Saturday night to support him at his gigs. Cooking him meals, giving him massages, and running him baths when his old back injury flares up and he's in pain, and sucking his dick like a motherfucking pro. Garrick loves my blowjobs, and it's our mutual favorite way to let off steam.

I know I'm lucky to have found him. That we're lucky to have found one another. I appreciate him so much, and my life is much happier having him in it.

But the intensity of my feelings for him, and his for me, still scares me. This is all new, and I don't want to rush into anything. I don't see the need. We are still young, and we have our whole lives ahead of us.

Right now, I'm enjoying spending time with him, being in love, and managing to focus on my relationship while not sacrificing my goals. I'm not sorry to be proven wrong about distractions or that Garrick has opened my eyes to possibilities. I'm content, and I don't need anything else. Except for him to be content going at this pace and not to push for more before we're both ready.

"Earth to my sunshine." He tips my face up, fixing me with a crooked grin. "Where'd you go, babe?"

"Sorry. I just zoned out."

"Please don't worry." He laces his fingers in mine as he leads me toward the passenger side of his Range Rover. "I promise it'll be fine. I will be by your side the entire time, and

I'll keep Mom in check if she gets out of line. Winston too, if he acts his usual asshole self."

"I just want to make a good impression, and first ones count." I glance down at myself. "Are you sure this is fancy enough?"

I'm guessing his mom's house is some big posh mansion, and from what Mom's told me, she is always dressed to the nines, so I put extra effort into today. I don't want to let Garrick down. But I don't have the money for expensive dresses or jewelry or matching bags and shoes. I splurged on a designer dress I found on sale in a department store in Seattle. It's a patterned A-line black silk dress with gorgeous purple, green, and white flowers all over it. It has long sleeves and a deep vee at the front. While it showcases cleavage, it's classy. It stops just under my knee, and my legs look long and slim in my skyscraper black heels. Nana loaned me her emerald necklace, and Mom loaned me her black Gucci purse. Hadley helped me with my hair and makeup, and I feel great. However, I still worry my efforts will fall short of Ivy Allen-Golding-Smith's exacting standards.

"Baby, you're perfect. You couldn't be any more beautiful if you tried. She will love you. She just hasn't had a chance to get to know you yet."

I wish it were as simple as that.

Garrick's naivety when it comes to his mother is a weakness but one I can't fault him for. He's a good son. A good boyfriend. And today I'm going to do my absolute best to turn his mother around.

For him.

Chapter Twenty-Eight
Stevie

My eyes are bugging out of my head as we drive through high wooden gates and along a winding gravel driveway, bordered by mature trees and colorful shrubs on both sides, heading toward the extravagant property looming in the near distance. A shocked gasp escapes my lips when we round the bend and the house comes into full view.

I was partly right in my assumption, but calling this palatial home a 'posh mansion' is doing it a disservice. Positioned at the bottom of the driveway, surrounded by tall trees and land-scaped lawns on either side, is a vast, highly impressive modern two-story building, comprising various outhouses and side structures, and constructed mainly of glass and gray stone. Different size vaulted roofs highlight a myriad of solar panels, and it's clear no expense has been spared on this property.

It's like something you'd see in a celebrity magazine, and my nerves are presently jumping through the roof.

"Breathe, babe," Garrick murmurs, helping me out of the car.

"This place is something else." My eyes are out on stalks as I try to drink it all in.

He shrugs, taking the flowers from my hand. "It's just a house." Only someone who has grown up surrounded by this kind of wealth could be so flippant. I like that Garrick isn't flashy, but it's possible a little reality check is needed now and then.

I hug the cake carrier to my chest as we walk up the steps toward the entrance door. Before we've had time to knock, the door swings open, and a stately gentleman with salt-and-pepper hair bows his head and steps to one side. "Mr. Allen. Do come in. Your mother is expecting you in the rear living room."

Garrick grasps my free hand firmly in his as we enter the hallway of his mom's home, stalling until the man in uniform has closed the front door and urged us to follow him. Butterflies float anxiously in my belly as I realize I am completely out of my depth.

Garrick should have prepared me better.

This kind of wealth is obscene, and this house is nothing like his dad's and Dawn's homey place in North Bend. Don't get me wrong, that's a massive house and very impressive too but in a much more subtle manner. It's a true family home with dogs running around, toys, games, and sports equipment underfoot, and it's lived in. I feel comfortable there, whereas I'm immediately uncomfortable amid all this opulence.

It's not at all what I was expecting either. I thought his mother would go for an old-worldly charm with wood paneling, ornate papered walls, patterned rugs and carpets, and antique mahogany furniture. Instead, the house feels light and airy as we follow the butler on pristine gray-and-white-marble tiled floors, passing by light-colored walls adorned with modern art, and tall tables housing glass lamps and vibrant vases filled with white roses.

I can't deny how stunning this house is, but it feels more like a model home than somewhere you'd actually live.

As we bisect other hallways, bypassing rooms exquisitely decorated with contemporary furniture and glossy hardwood floors, I feel like I might be sick. I don't belong in a place like this, and I instantly feel underdressed and out of my comfort zone.

Today is going to be ten million times worse than I imagined.

Sensing my inner panic, Garrick rubs soothing circles on the back of my hand with his thumb, but it does nothing to quiet the mounting alarm invading every nook and cranny of my being.

That sensation multiplies when the butler leads us into a long wide room where several people wait for us.

So much for it just being his mother and her boyfriend Winston.

The governor, his wife, Cristelle, Pepper, and an unfamiliar man all turn around to greet us with matching tight smiles. The three women are wearing expensive over-the-top ballgowns, and I feel like I've shown up in my nightgown.

Anger radiates off Garrick in potent waves as he tightens his hold on my hand and glances at me. His eyes plead for understanding behind his fury, and I'm glad he's surprised. If he had been a part of this ambush, I would turn around right now and walk out of his life.

Garrick leans in to kiss my cheek, brushing his lips against my ear. "I swear I didn't know she'd invited them."

I squeeze his hand in reply as I swallow back nerves and plaster a fake smile on my face. It will just be like at Sand Point during any of those times I had to wait on pompous rich pricks and their bitchy wives and girlfriends. I can fake it with the best of them, and I'll hold it together until we can make our escape.

"Darling. Don't whisper. It's rude." Ivy strides toward Garrick wearing an elaborate blue ballgown that sweeps the floor as she walks, not even looking in my direction.

Garrick is like a pot ready to boil over. I can almost see the steam billowing from his ears. Judging by the looks exchanged between the governor and his wife, it's evident they spot it too.

The way I see it, we have two choices. Leave now and make it clear we don't appreciate being ambushed. Or suck it up for a few hours, bite our tongues, and play this stupid charade until we can leave at the earliest opportunity.

As much as I loathe his mother, and I really do, she would not take kindly to being shunned by her son in front of her VIP guests. Garrick has only just repaired his relationship with his mother after it broke down over me. There are plenty of other reasons for him to cut ties with the interfering bitch, and I would prefer that over something that potentially has the power to come between us in the future. So that only leaves option number two.

Sucking it up and pretending.

Staying here, in the face of a setup, requires enormous lady balls, and I intend to prove to Ivy bitchface that I have them. It also sends a message to Pepper that I'm not threatened by her.

So, I'm going nowhere.

Even if I'd rather bathe in hot oil than sit through Thanksgiving dinner with these obnoxious people.

Digging my nails into Garrick's hand to reclaim his attention, I subtly shake my head just as he prepares to give his mother hell. His brow puckers momentarily as he stares at me, and his Adam's apple bobs pointedly in his throat. Quickly recovering his composure, he smooths out his expression and bends down for his mother to kiss him on both cheeks.

"It's so wonderful to see you," Ivy gushes before her mouth pulls into a narrow line. "Did you forget your tie?" She snaps her fingers over her head, and a young man, dressed in a similar uniform to the butler, races across the room from his stationary position at the wall.

"Mom, don't start," Garrick says as Ivy eyeballs the poor server and demands his tie. The man raises fumbling fingers to the black tie around his neck as Garrick's jaw pulls tight.

There is nothing wrong with what Garrick is wearing. He has on a light-blue dress shirt, open at the top, and pressed black slacks with matching dress shoes. He looks handsome and smart though he's underdressed compared to Winston, the governor, and the unidentified man shuffling awkwardly on his feet behind Pepper, who are all dressed in custom suits with ties.

"Leave it," Garrick snaps at the poor server before whipping his head around to his mom. "Drop it," he says under his breath. "Or I'm leaving."

Ivy looks momentarily annoyed before she plants a false smile on her face to match the false laughter that falls from her lips. She casts a quick glance in my direction for the first time. "It's clear neither of you got the dress code memo, but never mind." Her disdainful eyes are like claws raking down my body. "It's your presence that matters," she adds as Garrick moves in closer, wrapping his arm protectively around my shoulders.

"These are for you," Garrick says in a clipped tone, thrusting the bouquet at his mother.

"Oh, how lovely." Taking the pink, white, and purple floral arrangement from her son's hands, she barely glances at them before handing them off to the server.

"They are from Stevie," Garrick adds, tightening his hold on me. "From her nana's greenhouse. Stevie picked and arranged the bouquet especially for you."

"Garrick said gardenias were your favorite," I say in my most serene tone. "I hope you like them."

"I prefer roses." She offers me a tight smile that is completely insincere, and I just know it's going to set the tone for the day.

"Oh, I adore roses too." I smile prettily like she hasn't just offended me. "I'll remember that for next time." I let my smile grow bigger, enjoying the way her eyes narrow suspiciously on me.

Ha! As if there will be another time. The only way this bitch will ever get flowers from me again is if I'm putting them on her grave.

"This is for you too." I pass the cake carrier to her, keeping the smile supplanted on my face. "I got up early this morning to bake a Black Forest gâteau."

A visible shudder works its way through her. "Well, with all those calories, I certainly won't be eating it."

"Black Forest cake is my favorite," Winston says, stepping forward to meet us while Pepper and her family huddle next to the floor-to-ceiling window, talking in hushed tones while they drink champagne and pretend this entire situation is not all kinds of awkward.

"Did you know I'm of German descent?" he asks, taking the carrier from Ivy's hands, prying the lid off and licking his lips as he stares at my creation.

"Of course," I lie, knowing this will wind Ivy up. "I chose this particular cake after Garrick mentioned it." It's pure coincidence, but he doesn't need to know that. The only things Garrick has mentioned to me about the man his mother hopes will be hubby number four are unflattering in the extreme.

"A woman after my own heart." Winston guffaws before waggling his bushy brows and looking at me with uncomfortable appreciation. Ivy barely hides her glare, and I feel a smug sense of satisfaction. Perhaps I shouldn't have encouraged her beau, but fuck that bitch. She's already been super rude, and I know she'll be even ruder to me before the day is out.

Ivy doesn't disguise her disgust when Winston swipes a digit through the top of the cake, groaning as he licks cherry, chocolate, and cream from his meaty finger. I bite on the inside of my cheek and keep a fake smile plastered on my face as I internally scream. That fucking selfish twat has ruined the cake I spent hours making. I even made the morello cherry jam myself earlier in the week, and now that fat prick has put his grubby finger in it as if he's five years old and he can't contain himself.

"This tastes incredible. I look forward to eating it later." Winston pats his portly tummy before handing the cake to the sever and fixing me with a leering smile. "I do love a woman who is creative with her hands."

Rage rolls off Garrick in waves at Winston's blatant innuendo, and I'm ready for World War Three to kick off when Pepper rides to the rescue.

"Garrick, you're looking well, and it's so good to see you again, Stevie," she says, materializing at my side and redirecting Garrick's attention from Winston. She darts in to kiss me on the cheek, acting as if we're the best of friends. "I got you a glass." She hands me a flute filled to the brim with champagne, and I have a sudden urge to knock it back. Alcohol would help me get through this ordeal, but getting drunk would not be smart. Who knows what's liable to pop out of my mouth uninhibited?

Pepper pulls me and Garrick away from his mother and Winston, leading us over to the window and introducing us to her date, Randall Clemmings VI. She actually introduces him like that. The poor fucker looks suitably embarrassed, gulping back his champagne and looking nervously out the window.

Apparently, he works for her father, and Pepper got to know him over the summer when she was interning. They have just started dating. Pepper dropped that information dump in the first few minutes of conversation, and I'm sensing it was intentional.

I'm just not sure whose benefit it was for—mine or Garrick's.

Garrick keeps his arm around my waist as we chat, while the older couples congregate at the bar behind us, perched on tall stools. My eye is drawn outside to the lavish pool area, gorgeous grounds, and the dock at the back leading to the lake. A large boat is stationed behind the property, and I'm guessing it belongs to Winston or Ivy.

After a tedious hour of forced conversation with Pepper and her date—and restrained drinking on my part—we are ushered to a grand dining room and escorted to our assigned seating at the opulently decorated table. A large crystal chandelier hangs overhead, matching the lit crystal candelabras up and down the center of the table. Plain gold-colored vases hold bunches of white roses, complementing the white and gold table linen.

I'm already terrified of spilling something and being chastised.

"Darling, you're seated beside Pepper," Ivy tells Garrick when he moves to claim the seat beside me.

Of course, he is.

This woman has no shame.

A card with Randall's name is propped on the table in front of Garrick, and I wonder if Pepper was told to bring a date purely so they could foist him on me.

I'm hurt and fuming on Garrick's behalf. He accepted his mother's olive branch in true faith, but she had no intention of making any effort with me. I am not sure exactly what her agenda is today, but it's definitely not welcoming me to the family.

Garrick drills an angry look at his mother. "I'm sitting beside my girlfriend, or we're leaving."

Ivy emits a high-keeled laugh. Everything about that woman is fake from her plastic face to her plastic tits, her pretend posh accent, her nauseating compliments-slash-ass-licking to the governor, and her obvious false humor. "There's no need to get your panties in a bunch, darling." She flashes us a syrupy-sweet smile laced with hidden venom. "I don't know where your newfound dramatics have come from, but it's rather unbecoming. I did not raise you to conduct yourself in this manner."

She barely raised him from what I've been told. Dawn and his dad had a strong influence on Garrick growing up, and he spent most of his time in North Bend even if the divorce granted them joint custody of their only son. Ivy was often busy with society events, whichever husband she was married to at the time, or abroad on overseas trips, so he grew up largely with his father, and it shows. It's lucky for Garrick his father and stepmother were the main influence in his life. I shudder to think of how conceited he might be if his mother had had more of a role in his life.

"I don't see how speaking the truth amounts to drama, and what is wrong with my boyfriend wanting to sit beside me?" I ask before swigging from my champagne.

Across the table, Randall sits down beside Pepper in the seat that was meant for Garrick. Her mother is on her other side. Ivy and the governor have taken up position on either end of the table, and Winston slides into the seat beside me, much to my distaste.

"I don't expect you to understand how things work in high society, dear," Ivy says, her patronizing tone laced with sarcasm. "But it's traditional to sit apart from one's spouse or date at formal events."

"We're not royalty," Garrick hisses, glaring at his mother. "This is supposed to be a family Thanksgiving dinner. One I fully expected to attend with my girlfriend by my side."

Ivy sucks in her cheeks before her features smooth out. She claps her hands, choosing to ignore her son's statement. "Let's eat!"

Chapter Twenty-Nine
Stevie

I hold on to Garrick's hand under the table during the meal, and I'm on a countdown to when we can leave. Pepper makes polite conversation with me from across the table while Garrick and Randall talk sports, music, and wine. She asks me about college and my jobs, and she seems nice and genuinely interested, but I don't know if it's all a front. I ask her about her poli-sci major and her plans for the future, and she's animated and bubbly when discussing following her father into politics.

Ivy's heated glare sits firmly on my shoulders, and after a while, and probably too much champagne, I decide to challenge her on it. "Do I have something on my face?" I ask, sitting up straight in my chair and angling my body so I'm looking Garrick's mother straight in the eye. "Or perhaps you're staring at me nonstop because you'd like to know where I get my hair done?" I smooth my hand over my long glossy locks. "If you're considering a hair color change, I can highly recommend red. It's certainly classier and less common than blonde." I keep a sweet smile affixed to my face the entire time

I'm insulting her, purposely focusing on her bottled-blonde shade. "Though mine is natural and almost impossible to replicate with a dye."

"I have never had any desire to color my hair red," she drawls, lifting her wineglass and stabbing me with a sharp look. "Even less so now." She guzzles her wine while I count that a win.

Then she pointedly steers the conversation at the table to politics, purely to end the discussion I'm having with Pepper and most likely to embarrass me. As soon as the conversation turns political, I'm out of my comfort zone and forced to remain quiet because I can't contribute anything. Ivy wastes no opportunity to take a potshot at me, chipping away at my bravery, and I wonder how much more of this I can withstand.

Garrick growls at his mother, constantly intervening to shut her up. Until the next time, and we do it all over again.

It's exhausting, and I'm slowly losing the will to live.

The array of silverware on the table confuses me along with the convoluted menu consisting of amuse-bouche, soup, scallops, crab claws, and caviar to start and lobster as the main event with a host of different accompaniments. Ivy laughs when I pick up the wrong utensil and laughs again when Garrick subtly points out the silverware to use.

You just can't win with that bitch.

"We regularly have dinner at Dad and Dawn's," Garrick says, angrily forking some gratin potatoes on his plate in between shooting contemptuous looks at his mother. "They don't feel the need for all of these silly trappings. This is supposed to be a family dinner. We're not at some stuffy social event, and I don't see why there is a need for all this pomp and ceremony or your attempts to belittle my girlfriend. I'm running on limited patience, Mother, and I'd advise you to choose your words carefully. Unless your plan is to permanently drive a stake through the heart of our relationship? In which case, carry on and see what happens."

"Again with the dramatics," Ivy murmurs, looking like she wishes she could smother me in my sleep. "Everyone, eat." She waves her hands around. "The food is getting cold."

Her go-to MO seems to be ignoring shit she doesn't like and pretending it wasn't said. She truly is a piece of work.

Garrick spends the rest of dinner defending me, glowering at his mother, and whispering we can leave at regular intervals. I want to go, but I've come this far. I can make it until the end of dinner. Then I'm getting out of here, and I'm never coming back.

I pick at my food, appetite slaughtered thanks to the tension and stiltedness in the room. I miss good old-fashioned turkey, green beans, and mashed potatoes, and I wish I had turned down this invite and gone to my nana's. Memories of previous Thanksgiving dinners, surrounded by good company, traditional food, delicious wine, tons of laughter, and nonstop music surges to the forefront of my mind, adding to my misery.

Discussion among the women turns to haute couture while we're awaiting dessert, and I'm still out of my depth. "Your dress is pretty, Stevie," Ivy says, and I'm instantly on high alert. "Even I might be tempted to wear last season if I found something that complimented my hair so well. It must be challenging finding vibrant clothes that don't clash with the red."

"I don't have that problem, and Garrick loves my hair," I retort, struggling to keep the sickly-sweet smile on face as I drain my wine.

I ditched restraint the second I sat at this table. Right now, alcohol is getting me through this ordeal, and I couldn't give a flying fuck what might come out of my mouth. I am beyond caring. There is no way of salvaging anything with Garrick's mother, and I'm not going to sit here and take her bullshit.

"He's always finding ways to touch it." I bite my lip and wear my most suggestive expression as I blatantly eye fuck my boyfriend. "Especially in the bedroom. Isn't that right, babe?"

"Abso-fucking-lutely." Garrick doesn't let me down, gently fisting a hand in my hair, tipping my head back, and bringing his lips to mine. Ivy lets out a shriek of outrage as we kiss in front of everyone at the table, and I giggle against Garrick's lips. When we have pushed it enough, we break apart, and I rest my head on his shoulder as he plays with strands of my hair. "Your hair is stunning, like every part of you," he loyally supplies.

I hate he must choose between me and his mother, but she's the one who forced this, not me.

"That's enough." Ivy slams her clenched fist down on the table. "I won't have any more disrespectful behavior at the dinner table."

"Perhaps you should excuse yourself then," I say, unable to help myself.

Surprised shock splays across Cristelle's face while Ivy stares at me with barely concealed hatred. Garrick laughs and makes a point of lacing his fingers through mine on top of the table. The governor quietly sips his wine while Randall stares abjectly into space, looking like he wishes he could be zapped out of here—I can relate—and Pepper wears a worried frown as she looks at Garrick.

Winston chuckles. "You really need to remove that stick up your ass, Ivy." He waves his wineglass in her direction, spilling ruby-red liquid all over the white tablecloth. "Leave the girl alone." Winston tilts his head to look at me, planting his large hand down on my thigh under the table.

I jump, instantly removing it before Garrick or Ivy notices.

"I like your dress," Winston adds, slurring his words and hiccupping.

He's been knocking the wine and champagne back like it's

going out of fashion. Not that I'm one to talk. Although alcohol has loosened my tongue, I think I'm too angry to get drunk. Even though he's a bit of a letch, I would still take pervy Winston over evil-bitch Ivy any day. And honestly? If I was dating that witch, I'd be permanently drunk.

"Especially the front." Winston's eyes latch on to my cleavage, and it's not the first time.

I take back what I just said.

They're both as bad as one another and deserve to be miserable together.

"Keep your eyes on Stevie's face," Garrick barks, leaning across me to glower at Winston. "Or I'll fucking make you."

"Garrick!" Ivy feigns shock, placing her hand over her mouth. "Apologize right now."

Garrick throws his napkin down. "I'll apologize when he apologizes for leering at my girlfriend all through dinner." He stands just as the servers come into the room with dessert. "And after you apologize for your rude treatment of Stevie."

"This is supposed to a be a celebration," the governor says, projecting his voice around the room as he intervenes for the first time. "Everyone, just sit down and let bygones be bygones."

Fucking typical politician. I wonder would he be so dismissive if it was his daughter subjected to Ivy's verbal abuse?

Tugging on Garrick's leg, I implore him to sit with my eyes. "It's nearly over," I mouth as the servers set dessert down in the middle of the table. "We'll eat dessert, then make excuses and leave."

Reluctantly, Garrick reclaims his seat. "I'm so sorry, Stevie," he whispers in my ear. "We should never have come."

"We'll discuss it later," I whisper back, noticing the fresh frown crawling over his face.

"Where is Stevie's cake?" Garrick asks.

The servers are busy distributing crème brûlée and baked Alaska, but there is no sign of the cake I baked.

"In the trash," Ivy says, fighting a smug smile. "You can blame Winston for infecting it with his germs."

The cake was still edible. Just scrape off the top layer, cut it into slices, and it would have been fine. There was no need to toss the entire thing. It was pure maliciousness, and I've reached my breaking point. Swallowing painfully over the lump in the back of my throat, I force tears to retreat from the backs of my eyes. I will not let this bitch get to me, any more than she has, and I'm not staying here a second longer.

"I'm done," I say, standing and throwing my napkin on the table.

"Be a dear and fill me up before you leave." Ivy holds out her wineglass. "At least that should make you feel at home." An evil grin spreads over her mouth. "Maybe we should have had you serving us through dinner and show my son, once and for all, that you don't fit in his world."

Snatching the red wine bottle up, I walk quickly along the table, heading toward the bitch. She's so arrogant she actually believes I'm going to top off her glass.

What a dumb cunt.

Her strangled shriek as I empty the bottle of wine all over her hair, face, and expensive in-season ballgown is music to my ears. Winston's loud laughter bounces off the walls of the otherwise eerily quiet dining room.

I think I've managed to shock everyone else into silence.

Chapter Thirty
Stevie

The silence is shattered when Ivy emits a rage-fueled roar and lunges for me.

"Shit!" Garrick yanks me back before his mother reaches me, prying the wine bottle from my tight fingers.

"You stupid classless whore!" Ivy screams, wiping wine from her eyes before she lunges at me again. She wobbles on her heels and reaches out to clutch the edge of the table before she falls. I watched her push food around her plate while drinking glass after glass of wine and champagne, and it's quite possible she's very drunk.

"Enough!" Garrick bellows, stepping in front of me and partially shielding me with his body. "You deserve that and more." He jabs his finger in his mother's direction. "Just remember I gave you a chance to prove you could be a normal human. A normal mother. But you couldn't even attempt to try for my sake. You orchestrated this to humiliate Stevie, and I'll never forgive you for it. Never."

The governor and his wife stand on either side of Ivy, trying to keep a straight face, while Winston is slouched in his chair, eyeing proceedings with drunken amusement. I briefly wonder if their relationship will survive this dinner. Randall and Pepper are standing in the corner by the wall, attempting to smother their laughter.

At least I provided the entertainment.

Let's call it my legacy.

"She's not right for you!" Ivy screeches, sounding like a banshee as she plucks strands of wet hair off her face. "She's beneath you, and she's only after you for your money! Everyone can see it but you. She's a gold-digging harlot, and I'm not going to sit back and let her trick or trap you into marriage! This dinner was for you! It was about opening your eyes to the truth."

"The truth?!" Garrick yells, and I cling to his arm, offering silent support. "The truth is, you're a snob who cares more about appearances and social progression than her own son. If you took the time to get to know Stevie, you would realize how wrong you are, but you made your mind up from day one. You want the truth, Mother?" He leans toward her, shielding nothing from his face as he says, "I love Stevie!" He moves me under his arm, tucking me into his side. "I. Love. Her," he shouts. "She's the only one for me. Someday, soon if I have my way, Stevie will be my wife."

Ivy rears back in horror.

"That's right, Mother. I'm going to *ask her* to marry me, and there is nothing you can say that will change it."

I turn my head to the corner, watching as tears gather in Pepper's eyes. Shock is mixed with pain and longing on her face, and she's doing nothing to disguise it. Randall and I exchange a look, both understanding it. No one else has noticed, but it's plain to see. I can't say I'm hugely surprised.

Garrick clasps my hand in his. "You are dead to me," he tells his mother as I watch Pepper flee the room. "I am done making excuses for the shitty human you are. You need to take a long hard look at yourself, Mother, before you end up alone." He looks down at me, pain and resolve stretched across his strained face. "Come on, we're leaving."

We don't speak as we exit the room, leaving devastation in our wake. Garrick strides forward with purpose, like he can't wait to put distance between us and this disaster. Up ahead, I spot Pepper slipping into the bathroom. "I need to use the toilet," I tell Garrick when we reach the front door. "You go ahead." I stretch up and kiss his cheek. "Get the car started, and I'll be out in a few minutes."

"Stevie." He takes my hands in his. "I am so incredibly sorry about all this. I am ashamed and appalled at the way she has treated you. We should never have stayed. I should have made that decision the second we arrived when I saw the Montgomerys were here."

"I made the choice to stay, Garrick. You were willing to leave, and you did your best to defend me. This isn't your fault, and you need to stop apologizing for that woman. I'm done trying to seek her approval. She's your mother. What you do from here is your decision, but I will not be making any more effort, and I won't be having any contact with her ever again. I will not put myself through another nightmare like this one."

"I would not expect you to," he agrees, clasping my face in his hands and pressing a kiss to my brow. "I love you." He pecks my lips. "Go to the bathroom, and hurry. I need to get out of here before I'm tempted to murder my own mother."

The door to the bathroom is unlocked, and I slip inside, quietly closing it behind me. Resting against the solid wood door, I wait for the woman in the voluminous red dress to turn around and face me.

I could have left without confronting her, but I need to know.

Pepper is leaning against the counter, face forward, with both hands propped on the marble, her gaze fixed straight ahead as she stares into the mirror.

Tension bleeds into the air as she slowly turns to face me with tearstained cheeks and red-rimmed eyes.

I wet my lips and clear my throat. "How long have you loved him?"

"Forever," she whispers.

"Does he know?" I don't think Garrick does, but I have to ask. I need to know if he's just in denial.

She shakes her head. "He's clueless. I've ensured it."

"Why?"

"He doesn't see me like that. Not yet."

"Ah." I push off the door, knotting my hands in front of me. "You are biding your time. Waiting for the right moment to make your move."

"That was the plan, yes." She straightens her shoulders and brushes the moisture from under her eyes. "But I waited too long. You're different than the other girls he has dated. None of them were a threat. None of them were worthy of him, and I mistakenly believed you weren't either. But I was wrong."

"His mother would disagree."

"Ivy is a bitch and a snob, and what she did to you today was despicable."

"Yet you said nothing. All of you just sat there and let her treat me like that. You may not have gone out of your way to hurt me, Pepper, but you wanted me exposed. You were hoping to benefit by letting Ivy do the dirty work. If Garrick was free of me, you could finally make a move."

Her chest rises, and she audibly gulps as she stares at me. "You are right," she admits. "It was wrong of us to sit there in silence. Mom would never undermine her best friend in front of an audience, and Daddy values Ivy's connections too much to go to bat for someone he doesn't know. Randall is a stranger, and he couldn't speak out for fear of upsetting Daddy."

"But you could have. Yet you did nothing."

"I am sorry for not intervening, Stevie. I should have called her out on her treatment of you." Remorse undercuts her tone and flashes on her face, but I have no clue if it's genuine. These people are skilled manipulators, and she grew up in a world where it's acceptable to trample over everyone and everything to achieve the end goal. I doubt Pepper gives a flying fuck about me. All she cares about is Garrick.

"What do you think Garrick would do if he knew you purposely chose to remain silent for personal gain?"

"He may not know the real reason why, but he's disappointed in me. As his friend, he would expect me to take your side."

Yes, my boyfriend would. Hopefully, now he'll see her true colors and want to end this charade of a "friendship."

"I'm shocked Garrick stayed," Pepper continues, "but that was you, wasn't it? You didn't want to back down."

"I'm not a quitter, and I never wanted him to fall out with his mother because of me. I thought I could handle it for his sake, but I was mistaken. We should have left the instant we arrived when I saw it was another matchmaking attempt." I unknot my hands and stand tall. "Tell me, was Randall part of it? Did she tell you to bring him here for me?"

"Absolutely not. If she even attempted that with me, I would have told her to fuck off. I don't blame you for thinking the worst of me, Stevie, but I would never purposely hurt you. That isn't who I am."

"So why bring him then?" I cock my head to one side. "It's obvious you're not into him."

She winces, having the decency to look ashamed as she wraps her arms around her middle. "I knew you'd be here with

Garrick, and I wanted to bring a date. I couldn't sit through another dinner watching the man I love with someone who isn't me. Randall had been asking me out all summer, and I repeatedly said no. I decided to give him a chance. To see if I could move on, but I was delusional. Garrick is all I see."

At least she's being honest. I respect her for that. I hold Pepper's gaze as I make her a promise. "I won't step aside and let you steal my man."

"I wouldn't ask you too, and I never will. As much as it pains me, it's clear Garrick loves you and you love him. You make him happy. That's all I want for him. You're the one he wants forever, and I'll just have to find a way to make peace with it."

"You expect me to believe you'll just walk away?" Skepticism bleeds into my tone.

"No. You're too smart for that." We size each other up. "In different circumstances, I think we could be friends. It would be far easier for me if I hated you, but I don't. I couldn't hate any woman who brought the high and mighty Ivy Allen-Golding-Smith to her proverbial knees." Condescension rings clear through her tone before she laughs. "The look on her face when she lunged at you." More laughter bursts from her mouth. "It was priceless. I will never forget it. That woman has had that coming for a long time."

I shrug, needing to wrap this up before Garrick sends out a search party. Besides, I'm done wasting breath on that awful woman. "I don't want you around him," I say in a nonthreatening manner. I want her to understand my position and her place going forward, but I'm not going to sink to Ivy's despicable levels to make my point. "It's not fair to me, and it's not fair to him when he believes you only wish to be friends. Surely, it would be easier for you not to be around him either?"

Pain ghosts over her face as she clutches her arms more

tightly around her waist. "It would," she quietly admits after a few beats. "I don't think it will be a problem anyway. If Garrick is determined to cut ties with Ivy, and I believe he is, there'll be limited opportunities for us to meet." She loosens her arms, letting them drop to her side. "I know I have no right to ask anything of you, but I'd rather Garrick didn't know how I feel about him."

"We agreed to honesty in our relationship, and I don't like keeping secrets from him." Even if this one would work to my advantage. I don't particularly want Garrick to know Pepper loves him. But it's complicated now I have this knowledge. If he finds out some other way and he discovers I knew and didn't tell him, would he understand the reasons why?

"It's not your secret to share," she says, offering me an excuse on a silver platter.

"Why don't you want him to know?" I narrow my eyes in suspicion.

"What good would it do any of us? He doesn't love me. He loves you. He wants to marry you." Her voice chokes, and she briefly averts her eyes. "We will occasionally run into one another, and I'd rather it isn't awkward," she continues, lifting her head and piercing me with an earnest look. "Isn't it better to let our friendship peter out than dragging all this into the open? It will only hurt more that way."

"Okay." I nod. "I agree. I won't tell him."

"Thank you."

"I'm not doing it for you."

"I know."

We look at one another for a few seconds more before I turn and unlock the door.

"Stevie," she calls out as I swing the door open. I turn one final time to look at her. "Take care of him and love him good. He deserves to be happy."

Chapter Thirty-One
Garrick

"What time are you meeting Stevie at?" Will asks in between stuffing clothes haphazardly in his bag while I lounge on his bed, throwing a tennis ball up and down in the air. Classes ended today for the holidays, and we're all heading home for Christmas this weekend.

"We're meeting at Bumble Bees in an hour."

"Do you have any idea what the gift is?"

I shake my head, tossing the ball in the corner, and sit up. "All she said was she wanted to give me my Christmas gift early and we had to do it before we went back to Seattle."

"Intriguing." Will zips up his bag and flops down beside me. "How are things between you now?"

"Better but still strained. She has retreated a little since that disastrous dinner. Not that I blame her. It was awful. I should have left immediately. I made a mistake not forcing the issue. Stevie says she doesn't blame me, that it was her call to stay, but deep down, I suspect she is aggravated I didn't make the decision to leave when we got there and saw Pepper and her family."

"You can't change history, and you chose her over Ivy. You've cut your mother out of your life. That speaks volumes."

"Sometimes, it's hard to tell with Stevie. She's not like other girls, and she has big hang-ups about relationships." I gulp over the messy ball of emotion at the back of my throat. "I don't want to lose her."

"You won't. She knows how much you care, and she's always your priority."

"But am I hers?" I murmur, admitting something I've been terrified to confront.

"She's nuts about you, Gar. It's just a rough patch. You'll bounce back. Every couple goes through highs and lows. You two will last the distance. Just like Ellen and me."

"I want to believe that, but sometimes, I think she remembers how uncomplicated her life was before she met me. There were no annoying groupies, crazy exes, or bitchy mothers to deal with."

Air whooshes out of my mouth as I lean back against his headboard. "Stevie is so focused on her goals, and I'm really not sure where I land on her priority list." I angle my head to look at my buddy. "We had a fight on Monday because I brought up next year. She'll have built up enough credits to graduate in May. I asked her to consider holding off, to come back for senior year with me, and she accused me of being selfish."

"What did you say?"

"That I *was* selfish because I didn't want to be separated from her and I didn't want to lose her. She contended I wouldn't even if we have to do the long-distance thing. That it wouldn't be for long, and we could still see one another on weekends."

"That doesn't sound unreasonable."

"It's not." I cross my feet at the ankles. "But I don't want to be without her. It's more than just a wish. It's a physical need. I physically cannot be away from her for any length of time. She clearly doesn't feel the same way, and this relationship is starting to feel more and more one-sided."

"Have you told her that?"

"Yeah. She was hurt. Told me I was being unfair. That it would be hard for her to be away from me too, but we needed to maintain our independence within the relationship."

"And you haven't seen her since then?" Will arches a brow.

"Nope. We've been texting, but between exams and work, we haven't found time to meet up all week."

"It seems to me that Stevie needs more independence than most girls but the same level of reassurance. Just give her that, and trust things to work out. You two are meant to be, and it'll all be fine."

I wish I shared his optimism.

"Hey, you." Stevie hops up when I arrive at our table in Bumble Bees, flinging her arms around me and squeezing me tight. "Missed you."

"I missed you too." Wrapping my arms around her, I lift her off her feet and kiss her lips.

"I ordered you a black coffee and a chocolate chip muffin," she says when I put her down, smiling as Marie approaches with a tray.

"Thanks, babe." I kiss her cheek before she reclaims her seat, and I drop into mine.

Marie leaves our coffee and muffins and wanders off to attend to other patrons. "Can we clear the air?" Stevie asks, sipping her caramel macchiato and moaning as it tickles her taste buds.

My dick stirs at the sound and the look of abject pleasure on her face. "What else is left to say?" I shrug, taking a drink of my coffee. "We have a difference of opinion, and it's not like I'm going to force you into staying if you don't want to."

"It isn't about not wanting to stay, Garrick." Her hand slides across the table, and her fingers hook around mine. "If I had a choice, of course, I'd stay with you. But I set out on this path before I knew you. It makes no sense to hang around UO for another year when I can easily graduate in May. And this isn't just about me. Another college year means more money for food and accommodations, and it's one more year Mom will continue working her weekend job. I can't ask that of her. She has already given me so much."

When she puts it like that, I feel like a selfish prick. That thought hadn't crossed my mind. "I understand. I don't like it, but I understand."

"It's not even a full year, and we'll see each other on weekends and during the holidays."

"Maybe you could get a full-time job in Oregon?" I suggest, lifting her hand and kissing the tips of her fingers.

Her face twists into a grimace. "That's not an option."

"Why?"

"I have set ideas for my future career. I don't want to open a floral shop. I want to provide a professional service to corporate clients and provide a themed service for weddings. I won't be catering to the public or spending my days making bouquets."

My eyes pop wide in surprise. Of course, we've talked about our futures. I know her ambition is to run her own business after she has worked for others for a few years, to build up experience, but I didn't realize she had such set ideas. "What about your nana's place? Won't you be expected to take over?"

"Nana would never force me into anything. Mom will inherit the business, and either she'll take over the management of it, with some input from me, or she'll hire a suitably qualified person to run it. At some point in the future, I may change my mind. I might want to run it full-time, but for now, my goal is to start something of my own." She takes back her hand, straightening up and shrugging. "Who knows? Maybe, at some point, I can amalgamate the two businesses and run them together."

"So, how does this tie in with not being able to stay in Oregon?"

"The kind of business I want to run is quite niche. There's this start-up company in Seattle similar to the business model I have in mind. They are making a name for themselves, so I sent them my résumé." A massive grin spreads across her mouth. "And they have offered me a job!"

"You didn't even tell me you were applying for jobs." Hurt mixes with pride in my voice.

Her face falls. "I was going to tell you, but every time we talk about the future and me not being here for senior year, you get pissy. I wasn't going to say anything unless I got the job."

That she feels she can't tell me these things hurts even worse. "I thought we were a team. That I meant something to you."

"Garrick, of course, you mean something to me. I love you." She gets up and moves her chair over beside mine, snuggling into me as she tips her chin up. "I am serious about you. About us. But I've been honest with you from the start. I told you I have set goals and our relationship, while very important to me, can't take away from what I want to achieve."

"I love how ambitious you are, and I want you to succeed. But it seems like I'm relegated to the bottom of your list of priorities, and I'm scared I'm losing you." I'm aware I sound like a petulant child, but I can't help how I feel.

"I promise you're not, and I don't want to lose you either." Her fingers sweep through the stubble on my face. "We have to accept we need to give each other space to grow into the people we're going to be, time to develop our careers, and time to map out a plan for the future. We can still be together while pursuing independent paths."

She ducks down under the table, grabbing her purse and extracting an envelope. "I think this might help." Her eyes light up as she hands it to me.

"What is it?"

She nudges me in the ribs. "Open it and see."

I remove a square piece of paper from the envelope first, admiring the circular looped drawing. "Is this Celtic?"

She bobs her head, looking a little nervous as she explains. "It's a Celtic shield knot also called a dara knot. The Celts used the symbol in battle, but they also gave it to people they cared about the most. It's a promise to protect and look out for the person you love for all eternity. It's named after the Irish word for an oak tree, and it's said to mimic the roots of an oak tree. It's supposed to encourage and support people through challenging times. I think it's perfect to represent who we are to one another. Our love is as strong as the roots of a tree, and though they may branch out along different paths, we will forever remain interconnected."

She pulls out the other paper from the envelope and hands it to me. "That's an appointment for this afternoon at Mystical Tattoo. I thought we could both get this inked so we have a constant reminder of our love, no matter how many miles or how much time might separate us in the future." Her eyes glisten with emotion and a hint of vulnerability. "You know how I feel about tattoos. Anything I ink on my skin will become a permanent part of me." She taps the inside of her wrist. "I'm going to get mine here. I want this one visible, in a place where

I can touch it when I need to feel close to you, and somewhere others will see it and know how much you mean to me."

My lips crash down on hers as potent emotion replaces the blood flowing through my veins.

As gestures go, this is perfect. Stevie couldn't have suggested anything better. As we kiss, my heart swells with love for this woman, and I hope this blatant display of her commitment will settle that inherent restless fear of losing her that resides inside me.

Chapter Thirty-Two
Garrick

"Oh god, yes, baby. Right there." Stevie moans and writhes underneath me as I bury myself deep inside her before slowly withdrawing and thrusting back in. My gaze skims over the new ink on her wrist, visible through the clear Tegaderm bandage, while her hands are flung out to either side, and pride wells inside me. I opted to get my tattoo in the same place on my left wrist, and every time I look at it, it brings a huge smile to my face.

"You are so good at this," my girlfriend pants, wrapping her legs more tightly around my waist as I fuck her on the rug in front of the roaring fire at the cabin. We're spending Christmas with my folks in North Bend tomorrow. Monica and Betsy are joining us too. Tonight, I wanted my beautiful sunshine all to myself, so we snuck away to the winery earlier to enjoy some alone time.

Things have been perfect these past few days, and I'm happy our relationship is back on track. Not even my mother's pitiful weepy message has dampened my good mood.

Ivy made her bed, and she can lie in it.

"I love you," Stevie rasps, pulling my face down to hers for a passionate kiss as I drive in and out of her.

"Love you too." I nibble a trail from her lips to her jawline and along the elegant slope of her neck, dotting kisses along her collarbone and lower. Locking my lips around one nipple, I suck hard on the taut peak, basking in the noises she makes as I lavish attention on both tits.

"I'm close," she pants, lightly dragging her nails up and down my back.

"Stay with me," I grunt, picking up speed and ramming in and out of her with feverish need. I straighten up into a kneeling position and hold her legs around my waist as I pound into her. She looks like a fucking goddess underneath me with her gorgeous red hair fanned out around her, a pretty blush covering her chest, and her magnificent tits bouncing and jiggling as I fuck her into the floor.

My balls tighten, and delicious tingles build at the base of my spine. Rubbing her clit, just the way she likes it, I pivot my hips, hitting deep inside her, and we fall off the ledge together.

Sex with Stevie is out of this world, and I want to continue doing it forever.

We collapse in a heap of tangled limbs and sweaty skin, clinging to one another and softly kissing, as we come down from our high. After snuggling for a while, I wrap her in a soft blanket and head to the bathroom to get rid of the condom. Then I grab a chilled bottle of wine, two glasses, two spoons, and a tub of ice cream and return to my woman.

Stevie is propped against the base of the couch, swaddled in the pink and gray blanket as she stares into the crackling flames dancing around the hearth. "Penny for them?" I ask, handing her the ice cream and spoons before easing down beside her. Setting the bottle and glasses on the ground, I proceed to pour the wine while she pries the lid off her favorite black cherry chocolate chip ice cream. I always ensure the cabin refrigerator is stocked up with the stuff. I buy it from a local parlor in Woodinville. It's one of their most popular cartons, and they regularly sell out, so I like to pick up a few when they're back in stock.

Stevie turns on her side, handing a spoon to me. "I was just thinking about how this was my fantasy the first time I came here."

I hand her a wineglass and take a sip of my own drink before digging my spoon into the yummy, creamy goodness. "Eating ice cream naked in front of the fire?"

"Not that part," she says before licking her spoon and moaning.

My cock stiffens because those sounds she makes are my own personal aphrodisiac. "Which part then?"

"The sex part. The second I saw this rug and the open fireplace, I had a vision of us drinking wine and making love in front of a roaring fire, and now we've done it."

I lean in and kiss her chocolaty lips. "I want to fulfill all your fantasies."

"You do, handsome. You're the best boyfriend." She snuggles into my side, dropping kisses along my arm and my shoulder. "I mean it, babe." She looks up at me through a layer of long, thick, gorgeous lashes, looking sweet as sin and good enough to eat. "You look after me so well, and you make me feel loved and protected."

"Loving you is as easy as breathing."

"I'm happy we're all spending Christmas together."

"Me too. I want to prove you can join my family for the holidays and it will be normal and wonderful, not like that Thanksgiving nightmare." I leave Stevie to finish the ice cream while I savor the crisp sauvignon blanc.

"I already know tomorrow will be nothing like that disaster. It's going to be great."

"You better believe it." I tweak her nose before handing her the bag with the small gift-wrapped box. "I want to give you your gift now while we're alone."

Discarding the half-empty ice cream tub, she sits up straighter, placing the bag on her lap. The blanket falls from her shoulders, pooling at her waist. Strands of messy auburn hair tumble over her shoulders, brushing the tops of her perfect round tits. Her nipples are hard, and my dick is flying at full mast now, pointing at her like a loaded weapon.

I'm already salivating at the prospect of round two.

But I want her to open her gift first.

Stevie is quiet as she removes the package from the bag. Trembling fingers tear at the pretty purple wrapping. Her head jerks up, and panicked eyes meet mine when she reveals the small square jeweler's box.

"It's not what you're thinking. Breathe, baby. Please." My fingers caress her face and neck in a soothing motion.

Her chest rises and falls as she opens the box. Wide, dazed eyes stare at the custom piece of jewelry.

"It's a promise ring," I explain because she's gone deathly pale. I sit cross-legged in front of her, watching all manner of emotions flit over her face as she stares at the ring.

A layered red topaz stone occupies center stage, surrounded by small diamond edging, arranged to look like petals, resting on a rose gold band. I couldn't be more thrilled at how it turned out. "It's a poppy ring," I blurt, staring to panic when she still hasn't said anything. "I had it made especially for you. I wanted to give you a ring that was uniquely you and something that represented my commitment to us." I tap a gentle finger across my plastic-wrapped wrist. "In the same way you gave me a gift of your commitment."

"It's beautiful, Garrick," she whispers, looking up at me with glassy eyes. "But this is too much and far too expensive."

"You are worth it." I wind my fingers in her hair. "Put it on. It should fit. I measured your finger one night while you were sleeping. I wanted to ensure I got the right size."

"That was sneaky," she says, carefully removing the ring from the box.

"Here. Let me." Taking it from her, I slide it onto the ring finger of her left hand. "There. Perfect." I almost choke on emotion as I force the words out. I can't describe the joy I feel seeing my ring on her finger. If I had my way, it'd be an engagement ring, but I knew Stevie would balk if I proposed to her. I'll have to build up to that.

She holds out her hand, admiring it. "It's stunning." Biting on her lip, she stares at it like she's almost scared of it.

"If you don't like it, we can return it and pick something together."

"I love it, Garrick. I really do. I couldn't have picked anything more perfect."

"But?"

Air expels from her mouth in a rush. "I'm happy to wear your promise ring, Garrick, as long as we're on the same page about marriage, and I'm fearful we're not." She scoots in closer to me, her features softening with love as she peers deep into my eyes. "I want to marry you someday, but that's a long way away for me. I'm not even twenty-one yet."

"I know, and it's cool."

"Is it?" Her troubled eyes probe mine. "I don't want to hurt your feelings, but sometimes, it feels like we're on a high-speed train, and you're up there in the driver's cabin, screaming at him to go faster and faster, impatient to get to the destination, while I'm begging him to slow down so I can enjoy the scenery and savor every place we pass."

"Is it wrong I love you so much I want to marry you sooner than later?"

"It's not wrong to feel how you feel."

"But you don't feel it in the same way I do."

"I'm not saying that."

"Then what are you saying?" My tone is harsher than I intended, but hurt is mushrooming inside me. I wanted to give her something that was as thoughtful as the gift she gave me, but I seem to have completely misjudged the situation. "I'll take it back," I snap, reaching for her finger.

"Garrick, please." Tears well in her eyes, and her voice cracks. She whips her hand away. "I don't want you to take it back. I love it, but I want to ensure you're not reading too much into this. I'm not ready to get married, Garrick, and sometimes, it feels like you're smothering me."

I can scarcely breathe over the lump in my throat or the tight pain spreading across my chest. "I just want to love you." I scramble to my feet. "Why do you make that so hard?"

Chapter Thirty-Three
Stevie

"Talk to me," Nana says, resting her wrinkled palm on top of mine as we sit on the wooden bench outside. Classic Carpenters hits trickle out of the open glass double doors behind us as Garrick dances with Dawn. The twins are in the game room, playing their new Xboxes while Mom and Hugh sit at the kitchen table, chatting and drinking wine, as Garrick swirls his stepmom around the tile floor.

It's super sweet and a timely reminder of how good a guy my boyfriend is. The heightened emotion, mixed with obvious tension between Garrick and me threatened to break me apart. So, I fled to the safety of the patio, bundled in my coat, staring out at the blanket of trees curtaining the rear of Garrick's family home in North Bend, lamenting my insensitivity and wondering if there are critical cells missing from my brain.

"I hurt his feelings," I croak, "and I ruined Christmas for both of us, and I hate myself for it."

"Shush now, Little Poppy. Nothing was ruined. We had a lovely dinner, with lots of laugher and delicious wine, and the night is far from over."

"Why am I like this, Nana?" I turn to face her. "What is wrong with me?"

"There is nothing wrong with you, honey." Her eyes drift to the gorgeous ring nestled on the ring finger of my right hand.

Garrick's frosty gaze this morning when he noticed I'd changed it to my other hand could have cut glass. When I explained how everyone would jump to conclusions if I wore it on my left hand, he merely nodded and left the room.

"Is it something to do with this ring?" she asks, always uncannily observant.

"Yes." I fill her in briefly, careful to keep my voice low in case any of our conversation carries inside. "I should have waited to say anything, but we made promises to one another to always be truthful, and honestly, the intensity of his feelings for me, and the certainty he possesses about our relationship, really scares the shit out of me at times."

"You can't help how you feel any more than Garrick can." She cups my face. "You are mature beyond your years, Stevie, in so many ways."

"Except when it comes to love." I beat her to the punchline.

Nana's soft smile and loving gaze ghost over me. "I'm proud of you for knowing what you want and always prioritizing it. You should never beat yourself up over speaking your mind and sharing your truths. It is better to openly communicate instead of keeping things locked up inside. Perhaps compromise and a little sensitivity in relation to the timing of conversations might be something to work on."

"You're right. I should not have expressed those thoughts last night. He tried to do something romantic for me, and I trampled all over it with my words, and I hurt him. Maybe I'm too blunt. I need to stop and think before I open my mouth. I love Garrick. I truly do, but he wants to drive a thousand miles an hour and I can't keep up."

"You're both still so young, and you have your whole lives ahead of you. Now is the time to have fun and not worry about the consequences." She tucks a wayward piece of my hair behind my ear. "You're both intense in different ways."

"Is that a good or a bad thing?"

"It is neither good nor bad. It is what it is." Her papery lips kiss my brow. "We can't predict what is around the corner, and I personally believe one shouldn't spend too long trying to. Live in the moment is my motto. And what is meant to be is what will transpire."

"Am I interrupting?" Garrick asks, standing awkwardly behind us with his hands shoved deep in the pockets of his black pants.

"Never, sweetheart." Nana rises stiffly to her feet, and Garrick offers her his hand. She grips on to him with an affectionate smile. "There are so few gentlemen left in this world, Garrick, but you are one of life's rare treasures."

The look on his face conveys how much those words mean to him, and I couldn't love Nana any more than I do in this moment. Her words were not solely for him either, and I see what she's doing.

Nana slips quietly into the house, leaving us alone to stew in the strain.

I'm the one who did this, so it's up to me to mend it. I stand and turn around, wrapping my arms around my waist as I stare at my forlorn-looking boyfriend. "I'm so sorry, Garrick. I didn't mean to hurt you, and I hate that I did. Your gift was thoughtful and beautiful, and I was insensitive. My timing sucked."

He moves closer. "I'm sorry too. I promised I wouldn't pressure you and I keep fucking up."

"I love you so much," I whisper with tears in my eyes, closing the gap between us and leaning against him. "But I worry we want different things."

His arms encircle my waist as he hugs me close. "We want the same things, just at different times and in different ways." He rests his chin on top of my head. "I never want you to feel like you need to apologize for speaking your mind. I always want to know what you're thinking even if what you're thinking might hurt me. It's better than being lied to."

"I didn't mean to ruin Christmas."

"What are you talking about?" He tilts my chin up with one finger. My heart does a little dance when his golden-brown eyes latch on to mine. Those rich amber flecks sparkle as his eyes crinkle with a smile. Beautiful dimples I dream about come out to play, and I melt against him, hating all the cross words and silence between us today.

"You didn't ruin anything," he continues. "I have always said everything is right in my world as long as you are by my side, and that was true today. We might have been distant and upset with one another, but we still spent the day together. You are mine, and I am yours. That hasn't changed." He smooths his hand down my hair. "Our love will endure the challenges, and we'll come out stronger on the other side."

"There he is, my lyrical poet." Stretching up, I press my mouth to his. Our lips linger, gliding gently together in tender kisses that transmit all the unspoken words behind the potent emotion charging the air.

Garrick kisses me softly and lovingly, and my heart equally rejoices and melts.

I don't know what the future holds for us, but in this moment, he is all that I want and all that I need.

"I'm starting a new tradition," he purrs in my ear before pulling back, treating me to another glimpse of those dashing dimples. "Dance with me, sunshine?" he asks, extending his hand.

"I would love to." I place my hand firmly in his, smiling and full of his love as he leads me into the kitchen where he proceeds to spin me around the floor to The Carpenters with our families whoops and hollers ringing in our ears.

We return to campus in January, after a lazy Christmas break, with a greater understanding of where we stand as a couple. We love one another, and we're committed to making it work. I just hope that's enough.

The months race by in a whirlwind of classes, study, work, and nights spent huddled under the sheets in my bedroom, enjoying one another in a way that never ends in an argument. On Saturdays, the crew and I show up to Garrick's gig to support him, and I do my best to ignore the women who throw themselves at my boyfriend any chance they get. I know he has no interest in them, and I trust him, but it's annoying they act like such hobags when they know he has a steady girlfriend.

Sunday nights are date night, and we grab dinner out, or catch a movie, or I cook at home, and we make love for hours.

Thankfully, his friendship with Pepper is virtually nonexistent now, so that's one less complication to worry about.

Garrick is still giving his mother the cold shoulder, and he shows no sign of changing his tune. Especially after I played him the nasty drunken messages she left on my phone recently. Garrick refuses to speak to her, so he got his dad to talk to Ivy. Hugh made it clear her harassment had to stop. He was highly embarrassed telling us the things she accused me of. Dawn made a point of pulling me aside afterward to confirm how much she and Hugh adore me and love the relationship I have with their son. They have stated repeatedly they know our love is real and I'm not the gold digger Ivy is trying to paint me to be.

Is it wrong to want to make a voodoo doll in my boyfriend's mother's likeness so I can stick pins in her eyes any time she pisses me off? Because I have seriously considered it. I even went as far as googling how I could get a custom doll made and fell down a tempting rabbit hole of witchcraft and spells.

Spring break comes and goes. We forgo a Cabo trip with Will and Ellen, and Noah and his new girlfriend, to return to our cabin in Seattle. Our days are spent hiking, biking, kayaking, and walking the grounds of the winery. Nights are spent with family, or enjoying a romantic meal at the outdoor restaurant, or cooking together.

It's a nice sojourn before we return to UO for our last few months together at college.

In April, I surprise Garrick with a night away in a five-star hotel in Seattle for his twenty-first birthday and a couples boudoir photography shoot. The night after, we attend a party at the winery, organized by his dad, for family and close friends. It is a great weekend, and we are storing plenty of entries in the memory bank.

However, as the weeks close in, and exam stress piles on, we are arguing more and more, and I'm feeling the strain.

Chapter Thirty-Four
Stevie

Ellen and I grab the opportunity for a girl's spa day, one Sunday in May, a few weeks before exams start. The guys have gone to Sutherlin to hike the North Umpqua Trail. It's an organized event to raise money for a local kid with leukemia. Will's family knows the little girl, so he is keen to support the fundraiser, and he roped the guys in.

"Will is going to move in with me for senior year," Ellen explains as we're seated side by side in matching leather recliners getting pedicures.

"I'm glad you got the lease again and you're able to stay there over the summer. At least you won't have to pack up all your shit this time."

"I'm going to miss you like crazy. You better not forget your college bestie when you're a hotshot floral corporate exec high-tailing it with flashy bigwigs in suits."

I crack up laughing. "What the heck is a floral corporate exec? And you do know I'll be stuck in the office, behind a computer, most of the time, learning the management side of running the business?"

"Bish." She waves her hands in the air. "You'll be running the show single-handedly in no time."

"Thanks for the faith, but the closer it gets, the more terrified I am. A lot is hinging on this job. If I don't like it, it will throw all my plans into disarray."

One of the workers approaches, holding up a bottle of prosecco, and we both raise our glasses for a top off. We only come to this salon for the complimentary bubbly.

"I'm sure it'll work out, but if it doesn't, you have a degree, smarts, confidence, and other options. You also have a man who would walk through fire for you." She pats my hand. "You'll be fine."

"That's if I still have the man," I mumble under my breath, half hoping she hears me, half hoping she doesn't.

Ellen sits up straighter, and the girl painting her toenails shoots her an evil side-eye. "Why would you even say something like that?"

"Sometimes, my relationship feels like such hard work."

"*All* relationships are hard work."

"You and Will don't argue half as much as Garrick and I do."

"That's only because we do it behind closed doors."

I turn my head to the side and stare at her. "I love him, and I'm really going to miss him. I know I can handle the long distance. I'll throw myself into work, and I'm used to being by myself."

"But Garrick isn't."

"Exactly." I chew on the corner of my lip, staring up at the ceiling, counting the water stains on the off-white plasterboard. They really should hire a painter. Shaking myself out of my errant thoughts, I look back at my friend. "Garrick is used to being in a relationship and doing things with his girlfriend. Will is moving in with you, and Noah is all loved up. I don't see

Garrick hanging out with Cohen much, so what'll he do? He's going to get lonely, and all his little groupies will love I'm not there."

"You'll be here on weekends, or he'll be with you in Seattle. The groupies don't matter, and Garrick would never cheat. You need to have a little faith, boo."

Garrick plans to cancel his regular Saturday night gig, and our mutual boss has agreed he can switch from Friday nights to Thursday nights at The End Zone, so he'll be free on weekends to meet up with me. "Deep down, I know that."

"So, what are you saying?"

I sigh heavily. "I don't really know." Pain lances me through the heart. "Just that I don't know how this will play out or"—I draw a brave breath—"whether we're meant to be forever."

Ellen blinks profusely as she stares at me. She roughly clears her throat. "No one can say that with any guarantee, babe. Not even married couples. I think you're overanalyzing and reading too much into things."

"What would you say if Will proposed to you tonight?"

A dreamy expression appears on her face. "I'd say yes."

I knew she would. I drill her with a look. "If Garrick asked me, I'd say no."

"Of course, you would. You have big career plans, and you always said you didn't want to get married until you were thirty."

"But shouldn't I say yes? If he's the one, it shouldn't matter."

Ellen sits upright and glares at the beautician, daring her to say anything. "Babe, listen to me." She reaches over and grabs my hand. "You have yourself all worked up over this, and I blame Garrick. He has always come on way too heavy with the marriage stuff."

"He can't help it. It's how he rolls."

"Yes, but you don't, and compromise is the name of the game. I think that gets lost in translation sometimes. If he wasn't going on about marriage all the time, you wouldn't give it a second thought, and half of these doubts would disappear."

"True."

"The way I see it, you have two choices. Try the long-distance thing and hope your love is strong enough to survive. For the record, I believe it is. Or break up with him now. If it's meant to be, you'll find your way back to one another when the timing is right."

"I don't want to break up with him," I rush to admit, rubbing at the pain in my chest. "The thought makes me equally ill and tearful."

"Then you have your answer. Forget about proposals and weddings. It's simply a case of the wrong time. But it doesn't mean you're with the wrong person."

"Boo, Garrick is here," Ellen says, poking her head through my bedroom door.

"Tell him I'll be right there," I say, stuffing the last of my toiletries in my weekend bag. "Do I look okay?" I ask before she leaves, running a hand over the front of my tight, short green and gold minidress. I have teamed it with a pair of knee-high leather boots, and my hair is in a half-up, half-down style that is very sixties. I went heavy on my eye makeup and pale on the lips.

"You look beautiful, like always." She darts in and kisses me on the cheek. "Garrick is going to eye fuck the shizz out of you when he sees how sexy you look."

"Is it too much for Nana's birthday?"

"Are you kidding?" She cracks up. "Nana will love it."

Ellen hops from foot to foot, emitting a tiny squeal that is kinda weird.

I narrow my eyes at her. "What is wrong with you?"

"Nothing is wrong." She's practically bouncing off the walls now. "I'm just excited for you."

"Okay." I draw out the word. "Weirdo."

"What's taking so long?" Garrick asks, materializing in my room. "Wow." His gaze roams appreciatively over me. "Baby, you look sexy as fuck."

I give a little curtsy. "I aim to please."

Garrick grabs me to him, smacking a loud kiss on my lips as he squeezes my ass. "You're gorgeous, and I'm a lucky man."

"You're about to be a very lucky woman!" Ellen squeals, and I don't miss how Garrick shoots daggers at her.

"What's going on?" I ask, my gaze bouncing between them.

"Your bestie has no poker face." Garrick leans around me to grab my bag. "Come on. I've got a surprise for you."

The surprise is a new car. Some kind of flashy BMW SUV. I'm so stunned I can't even form words. Ellen and Will are opening doors and oohing and aahing over it while Garrick stands in front of me, looking increasingly alarmed.

"You bought me a car?" I splutter, shock rendering my voice barely louder than a whisper.

"Yes." He takes cautious steps toward me. "If you don't like the color or the make or model, we can get you something else."

"Why?" I stare at him as shock turns to anger. "Why did you buy me a car?"

"Because your car is on its last legs, babe, and I want you to have something safe for all the driving we'll be doing on weekends."

"I know my car has become unreliable, but it still drives fine." It's been in the garage a lot recently for one thing after another. "My plan was to save up to buy a car this summer."

"Well, now you won't have to." He smiles as he hands me the keys. "Take a look inside. Sit behind the wheel. See what it feels like."

"No." I throw the keys back at him, rubbing at a tense spot between my brows. "I can't let you buy me an expensive car, Garrick."

"Why the hell not?"

"Because it's too much! We've not even been dating a year!" I throw my hands in the air.

"Who gives a fuck how long we've been dating?" he shouts, my anger sparking his. "You're going to be my wife one day, and I want to know you're safe. Why does everything have to be such a big fucking deal with you? Most girls would be knocking me to the ground and dry humping me by now. But not you. You have to give me shit for doing something nice. What the hell is your problem?"

I shove my finger in his chest. "My problem is, I can buy my own fucking car! I don't need you bankrolling my future, Garrick! You know I like to be independent. Why is this such a surprise to you?"

"Maybe because I thought we'd moved beyond all this bullshit over my money, but I can see I was wrong."

Ellen and Will are nowhere to be seen, and I guess they must have slipped back inside the building when we started arguing. They're probably afraid it's contagious.

I work hard to calm down. I know he means well, and I'm coming across as ungrateful. But he just doesn't get it, and it's damn frustrating at times. "Garrick, I love you, and I love how generous you are."

"Obviously not enough, or you'd accept the fucking car," he hisses.

"Being independent is important to me. I've been raised by women who instilled that repeatedly in me." I thump a fist over my chest. "It's deeply ingrained in here. I know you only want to help, but you've got to let me do things my way. I want to support myself."

"Is that the whole truth, or is this to do with my mother?"

"It's mostly the truth, but I won't lie and say what your mother thinks of me has no bearing. If I accept this car, she'll feel vindicated in calling me a gold digger."

"Fuck what she thinks, sunshine." His anger fades as he steps up to me. "I just want you to be safe. Protected. Cared for."

"I know." I rest my head on his chest, clinging to him with pain in my heart.

"I don't want to undermine you. I'm trying here, Stevie. I'm really trying, but everything I do seems to be the wrong thing. I don't know what else to do."

"This isn't about you. It's my hang-up. I'll try to work on it, but you can't keep forcing the issue."

He sighs heavily. "It's getting late. We should make a move. Why don't you drive the car to Ravenna and see how it feels?" He holds up his palms. "No pressure or expectations. If you don't want it, I'll return it."

"Of course, I'll want it if I drive it! That's not the point." I step back and rub my temples. Who the fuck wouldn't want such a gorgeous car? She's a beauty, and if I'd bought it with my own money, I'd be champing at the bit to drive it. But I didn't pay a penny for it, and therein lies my problem. "How about I drive my CR-V home? You can park the BMW in my spot while I'm gone, and I promise I'll think about it?"

"You're not saying no?"

"I'm saying I'll think about it. It's not a yes or a no."

He considers that for a moment. "Okay. Let's go."

I let Garrick drive to keep the peace. I'm lost in thought most of the journey, wondering if I'm cut out for relationships. I don't seem very good at it. When things are great, they are incredible, and I'm deliriously happy. But when shit goes down, it makes me feel like a worthless piece of crap.

Garrick is a good guy, and I'm beginning to think he deserves someone better than me. Someone who appreciates everything he brings to the table. Not someone with deep-seated fears and multiple hang-ups who can't accept the intensity of his love or the many extravagant ways he likes to show it.

"I'll return it," he says when we're close to the exit for Ravenna. "I thought it'd make you happy. Instead, you're miserable."

"I told you I'd think about it, and I will."

"I already know what your decision will be, and so do you." He uses the blinker and takes the left exit. "Do you not see a future with me? Is this what it's really about?"

I sit up straighter. "This is about you buying me a fifty-thousand-dollar car."

"Ninety," he says, tearing around the bend too fast for my liking. "It was ninety thousand dollars."

My jaw slackens. I'm definitely getting him to return it now. I'd be a basket case driving around in a car that's worth so much.

"Slow down!" I shout as he almost hits the rail at the side of the road.

"Fuck!" His face turns ghostly white as the car hurdles down the last stretch of the exit toward the busy road.

"You're going too fast!" I scream, starting to worry. "Slow down!"

"I can't!" he yells, repeatedly pressing his foot down on the brake. "The brakes aren't working!"

"Oh my god." Terror, unlike anything I've ever felt before,

powers through me as we race downhill toward the intersection.

"Get in the brace position," Garrick shouts, turning the hazard lights on. Setting his palms down on the horn, he attempts to alert the traffic on the main road to our predicament.

Facing forward, with my head pressed firmly against the headrest, I pray like I have never prayed before. I'm shaking and trembling all over, and it feels surreal as my life flashes in front of my face. The busy road approaches, and nausea travels up my throat. We are powerless to do anything but brace ourselves and pray.

"Stevie!" Garrick yells, panic and fear lacing his tone. "I love you. No matter what happens, you are the best thing that ever happened to me."

I'm sobbing and screaming as we careen onto the main road, and my bones rattle as the first impact is felt when a vehicle viciously slams into us. Screeching metal, squealing tires, and the shattering of glass accost my eardrums as we spin round and round, hitting off other vehicles as we spiral out of control. White spots fly across my retinas, and I'm lightheaded and nauseated as I'm jostled violently behind my seat belt when the car flips upside down and spins. "Garrick!" I cry out in between screaming. "I love you!" My head slams brutally against the side of my CR-V, and the last thing I think before I black out is I should have accepted the car.

Chapter Thirty-Five
Stevie

An irritating persistent beeping noise rouses me from sleep. Hushed whispering tickles my eardrums as I slowly come to. Blinking my eyes open, I wince as the glare of the overhead light ignites a pounding in my head.

"Sweetie. It's okay. I'm here. Nana is too." Mom's soft voice is laced with concern as my eyes shutter, and a moan filters from my dry lips.

My tongue feels superglued to the roof of my mouth, and my throat aches as I swallow thickly. I attempt to move onto my side, but my limbs are lethargic, and they refuse to cooperate. Forcing my eyes to open again, I wince a second time as glaring light pummels my skull.

"I'm turning the main light off." Nana pads to the wall to flick the switch, plunging the room into semi-darkness. The only illumination now is from the recessed lighting by the door and trickles of sneaky daylight filtering in through the window blind.

Slowly, I take in my surroundings. My horror grows as I note the pale gray walls, my position on an elevated hospital bed, the dresser and table off to one side housing copious vases with vibrant flowers, boxes of sweets and chocolates, and cards, and a machine beeping someplace behind me.

Instant panic consumes me as the events of the car accident resurface in my mind, and it's like being punched in the gut. Air wheezes out of my mouth in strangled puffs as a surge of adrenaline courses through my veins. "Garrick," I croak as tears instantly form in my eyes. "Where's Garrick?" I frantically scan the small private room, but it's only me, Mom, and Nana in here.

Nana and Mom exchange a pained look, and terror has a vise grip on my heart. The beeping from the machine accelerates as I struggle to breathe. "Mom!" I rasp over a scraping throat. "Where is he?" I move onto my side, ignoring the heaviness cloaking my bones as I attempt to pry the covers from my body. Tubes run from my hand to a drip propped alongside my bed. "Where is my boyfriend?!" I scream, my gaze bouncing from Mom to Nana. "Tell me!" I try to get up as Mom stands, crouching over me with tears in her eyes.

The door to the room bursts open, and two female nurses rush in.

"Shush, honey," the older lady with the short gray hair says. "You need to calm down, Stevie."

"Nana." I turn pleading blurry eyes on my grandmother while the nurses add a different pouch to the drip. "Please."

She leans down, brushing delicate fingers against my cheek. "He's alive, Little Poppy. He's alive."

Temporary relief floods my veins until I see the doleful expression they share. The hand around my heart squeezes, constricting my oxygen supply until I can barely breathe. I force the question out of my mouth. "How...bad...is...he?" I can hear the hysteria peppering my stammering words as I try to force myself into an upright position.

The younger nurse gently pushes me back down, her mouth moving in speech, but I don't hear the words. All I can see are the tears clouding Mom's vision and the pain in Nana's eyes.

"Tell me!" I screech in a louder voice, barely feeling the pain the motion produces in my throat. Finding strength, I shove at the nurses and thrash around in the bed. "Take me to him!" I beg, fighting the nurses as they attempt to thwart my efforts to get up.

Nana leans down, putting her wrinkled face in mine. Her eyes are awash with compassion as she says, "Garrick is in a coma, sweetheart."

Her words hit me like a sledgehammer. A painful lump wedges in my throat, and an all-consuming pressure sits on my chest. "No!" I croak, sobbing as reality slams into me. "No!" I protest, slapping at the hands trying to restrain me as I lose it. "It's all my fault!" My eyes dart manically between Mom and Nana. "I should be in a coma, not him!" I can barely see through the tears falling relentlessly from my eyes. "I should have accepted the car, and I should have worn his ring on my main ring finger." I glance down at my right hand, and panic erupts from my chest. "My ring!" I shout in a hoarse voice. "Where's my ring! I need to find it!" I thrash around again, howling as pain rips through me of the physical and emotional kind.

"Sweetheart, it's okay, it's okay." Mom reaches out, trying to console me. "I have your ring and your locket. They were with the things recovered from the car. Relax."

"Here, Little Poppy." Nana slides the ring on my left hand as my sobs reach epic levels of hysteria.

"Garrick!" I slur, fighting to keep my eyes open as whatever sedative the nurses administered starts entering my blood stream.

"Shush, honey." Nana and Mom are both crying as the older nurse urges me to calm down before I exacerbate my injuries.

"It's my fault." Agony attacks my heart, battering it until it feels like there's nothing left of the organ. "It's my fault," I mumble just before the world goes dark and quiet again.

When I wake the next time, Mom is alone sitting by my bed with a book open on her lap. The room is much darker, and the only sound is the steady beep, beep from the medical machine.

"Honey." Mom sets her book down and pulls her chair in closer to my bed. "How are you feeling?"

"Garrick," I whisper over the clawing pain of my throat. Tears instantly well in my eyes as I look down and spot the poppy ring on my left ring finger. "How..." I can't get any more words past the ragged lump in my throat and the suffocating pain in my chest. It feels like I'm dying.

My sobs and the repetitive beeping of the machine are the only sounds in the room as I slowly self-destruct.

Sorrow is etched across Mom's face as she clasps my hand in her warm one. Moisture pools in her tired eyes, and dark circles cling to the skin underneath. "Garrick is a fighter, and I know he's fighting to come back to you. He has the best doctors working on his case, and he has youth on his side. We have to cling to hope and keep the faith."

"What if he doesn't ever wake up?" I wail.

"Don't think like that. It's early, and there is still hope. A coma is the brain's way of repairing itself after significant trauma. His brain and body are taking the time they need to heal, and when he's ready, he'll wake up."

I wish I had Mom's optimism. I know she fully believes if she says it enough she'll manifest it. But I'm a more pragmatic being, and I need more than hope and faith to cling to.

I will never forgive myself for this, and if he doesn't wake up, I don't want to live.

"It's my fault," I choke out as tears cascade down my cheeks. "This is all on me, and I hate myself."

"It was an accident, honey. A tragic accident. You have to stop hating yourself for something that wasn't your fault."

I shake my head, crying out when pain splinters my skull.

"Shush, sweetheart." Mom carefully brushes hair back from my brow. "You need to remain calm, Stevie, and you can't make any sudden movements. You have a concussion, a broken arm, and two broken ribs."

"I need to see him."

"Only family is permitted in ICU for now, but Hugh is working on getting you in to visit him." She kisses my cheek. "Hugh and Dawn have stopped by every day to see you, and Hugh even arranged for you to be transferred to this private room."

"How long have I been out?" I ask as Mom lifts a pink plastic cup with a lid and straw from my bedside table.

"It's been two days since the accident," she confirms, pressing a button on the bed to elevate it until I'm in a more upright position. "The nurses say it's important for you to drink plenty of water, or I can get you some ice chips if your throat is too sore." She places the straw to my lips. "Just small sips for now."

I take a few sips as Mom holds the cup and straw to my mouth. When she sets it back on the bedside table, I turn my head to stare at her. Dried tear tracks tighten the skin on my face. "How bad are Garrick's injuries?"

She rests her hand on mine while peering deep into my eyes. "He broke one arm, both legs, and three ribs, but the damage to his spine and his head trauma are the most concerning injuries. He seems to have borne the brunt of the initial impact." Tears pool in her eyes. "You are so lucky you weren't more seriously injured." She swipes at the tears coursing down her cheeks. "The terror I felt when I got that phone call will stay with me for the rest of my life. Nana and I were so worried. Scared of what we'd find when we got here. We prayed nonstop the entire ride to the hospital, begging God to let you be okay."

"Was anyone else hurt?" I brave asking.

"One male driver has whiplash and a concussion, and a couple of other people were taken to the hospital to be checked out, but they only have minor injuries. You two suffered the most severe damage."

A pregnant pause ensues as I let that intel settle in my tormented brain. "Where am I?" I ask, realizing I don't know which hospital I'm in.

"You're at UW Medical Center – Montlake, and you are both in the best hands."

"Garrick bought me a car, and I refused it." A sob erupts from my lips as more tears spring to my eyes.

"I know, honey. Ellen explained. But that doesn't mean this is your fault. It was an accident. You can't blame yourself."

"Ellen was here?"

"She came immediately when she heard the news, and she stayed here all day yesterday. Hadley too. I made them leave last night. I knew you wouldn't want either of them missing their exams, and before you panic, I have spoken with UO, and they'll let you take your exams over the summer break, whenever you feel ready, so you don't need to worry about that."

Right now, that's the least of my worries. "Garrick wouldn't be in a coma if I'd said yes to the car. Even if I'd just agreed to drive it without making a commitment, like he suggested, this wouldn't have happened." Anguished sobs rip through the air as I cry. "Why did I have to be so stubborn? Why couldn't I have just accepted it? Why am I so selfish and stupid?" Pain spears me all over, and I'm choking on air as I struggle to breathe. "I want to die!" I howl. "I want to trade my life for his because he doesn't deserve this, but I do!"

"No, honey. Don't say that. Neither of you deserve what happened." Mom perches on the side of my bed, wrapping me in a gentle embrace, holding me tenderly against her chest as I cry and cry, soaking her blouse and making my eyes sting. Her tears mingle with mine for a few minutes before she pulls herself together. "Honey, please, you need to calm down. The best thing you can do for Garrick is to get better so you can be there for him. He wouldn't want you blaming yourself. You didn't know the brakes would fail. It's not your fault. It was a terrible, terrible accident."

The door opens and closes, and Mom briefly glances over her shoulder, getting rid of whomever it is with a look of silent communication. "Garrick will need you to be strong for the both of you," she adds, softly stroking my hair. "And you need to prioritize your recovery."

"How long do I have to be here?" I ask when I finally stop crying, looking up at her through bloodshot throbbing eyes. My head is killing me, and I ache all over. It seems there is no part of me that isn't sore. My gaze treks over the multitude of bruises covering my arms, and I'm glad I'm suffering. I deserve every bit of pain I'm feeling and more.

"They want to keep you under observation for another few days, but you should be able to go home by the weekend." She dots kisses into my hair. "You're going to need a lot of rest, but we'll make sure you get to visit Garrick every day."

"Where is Nana?"

"I sent her home to get some sleep. She was exhausted." Mom kisses my head one final time before releasing me. "You should try to sleep more too. Your body needs it to heal."

The following morning, I'm taken in a wheelchair to the ICU to visit my boyfriend. Only two to three visitors are allowed in at one time. Garrick's parents are with him now, and I figure they want privacy, so I wait with the nurse and Mom in the private waiting room until Dawn and Hugh leave Garrick's room.

They join us in the waiting area a few minutes later. "Sweetheart, it's good to see you awake." Hugh leans down and hugs me.

"I'm so sorry," I cry, hating how tears instantly swim in my eyes. It's like my tear ducts got injured in the accident as well. "This is all my fault." Choking sobs cleave from my mouth as pain tears across my chest, adding to my heartbreak.

When I'm conscious, I exist with a constant constricting pain in my chest. My heart is a shredded mass of tissue, broken beyond repair.

"I'm glad we are on the same page about something," a snooty unfortunately familiar female says as the door flies open behind me, admitting another visitor.

"That's uncalled for and untrue, Ivy," Hugh says, straightening up as Mom places her hand on my arm and stands stoically by my side.

"It was a tragic accident," Dawn agrees, softly squeezing my hand.

"Garrick would want us rallying around Stevie, not blaming her for this," Hugh adds, and I wonder if he knows about the BMW. I doubt he does. I know Garrick's dad is a good man, but surely even he would struggle to accept I'm blameless if he knew the truth.

"Everything turned to shit for my son the moment he met

that gold-digging slut," Ivy hisses, her words infused with the usual poison she reserves for me.

Mom spins around with fire in her eyes. "Would you like to say that to my face?"

"Garrick loves Stevie, and your hurtful accusation is the last thing anyone needs right now." Dawn levels Ivy with a cool glare.

"You agreed not to come until twelve," Hugh says, sliding his arm around Dawn's waist.

"You knew Stevie was coming to see Garrick, and you planned this on purpose," Dawn adds in a clipped tone. "You should be ashamed of yourself, Ivy. Look at the poor girl. Stevie is as devastated as we are. Bickering about blame is pointless when our son is in there fighting for his life." Her voice cracks, and she bursts out crying.

Hugh is barely holding it together, and silent tears crawl down my face and drip over my chin.

Mom squeezes my hand, and when I look up at her, she is crying too.

"Don't lecture me about how I feel," Ivy snaps. She's the only one in the room with dry eyes. "Garrick is my only flesh and blood. He's my everything, and all that little bitch has done is try to take him away from me." Ivy shoves Dawn out of the way and thrusts her cosmetically altered face all up in mine. "You better hope and pray my son recovers because I will make your life a misery if he doesn't."

Chapter Thirty-Six
Stevie

"Don't mind her, Stevie." Dawn crouches down in front of me, gently wiping the tears from my face. Ivy departed after making her threat and it's good riddance. "She's a miserable bitch who takes her unhappiness out on everyone around her."

"She's upset and not able to express it," Hugh says.

I can see where Garrick gets this side of his personality from now. I don't think Hugh Allen has said a bad word about anyone at any time in his life. He always tries to see the best in everyone. It's probably how that poisonous bitch managed to get him to marry her.

Dawn straightens up, leveling her husband with a stern look. "You need to stop making excuses for that woman, and I'm done biting my tongue. She's a horrible, selfish, uncaring bitch, and I hate that we're saddled with her."

Internally, I'm fist pumping the air and high-fiving Garrick's stepmom.

"I don't want her upsetting Stevie," Mom says.

"We'll work out a roster of visiting times," Hugh confirms.

"We're both listed as family spokespersons, so I'll talk to the nursing staff, and I'll talk to my ex-wife." He pats my shoulder. "I'll ensure she stays away from Stevie."

"Make sure she doesn't try to have her banned," Dawn adds.

"I will ensure the nursing staff knows Stevie is on the priority list and no one is to remove her visitation rights without consultation with me. If she tries anything, I'll deal with it."

"Thank you, Hugh," Mom says.

"I'm sorry," I whisper, "I don't mean to cause extra trouble."

"You're not, sweetie." Dawn's smile is sad. "This isn't on you."

Yeah. Pretty sure it is.

But I don't argue the point.

I just want to see him.

"Can I go in now?"

"Of course." Hugh gently pats my shoulder.

"You should prepare yourself, Stevie." Dawn bends down in front of me again. "He doesn't look much like himself."

I nod even though I'm in no way prepared.

Pain has a stranglehold on my throat and my heart as the nurse wheels me out of the waiting room and down the hallway toward Garrick's ICU room. I sanitize my hands and put on a medical mask at the door. "Do you want me to come in with you, honey?" Mom asks. A veil of concern shrouds her face.

"No," I whisper. "I need to do this alone."

"I'll be right out here if you change your mind."

My heart plummets to my toes, and acid churns in my gut as the nurse wheels me into Garrick's room.

I desperately need to see him, but at the same time, I don't want to.

It's going to make this real.

And I don't know if I'm strong enough to handle this horrific new reality.

It seems there is no limit to my cowardice.

Every time I think about my boyfriend being in a coma, I break down in floods of tears.

Garrick is always so full of life, and I don't think I can bear to see him any other way.

Especially when I know I'm responsible for his condition.

Tears are already forming in my eyes. This is going to hurt so bad.

I don't look up at him as the nurse positions me alongside his bed, fixing the freestanding drip beside my wheelchair before she discreetly slips out of the room. It's eerily silent in the room except for the annoying beeping of monitoring devices and a sucking mechanical sound emitting from the machine that's helping him to breathe.

Tears roll down my face, plopping onto my clasped hands on my lap. I draw in big lungsful of air as I try to pluck up the courage to look at Garrick.

I'm petrified.

Shaking and trembling all over.

Scared to be confronted with the evidence of every mistake I have ever made when it comes to this man.

It feels like my heart is disintegrating behind my rib cage.

I don't know if I'll ever be able to look at myself in a mirror again, knowing I did this to him.

Finding strength from somewhere, I lift my head and look up at him. More tears spill from my eyes as I stare in horror at my love. His arms are visible under the short sleeves of his hospital gown, and a cast covers one while the other is heavily bandaged. Both legs are encased in plaster and slightly elevated within some metal contraption.

I'm shaking all over and sobbing as I reluctantly drag my

gaze up his body to his face. My hand goes over my mouth of its own volition when I stare at Garrick's almost unrecognizable features.

The head of the bed is elevated, and his neck is in some kind of brace. Garrick's cheeks are puffy, one eye is red and swollen, and his entire face is bloated underneath a multitude of cuts, abrasions, and bruises. His hair—his beautiful, gorgeous hair—is all gone, shorn tight to his scalp and completely shaved on one side of his head. A large incision runs from just in front of his ear, curving along his skull and ending at the top center of his forehead. Steel stiches hold the sealed skin in place, and a cluster of rectangular white bandages cover the back of his head. Small tubes run from his nose and mouth into larger tubes hooked up to a ventilator.

My sobs ring out in the room, audible over the beeping of the machines and the mechanical clacking sound of the machine as it helps him to breathe. Pain eviscerates me on all sides, and I clutch an arm around my middle, whimpering and sobbing as I stare at my comatose boyfriend.

Nothing could have prepared me for this.

This is truly awful.

Way worse than I imagined.

I want to die.

I want to trade places with him and be the one hooked up to machines and tubes with half my body in a plaster cast. "I'm so sorry, Garrick," I sob. "This is all my fault, and I am so, so sorry. I wish I could go back and do everything differently," I cry, tentatively reaching out to touch his hand. His flesh is warm, but it offers little comfort. Curling my hand underneath his, I am careful not to displace the tubing that links to a drip. "I love you, and I need you to wake up, baby. Please wake up. Please be okay." I cling to his hand, dusting soft kisses over his skin as I pray and beg and plead.

"Come on, honey," Mom says sometime later, materializing at my side with the nurse. I hadn't even heard them coming into the room. "You need to rest."

Sympathy splays across the young nurse's face as she hands me a box of tissues. I wipe my nose and rub at my eyes as tears continue to leak my sorrow. Placing one last kiss on his hand, I raise bleary eyes to his face. "I love you, Garrick. Please don't give up. Keep fighting. I'll be back. Every day. I'm not going anywhere. I won't ever leave you."

Silent tears stream down my face as I'm wheeled out of the room. Ivy bitchface is out in the hallway, waiting to see her son, but we purposely avoid looking at one another. Tracing the ink on my wrist with my fingers the entire way back to my room, I hope the matching Celtic shield knot on Garrick's skin lives up to the symbolism. That it protects him and imbues him with power, strength, and endurance because he's going to need every bit of help he can get.

***

The next few days pass by in a numbed daze. It seems I've broken my tear ducts, and now I can't produce a single tear. My vocal cords won't cooperate either. I'm like a living corpse. A shell of a person who has lost the will to survive. Seeing Garrick like that has irreparably broken me. I'm drowning in guilt and self-loathing, and I pray every night, begging God to take my life force and funnel it to Garrick. To sacrifice me so the best man I know can live.

Mom and Nana sit by my bed all day—taking it in turns at nights—and they chat away, trying to engage me in conversation, but I just lie there, staring into space, running everything through my sore head, wishing I had a time machine so I could go back and change the events of that day.

Hadley shows up every evening after her exams, and she does her best to cheer me up as well, but it's useless. She burst into tears when she visited Garrick, and I know she's been in contact with Hudson. Poor Hudson. He wants to be here, but he's on the East Coast, taking his finals this week at Brown. I've been texting with him every day, and I know he's purposely checking in on me because it's what Garrick would expect of him.

I know everyone is worried about me, and I want to stop moping so it lessens their concern, but I can't summon the strength to fake it. Mom, Nana, and Hads play my favorite music, bring my favorite foods, and stream my favorite movies and shows to raise my spirits, but it's a futile exercise.

The only thing that would lift my spirits is Garrick waking up, and he's showing no signs of it.

Dawn and Hugh have been keeping us updated, much to Ivy's disgust. If she had her way, I'd have been kicked out of the hospital by now and banned from visiting her son's bedside. Hugh has promised me he won't let her do that, and I'm so grateful for his support and graciousness.

I hate seeing Garrick in such a condition, but it would be so much worse if I couldn't see him at all.

I have been visiting him as much as I can in between sleeping and trying to heal.

Hudson's father, Harvey Edwards, is one of the country's most skilled neurosurgeon's and he is the primary neurosurgeon assigned to Garrick. It's fortunate he works here, and this hospital is an acute care hospital and home to one of the largest and most experienced neurology and neurosurgery teams in the US.

Harvey has consulted with esteemed colleagues, and they are discussing every aspect of Garrick's case. The more time passes without him coming out of the coma, the less likely it is he will, or so we've been told. Nerves have been severed in his spinal cord, and Harvey has warned us it's likely he'll suffer some form of paralysis. He underwent brain surgery to relieve pressure on his brain, and while the surgery was a success, they can't say what the aftereffects of his brain trauma might be either.

Hugh relayed that shocking news this morning, and after initially being inconsolable, I've decided to worry about one thing at a time. Right now, Garrick waking up is the priority, and it's what I'm focusing on.

As long as he is alive.

What happens after that can be dealt with one step at a time. So, for now, I'm trying to put those other fears into a box to worry about at a later point.

When Saturday rolls around, my doctor arrives to confirm I'm being discharged at noon. While Mom handles the paperwork, I get dressed and pack up my things. The nurse helps me with my arm sling, and then I make the solo journey on foot to Garrick's room to see him. I'm still weak, and my ribs throb like a bitch, so it takes far longer to get to the ICU, but I need to start reclaiming some independence.

A set routine is in place where I visit him for an hour in the morning and an hour in the afternoon after Ivy is gone, and I usually spend a couple hours at night sitting with Hugh by Garrick's bedside. We talk to him and among ourselves, trying to remain upbeat, but it's challenging.

Hugh regales me with stories from Garrick's childhood, and it's bittersweet learning of all his boyish escapades. Sometimes, we're too heartsore to talk, so we play Garrick's favorite songs. I asked Dawn and Mom to bring in some photos, and I pinned them and some of his get well cards to the walls because you're not allowed plants or flowers in the ICU, and I wanted to do something to make it look less clinical and more homey.

Dawn visits every day, but she can't stay for too long as someone has to be home for the twins. They are still at school, and they have a ton of after-school activities. Dawn and Hugh are keen not to disrupt their schedules, believing normalcy is important. John and Jacob are only eight and this has been super hard on them. They adore their big brother, and seeing him like this reduced them to tears, so the decision was taken not to have them visit every day. It's too much for them to handle.

I'm seated by Garrick's bed, holding his hand and staring at his face, willing him to wake up, like I always do, when there's a knock at the door. I glance over my shoulder as Ellen and Will step into the room. They haven't been able to visit all week because of exams, but Ellen has been calling and texting when she can.

"Hey, babe," Ellen rushes to my side, leaning down to hug me gently. "How are you holding up?"

I offer her a feeble smile and a weak shrug. Behind her, I watch the devastation wreaked on Will's face as he sees his friend for the first time since the accident. Tears prick his eyes, and he scrubs a hand back and forth across his mouth as he stares at Garrick. Will is leaning against the wall, like he needs it to prop him up, struggling to hold back tears.

"Oh god," Ellen whispers, tears instantly pouring down her face as she stares horror-struck at Garrick.

The shock of seeing him like this never subsides. Every time I visit, I have to suck in brave breaths before opening the door. It doesn't get any easier seeing him lying there, so still and quiet, his broken body supported by braces and casts, all the color gone from his cheeks. Not getting to look into his gorgeous golden-greenish-brown eyes is torture as is not feeling his fingers curling around mine when I hold his hand.

Tears stab the backs of my eyes as I watch my best friend

cry and her boyfriend fight a multitude of emotions. But my tears don't fall. I feel weirdly numb even though I'm awash with powerful emotions that keep me awake at night.

"It doesn't look like him at all," Ellen wails, dropping into the chair beside me and clinging to my arm.

I stare at Garrick, seeing everything she sees, agreeing with it, but unable to voice those thoughts.

"This is awful, so awful." She clings to me harder. "I'm so sorry for your pain, babe. I can't even begin to imagine what you are going through."

"What *she's* going through?" Will barks. He stalks over to the bed. "What about what Garrick is going through?!" He jabs his finger in my face as he pins angry eyes on me. "Do you even care?"

"Of course, she cares!" Ellen retorts when I'm incapable of a response. "Why the hell would you say that?"

"Doesn't much look like it from where I'm standing."

I stare at him in a daze, wanting to defend myself, but how can I? We all know I'm responsible for this, and Will has every right to his rage.

"Cat got your tongue, Stevie? Or are you doing what you do best? Retreating into your selfish shell and pushing everyone else away?"

"Stop it!" Ellen stands, spitting fire at her boyfriend. "I know you're upset and angry, we all are, but you can't take it out on Stevie."

"Why not?" He folds his arms and glares at me. "Let's not beat around the bush. Everyone knows why my best friend is lying in this bed." His voice cracks, and he pauses for a few seconds to compose himself. "This is your fault." He waves his finger in my face. "You turned him down, *again*, and he was only driving that piece-of-shit car because you refused the new one he bought you because *he wanted you to be safe!*" He roars the last part, dragging out the words.

"Will, stop this. Please." Ellen reaches for her boyfriend, but he shoves her away. "It's not fair. It was an accident. Stevie didn't want this to happen, and look at her! She's traumatized, and you're only making it worse."

"I should've told him to break up with you when he sought my advice," he continues, tearing another strip from my fragile heart. "I selfishly kept my true thoughts to myself because I didn't want shit to get awkward in my relationship, but he deserved better than you. You were pushing him away and sabotaging the relationship on purpose. Were you going to break up with him? Is that what you were planning after summer break?"

"Okay. That is fucking enough!" Ellen roars at her boyfriend while I sit there in the same numb fugue state. "You are way out of line, Will. Garrick would not want you speaking to Stevie this way or pointing the finger of blame in her direction."

"It doesn't matter what Garrick would want," he chokes out, swinging his gaze to his friend on the bed. "He's incapable of voicing his opinions." Tears stream down his cheeks. "If he doesn't come out of this, I will never forgive you. Never." He drills me with a dark look before storming out of the room, leaving thick tension in his wake.

A shuddering breath escapes Ellen's lips as she slumps into the chair beside me, briefly burying her head in her hands. Tears are stuck to her lashes when she lifts her chin. "He doesn't mean it, babe. He's just really upset. He's been lashing out all week. Don't take any of that to heart because it's not true. Deep down, Will knows that."

"It is true though," I croak, almost choking over the emotion clogging my throat. "Will is right to throw all of that at me and more." I stare into her forlorn eyes. "It *is* my fault. I'm the stupid bitch who refused his sweet, loving, protective gesture, and I'm going to have to live with the guilt of that decision for the rest of my life."

***

The story continues in **Say It's Forever**. Available now in ebook, paperback, alternate paperback and hardcover.

This is Garrick's twenty-first birthday scene.

GARRICK

"I think we have a plan," Bria says, smiling as she stands. The hip single-mom with a quirky sense of style is the photographer assigned to us today for our boudoir couples shoot. Something Stevie just sprung on me an hour ago when we checked in to one of Seattle's best five-star hotels for the night. "I'll leave you to get changed," she adds, eyeballing my girlfriend. "Pop into the room next door when you're ready, and Steph will do your hair and makeup." Bria slips out of the room.

"Are you sure you're okay with this?" Stevie asks, coming up to me and placing her hands on my chest.

"Hell yeah. What's not to love?" I lean down and plant a passionate kiss on her lips. "You are spoiling me, sunshine."

"You're only twenty-one once, and I want to ensure you have the best time."

"I'm with you. Of course, I will."

"Always so romantic." She runs her fingers along the light layer of stubble on my chin and cheeks.

"I understand why you made me pack my guitar now."

Stevie waggles her brows, tossing me a flirty grin. "That's not all I packed."

My cock jerks at her insinuation, and my mind goes into overdrive imagining what she has brought to wear. "I can't wait to see."

"I love you." She stretches up to kiss me.

I love how easily those words slip from her lips now. There was a time I wondered if I'd ever hear them. Our one-year anniversary is approaching, and I can't wait to celebrate the best year of my life with the only woman who will ever hold my heart. "I love you so much. More than I can express."

Her features soften as she slides her arms around my neck. "Happy birthday, Garrick."

"Go get ready, babe." I squeeze her ass. "We have some sexy pics to shoot."

***

The bulge pressing against the side of my unbuttoned jeans only adds to the electricity zinging in the air as I sprawl on a chair, bare-chested, with my legs spread, naked feet to the floor, as my love stands in front of me looking like she stepped straight out of a dream. For our first scene, Stevie is a dominatrix in a skimpy, black corset-top with a matching thong. Red garters hold sheer black stockings in place, and she holds a leather whip in one hand. Her fiery hair is hanging down her back in thick, lustrous waves. Vibrant red lips stir my blood, and my erection swells imagining her mouth on my cock.

"That's it," Bria says as I eye-fuck my love like I'm seconds from shoving her up against the wall and driving inside her.

Stevie is a natural, switching into different poses as Bria works around us. I have almost forgotten the photographer is here. A couple of glasses of champagne while we were getting ready has helped to settle any nerves, and I'm really enjoying this.

My eyes are out on stalks as Stevie stalks toward me with a seductive, confident strut, sashaying her hips and thrusting her chest out. Her tits are pushed up high in the corset, and when she leans down over me, I bury my face in her chest and inhale deeply. All while Bria clicks away in the background.

My hands roam her gorgeous body as she stretches out over me with her legs arched over the side of the chair. Her grin is downright devilish as she leans in, grabbing one of my nipples with her teeth and tugging. I claim her lips in a punishing kiss as my cock leaks precum.

Our second scene is a bedroom scene and there's no disguising my boner in the form-fitting black boxers I'm wearing. Stevie is wearing a virginal white silk nightie as she lies provocatively on the bed while I crawl over her tempting body. We kiss and grope as I settle between her legs, pushing my crotch against her quickly dampening panties.

Our third scene is on a window seat that looks out over a courtyard garden. Stevie straddles my legs in a pretty gold bra and panties set while I serenade her with my guitar. After I set it down, she grinds on top of me as I grab her ass and we kiss like the world might be ending.

Bria finishes with a few more romantic shots of me holding Stevie in my arms as her back rests against my naked chest. It's probably the most intimate pic of the shoot. Other less-sexy pics are close-ups of us staring into one another's eyes or tenderly embracing.

"That's a wrap, guys," Bria says. "I have photographed a lot of couples, but this was definitely one of my hottest shoots. Your intense chemistry will look incredible in these pics. I can't wait to see them."

"Thanks, Bria." Stevie slides off my lap. "This was so much fun. Even better than I expected."

"You're welcome." She waggles her brows as she backs away. "I'll give you two a little time to...get dressed." Her grin is so wide it threatens to split her face in two. "When you're ready, come out to the office, and we can look at some shots."

She slips out of the room, and I waste no time scooping my love up and tossing her over my shoulder.

"Garrick!" Stevie is giggling as I all but race to the changing room.

"You heard her. We basically have permission and it's just as well because if I don't get inside you stat, I'm liable to explode in my jeans."

I slam the door shut with my foot before placing Stevie on the ground and backing her up against the wall. "That was incredible, and I have never been so turned on," I admit, pushing her panties aside and driving two fingers inside her. A smirk plays over my lips. "Seems I'm not the only one."

Stevie yanks my boxers down to my knees and curls her warm fingers around my dick.

"Fuck," I rasp, jerking in her hand as I circle one finger around her glistening clit and suction my mouth around her nipple through her bra.

"Fuck me now, Garrick." Stevie strokes me fast. "I need you."

I make quick work of removing my boxers and her bra and panties and then I grip her hips, urging her to jump up and hug me with her legs. When she's in position, I push her against the wall and thrust inside her in one fast drive, swallowing her cries with a brutal kiss.

Stevie digs her nails into my back as I fuck her hard and fast against the wall. My lips travel from her delicious mouth to her fabulous tits as I pound into her with all the pent-up need that has been building for the past two hours.

"Garrick, fuck," she pants, grabbing handfuls of my hair. "I can't last. I'm going to come."

"Right there with you, babe," I grunt out, grabbing onto her ass as I thrust in deeper and harder.

We fall off the ledge together, kissing passionately to disguise our mutual moans.

After, I hold her against the wall with my dick still inside her, peppering soft kisses along her neck, never wanting to let go. "Best birthday ever," I mumble against her ear, and her chest rumbles with soft laughter.

Carefully setting her feet down on the carpet, I bundle her into my arms and hug her, soaking up every soft whimper, tender caress, and satisfied sigh, committing them all to my memory bank. "I love you," I say, pressing my lips to the top of her head.

"I love you too." She peers up at me. "I'm so glad we did this. I have never felt closer to you than I do at this moment."

"I know. I'm feeling it too." We continue to embrace, and I never want to break the spell, but Bria is waiting, and we can't stay here all night.

We get dressed and head out to the office where Bria shows us some photos from the shoot and we pick a few favorites. She'll have two twenty-page leather albums ready in a week for us to collect. I can't wait.

Exiting the studio hand in hand, we set out under a darkening sky and I'm happier than I've ever been walking the streets of the city I love with the girl I adore by my side.

Back in the hotel, we shower together, which leads to shower sex, and then we get dressed for dinner. Stevie has booked the rooftop restaurant in the hotel, and we enjoy a sumptuous dinner with cocktails and more champagne. After making love to my girl, I fall asleep with Stevie in my arms and the biggest smile on my face.

"Happy birthday to you. Happy birthday to you..." Stevie joins Dad and Dawn, the twins, Hudson, and my other friends, and extended family members, as they sing happy birthday to me the following night. Dawn organized a surprise party at the winery, catching me completely unaware. I thought we were just coming here for dinner with my dad, stepmom, and my brothers.

"Speech!" Will calls out after the singing has ended. He's smirking as he sways, with Ellen in his arms.

I'm not one to shy away from public speaking, so I have no issue in making an improvised speech. "Thank you all for coming. It's rarely I'm surprised, but Dawn and Dad did it tonight." I turn to where my dad and stepmom are hugging. "Thank you so much for organizing this tonight and for everything you have done for me over the years. I know I haven't always been easy to live with"—laughter rings out—"but you never begrudged me my feelings." They'll know what I'm referencing. "I love you."

Dawn rushes forward, enveloping me in a hug. "You make it easy to love you, Garrick." She clasps my face in her hands and tears are shining in her eyes. "The day I married your father, I knew I was getting a two-for-one special. You make me proud." She presses a kiss to my cheek. "It's been an honor watching you grow up."

A lump forms in my throat as I hug her tight. My eyes meet Stevie's over Dawn's head, and she's wiping tears while smiling.

When Dawn pulls back, I reach out my arm for my love. "I have someone else to thank." I reel Stevie into my body, wrapping my arm around her shoulders. "Stevie has made my birthday weekend extra special and just having her in my life is the icing on the cake." I peer deep into her eyes. "I love you and

I can't wait to spend every birthday with you." The crowd oohs and ahhs as I kiss her.

Music thumps out of speakers, and beer, wine and bubbly are freely flowing. Servers deposit platters of finger food on crowded tables as I mingle with guests, accepting congratulations, and making small talk. I keep one eye on Stevie, ensuring she's okay. She's currently talking with Hadley, Will, Ellen, and Noah and his new girlfriend, looking chill and relaxed.

"Happy birthday, dude." Hudson slaps me on the back. "I heard you had an interesting afternoon yesterday." He waggles his brows and smirks.

I let a grin run loose on my lips. "Hottest thing I've ever done."

"She's so good for you," he says, before lifting a beer bottle to his lips. "I've never seen you so happy."

"She's it for me. I'm going to marry her. Soon if I have my way. I have never been surer about anything."

"That's great, Gar. Stevie is amazing. Just apply the brakes a little, yeah? Not everyone is as self-assured as you, and you go a hundred miles an hour when it's something you want. Stevie strikes me as the type of girl you can't rush."

"I know who my girlfriend is." Irritation pricks my skin at his words, even if I know he means well. I'm a little touchy because Stevie and I are still arguing over her plans to graduate early and move to the city. No one needs to tell me how stubborn my girl is because I'm confronted with that reality all the time. I know I have to take it easy with her. I don't need my best buddy stating that fact.

He raises his palms. "I'm not saying you don't. Just give her time to get used to the idea. Like you did at the start. That's all I'm saying, and it's because I love you like a brother."

"Love you too, man." I pull him into a brief man-hug.

"Garrick. Sorry to interrupt," Dad says, materializing at our side. "Could we talk in private? I have something I want to show you outside."

"I'll catch you later," Hudson says, before walking off toward Hadley.

"Let me check in with Stevie, real quick," I tell Dad, making my way across the room to my girlfriend. Sliding my arm around her waist, I tug her in close. "Dad wants to show me something, so I'll be gone for a bit," I whisper in her ear. "Are you okay?"

"I'm fine." She beams up at me. "Go spend time with your dad."

I kiss her deeply, ignoring the catcalls and whistles from our friends. Breaking our kiss, I place my mouth to her ear. "I won't be long. Behave."

She blows me a kiss as I walk off, sporting a wide grin.

Dad and I head outside together, making casual talk as we walk away from the main part of the winery toward the private residential area at the back of the property.

"How are things going with Stevie?" he asks as I shove my hands in my pockets to keep warm. Although it's April, and the weather is warmer, it still gets chilly at night.

"Great. Everything is perfect."

"She's a lovely girl and we're both very fond of her."

"She likes you and Dawn, too." Neither of us mentions the elephant in the room because talk of Mom has no place on a night like tonight.

"You did a great job here last summer." Dad says. "And I want you to know I'll be signing the winery over to you officially after you graduate."

My eyes pop wide. "Seriously?" I knew it'd all be mine one day, but I didn't think Dad was going to do this.

"You have a maturity and business acumen that belies your age," he adds, as we round the bend and bypass the family cabin. "And I know your enthusiasm is genuine." He pins admiring eyes on me. "Honestly, it's more than I dared to hope for. I would never have pushed you into the business if you didn't want it. The same way, I won't force the twins either. I plan to give you the winery and the twins can share responsibility for the lumber yard if they want it. If not, that will be yours to run too someday."

"I don't know what to say."

"You don't have to say anything, Garrick. I just want you to know I believe in you, and I want to help you plan for your future." He stops before an unspoiled area in front of the forest with magnificent views over the winery. "I thought this plot would make an excellent home," he adds, handing me the envelope he's been holding in his hand the entire time. "Planning permission is approved for a six-bedroom, two-story home. You can work out the details with the architect and building contractor I hired. It's on our dime. We want to give you the best start in life."

My jaw trails the ground. I was not expecting this at all.

"Consider it a combined birthday and wedding gift." Tears well in his eyes. "I'm proud to call you my son, Garrick, and so proud of the man you're becoming." He grips my shoulders tight, as I swallow over the messy ball of emotion in my throat. "You remind me a lot of me at your age. You know what you want, and you go for it." He squeezes my shoulders. "I wish you every happiness for the future and I'm excited about all that's coming for you."

"Thanks, Dad." I drag him into an embrace. "Thanks so much for everything."

"We should get back. Our women are waiting."

I'm floating on a cloud as we walk back to the party, and I'm bursting to tell Stevie the news. We get to build our own house! In a special place, that means a lot to both of us. But

Hudson's earlier warning is playing on a loop in my mind. I'm not sure Stevie will appreciate Dad's gesture as much as I do. She's got some serious hang-ups about money. I partly blame my mother for calling her a gold-digger, but Stevie's fierce need for independence is behind a lot. I love that she's independent, and she isn't after me for my money, but it's aggravating when I want to shower her with gifts and treat her like a princess, and she won't let me.

Laughter and warmth greet us as we step back inside the function room, where the party is in full swing. My eyes gravitate to Stevie, like always. She's laughing with Hudson at something Hadley is saying. I love her, and I want to tell her what Dad has done for us, but this isn't the time. So, I stow the secret deep down inside, deciding I'll tell her when the opportunity is right.

***

The story continues in **_Say It's Forever_**. Available now in ebook, paperback, alternate paperback and hardcover.

I was suffocating under an avalanche of guilt and grief until *he* entered my life.

The hot, slightly older guy who looked like a cross between a tatted biker and a billionaire businessman.

Beck understood me, and our situation, in a way no one else could.

As a friend, he held me together and helped to piece back the shredded fragments of my heart.

I didn't mean to fall in love with him—it just happened.

No one understands, least of all me.

Now my heart is split in two, and I don't know what to do.

Is my first love my one true love? Or do I belong with the man who brought me to life?

CLAIM YOUR FREE EBOOK – ONLY AVAILABLE TO NEWSLETTER SUBSCRIBERS!

The boy who broke my heart is now the man who wants to mend it.

Jared was my everything until an ocean separated us and he abandoned me when I needed him most.

He forgot the promises he made.

Forgot the love he swore was eternal.

It was over before it began.

Now, he's a hot commodity, universally adored, and I'm the woman no one wants.

Pining for a boy who no longer exists is pathetic. Years pass, men come and go, but I cannot move on.

Tell it To My Heart

I didn't believe my fractured heart and broken soul could endure any more pain. Until Jared rocks up to the art gallery where I work, with his fiancée in tow, and I'm drowning again.

Seeing him brings everything to the surface, so I flee. Placing distance between us again, I'm determined to put him behind me once and for all.

Then he reappears at my door, begging me for another chance.

I know I should turn him away.

Try telling that to my heart.

This angsty, new adult romance is a FREE full-length ebook, exclusively available to newsletter subscribers.

Type this link into your browser to claim your free copy:
https://bit.ly/TITMHFBB

OR

Scan this code to claim your free copy:

About the Author

Siobhan Davis is a *USA Today, Wall Street Journal*, and Amazon Top 5 bestselling romance author. **Siobhan** writes emotionally intense stories with swoon-worthy romance, complex characters, and tons of unexpected plot twists and turns that will have you flipping the pages beyond bedtime! She has sold over 2 million books, and her titles are translated into several languages.

Prior to becoming a full-time writer, Siobhan forged a successful corporate career in human resource management.

She lives in the Garden County of Ireland with her husband and two sons.

You can connect with Siobhan in the following ways:

Website: www.siobhandavis.com
Facebook: AuthorSiobhanDavis
Instagram: @siobhandavisauthor
Tiktok: @siobhandavisauthor
Email: siobhan@siobhandavis.com

Books By Siobhan Davis

NEW ADULT ROMANCE
The One I Want Duet
Kennedy Boys Series
Rydeville Elite Series
All of Me Series
Forever Love Duet

NEW ADULT ROMANCE STAND-ALONES
Inseparable
Incognito
Still Falling for You
Holding on to Forever
Always Meant to Be
Tell It to My Heart

REVERSE HAREM
Sainthood Series
Dirty Crazy Bad Duet
Surviving Amber Springs (stand-alone)
Alinthia Series ^

DARK MAFIA ROMANCE

Mazzone Mafia Series
Vengeance of a Mafia Queen (stand-alone)
*The Accardi Twins**

YA SCI-FI & PARANORMAL ROMANCE

Saven Series
True Calling Series ^

**Coming 2024*
^Currently unpublished but will be republished in due course.

www.siobhandavis.com

www.ingramcontent.com/pod-product-compliance
Lightning Source LLC
Chambersburg PA
CBHW061622210726

48287CB00001B/245